PRAISE FOR
THE NEIGHBOR FAVOR

• • •

"[A] warm and welcoming new contemporary. . . . The book breathes easily and pulls you right into its world. Especially recommended for anyone who ships Janine and Gregory from *Abbott Elementary*." —*The New York Times Book Review*

"Warm, witty, and deeply romantic. Kristina Forest is a fantastic storyteller, with an eagle eye for detail and a knack for crafting lovable characters. It's impossible not to smile while reading this book!"

—Rachel Lynn Solomon, *New York Times* bestselling author of *Past Present Future*

"*The Neighbor Favor* is the type of charming, feel-good story that reminds me why I love romance. I dare anyone to try reading Lily and Nick's adorably awkward encounters without smiling, impossible."

—Farrah Rochon, *New York Times* bestselling author of *Pardon My Frenchie*

"I fell head over heels in love with Lily and Nick. *The Neighbor Favor* is sweet, swoony, and full of heart. I didn't want it to end!"

—Lynn Painter, *New York Times* bestselling author of *Accidentally Amy*

"Anchored by two endearing leads and a touching plot filled with a wonderful cast of side characters. . . . *The Neighbor Favor* is as comforting as it is lovely—an admirable example of everything a heartwarming romance can be."
—Claire Kann, author of
Looking for Love in All the Haunted Places

"In a world of swipe right for love, this electric debut crackles with old-fashioned chemistry. Forest writes with so much heart. Nick and Lily absolutely simmer together and make you feel like 'high fantasy' could be right next door!"
—Nikki Payne, author of *Sex, Lies and Sensibility*

"Forest expertly balances this perfectly matched duo's emotional connection with their physical chemistry, making them easy to cheer on. This is a winner."
—*Publishers Weekly* (starred review)

"This swoony contemporary romance with fully realized characters will have readers hooked from the first page, and the protagonists, who are Black, have deep, relatable backstories."
—*Library Journal* (starred review)

PRAISE FOR
THE PARTNER PLOT

• • •

"A top-tier second-chance romance. . . . Kristina weaves a love story that feels familiar yet entirely fresh. Xavier and Vio- let jump off the page and directly into your heart. . . . Kristina "could write my to-do list, and I'd read it faithfully. This fantastic book is no exception."

—Erin Hahn, author of *Even If It Breaks Your Heart*

"*The Partner Plot* is everything I'm looking for in a romance. Violet and Xavier's swoonworthy second-chance journey stole my heart—a chemistry-filled and thoroughly satisfying exploration of what it takes to turn first love into forever love. I'll read anything Kristina Forest writes!"

—Ava Wilder, author of *Will They or Won't They*

"Forest's novel is a sweet portrayal of first love and second chances. Violet and Xavier are memorable, real, and vulnerable as they struggle with career sacrifices and the fear of more heartbreak. Yet they were destined from the start—and Forest's romance never misses a shot. A second-chance slam dunk."

—*Kirkus Reviews* (starred review)

"Readers will root for Violet and Xavier as they come to understand that career success means little without a special person to share it with."

—*Publishers Weekly*

"A fun, breezy rom-com that will please fans of fake-relationship stories."

—*Library Journal*

The Love Lyric

Kristina Forest

BERKLEY ROMANCE New York

BERKLEY ROMANCE
Published by Berkley
An imprint of Penguin Random House LLC
penguinrandomhouse.com

Library of Congress Cataloging-in-Publication Data

Names: Forest, Kristina, author.
Title: The love lyric / Kristina Forest.
Description: First edition. | New York : Berkley Romance, 2025.
Identifiers: LCCN 2024024390 (print) | LCCN 2024024391 (ebook) |
ISBN 9780593817100 (trade paperback) | ISBN 9780593817117 (ebook)
Subjects: LCGFT: Romance fiction. | Novels.
Classification: LCC PS3606.O7474 L68 2025 (print) | LCC PS3606.O7474
(ebook) | DDC 813/.6—dc23/eng/20240604
LC record available at https://lccn.loc.gov/2024024390
LC ebook record available at https://lccn.loc.gov/2024024391

First Edition: February 2025

Printed in the United States of America
1st Printing

For my grandma Peggy

Author's Note

In this book, there are scenes where one of the main characters reflects on their grief from losing a partner. If this topic is sensitive to you, please read with care. However, as with all of my books, I promise that there will be laughter, love, joy, and a happily ever after. Thank you for reading, and I hope you enjoy Iris and Angel's story.

The
Love
Lyric

PROLOGUE

ANGEL DIDN'T REALLY KNOW ANYONE AT THIS PARTY.

That had more or less been the norm since he'd left small-town Georgia behind for Los Angeles, where every-one seemed to know everyone, and he stuck out like a sore thumb. Even after four years of having a Los Angeles ad-dress, his Southern accent felt too strong and noticeable. His clothes weren't trendy enough. He was a needle in a haystack of talented, beautiful people. It was hard not to fear that maybe he wasn't anything too special, and maybe he shouldn't have abandoned his gospel roots to pursue a career in R & B. Or *that sex music*, as his mother liked to say.

Tonight, however, Angel wasn't at a party in Los Ange-les. He was at a wedding hall in New Jersey because his new stylist, Violet Greene, was having an "anti-wedding" party to celebrate the dissolution of her engagement.

An anti-wedding party was exactly what it sounded like. Guests had been told to wear all black. On the makeshift stage, Karamel Kitty, a popular rapper and another one of Violet's clients, rapped into the mic. Violet was there in the middle of the crowd, her brown cheeks flushed red as she rapped along. Violet's ex-fiancé, Eddy, had been Angel's previous manager. After Violet discovered that Eddy had cheated on her two weeks before their wedding, she'd called it off. But instead of canceling the venue and the catering that they'd already paid for, Violet had decided to throw a party.

Cheating scandal aside, Angel hadn't been too crazy about Eddy from the beginning. Eddy was a terrible communicator and had always put Angel on the back burner in favor of his bigger clients. After Angel discovered how Eddy had cheated on Violet, he'd fired him because he didn't want a slimeball like that on his team. Luckily, Angel's record label had quickly paired him with a new manager who actually seemed like she might be able to help Angel's career progress. His label had also set him up with a physical trainer and enrolled him in dance lessons. He was working with the hottest new producers for his debut R & B album. His team wanted him to be the next big star of his generation. After almost half a decade of struggling to be noticed in the industry, Angel was finally beginning to feel hopeful that his R & B career might actually take off.

After Karamel Kitty finished her set, the DJ switched to the Electric Slide. Angel smiled as he looked around at the sea of unfamiliar faces, Violet's family and friends on the dance floor. Here, Angel felt less self-conscious about his outfit: a basic black button-up, black jeans and a pair of black Vans. Violet had officially taken him on as a client only two weeks ago, and they hadn't yet had their first fitting. He hoped she'd be able to fix his image and help him appear less boy next door, less like a twenty-five-year-old who'd lived the majority of his life in a sheltered bubble.

He walked toward the dance floor to join the Electric

Slide, eager to strike up conversation with someone instead of standing alone, hovering on the outside. When he glanced toward the bar, he spotted another person he knew: Violet's younger sister, Lily. She leaned against the bar, looking a lot like Violet with her heart-shaped face and glowing brown skin. He and Lily had spoken before at Violet and Eddy's engagement party a few months ago. Violet had attempted to set him and Lily up, but the vibe with Lily had immediately, and mutually, felt platonic. And he was pretty sure that Lily had a boyfriend now. He walked over to say hello.

"Hi, Lily," he said as he approached.

Lily turned to him, blinking in surprise. "Hey, Angel." Her face broke into a warm smile. "How are you? I didn't expect to see you here."

He smiled too, shrugging. "I took Violet's side in the breakup. Eddy wasn't a good dude." The last time they spoke, Lily had told him that she was an editor of nonfiction books. "Are you still working on books about dictators?"

Lily laughed and shook her head. "Thankfully no. How's the album coming along?"

"*Great.* I've been collaborating with this new producer who—"

Abruptly, Angel trailed off as his attention was caught by a petite woman in a short black dress, who was making a beeline toward them. Dark lipstick painted her full lips and shimmer lightly decorated her Cupid's bow. Her light brown eyes were lined in black liner, and her short hair was slicked down. A black rose was tucked behind her ear. Her hips swayed as she approached them. She wasn't smiling, but she

wasn't frowning either. Her even expression was somewhere in between.

Angel blinked, trying to conjure words to finish his sentence. *What had he been saying?* He had no idea. All he knew
was that he couldn't stop staring at this beautiful woman.

"I think Karamel Kitty's lyrics are going to give Great-
Aunt Portia a heart attack," the woman said to Lily, leaning
her elbows against the bar top. Her voice was low and sultry. She took a sip from the drink beside Lily and she glanced
at Angel. The corner of her mouth lifted in a smile. "Hello."

Angel's heart began a heavy gallop in his chest. The
pounding traveled to his throat and hands. Belatedly, he realized she'd greeted him and he was too busy gaping at her
to answer. He wished he was smoother, but thanks to that
previous sheltered life of his, he had no game to speak of,
and despite his best efforts, his game hadn't improved in LA.

"Hey, what's up," he said, stumbling over his words.
"What's good?"

"Iris, this is Violet's friend Angel," Lily said. "Angel, this
is our other sister, Iris."

Iris. Even her name was beautiful.

Iris gave a slight tilt of her head. "You're the musician."

"*Yes,*" He blinked in disbelief. She knew him? "You've
heard my music before?"

He wasn't getting any major radio play yet, but some of
his SoundCloud songs were still floating around, and of
course there were the songs from his gospel days.

"No," Iris said simply. She returned her attention to Lily.
"Calla's sitting with Mom. I'm going outside to get some
fresh air if anyone's looking for me."

Without another word, she walked away. Angel stared

after her. The black rose slipped from its place behind her ear and landed on the ground. Unaware, Iris kept walking.

"It was nice seeing you again, Lily," Angel said, already moving to retrieve the rose. His voice sounded like it was coming from far away. "I have to . . . go check on something."

A ghost of a smile lingered on Lily's lips as she watched him. "Nice seeing you too."

Angel scooped the rose from the floor and jogged to catch up with Iris. He didn't know what propelled him. Maybe he wanted to make up for his fumbling attempt at conversation, or to apologize for gaping at her so openly. Or maybe it was something else. His parents and other people from his old church had often talked about otherworldly, divine interventions. The heavens or angels leading people to make decisions that made sense only in retrospect. Angel didn't know if this was one of those situations. But he felt moved by some kind of unnameable force as he held Iris's rose in his hand.

Iris walked into the hallway and made a left turn toward the exit. As she pushed the door open and stepped outside, she tripped over the threshold. Angel broke into a run and caught her at her elbows before she tipped completely forward. She let out a gasp as she fell backward into him. She turned her head and glanced up at him with wide, startled eyes.

"I've got you," he said, holding her. He helped her stand upright and she kept her hands grasped in his as she wiggled her foot in her loose heel.

"Thank you," she breathed, pulling away once she regained her balance. "I assure you that I'm not a clumsy person. It's these shoes."

He looked down at her strappy black heels. They were at least five inches tall, but she reached only to his collarbone, which let him know that she was much shorter than him normally.

"They're Violet's," she said, grimacing at the shoes. "She believes that beauty is pain. I wanted to wear flats, but she threatened to kill me."

Angel laughed. "They do look complicated." His hands were still buzzing from holding her. He remembered the rose. "You dropped this back inside."

"Oh." She reached for the flower. The petals were slightly bent from when she'd grabbed his hands to break her fall. "Thank you."

"Of course." There were a few other partygoers milling outside, talking and smoking. The sun was beginning to set, and Iris's honey brown skin glowed. He wondered if she had come tonight with a date.

"I guess I'll have to look forward to her threats soon too," he said. At Iris's confused expression, he clarified, "Oh, I mean Violet. She's my new stylist."

"Don't worry. She won't kill you since you'll be paying her." Iris smiled a little, the corner of her mouth hitching up a millimeter. "She's amazing at her job. You're in good hands."

"Yeah, I've seen."

What else could he say? *Think, think.*

"What do you do for work?" he blurted, then winced. It was such an LA question.

"I work at a makeup company," she said.

Despite having a younger sister whom he was very close to, he knew squat about makeup. "Really? That's cool."

Whack, so whack. He was blowing this. He shouldn't have been surprised, though. His roommate, Ray, liked to joke that while Angel could easily reel in women thanks to his face, he often ruined his chances once he opened his mouth.

"And you sing?" she asked.

"Yeah, I do," he hastened to say, grateful that she'd given him a chance to redeem himself. "What kind of music are you into?"

"All kinds," she said. "R & B. Soul. Pop. Afrobeats. Soft rock on occasion."

"Soft rock?" He grinned. "You a fan of the Bee Gees?"

"Yeah. But mostly Hall and Oates. Feel free to judge me there."

Angel held up his hands. "Hey, no judging from me, es-pecially not on someone's taste in music. Hall and Oates is a solid choice. Is a movie montage or toothpaste commer-cial even good if 'You Make My Dreams (Come True)' isn't playing in the background?"

Iris's smile inched wider. "What do you sing?"

He started to tell her that his heart was in R & B, really soul, even though his label was pushing him in a pop direc-tion, but before he could answer, a little girl ran straight toward them. She looked a bit like Iris with the same com-plexion and light brown eyes.

"Mom," she said, throwing her arms around Iris's legs. She glanced at Angel shyly, and he waved. She turned back to Iris and whispered, "Come dance with me."

Angel took that moment to quickly observe Iris's left hand. No wedding ring.

Iris gazed into her daughter's face and smiled. "Okay, let's go back inside."

Her daughter eagerly pulled her away, and Iris laughed, shaking her head.

"Enjoy the rest of your evening," she said, glancing at Angel over her shoulder. "Thank you again for catching me."

"You too," he said, lifting his hand. "And you're welcome."

Iris spared him one last soft smile before she and her daughter walked back inside.

Angel breathed a deep, wistful sigh.

He'd had a difficult relationship with religion since leaving Georgia. It was tainted with his mother's judgments and her harsh black-and-white ideals. He hadn't prayed consistently in years.

But right then, Angel prayed that he might one day see Iris Greene again.

Three years later

IRIS GREENE WONDERED IF THERE WAS SOME SORT OF Bat-Signal that appeared in the sky whenever she walked into a room. But instead of seeing an image of a winged mammal hovering between the clouds, people saw the words *Eldest Daughter*, and they released a collective sigh of relief, knowing that they were in the presence of a proper problem solver.

It would explain why tourists frequently singled Iris out on the busy New York City streets and asked her for directions, or why disgruntled parents at the grocery store felt comfortable asking her to watch their toddlers in line for just one quick minute while they ran to grab that forgotten box of frozen chicken nuggets in aisle seven. It would explain why her boss often requested that she sit in on meetings outside of her purview because she needed Iris to lend *her ear to the matter at hand.*

Or in this particular moment, it would explain why, in the middle of her younger sister's wedding reception, the wedding coordinator had shoved her binder into Iris's arms, begging Iris to take over, as she sprinted to the restroom, face and neck covered in hives because she hadn't been told that the pasta salad contained shellfish.

Iris had been leaving the restroom herself, headed back toward the dance floor, and she fumbled to catch hold of the binder before it clattered to the floor. Iris blinked and hardly had a chance to gather her bearings before her great-aunt Portia took the opportunity to approach Iris and corner her in the restroom alcove.

"Can you *please* tell them to change the music?" Great-Aunt Portia asked, wincing. She grabbed onto Iris's elbow. "I don't understand how anyone can dance to this!"

Iris glanced toward the DJ, who was deep in his mix, spinning an edited version of a rap girl duo's song. Out on the dance floor, Iris's younger sister Violet, the blushing bride, danced with her new husband, Xavier. Violet had two rules for her wedding: one, everyone had to come dressed to impress—she was a celebrity stylist, after all. And two, she and Xavier wanted their wedding to feel like a big party. It was why they'd hired a DJ who usually worked at nightclubs in the city.

"It's not all that bad, is it?" Iris asked, patting her aunt on the shoulder in an attempt to appease her.

Other than Great-Aunt Portia, most people seemed to be enjoying the music. Sprinkled throughout the sea of family and friends were Violet's famous clients, and Iris spotted her parents laughing with her aunts and uncles by the bar. She located her youngest sister, Lily, and Lily's boyfriend, Nick, dancing with Iris's six-year-old daughter, Calla. Nick lifted Calla onto his shoulders and spun her around in a circle. Calla laughed, keeping her hands firmly placed on top of Nick's head. Iris smiled, eager to return to her daughter. She hated missing moments like this, especially since Calla's father couldn't be there to witness them too.

Well, her late husband, Terry, wasn't there *physically*, but Iris liked to think that he was watching over her and Calla and that his life was continuing on, just elsewhere. She preferred that perspective to thinking that for the past five years, he was ashes in an urn, never progressing beyond twenty-seven years old.

"She said she's going to ride *what* like a rodeo?" Great-Aunt Portia asked, aghast, listening closely to the song's lyrics.

"I'm sorry, what?" Iris turned to her great-aunt, who continued to complain about the DJ. Great-Aunt Portia might as well have been speaking the slow, garbled language of Charlie Brown's schoolteacher. Iris could barely hear her aunt as she waited for the quick sting of grief to recede.

Since Terry's death, she'd learned that grief was like an ocean. Sometimes the tide was high, and her grief built itself into waves that crashed down and knocked her over, surprising her. And other times, like just now, her grief was a low tide. Gentle waves quietly rolled ashore to wash over her feet and brush against her ankles, reminding her that it was still there, even if she wasn't looking at it directly. These days, the low tide was more of the norm. Her grief was part of her, just like Terry's memory.

"The music, Iris," Great-Aunt Portia insisted. "Can you do something about it, please?"

Iris took a moment to gather herself, and once she felt steady, she dug in her clutch and retrieved her AirPods and her spare iPhone that could be used only when connected to Wi-Fi. She usually kept it with her in case Calla needed to be entertained with an educational game. Iris pulled up YouTube and found a channel that played a continuous mix of Luther Vandross hits. She offered the phone and earbuds to her aunt.

"Here," she said. "I think this should do perfectly."

Great-Aunt Portia smiled and gratefully accepted her auditory escape from modern-day rap.

One fire doused. Now, onto the next. Iris flipped open the binder and scanned the schedule. It was time to cut the cake. Binder in hand, she walked back into the open area of the banquet hall and set her sights on the waitstaff gathered by the buffet table. She side-skirted the dance floor, double-checking and confirming that Calla was still safe with Lily and Nick, and she wound through the tables and chairs, her sleeveless champagne-colored gown swishing against her curves.

The wedding was being held on the grounds of a vine-yard in upstate New York. (Upstate, depending on who you asked. It was only an hour north of New York City.) And the ballroom with its high ceilings and sparkling chandeliers made the entire evening appear elegant and grand. The waitstaff even wore matching bow ties. Before Iris could reach them, the group dispersed, moving throughout the room to gather plates and offer refreshments. One young guy, tall, skinny, and pale with long dark hair, remained lingering by the buffet table.

"Hi," Iris said, approaching him. She tapped the wedding binder. "I'm the sister of the bride and the interim wedding coordinator, it would seem. It's time to cut the cake."

The guy blinked at her. "Oh, um, I'm only a trainee. I just got hired yesterday. I don't—I mean, I . . ." He pulled nervously at his bow tie and glanced about the room. He returned his attention to Iris, who eyed him with a steady gaze. She continued to tap her fingers against the binder. He gulped and cleared his throat.

"What's your name?" she asked.

"Ethan."

Iris had been told on more than one occasion by her younger sisters that she had a no-nonsense demeanor that many people found "intimidating as fuck." In Iris's opinion, whether or not someone felt intimidated by her sounded like a personal problem on their end. But in the interest of time, she decided to throw Ethan a bone.

"Ethan," she said calmly, "can you please take me to the kitchen so that I can tell someone it's time to bring out the cake?"

"Yes, yes, absolutely," Ethan quickly pushed up off the wall and gestured for Iris to follow him out of the ballroom and through the venue, down a winding hall that led to the bustling kitchen.

Servers moved in and out of the kitchen area, and thanks to the seven months she'd spent hostessing at TGI Friday's during her sophomore year of college, Iris expertly dipped and dodged each moving body. The three-tier wedding cake was placed atop a tray with wheels in the center of the kitchen. The shimmery white icing sparkled under the ceiling lights.

"It's perfect," Iris said. "Now we just need the cake knife and we can get this wheeled out to the ballroom."

Ethan quickly produced a cake cutter and handed it to Iris, beaming, proud to have accomplished a task so quickly. Iris turned the cutter over in her hands and frowned. "No, there's a specific cake knife. The word 'Greene' is inscribed on it."

The cake cutter was sterling silver and had been used in her parents' wedding and her paternal grandparents' wedding as well. It was a family heirloom . . . an heirloom that Iris hadn't used in her own wedding. That had been a much different scenario. She and Terry had gotten married at the city hall on Court Street in downtown Brooklyn. She'd been twenty-five years old and eight weeks pregnant. Afterward, the two of them, along with her sisters and their parents, had crowded into a random Italian restaurant down the street and filled their stomachs to the brim with pasta. There had been no cake. Iris hadn't cared. The day had had been perfect in its own way.

"The cake knife," she repeated. "Where is it?"

Ethan bit his lip and mumbled, "Um."

Iris glanced around at the other staff in the kitchen, who stared back at her in confused silence. She flipped through the binder, hoping to discover some information regarding where the special cake knife might be stored, but she found nothing.

Okay, she just had to think. There was a solution for every problem. The cake knife had to have come from her parents' house, which meant that the wedding coordinator most likely had the knife when she brought in the decorations for the centerpieces.

"Do you have a storage room?" she asked.

"Yes!" Ethan said, and he led her back to the ballroom and past the dance floor once more.

"Iris," her mother, Dahlia, called, catching sight of her as she hurried behind Ethan. "What's going on? Where's the coordinator?"

"Everything's fine, Mom!" Iris waved her hand and affected an easy smile.

To most, using the family cake knife might seem inconsequential. But Dahlia had already been disappointed that Iris, her first daughter to be married, hadn't used the knife for her own wedding. Making sure that Violet used the knife for her wedding was one small gift that Iris could give their mother. And after everything Violet had gone through with her ex, she deserved a perfect wedding day to start her new life with Xavier, her former high school sweetheart.

Plus, if Iris didn't find the knife, she and her sisters would never hear the end of it from Dahlia.

Ethan stopped in front of a door right beside the coat check. He turned the knob and revealed a room filled with boxes and decorations. Iris immediately spotted a box of vases that looked just like the ones used for centerpieces on the tables in the ballroom. She crouched by the open box, and there, wrapped in crisp black linen, was the Greene cutting knife.

"Found it," she said, standing.

Ethan gazed at her, awed. "You're like Sherlock Holmes or something."

Iris almost laughed. Compared to what she dealt with at her job and/or family on a normal day, this was light work. She handed the knife to Ethan.

"Can you please clean this and meet me back in the ball-room in three minutes?" she asked.

He saluted her. "Yes, ma'am."

Ma'am? Jeez. No need to make her feel ancient. She was only thirty-two.

"Three minutes," she repeated. She held up her hand and wiggled three fingers. "*Three.*"

Ethan nodded before hurrying off to the kitchen.

Iris took another deep breath and squared her shoulders. Time for the next task. She reentered the ballroom and made a beeline for the DJ. He wore large headphones and nodded his head so intensely, Iris worried he might throw out his neck. She had to tap his shoulder to get his attention. He startled and turned to her, then the edges of his lips curled into a smile.

"What's up, beautiful?" he shouted over the music. "A song request for the maid of honor?"

"Co–maid of honor," she corrected. She and Lily shared the title. "Can you announce that it's time to cut the cake, please?"

"You said you wanna hear 'Cake' by Rihanna?" he asked.

"I got you, girl!"

Iris groaned and leaned over to grab the mic before he could change the song. "Hello, friends and family!" She looked toward her radiant sister and her new husband. "Newlyweds, it's time to cut the cake."

Violet and Xavier, followed by their guests, herded in the center of the dance floor, just as Ethan and two other servers rolled out the cake. Iris joined the crowd and she thanked Ethan for his help before inspecting the knife for cleanliness and handing it to her sister. In gratitude, Violet gave

Iris a loud smacking kiss on the cheek and angled herself toward Xavier.

Iris stepped back, allowing space for the newlyweds to have their moment and photo ops. She found her way to Lily and Nick. Calla was still propped on Nick's shoulders so that she could see the action.

"Hi, Mom," Calla said, grinning, "Look, I'm taller than Nick."

"Hi, baby," Iris smiled as she reached up and squeezed her daughter's hand. Calla had been the flower girl during the ceremony, and like Iris and Lily, she wore a champagne-colored dress, but hers was short-sleeved with an empire waist. Iris had blown out Calla's thick curls this morning and adorned her hair with matching bows. She stepped closer to her daughter and looked at Nick. "You okay holding her like that?"

Nick shrugged. "She weighs almost nothing." He jiggled his shoulders up and down, causing Calla to shake with him, and she burst into laughter.

Nick was basically family now. He and Lily had been dating for three years, after first meeting over email and then somehow ending up neighbors. The kind of love story that could happen only in New York City.

"Where have you been?" Lily asked, poking Iris in the arm. Like Iris, Lily's eyelids were covered in light gold shimmer. Her curls were pulled back into a French twist. Iris's hair had been long like that once too. But after Calla was born, she'd cut it short. She'd been growing it out for the last few months, though. Today it was styled in a wavy chin-length bob. "You went to the bathroom and then disap-peared."

Iris sighed, shaking her head. "You wouldn't believe the journey I've been on."

Their conversation was interrupted by a spattering of applause. Violet and Xavier were feeding each other cake. They pretended like they were going to smash cake in each other's faces, but instead, Xavier wrapped his arms around Violet and kissed her deeply.

Iris had another flash of her own wedding day. She'd worn a simple white long-sleeved, A-line dress. Her hair had been longer. Her face had been fuller. They'd gotten married on a Tuesday afternoon, because as NYU Stern School of Business students at the time, they hadn't had classes that day. The smell of fresh paint and linoleum in the courthouse had made Iris slightly nauseous as they'd waited for their turn to be wed. Terry had handed her a bottle of water and gently rubbed his palm against the small swell of her stomach—a surprise neither of them had anticipated only six months into their relationship. Terry had looked so handsome. His light brown skin was smooth. His chocolate brown eyes sparkling. He'd been average height, so he hadn't towered over Iris as they'd said *I do.*

Their decision to marry had been swift and impulsive—probably the only impulsive decision Iris had ever made in her life. It was a decision she'd never regret despite the heartbreak that came after.

It was moments like this, while surrounded by family and celebrating, that Iris was reminded of Terry's absence the most. He wasn't there to see Violet, whom he'd loved like a blood sister, get married. He wasn't there to convince Iris to take a moment to relax and slow dance with him, just once. And he wasn't there to sit Calla on his shoulders so that she could see her aunt cut her wedding cake.

A tear escaped down the side of Iris's face, and she hastened to wipe her eyes.

Lily was watching her. She leaned closer. "Hey," she said quietly. "You okay?"

Iris froze. She didn't want to call attention to herself, especially not when this day was supposed to be about Violet. She cleared her throat.

"I'm just gonna . . ." She pointed her thumb in a random direction that signaled away. She glanced up at Calla, who was oblivious to her mother's wavering resolve.

"Don't worry," Lily said softly. "We've got her."

"Thank you," Iris whispered.

She fixed her lips into a smile as she told Calla she'd be back in a few minutes. Then she slipped through the crowd, trying her best to avoid being stopped by another one of her family members. She kept walking until she reached the back door of the banquet hall, which led outside. The patio space was empty, for which Iris was thankful. She hated crying in front of people, always had, even before having a deceased husband gave her a reason to cry. Violet liked to say this was because Iris's moon was in Capricorn. Whatever that meant. Iris didn't believe in astrology. She talked about her feelings in therapy, and often, that was about as much emotional unpacking as she was comfortable with.

She looked out at the expansive vineyard before her, rows and rows of grapevines as far as she could see. Spacious, quiet. She wanted to be alone, just for a few quick minutes. She headed toward the vineyard. The sun was beginning to set, and it made everything look beautiful and serene. It was early June, so the weather was warm but not unbearably hot. She felt her pulse rate slow as the walk calmed her.

Soon, she came to a clearing. A large oak tree reached up toward the sky. Several names were carved into the bark. *Annie + Jeff. Kimmy and Ryan Forever. Ben loves Frank.* She walked behind the tree and discovered a rope swing attached to one of the sturdy branches. She brushed leaves and debris off the seat of the swing and sat down, slowly pushing herself back and forth. She'd give herself another five minutes of quiet. Then she'd head back to the venue. Given the circumstances, she accepted that she was having a moment, but like everything else, it would pass.

Maybe the last couple months were finally catching up to her. Save Face Beauty, the company where she worked, had taken a huge hit to its reputation after a brand trip had turned disastrous. Back in February, they flew twenty-five popular makeup influencers out to a five-star resort in Turks and Caicos, and after days spent doing excursions and eating fancy meals, over half of the influencers got sick with food poisoning. Of course the influencers documented the entire ordeal, and suddenly Save Face Beauty became public enemy number one. They were accused of not caring enough about the influencers by choosing a resort that served food that made people sick. Once beauty-world darlings with several hero products on their roster, SFB suddenly was deemed problematic and overrated. Many influencers declared that they'd never purchase an SFB product ever again. It became a dogpile online, people dunking on SFB left and right. For a week straight, "Save Face Beauty Turks and Caicos controversy" was one of the most searched phrases on social media.

Even worse? As the director of partnerships, Iris had large involvement in the brand trip, and *she'd* chosen the resort. Weeks before the trip occurred, the resort switched their kitchen management staff, a decision totally out of Iris's control, but she couldn't have predicted the horrible turn that the trip would take. In the months since, people had moved on to other stories, but overall sales remained low, and even though Iris knew that the food poisoning ordeal wasn't her fault, she carried deep guilt over what happened.

As a Hail Mary to restore the company's reputation, as well as her own, Iris had come up with the idea to launch their new skincare line with a celebrity brand ambassador. Planning the campaign had meant many late nights at the office, and she and Calla had eaten a lot more meals from DoorDash than she cared to admit. She'd been exhausted lately, but she needed this new endeavor to work.

Iris never struggled to pour into her professional life. But with the exception of caring for Calla, Iris's personal life was not so well watered. It was a topic that she'd been discussing in therapy lately because after five years of being single and widowed, she was working herself up to dipping her toes in the dating pool again. There would never be another Terry, and she wasn't seeking to replace him in her heart. But the truth was that she was lonely. She wanted companionship. She was still young, and she knew that Terry wouldn't have wanted her to be alone forever. She hoped maybe one day she'd meet another man who had similar qualities to Terry, like his abundance of patience, his steadfastness and intelligence, his kind heart. This new person would need to like kids, and he'd need to have a loving relationship with Calla. Iris wasn't asking for much. She wanted to live a simple, low-key life, and she hoped to eventually meet a man who wanted the same.

She'd had yet to go on a first date, though. She'd been too busy lately with work. Or at least that was the excuse she gave her therapist.

The sound of shoes crunching against grass snapped Iris out of her moment of quiet. The footsteps paused on the other side of the vast tree.

"Hey, cutie," the person cooed. Their voice was deep, masculine. "How's my little cutie doing?"

Iris stopped swinging. Something about the voice was vaguely familiar. She tried to recall if any of her cousins had just had a baby whom they might FaceTime, but she couldn't think of anyone. Maybe this person was related to Xavier?

"You are beautiful, missy miss," they continued, making their tone of voice higher. "Yes, you are. So beautiful. I love you so much. Woof, woof."

Woof, woof?

Now Iris was curious. Stealthily, she rose from the swing and crept around the base of the tree trunk. When she leaned forward for a quick peek, she froze, realizing whom the voice belonged to.

He was tall with an athletic physique and brown skin. His hair, shaved close to his scalp in a fade, was probably dark brown or black naturally, but it was dyed a deep burgundy shade. He had a gold hoop nose ring in his right nostril. His cream suit clung expertly to his frame like he'd been born into it. He leaned back against the tree with slow ease, containing the grace of a dancer, of someone who was comfortable in his body.

Iris knew him.

Well, that wasn't saying much, really. Millions of people knew him. Iris's sister, Violet, was his stylist, which explained why he was here at the wedding.

He was a famous singer, and he was Save Face Beauty's new brand ambassador.

His name was Angel.

2

IRIS DOUBTED THAT ANGEL REMEMBERED HER. THEIR brief conversation at Violet's anti-wedding party three years ago had predated his rise to megafame, and his life had drastically changed since then. Before, Iris hadn't heard much about Angel outside of the few times Violet had mentioned him, and Iris had certainly never heard any of his music. He'd also looked slightly different—no burgundy hair or nose ring, and no expensive clothes, as Violet hadn't yet worked her stylist magic on him. Now Iris couldn't turn on the radio without hearing at least one of Angel's songs. He was on television, starring in Adidas and Peloton commercials. He was on the cover of magazines, flexing his muscles, gazing at the camera. She'd even once seen an ad for his last album on the side of a New York City bus. His sound was like upbeat R & B. People obviously liked his music, because he'd won a Grammy and consistently topped the *Billboard* charts.

The *Save Face Beauty* team's intention had been to share the message that skincare should be a universal topic, regardless of gender. And because Angel was the current man of the moment, he'd been Iris's first choice for the brand ambassadorship.

Over the last few months, she had gotten to know the details of his face intimately as she pored over images from his Save Face Beauty photo shoots. She'd worked with the PR team to orchestrate a weeklong meet-and-greet tour at several Refine stores across the country, where Angel would promote their new skincare line. Refine was one of the leading retailers of personal care and beauty products. The Refine customer demographic was made up of people aged eighteen to thirty-four, which was the same demographic as Angel's fan base.

The tour was set to take place in a couple weeks, and Angel would be accompanied by Iris's colleague Paloma, the head of PR. Iris's hope was that Angel's involvement would help turn things around for the company.

She peered around the tree trunk as Angel angled his face closer to his phone camera and grinned. Iris was still thrown by the *woof, woof* he had spoken into his phone a moment ago. Was he talking to a girlfriend? A woman with a kink who liked when he used canine speak? Over the past three years, Angel had been tied to a string of beautiful starlets. While waiting in line at the grocery store, Iris often saw pictures of him on the front cover of gossip magazines, arm in arm with another gorgeous, long-legged woman. Most recently it had been Gigi Harrison, the lead actress in several action and superhero films.

"Woof, woof, pretty girl," he sang.

Iris couldn't help it. She laughed.

Angel's head jerked up. He glanced over and caught eyes

with Iris. A deep pink hue spread across his brown cheeks, and Iris backed away, embarrassed to have been caught.

"I'm sorry," she said quickly. "I didn't mean to eavesdrop." Although, she clearly had meant to do just that.

Angel blinked at her, then glanced at his phone. "Bye, girl," he whispered, waving at his phone's camera. He slipped his phone in his pants pocket. He turned to look at Iris again, leaning his shoulder against the tree. The corner of his mouth hitched up, the beginnings of a smile.

"So," he said, "that's what I sound like when I talk to my dog."

"Your dog?" Oh, she had been so wrong. "That makes *a lot* of sense."

"Yeah, she has separation anxiety, so I put one of those doggy cameras in my place to check in on her when I'm gone."

"I see." Iris didn't know what else to say. She'd never had a pet growing up and therefore didn't understand Angel's dedication. Lately she'd considered getting an easy pet for Calla, though. A hamster or gerbil. Maybe a goldfish.

She wondered if she should properly reintroduce herself. Since Violet was Angel's stylist and had styled him for the SFB campaign shoot, Iris knew that Violet had told Angel that she worked at SFB, but Iris hadn't been at his photo shoot to meet him, so she didn't know if he was aware of her level of involvement in his campaign.

But she had rudely listened in on his conversation just now, so she should probably give him some privacy. Also, it was the weekend, she was at her sister's wedding and she didn't want to talk about work. Given the way that Angel disappeared from the party to FaceTime his dog, she would hazard a guess that he didn't want to talk about work either. She'd have a chance at a professional redo at some point in the future. Plus, her role was more behind the scenes. Client care was a job for Paloma and the PR team.

"Again, I apologize," she said. "Please call your dog back and continue your conversation." She waved politely and set off through the vineyard back toward the venue.

"Hey, wait," Angel said, jogging to catch up with her. He easily maneuvered his body, managing not to be sideswiped by an overgrown grape bush. "You're Violet's sister, right? Iris?"

Now it was her turn to blink in surprise. He remembered her.

She slowed her walk, angling herself toward him. "Yes. Hi."

"Hi." He smiled, and it was as though Iris watched the act in slow motion. His full lips lifted then curved. His straight white teeth revealed themselves. His eyes crinkled in the corners. A picture of warmth.

Gorgeous, her brain said.

Well, obviously he was gorgeous. His voice wasn't the only reason that a good portion of the country was currently obsessed with him. Saying that he was gorgeous was simply a fact. She'd noticed that about him when they'd first met, before all the glitz and glam.

"I'm Angel." He held out his hand. "We met a couple years ago. You probably don't remember."

Iris almost laughed to herself again. To think that he thought that *she* didn't remember *him*.

"I remember," she said. She placed her hand in his, and she felt a zing shoot straight up her arm, from her fingers to her shoulder, as his hand engulfed hers. He didn't break eye contact as their palms pressed together. She took a deep breath and cleared her throat. "I work at Save Face Beauty," she said, deciding that now would be the best time to tell him. "We're so thrilled to have you as our brand ambassador."

"Violet did tell me you worked there." He grinned. "Thank y'all for giving me the job."

Iris felt her stomach do something funny as he grinned at her.

"Do you always introduce yourself that way?" she asked after a moment.

Angel lifted his chin, tilting his head slightly. "What do you mean?"

"Angel must be your stage name, right?"

"Oh, nah." He laughed softly. It had a melodic quality. "I was intentionally named Angel at birth. My mom is very religious."

"Really?" Iris thought of the images her team had displayed during their many ambassador strategy meetings over the last few months. Photos of Angel shirtless, his abs and muscles lathered in baby oil. Clips from his music videos as he grinded with his backup dancers. She wondered how his mom felt about that.

"Yeah, she's hard-core," he said. "Why are you out here and not inside?"

His thumb brushed against the knuckle of her pointer finger and that was when Iris realized that their hands were still clasped together. Blinking, she let her hand drop and she pivoted forward, continuing to walk.

"I just wanted some fresh air," she said, glancing at him

sidelong as he walked beside her. He was very tall. And he smelled nice. Like cinnamon.

It was a simple observation. For research purposes. She could now confirm that cinnamon-scented cologne smelled nice on a man. Maybe Save Face Beauty could incorporate cinnamon scents into their products. She'd float the idea at a meeting. That was all.

"I feel you," Angel said. He spread his arms wide. "It's beautiful out here. I thought I'd give my lady a call and let her see some nature."

Iris quirked an eyebrow. "You mean your dog?"

"Yeah, Maxine. She's the only lady in my life at the moment."

Well, it looked like things were over with Gigi Harrison, then.

"Maxine?" Iris repeated, smiling a little. "That's an elegant name for a dog."

"Maxine is an elegant lady." He pulled out his phone and showed Iris a photo of a brown boxer puppy with a black satin bow tied around her neck. Her tongue lolled out the side of her mouth as she chewed on a bone.

Iris's smile broadened. "Elegant indeed."

"Thank you." Angel's eyes twinkled as he looked at her. "I won't lie, though. I also came out here to escape your younger cousins. They kept taking pictures of me while I was trying to eat. Tomorrow photos of me covering my steak in mashed potatoes will probably be reshared all over Instagram."

Iris laughed, thinking of her teen cousins, who mostly wanted to come to Violet's wedding so that they could get a glimpse of her famous clients. Somewhere, back inside the venue, Karamel Kitty was probably being bombarded for photos as well.

"Wait a minute," Iris said. "You cover your steak in mashed potatoes? Is that like a Southern thing?"

Angel shrugged. "More like a me thing, I think. How did you know that I'm from the South?"

There was the slight twang in his accent for one, less prominent now than it had been three years ago. From her team's research, she knew that Angel had been born and raised in a small town in Georgia. But so much about him was common knowledge to the average citizen.

"Oh, there's this thing called the internet," she said. "If you use a tool called a search engine, you can find the answer to almost any question."

His brows lifted. "Really? *Any* question? Sounds fake."

"It also lies, so sometimes it is fake."

"See, now that's confusing," he said. Then, "But . . . what you're trying to say is that you googled me?"

She brought her index finger and thumb together. "Only a little."

"Oh, just a little, huh?" he said, laughing. And Iris laughed too. It felt nice to laugh so easily this way. She noticed another obvious change in Angel since their previous conversation three years ago. Back then, he'd seemed a little nervous, but now he was clearly much more comfortable in his own skin. He was dripping in charisma.

Dusk was beginning to settle, and fireflies swirled in and out of the vine rows, passing in front of her and Angel.

"So, what were you escaping from?" he asked.

Iris looked at him, taken by surprise at his question. She

hadn't been escaping, had she? She'd just needed a moment of quiet. Escaping made it sound as though she were trying to outrun her feelings, which, from experience, she knew was impossible.

Angel watched her closely, waiting for her reply. The only thing he knew about her was that she was Violet's older sister and she worked at SFB. He didn't know about Terry or her unfortunate backstory. He didn't see *widow* written across her forehead, like so many others saw. To him, she could have been anyone.

"I guess you can say I've had a long day," she supplied.

"Me too."

Up ahead, she could see the twinkle lights hung on the back patio. Silhouettes of servers taking smoke breaks moved in and out of her view.

"You know this is the first wedding I've been to in my twenties?" Angel said. "People aren't getting married like that anymore."

"Half of marriages do end in divorce." She lifted her shoulder in a shrug. "But this is the first one of your twenties? How old are you?"

She'd looked up his age at work, but as she'd already noted, sometimes the internet lied.

"I'll be twenty-nine in a couple weeks," he said. "You?"

"Thirty-two."

He was younger than her, but not by that much.

"The last wedding that I went to was back home in Georgia," he said. "I was sixteen and they asked me to sing 'Amazing Love' by Fred Hammond. You know it? It's a gospel song."

Iris shook her head. Her parents had taken her and her

sisters to church every Easter and Christmas Eve as kids, but that was as far as her experience with religion went.

"It's a good one, but anyway, it was the middle of August, and the church was blazing inside. I mean, *blazing*. My button-up was so covered in sweat, you could see right through the cotton. The bride passed out on her way up to the altar."

Iris burst into laughter. "Stop. You're messing with me."

"I'm so serious," Angel said, smile widening as he looked at her. "And while they fanned off the bride, they made me stand up and sing way before I was supposed to. I was so dehydrated, I almost passed out myself! My voice was trash that day."

Iris was still laughing. "Did you at least get paid to sing?"

"Of course not. My mom was friends with the bride and she told them I'd do it as a favor."

"Child labor exploitation. Terrible."

"Right? That wasn't my real job, though. I was cleaning toilets at Cook Out and getting chased by dogs on my paper route." He smirked at her. "What about you? You look like you had a nice, chill job. Like selling perfume at the mall or something."

She shook her head. "Not exactly. Aside from the semester that I worked at TGI Fridays, I worked at my parents' plant nursery. I was elbow- and knee-deep in soil every weekend."

"Ah," he said, nodding. "Makes sense now. Daughters named after flowers."

"And a church boy named after a spiritual being."

He grinned, inclining his head toward her. "Sometimes I wish my mom named me something more common. Like Jim."

"Or two common names together," she said. "Jim Bob."

"Bobby Tom."

"Tom Wyatt."

"Tom Wyatt," he repeated. "That's got a ring to it. Maybe I should make that my stage name."

"Don't forget to give me credit," she said, and Angel laughed.

"What about you?" he asked. "What's the last wedding you went to?"

It had been Paloma's wedding two years ago. And before that, it had been her own ceremony.

"It was a while back," she said.

They were close enough to the venue now that she could hear the faint sound of music playing. It was a slow song. "Spend My Life with You" by Eric Benét and Tamia.

Iris stopped abruptly. This song had always reminded her of Terry.

"You okay?" Angel asked.

Iris blinked quickly, glancing at him. She remembered that he didn't really know her. Maybe that was why she answered truthfully.

"Not really," she said quietly. "Today has been . . . off."

He nodded slowly, expression devoid of judgment. "It be like that sometimes."

"Yeah." She stared down at the straps of her gold open-toe heels.

"Too much maid of honor pressure?" he asked.

Iris managed a small laugh. She brought her gaze back up to his face and found that he was smiling at her.

"Definitely," she joked. "Try to avoid being a maid of honor if you can."

"I'll take that advice to heart."

She glanced toward the open doors of the venue again. Inside, she spotted her parents swaying together. Somewhere, Lily and Nick were probably holding hands with Calla, slow dancing too, or maybe the three of them were eating cake. She should probably go back inside and join them.

"Hey," Angel said. "You wanna dance?"

She squinted. "Out here, you mean?"

"Sure." At her skeptical expression, he smiled innocently. "Once I step inside, your cousins will go back to recording my every move. This might be my only chance to slow dance all night in peace."

Iris was unable to hold back her chuckle. The song changed. "I Want to Be Your Man," by Roger filtered outside. The DJ was really throwing it back with that one.

"What do you say?" Angel asked, holding out his hand.

Iris stared at his long, outstretched fingers. His nails were buffered shiny and clean.

It had been so long since she'd danced with someone. She looked up at Angel, who waited patiently for her answer. His mouth curled into a soft smile, dimples deepening. She couldn't say exactly what she saw there in his expression, but whatever it was made her step forward and take his hand. He pulled her close and brought her arms up to loop around his neck. He gently rested his hands at her waist. Slowly, they began to sway from side to side.

"This is nice," he said quietly.

Iris nodded, watching his pulse jump at the base of his throat. She rarely found herself feeling nervous or flustered in the presence of a man these days, but for some reason,

being this up close to Angel, a literal superstar, she was suddenly tongue-tied.

He began to hum lowly, tapping his fingers against her
waist in time to the music. "You're a good dancer," he said,
keeping his voice at that deep, low tone. She swallowed
thickly as goose bumps spread across her arms.

"I bet you say that to all the girls," she managed.

"No," he said simply.

He gazed down at her, and Iris, who was usually made of
much stronger stuff, could only gaze back. The song was
winding down. Their moment in time was coming to a
close. At the end of this song lay real life back inside of the
venue.

Angel's eyes slowly lowered to her mouth. Iris felt her
heartbeat pick up pace.

"Do you . . ." he started, then stopped. "Would you maybe
be interested in taking another walk on a different day?"

Iris was shocked by how quickly the word *yes* almost
tumbled off her tongue.

What was she *doing*?

"I'm sorry, I can't do that." She stepped out of his embrace, a quick, jerky movement.

Angel blinked, his empty hands grasping at air. "Wait—"

"Have a good night," she mumbled.

Before he could say anything else, she hurried back into
the ballroom, forcing herself to keep her gaze forward. She
saw both of her sisters holding hands with Calla, dancing
and laughing in the center of the dance floor. They waved
when they saw Iris. She didn't slow down until she reached
Calla, wrapping her arms around her daughter and squeezing her close, reminding herself of who she was.

Iris was capable. Reliable. She was a problem solver. Ambitious and motivated. She was often tired. Often lonely. And she didn't live a life where a dance with a famous singer at dusk might lead to a magical love affair.

That wasn't her story.

She'd already met the love of her life and he'd died. On the most ordinary of Sunday afternoons, he'd left to buy more diapers, and the next thing she knew, police officers were at her door, saying words like *car accident* and *deepest apologies* all while Calla cried and squirmed, fussy in her arms. Their lives had changed in a millisecond.

Most people didn't end up with their soulmates. They settled for whoever was there at the right time. Or they ended up alone. Iris was lucky to have experienced the years she had with Terry, luckier than most. If she was going to risk putting herself back out there again, she wouldn't be silly enough to think that things would work with someone like Angel, because there were several reasons to prove otherwise. One, she wouldn't risk getting romantic with the new brand ambassador because Save Face Beauty couldn't handle another controversy. Two, Angel was a celebrity who didn't seem to have plans to settle down anytime soon, least of all with an ordinary person like her. Why would he, when he had access to the Gigi Harrisons of the world? And most important, she had Calla to consider. If she was going to bring someone into her and Calla's fold, he'd have to be capable of stability, and Angel's life seemed to be the opposite of that. His lifestyle was too different.

Iris wanted companionship, true, but she was going to be practical about finding it.

"You having fun, baby girl?" she asked Calla.

Calla grinned, hugging Iris tightly. "Yes! I've had *so* much cake, Mom."

Iris laughed and pretended as though she couldn't still feel the sensation of Angel's fingers pressed gently at her waist.

3

WAS IT SOMETHING I SAID?

Perplexed, Angel stared after Iris's quickly retreating form until she melded into the crowd on the dance floor. He stuffed his hands in his pockets and stood motionless, replaying and dissecting each moment of their interaction. Had he made her feel uncomfortable somehow? From the way she'd easily leaned into him, it seemed like she'd been enjoying their dance. Maybe he'd put his foot in his mouth by blurting out the suggestion that they take another walk on a different day. In retrospect, the line sounded corny to his own ears. It was just . . . after all this time, he still remembered everything about their conversation from three years ago. He remembered the sound of her sultry laugh and the slight tilt of her lips when she smiled. She looked almost exactly the same, except now her hair was longer.

Over the years, as he and Violet worked together and grew closer, Angel had expressed interest in Iris. He'd asked Violet to bring Iris to one of his shows, and Violet had vaguely told him that she didn't think it would be a good idea. She'd gently encouraged him to aim his attentions elsewhere. Angel had been confused and disappointed by Violet's response, but he'd respected the boundaries that she'd placed before him, figuring that she was trying to be protective of her sister. He'd tried not to mention Iris too often, but he'd been incapable of forgetting her completely, even if she'd slipped to the back of his mind.

Shortly after Violet's anti-wedding party, Angel's career had blown up overnight. His first single, "Better for You," had gone viral and was declared the song of the summer. It rose to the number one spot on the *Billboard* charts, and Angel became top priority at Capitol Music Group. They'd thrown everything into the rollout for his first album. The budget for his music videos had been astronomical. He'd performed at almost every music award show. He'd signed endorsement deals left and right, and his newfound success gave him social currency. He sat courtside at Lakers games and was invited to birthday bashes thrown by celebrities he'd only dreamed of meeting. He was in the studio, on tour, back in the studio, onstage. It was never ending. A year later, when his second album dropped, and he'd evaded the sophomore slump and won a Grammy, his star had risen even higher.

And the women. They were everywhere. In his DMs. At his shows. Waiting outside his hotel with their phone numbers written on pieces of paper. They were his peers whom he met at industry events and parties and clubs. Beautiful women, talented women, who probably wouldn't have given him the time of day before. At first, he hadn't had the faintest idea of what to do with so much attention. A few of the women he'd been involved with over the years had been really lovely and accomplished and fun. But for some reason, Angel failed to feel a real, lasting connection with any of them, and that made him feel only lonelier.

Then tonight, he'd seen Iris standing there as the maid of honor. The initial potency of his crush on her had dulled for sure, but during the ceremony, his eyes kept drifting toward her. During her speech, Angel was spellbound as Iris shared the mic with Lily, speaking eloquently in her alluring voice. Throughout the reception, he'd kept his distance, remembering Violet's directive about aiming his attentions elsewhere. He'd talked with other wedding guests and signed some autographs. He'd posed for picture after picture with the teenage cousins. And then when he'd realized that they were recording him, he began to feel self-conscious. The idea of being constantly perceived and picked apart by anyone with a smartphone was still difficult to get used to. Leaving his dinner half-eaten, he'd quietly slipped outside for a moment of solitude. And he'd wanted to check on Maxine. He'd found the oak tree in the middle of the vineyard . . . and then Iris had appeared.

Seeing her there had felt too good to be true. Like his long-ago prayer had been answered. He thought it might have been something like fate. Especially since he was the new brand ambassador for the company where she worked.

But given the way she'd practically run from him just now . . . maybe not.

An alert chimed on his phone, snapping him to attention. It was a text from his driver, Gabriel. Outside, boss.

Angel texted back, Thanks, coming now. Want some cake?

I shouldn't, Gabriel responded. Then, But yes.

Angel laughed and walked back inside. The younger

cousins whipped their phones out again. Angel searched
the crowd for his best friend and bodyguard, Ray, and he
found him slow dancing to a fast song with another wedding guest. The woman gazed dreamily up at Ray, like she'd
been in love with him for decades and hadn't just met him
less than an hour ago. Ray often had that effect on women.
Standing at six foot four with arms that looked like they
could snap a tree trunk in half, a bald head and neck tattoos, there was something about Ray that women couldn't
resist. He'd moved to LA with dreams of becoming a professional bodybuilder, and he'd been Angel's first roommate
after connecting on a roommate app. They'd shared a crappy
one-bedroom in West Hollywood that had low water pressure and frequent mice. To make money, Ray had worked as
a bouncer at nightclubs, and Angel had bussed tables and
sang at open mic nights. Ray eventually gave up on his dream
of becoming a professional bodybuilder, but now he was
paid very well to protect Angel.

Last year, after a fan had waited outside of Angel's gated
community and lain down in front of his car, his team had
decided that it would be best if he didn't leave the house
without security. Angel had jumped at offering the job to
Ray. If he had to have someone with him all hours of the
day, he at least wanted that person to be a friend.

Ultimately, his level of popularity was what had influenced him to move to Manhattan last year. He was still recognized, but in the city, he had more anonymity and there
were fewer paparazzi. New Yorkers didn't care that he was
famous. They'd still tell him to move out of their way if he
was walking too slow.

Ray smiled at the woman and leaned down to whisper

in her ear. The woman tightened her hold around Ray's torso, and Angel laughed. It was funny that *he* had the reputation for being a Casanova or whatever when that title really belonged to Ray.

Angel kept walking in Violet's direction, who stood arm in arm with her husband, surrounded by a group of older relatives. Angel waited patiently while Violet's family members wished the bride and groom congratulations. When they walked away, he took his chance to slide in front of Violet and Xavier.

"Hey, you!" Violet beamed as she hugged Angel tightly. "I feel like I haven't talked to you all night!"

"You've been too busy for me," he joked, and Violet lightly swatted his arm. "I'm kidding, I wanted to say congratulations again before I left."

"You're leaving already?" Violet pretended to pout. "You can't stay for late-night tacos?"

"We've got chicken, pork, barbacoa, *and* vegan, if you're not into meat like the rest of her friends," Xavier said.

"That sounds bomb," Angel said. "But unfortunately, duty calls. Gotta go to the studio." He dapped Xavier up. "Congrats, bro." Then he leaned down and hugged Violet. "I'm happy for you, Big Sis."

He'd given her the nickname shortly after they'd started working together, because Violet had always looked out for Angel and treated him like a person and not a product. She'd helped him develop his own sense of style. His clothes had become a unique avenue for him to express himself after spending most of his life doing the opposite. And she was genuinely his friend.

As he hugged Violet, he glanced up and caught eyes with

Iris, who stood several yards away, holding hands with her daughter and speaking to Lily and her boyfriend. Their gazes held across the tables and chairs separating them. Spots of pink bloomed on Iris's cheeks, and Angel's pulse stuttered. Their gazes locked long enough for Violet to lean away from Angel and follow his line of sight.

"Let me guess," she said quietly, smirking. "You still have a thing for my sister?"

Angel reluctantly pulled his eyes away from Iris. Violet's head was tilted, observing him.

"I—" he started. "We went on a walk earlier and I basically asked her out. I think I might have made her uncomfortable somehow. I'm sorry."

Violet looped her arm through Angel's and began to pull him away, signaling to Xavier that she'd be back in a moment. Confused, Angel let Violet lead him to an unoccupied table. She leaned closer and lowered her voice.

"If Iris rejected you, don't take it personally," she said.

He glanced toward Iris again. Her back was facing him now as she talked with Lily. He studied the elegant slope of her neck and shoulders. Was it something about him that Iris found particularly unlikable?

"Why not?" he asked.

Violet bit her lip. "She's been through a lot. I don't think dating is really one of her priorities right now."

Angel nodded slowly. He wanted to ask for more clarification, but he didn't feel like it was his place. He glanced up, searching for Iris again, but she'd disappeared from her previous spot in the ballroom. He thought of the troubled look on her face when he'd asked her out.

"Understood," he said quietly.

Violet wrapped Angel in a hug. "For the record, I do think you'd make a nice couple. You're ridiculously easy-going and she's not. It's a whole opposites-attract vibe." She pulled back from Angel and smiled. "I'll see you in a few weeks for your next fitting?"

"Yeah." Angel fought the urge to glance around the room for Iris one last time. He kept his gaze fixed on Violet's joyful face. "Enjoy your honeymoon."

After stepping away from Violet, he waved to Ray, who looked reluctant to separate from his dance partner.

"Sorry to bust up your groove," Angel said, once he and Ray met halfway.

Ray shrugged. "It couldn't have gone anywhere. She's a marine biologist in Alaska, which is cool as shit, but I'm not tryna freeze my balls off whenever I have time to visit her."

Angel snorted and swiped two slices of cake on their way out the door. Three women, fellow wedding guests, were waiting for valet to bring their cars around in the horseshoe driveway. They whispered to one another as Angel and Ray passed them. Angel smiled politely.

"Can we get a selfie, please?" one woman asked, already holding up her phone.

Angel doubled back toward them. "Sure," he said.

He was tired, but during these moments, he always heard his mom's voice in his ear, reminding him to be thankful for all the good that he had in his life. He wouldn't be here without the fans who listened to his music.

He leaned down between the women and smiled as they snapped several selfies. Then he thanked them for their support and smoothly excused himself. He heard them giggling as he and Ray approached a black Mercedes with tinted windows. Angel tapped the back window and Gabriel unlocked the doors. Angel and Ray slid into the backseat and Angel passed a plate of cake up front to Gabriel.

"Got you a vanilla slice," he said.

Gabriel nodded in thanks. He tucked a napkin in his shirt, always careful not to mess up his clean black suit. With one hand, he stuck a fork in the cake, and with the other he put the car in drive.

"Home or the studio, boss?" Gabriel asked.

"The studio," Angel said, which was basically his home lately.

Gabriel kept his eyes on the road. "Did you have a good time?"

Ray stretched out his long legs and cracked his neck. "I'm gonna need to soak my feet after all that dancing. They couldn't get enough of me."

Gabriel laughed and looked at Angel in the rearview mirror. "And you?"

Angel pictured Iris's face again and realized that tonight would probably be the last time he'd ever talk to her.

"Yeah," he said. "It was beautiful."

AS ANGEL ENTERED the recording studio in Chelsea, a familiar sense of calm washed over him. For as long as he could remember, music had always been his outlet.

There had been many rules in his house growing up. No swearing. No lying. No suggestive television or movies. No suggestive music. Activities that were allowed: school, church, Bible study and choir practice. His parents' main goal in life had been to keep Angel and his younger sister,

Leah, on the straight and narrow path. At night, while the rest of his family was asleep, Angel huddled under the covers in his bedroom, listening to CDs on an old portable CD player that he'd found at the thrift store.

His favorite artists were the greats like Marvin Gaye, James Brown, Al Green and Prince. But he loved nineties R & B too. Groups like Jodeci and H-Town and Next, and solo artists like Maxwell and Ginuwine. They sang songs that talked about women—songs that talked about sex. Angel loved the passion in their voices. As a sixteen-year-old virgin, Angel hadn't done even so much as kiss a girl, but he wrote his own passionate love songs, inspired by the music that he loved. He'd been blessed with the gift of song himself, but his talents were solely reserved for singing solos before the congregation with the youth choir every Sunday.

Once, while cleaning his room, his mom had discovered his notebook of songs and his secret stash of albums, and she'd been beside herself as she'd shouted and lamented about Angel's sinful thoughts. She'd grounded him for an entire month and made him meet weekly with his youth pastor. Angel always seemed to be getting in trouble somehow. At school, he was written up on multiple occasions because he couldn't stop humming in class. At home, he forgot to take out the trash or fold his laundry because his head was stuck in the clouds, imagining a life outside of his bubble of Maren, Georgia, where he could sing the kind of music that he wanted to.

A few weeks shy of his eighteenth birthday, a visitor who worked for a small Christian record label in Atlanta happened to attend church service. The label rep saw something special in Angel and extended an invitation for him to audition for the larger team. Angel's mother, Cora, had joined him on the drive to Atlanta, and after singing for the label execs, they offered to sign him on the spot. Cora had been hesitant because Angel still had two months of high school to finish, but after the execs assured her that Angel's music wouldn't interfere with his studies, she became more agreeable. Angel signed a one-album contract, and that day, Cora instated herself as Angel's manager, because, in her opinion, he needed her there for his protection.

Angel loved singing gospel. He felt overwhelmed with a deep sense of joy whenever he sang in church. But it didn't change the fact that his dream was to be an R & B singer.

His gospel album, while well reviewed, had performed to middling success. But it was enough to encourage him to chase his real dream. Shortly after turning twenty-one, he moved to LA. He hadn't known a soul, and most of the money he'd made from his small gospel deal had gone toward helping his family, so he didn't have much liquid cash. And, of course, his parents—particularly his mom— were against his decision to leave gospel behind for secular music, so that weighed on him too. But Angel tried to break into the industry in every possible way. In addition to the billions of open mic nights he attended, he posted his original songs on SoundCloud and made YouTube videos singing covers of popular songs. A video of him singing a D'Angelo cover got the attention of an R & B showcase organizer, who invited Angel to perform at their next event. That night, an A&R rep from Capitol Music Group listened to Angel sing and told him that he could be the next big thing in R & B, and Angel signed with the label.

The A&R rep had been correct in one regard: eventually, Angel would turn out to be the next big thing. But straight up R & B? Not exactly. For his first album, his label had pushed him in a pop-ish direction, saying that the sound would help break him out, and later he could transition to full-on R & B. Angel had believed them. He'd worked with their appointed physical trainer and changed his eating habits so that his body was perfectly sculpted for photo shoots. He'd taken the dance lessons and learned the choreography for his music videos. His first two albums had been filled with up-tempo tracks. He'd garnered the popularity and sales that the label had been hoping for. He'd even won a Grammy for Best New Artist.

Now he was working on his third album. His soul R & B album, supposedly. But every time he recorded a new song and turned it into his label, the song was swiftly rejected. This runaround had been happening for the last three months.

"Yo, bro," Angel said, greeting his friend and producer, Malik, who sat at the mixing booth, nodding his head to a newly created beat.

Malik stood and dapped Angel up, then Ray. Ray sat on the couch and quickly fell asleep, which is what he usually did whenever he joined Angel at the studio.

Angel and Malik had been paired together for his first album, and even though Angel had worked with other producers since, he preferred working with Malik the most. They just vibed. Maybe it was because Malik was from Atlanta, which felt closer to home for Angel.

"Made some beats for you," Malik said, sliding back into his seat. "Wanna hear 'em?"

"For sure." Angel took the open seat beside Malik, loosened his tie and shrugged off his suit jacket.

Malik played a new beat. It was up-tempo, something you usually heard at clubs and parties. The same kind of music on his first two albums.

"Sounds dope," Angel said.

Malik smirked at him. "You don't like it, though. They keep rejecting everything else, so." He shrugged.

"I know," Angel said, sighing. "They'll probably love this beat."

Lately, his artistic integrity was in a constant war with his practicality. This kind of music had made him popular. It sold well and led to endorsement deals that lined his pockets and made it so that he could live his current lifestyle and pay for his parents' mortgage and his dad's diabetes medication and doctor visits and Leah's college tuition. Being able to take care of his family was important to him.

So, if it wasn't broke, why fix it? At the same time, he craved creative freedom.

He was exhausted by the current stalemate, though.

"Let me see if I can come up with something," he said.

He pulled out a pen and his small notepad that he usually carried with him because he wrote the majority of his own songs and never knew when inspiration would strike.

He listened to the beat on several loops, gaining the rhythm, and waiting to see if any words or hooks jumped out at him. Nothing.

"Can we turn that off for a second?" he asked.

"Of course." Malik cut the music.

Angel sat at the electric keyboard across the room and plucked a few notes. That was how some of his best song-writing sessions started: a pen, a paper, an instrument and a question. What did he want to say? What was on his heart? Ideas for songs usually came to him while he was focusing on other things, like showering or doing vocal exercises. He'd have to stop midtask and jot words down in his Notes app if he couldn't get to his notepad. In high school, he used to carry around sticky notes and a pen.

He leaned back and closed his eyes. An image of Iris materialized in his mind. She was smiling at him as the sun set in the background. Wearing her light gold dress. No, it had been champagne gold. Angel played a few more keys and began to hum.

She'd been wearing a dress . . . the color of champagne.

He tapped his pen against his notepad and played the keys again before transcribing the words to paper.

> *You in that dress, the color of champagne.*

He needed something to rhyme with *champagne*.

If he could go back in time, he'd try to make it clear that whatever he'd done, he hadn't meant to upset Iris. He hurried to write again.

> *I don't know how else to say it. How can I make it plain?*

He was starting to find a groove. Her name was a flower. What rhymed with flower?

> *Your name's just like a flower . . .*

Someone he could think about every hour.

He felt the headlong rush of a creative flow underway. The words poured out of him, quicker than he could write. When he put them to music, lightly pressing his fingers against the keys, the song was soft and slow. The way he wished he could record it.

"That's dope," Malik said, listening quietly.

Angel grinned. But just as quickly, his smile fell as realization dawned.

"I need the label to finally approve something," he said. He sighed and stood, approaching the recording booth. "Let's record it over your beat."

He spent the next hour recording, changing the lyrics when necessary. By almost midnight, the song was finished. Malik played it back a few times, tweaking here and there. The final product was good, something Angel pictured people blasting in their cars all summer. It wasn't the sound he would have chosen but whatever. He'd send it to his manager in the morning to share with the label. Hopefully this song would be approved.

After leaving the studio, Gabriel dropped off Ray and drove Angel to his condo, which was also in Chelsea. As Angel exited the elevator and walked to his door, getting his keys out of his pocket, he heard Maxine whining and scratching at the door. She catapulted into Angel's legs the moment he stepped inside.

"Hey, pretty girl," Angel cooed. Maxine beat her tail against his thigh as he bent down to scratch behind her ear. She covered his face in exuberant kisses. She was too big to be carried now, but Angel scooped her up anyway and carried her into the living room, where he found his sister sprawled out on his couch, digging into a bag of Funyuns.

"You're home earlier than I expected," Leah said, sitting up. She was wearing an oversize hoodie, and when her hood fell back, revealing her head, Angel blinked. She'd buzzed off half of her curly hair.

"Leah . . ."

"Yes?" She stretched her arms and smiled innocently, picking up one of Maxine's toys and tossing it across the room. Maxine jumped out of Angel's arms and raced for it.

"When did you do that to your hair?" Angel asked, standing at the arm of the couch.

"About an hour ago." She moved her head from side to side. She looked so much like their mom with her almond-shaped eyes and high cheekbones. "Do you like it?"

Angel sat next to her and inspected her hair more closely. Lucky for Leah, she had a nice-shaped head. The look was actually pretty dope.

"I do, but you know Mom is gonna say this is my fault."

Leah smirked at him. "What else is new?"

Every time that Leah did something that their mother deemed rebellious, she blamed Angel's influence. Leah's decision to go to NYU instead of staying close to home in Georgia? It was because of Angel. Leah getting a tattoo of a butterfly on her arm? That was because of Angel too, even though he didn't have any tattoos himself. And most definitely, Angel, who dyed his hair frequently, would be to blame for Leah's new halfway buzz cut. But Leah was twenty years old. Her frontal lobe might not be fully developed yet, but she was capable of making her own choices, despite what their mom thought.

"You know," Angel said conversationally, as he took the bag of Funyuns from his sister and shook some into his palm, "I don't pay all that money for your on-campus housing just for you to be here all the time."

"My roommate's girlfriend is over, and I'm tired of being a third wheel." Leah rolled her eyes. She was taking summer courses to complete her degree in sociology early. "How was the wedding?"

"It was nice."

"Did you bring a date?"

Angel laughed midchew. "If you count Ray, then yeah."

"I don't count Ray." Leah snorted and took the bag of Funyuns back. "You and Gigi broke up almost two months ago. I'm surprised you haven't already found someone new yet."

Angel shook his head and laughed again. "You make me sound like a ho."

"You kind of are, but I'm not judging." Leah shrugged. "I liked Gigi, though. She was nice."

"She was," Angel said. "But we agreed we're better as friends. We're cool."

"You said the same thing about that singer Shana Shah and that actress Tracey what's her face, and then that model—"

"Okay, *okay.*" Angel plucked Leah in the arm. Sometimes he missed when she was the little girl who followed him around adoringly and didn't comment on his failing love life. "Your point has been made, ma'am."

"As your sister, it's my job to be in your business like this."

Angel rolled his eyes but smiled.

Each of his relationships (and the situationships too) had ended on good terms. There was no bad blood with any of his exes. At first, dating had been an exciting, new experience, because he hadn't dated at all as a teenager and during his first few years in LA, he was practically broke and entirely too focused on trying to get signed. But when he did start dating, the fleeting relationships grew old pretty fast. They had been fun and new, but they hadn't been anything deeper than that. He wanted something beyond the superficial.

Before he'd become famous, Angel had always known that he wanted to share his life with someone. He wanted to get married and have a family. Maybe he was a traditional Southern guy in that way. He craved a real connection with someone. With his kind of career, it wasn't always easy to feel grounded. He just wanted to be with someone he could really talk to.

Leah rolled up the bag of Funyuns and yawned, standing. "Mom asked which day we're coming down for the ceremony next month, by the way."

Angel was being honored in his hometown Maren as a thank-you for funding renovations for his parents' church and donating new equipment and instruments to the school district's music department. The ceremony was held every year to celebrate different people in the community. His mother had been honored twice for her work with the church.

When he'd heard about the honor, he hadn't planned on attending. He didn't visit home very often. Mostly because his mom made his visits so stressful. But if the town was taking the time to honor him, and his old pastor was presenting him with the award, Angel figured at the very least, he could be bothered to show up.

"I'll handle getting our flights booked," he said. "Don't worry."

"Cool." Leah began to walk toward one of the guest rooms that she reserved for herself, but she doubled back. "Hey, do you want to come to church with me tomorrow?"

Angel shook his head. "I'm good, but thanks."

Leah smiled softly. She was used to this answer. She'd found a church in the city that she really liked. Angel hadn't been to church in years.

"Okay. Good night," she said.

"Good night."

Maxine trailed behind Leah, and when she realized that Leah was going to bed, she returned to the living room and clambered onto the couch, dropping her slobbery bone toy in Angel's lap. Technically, Maxine was Leah's dog. She'd begged Angel for one since their parents hadn't allowed them to have pets growing up. But Maxine lived with Angel, and he took care of her, so she was his too. He picked up her squeaky toy and threw it across the room. Maxine lunged and scrambled across the carpet.

Angel laughed and eased back onto the couch. He'd be separated from her in a couple weeks. He was going on a makeup tour for Save Face Beauty. No, wait, it was skincare. He'd been paid a lot of money to shoot ads and videos looking at his reflection in the mirror as he covered his skin in face jelly or moisturizer. Something to prevent dry skin and acne. He rarely said no to opportunities because, one, he never knew if or when they'd stop coming, and two, a check was a check. It was more money to ensure he'd be able to buy his parents a new house if they ever let him or to help Leah with whatever she needed once she graduated. He had a series of meet and greets scheduled throughout the country to promote Save Face Beauty's new skincare products. He was traveling with a woman named Paloma and her assistant. Foolishly, he wished that Iris was the one accompanying him.

Maxine brought the toy back to Angel, and they played their rowdy late-night game of fetch for another hour.

In the morning, Angel received news that the label loved the new song. They changed his original title from "Infatuated" to "Summertime Fine."

When it released two weeks later, it debuted at number four on the *Billboard* Hot 100 chart.

4

IRIS'S PHILOSOPHY WAS THAT MAINTAINING A GARDEN was a lot like maintaining one's life. After a seed was planted, its development depended on how well it was nurtured. If watered appropriately and given the right amount of sunlight, the seed could bloom into a beautiful plant. A healthy garden required consistency and dedication. It also required a sense of order, and Iris had orderliness in spades.

She loved her garden. It was her happy place.

The morning sun shone down on her as she took a cursory stroll through her garden in her backyard before work. Her hydrangea bushes were thriving, and purple flower buds were beginning to open. Her orange and yellow marigolds looked good too, which relieved her. Two summers in a row, she'd planted marigolds only for the flower heads to mysteriously disappear overnight. She'd discovered that deer had been sneaking into her backyard and snacking on her marigolds specifically. The trick now was to spray her flowers with deer repellant.

She crouched down and peered closely at her pink begonias. Two bumblebees hovered around the flowers, collecting pollen and paying Iris no mind. Bumblebees were mostly harmless and tolerant of people, unless you did something dramatic to threaten them. Iris considered the bees part of her garden's ecosystem. Similar to the big spider who lived in the web above her peonies. Every spring, he reemerged and trapped the bugs that tried to eat her plants.

Everything that she knew about gardening and plants she'd learned from her parents, thanks to the many summers she'd spent working at their florist/nursery shop, Greene-house. Then after college, she'd joined corporate America and never looked back. Now gardening was her hobby, but sometimes she wondered what her life might have been like if she'd taken that other path and stayed in the family business.

She stood upright, brushed the soil debris off her hands and walked inside. Their house was two stories with three bedrooms. Iris used the third bedroom as an office and storage space. Admittedly, the house felt too big for just her and Calla. When she and Terry had first moved here almost seven and a half years ago, they'd done so with the assumption that they'd have more children down the line. Their studio apartment on the Lower East Side with its uneven floors and unreliable heating system hadn't been large or safe enough for a baby. Moving back to Iris's New Jersey hometown, Willow Ridge, had made sense. It was only an hour train ride away from the city, and Iris couldn't imagine taking care of a newborn without her parents' help, especially since Terry's parents were hours away in DC. They'd gifted Iris and Terry with the money for the house's down payment.

Iris walked upstairs and paused in Calla's bedroom doorway. Calla unabashedly loved the color pink. Her walls and bedspread were pink. Pink teddy bears sat atop her little bookshelf, which housed tons of books gifted to her by Lily, who now was a children's book editor. And the window drapes were pink too. Wearing a light pink short-sleeved sundress, Calla kneeled in the center of her room, carefully tying the laces of her white sneakers. She'd recently mastered the bunny ears method. She was graduating from kindergarten at the end of the week, and soon she'd be a child of summer, juggling day camp, swimming and karate.

Iris quietly observed her daughter's quirked lips and pinched brows as she tied her shoes. Calla wore such a serious expression sometimes, like she'd experienced much more life beyond her six years. When she'd been a newborn, cute and soft and fragile, everything that she did had seemed like a wonder to Iris and Terry.

Did you see the way her mouth moved? I think she's smiling at us, Iris would say.

Look at the way she stretches her arms. She's going to be so strong, Terry would say.

They'd been new parents, exhausted and bleary-eyed, whispering to each other in the early-morning hours as Calla dozed on the bed between them. Their lives had turned out so differently from what they'd pictured when they'd first bumped into each other at NYU's Bobst Library. That first year of business school, Iris had seen Terry around here and there. They'd even shared the same Foundations of Finance class. She'd noted that he was handsome and well-spoken, often raising his hand to answer questions. But she hadn't talked to him directly. After graduating from Princeton at the top of her class and landing an entry-level job at Save Face Beauty, Iris had been focused on moving up in the corporate world. Not on spending time with handsome young men.

One night during their first semester, she'd been in the library studying after class, and Terry had been there too, seated a few tables over. They'd stayed until the library closed, and it had been raining when they'd stepped outside. Iris usually came to her evening classes straight from the office, so she hadn't thought to bring an umbrella. As she stared at the rain, annoyed with herself and her unpreparedness, contemplating a mad dash to the F train at West 4th Street, Terry had appeared beside her and opened his wide umbrella over both of their heads.

"I can walk with you to the subway," he'd said quietly. "If you'd like."

He had impeccable manners. That was the first thing Iris noticed about him. He knew to walk on the side of her that was closest to the street to protect her from getting splashed, and he lightly held on to her elbow and steered her around trash in the middle of the sidewalk. He wore a classic digital Casio watch, wrinkle-free slacks, a button-up and a tan trench coat. She didn't recall ever seeing him wear jeans to class. During their walk, they discussed their courses and what had brought them to New York. Terry was originally from DC and had graduated from Hampton four years prior. He was getting his business degree and then planned to return to DC to work for his father's financial advisory firm. He spoke in a direct, matter-of-fact way that Iris appreciated.

When they reached the West 4th station, he'd politely bid her good night. The following evening, he'd sat beside her in class, and later they'd walked to the library and discussed their notes. It became their routine, soon followed by late-night walks for slices of pizza, where they shared their ambitions, like Terry's desire to expand his father's business and Iris's desire to learn as much as she could from her boss, Dominique. He told Iris about how he liked playing basketball for fun but was only passably good. She told him about how she loved gardening and had her parents to thank for it.

She fell in love with Terry the way that she did most things: methodically. First there was the spark of physical attraction, then she fell in love with his mind. At the end of the semester, when their cohort went out for drinks on the last day of classes before winter break, Iris stared at Terry's mouth the entire time that they talked at the bar. She was single-minded in every aspect of her life, and when Terry finally kissed her outside the bar, she knew she'd become single-minded about him too. Falling for him hadn't been part of her plan. But life was full of surprises. Iris knew that all too well now.

"Ready for school?" Iris asked Calla, leaning against the doorjamb.

Calla glanced up. She had Terry's dimpled chin and the shape of his nose. The traits she'd seemed to inherit from Iris were her thick, curly hair and her penchant for organization. She stood and grabbed her Little Mermaid backpack, placing her hands on her hips in satisfaction.

"Yes," she said, smiling.

Calla followed Iris downstairs and they ate bowls of cereal. Then Iris packed Calla's snacks in her backpack and grabbed her travel mug. Calla was newly obsessed with dinosaurs because they'd watched the most recent *Jurassic*

Park movie over the weekend. She'd been talking about dinosaurs nonstop since, and she provided Iris with random facts as they walked outside to the car.

"Mom," Calla said contemplatively. "Did you know that the longest dinosaur was the same length as *four* fire trucks?"

"I didn't know that." After they climbed inside, Iris made sure that Calla was safely buckled up before she pulled out of the driveway. "What else can you tell me?"

"The first dinosaur was called the *Megalosaurus*."

"That's a mouthful," Iris said, smiling.

"Mom, I want to be an arch . . . archeo—" Calla frowned, and her tongue continued to trip over the word.

"Archaeologist?" Iris supplied.

"Yes. I want to find dinosaur bones."

Iris nodded, encouraging this new idea. A few weeks ago, Calla had declared that she wanted to be a gymnast, and a few weeks before that, she'd wanted to be a teacher. Iris took each of her ideas seriously. She wanted Calla to know that she could be anything that she put her mind to.

"Did you know that the museum of natural history in the city has an exhibit on dinosaurs?" she asked.

Calla's round eyes widened. "They do?"

"Yep. They even have life-size replicas of dinosaurs."

Calla gasped. "*Wow*," she whispered. "I want to go. Can we go, please? *Please?*"

"Of course. We have all summer."

Minutes later, she pulled into the drop-off line at Calla's elementary school, and the radio caught her attention.

"We got some new songs taking up our top ten spots this morning," the Power 105.1 DJ announced. "A new hit from Angel coming up after these messages."

At the sound of Angel's name, Iris stilled. She'd thought about him in the couple weeks since Violet's wedding, of course. Mostly, she'd been embarrassed at how she'd experienced a small freak-out at his suggestion that they see each other again. She'd since realized that she'd completely overreacted. He was probably just trying to be nice because he could tell she'd been feeling sad. It had been kind of him to dance with her in an attempt to cheer her up. There was no way he'd actually been interested in her romantically. He was famous! And she was . . . well, she was a decidedly unfamous person who lived in the suburbs of New Jersey and took the commuter train to work in the city after dropping her daughter off at school.

"Mom?" Calla said, waiting for Iris to get out and walk her to the front doors. She was eager to be at school today because they were having a pizza party for lunch.

"Sorry, baby," Iris said, snapping to attention.

She walked Calla to the school's main entrance and gave her a big hug and kiss goodbye.

"Have a good day, honey," she said. "I love you."

"I love you too." Calla smiled and darted away. Iris was grateful that Calla was still at the age where she didn't mind being hugged and kissed by Iris in public. Iris felt like just yesterday she'd held a newborn baby in her arms, and now her baby was graduating from kindergarten. Time was moving so quickly.

Iris watched as Calla joined the group of students walking down the hall. Then Calla paused and quickly doubled back. When she reached Iris, she leveled her with a serious stare.

"Mom, remember, karate ends at six thirty," she said.

Usually, Iris's mom or dad, who also lived in Willow Ridge, picked Calla up from school and dropped her off at karate class. Iris insisted on being the person to pick her up. But dealing with the unreliable MTA and NJ Transit during rush hour was a lawless gamble. More often than not, Iris was late to the karate dojo and Calla was one of the last kids to be picked up. A huge no-no in the little-kid rule book. But today, Iris planned to leave early anyway since she had her scheduled therapy appointment.

"I remember," Iris said. "I'll be there on time today. Promise."

"Okay, bye." Calla waved as she hurried back inside, her book bag bouncing against her back.

Once Calla was safely on her way to her classroom, Iris walked back toward her car. A few feet in front of her on the sidewalk, she spotted Janet and Viv, two women who had daughters in Calla's class. Their daughters also took karate with Calla, which meant that the girls were friends and had playdates often. Janet and Viv were fine in small doses—chatting idly before tournaments or in the dojo parking lot. But Iris was fully aware that if she didn't have a daughter who was the same age as theirs, she probably wouldn't be friends with Janet and Viv. They were about a decade older than her, but that wasn't the issue. Mainly, she didn't want to get that close to them because they were nosy, and if she told them anything personal, she couldn't trust that they wouldn't share her business with someone else. But that was the problem with a small town like Willow Ridge in general.

"Iris, hey!" Janet said, waving Iris down.

She and Viv were wearing pastel-colored workout sets and holding iced coffees. Their hairstyles also matched, each donning jumbo knotless box braids. They'd been best friends since high school, and their husbands were best friends as well. Janet had dark brown skin and was tall and slender, while Viv was light-skinned, medium height and curvy, but they liked to tell everyone that they were fraternal twins. They went to barre classes during the week and often invited Iris. She wished that she had the freedom to go to a workout class on a weekday morning.

"Hey there," she said, slightly slowing her walk. She didn't really have time to talk, but she didn't want to be rude. "How's it going?"

"Good!" Janet said brightly. "You know, same old, same old. Trying to get my ten thousand steps in every day but failing!" Dramatically, she looked to her left, then to her right, and lowered her voice. "Viv and I were just talking about Adrienne and Lamar. Have you heard what happened?"

Adrienne and Lamar were the parents of Lamar junior, another one of Calla's classmates. Iris glanced at the time on her phone screen.

"I haven't," she said. "I wish I could stay and talk, but—"

"They're *separating*," Viv whispered, eyes widening. "Adrienne said she caught Lamar texting his secretary. I mean, how stereotypical can you be?"

She and Janet tutted, shaking their heads. Iris didn't know Adrienne or Lamar that well, so talking about their personal business made her uncomfortable.

"That's, um, really sad to hear." She continued edging away. "I'm sorry but I've got to head to the train."

"Don't worry, we'll share the rest of the story through text," Janet said, tapping her phone.

That was another thing. Last year, they'd created a group chat with a couple other karate moms. It was their water cooler for town gossip. Iris never looked at the chat and had it silenced.

"Have a good day!" she called, breaking into a light jog, waving over her shoulder.

Iris knew that Janet and Viv had singled her out and made continued attempts to bring her into their fold because they felt sorry for her. It was the whole being-a-young-widow thing. In a way, Iris appreciated that they had good intentions where she was concerned. That was probably why she literally ran away from conversations with them instead of straight up saying that she'd rather stick to discussing matters that mutually involved their children and nothing more.

Iris climbed back into her car and began her drive to the train station at the same time that the radio DJ finished his commercial break.

"Okay, so this new song from Angel is a nice lil summer turn-up," the DJ said. "Let's get into it."

Iris perked up in her seat, realizing she was relieved that she hadn't missed hearing the song. She turned the volume up as the song began to play. The beat was smooth and fast, something to easily dance to. The kind of song that she was used to hearing from Angel. His dulcet tones filtered over the airwaves.

> *Your name is like a flower. I think about you every hour.*

Iris blinked and stared at her dashboard. The driver in the car behind her honked their horn as the stoplight turned green. Iris put her foot on the gas.

A name like a flower. That could mean anything. He'd probably needed something to rhyme with *hour*.

The song continued, and Iris listened more closely.

> *You in that dress, the color of champagne. I don't know how else to say it, baby, how can I make it plain? I remember every move of our dance. Even though I know I'll never have a chance.*

Iris gasped.

Wait a minute . . . Was this song about *her*?

No. No way. It couldn't be. Could it?

She pulled into the train station parking lot and cut the engine. She was scatterbrained as she raced up the staircase and onto the platform. The two-decker train came roaring into the station, and Iris entered the train and moved to the designated quiet car. She found an unoccupied window seat and opened the music app on her phone. She didn't even need to search for Angel's name. His new song "Summertime Fine" was being advertised on the app's home page. She popped in her headphones and clicked play, listening to the song again.

She hadn't imagined things. Those lyrics were real.

Her name was a flower.

She had worn a champagne-colored dress as *they* had danced together.

Blood rushed to Iris's face. She glanced around at the other commuters, as if they could hear what she was hearing. She had the weird fear that everyone in the world was staring at her, which obviously couldn't be further from the truth. No one on the train was looking in her direction. Why did he write those lyrics? What did it mean? And why was her heart pounding so painfully?

She was in a confused daze as the train pulled into Penn Station and she took the downtown A train to the Financial District. She waved hello to the doormen at the Save Face Beauty building and took the elevator up to her floor. When she reached her office, she placed her bag on her desk and flopped into her chair. All the while, Angel's voice continued to croon in her ears. She'd listened to the song on a loop at least ten times.

She was flattered—how couldn't she be?! It was Angel! But she was also so, so confused. Why had he written a song about *her*, of all people?

A knock sounded at her door. "Good morning!"

Startled, Iris glanced up at her assistant, Bree, who stood in her doorway, a ready smile on her lips. Bree wore a black turtleneck and black jeans even though it was mid-June. On Bree's first day, Iris had told her that she mostly wore black because it was easy and always looked professional. That was two years ago, and Bree had taken that little nugget of information to heart. Her blonde faux locs fell midway to her back, and she smoothly brushed her hair over her shoulders as Iris hastened to sit up and pull her headphones out of her ears.

"H-hi, good morning."

"Sorry to interrupt," Bree said, approaching Iris's desk. "I didn't mean to startle you."

"It's okay. Do you need me?"

"Dominique wants to see you."

Iris glanced at her monitor. It was 8:53 a.m. She still had seven minutes left until her day started. "Right now?"

Bree nodded. "She said it's urgent."

Iris shrugged off her white Nike trainers and slipped on her black single-sole heels. She grabbed her legal pad on her way to the door. "Any idea what this is about?"

"No," Bree said, keeping up with Iris's brisk stride. "I asked her assistant for extra info, but she didn't give much away."

"Right." This wasn't untypical. Dominique, Iris's boss and the president and CEO of Save Face Beauty, relied on Iris's input for a handful of things. This meeting could be about Dominique's desire to know Iris's thoughts on a new employee's performance or she might ask if Iris had any ideas for this year's company retreat. It really just depended on the day.

Iris and Bree rounded the corner that led to Dominique's office. Dominique's door was open, and she sat behind her desk as Paloma sat across from her. A life-size cutout of Angel wearing an all-white sweat suit and holding the new facial moisturizer was positioned right behind Dominique. It was a literal jump scare. Like he'd leaped from Iris's thoughts right into the room. She yelped and froze in the doorway. Bree stumbled into her back.

Dominique snapped her head up, and Paloma, who was resting her hands on her stomach, whipped around to face Iris. They stared at her, brows raised at her sudden outburst.

"Are you okay?" Bree asked, tapping Iris on the shoulder.

"Sorry," Iris said, regaining her composure. She let out a

shaky laugh. "We did such a great job with those cutouts. They look so real, I thought it was actually him."

Dominique and Paloma laughed, and Iris secretly released a sigh of relief that they'd bought her lie.

"That was all you," Paloma said.

The promotional cutouts had been Iris's idea to place inside Refine stores. Iris swallowed hard, hearing the melody of Angel's new song again in her head.

"Don't hover in the doorway. Come in, come in," Dominique said. She looked at Bree. "Bree, hun, no need to join this meeting just yet."

Iris and Bree exchanged a quick look. Bree usually sat in on all of Iris's meetings to take notes. If Dominique didn't want Bree there, the subject matter must have been of a confidential nature. Bree whispered to Iris that she'd be at her desk if Iris needed her, and she quickly left the room.

"Good morning," Iris said, taking the open seat beside Paloma.

"Hi, lady." Paloma reached over and lightly touched Iris's hand. Paloma's wavy hair was dyed honey blonde and she wore her signature blue-red lip that popped against her brown skin. Iris and Paloma had started at Save Face Beauty right out of college. Iris had been hired as a marketing assistant and Paloma had been an assistant in PR, and they'd become quick friends. In the past decade, they'd both climbed their way up the corporate ladder.

As director of partnerships, it was Iris's job to cultivate Save Face Beauty's expansion. She led the team that secured endcap displays and exclusive gift bundles and sales with companies like Sephora, Ulta, and Refine. The work that Iris did used to give her a rush. But for the better part of this past year while finalizing Angel's meet-and-greet tour for their skincare line, something had changed. She felt less inspired. Maybe it was because of the Turks and Caicos food poisoning situation. The constant online bashing had resulted in record-low sales and had even led to a round of layoffs at the end of spring. It had affected overall morale. Iris could feel the difference in herself and her colleagues as they sat in meetings and walked through the halls. It was an eerie feeling, like they were all waiting for the other shoe to drop. Everyone was hoping that this new skincare venture would help turn things around. Maybe the pressure Iris put on herself had depleted her creativity.

It was also highly likely that she was burned out and just needed a vacation.

"So, we have some news for you," Dominique said. Her gray braids were pulled into a bun high on top of her head. Pearl drop earrings dangled from her ears.

Iris glanced back and forth between Dominique and Paloma. "What's going on?"

"I have to take early pregnancy leave." Paloma pointed at her stomach. "Just found out yesterday evening. Doctor's orders."

Iris knew that Paloma, who was seven months along, had been experiencing a difficult pregnancy after she and her wife had finally conceived last year through IVF. Iris squeezed her friend's hand. "Oh no, babe, I'm sorry."

"Yeah," Paloma said, sighing. "I guess it gives me more time to catch up on *Grey's Anatomy*. Be prepared to receive several live texting updates." She laughed, and Iris laughed too. "I'll still be working from home, but I won't be coming into the office. The daily commute is too much."

Iris nodded. "If there's anything I can do to help, let me know."

"Well . . ." Paloma looked to Dominique.

"That's why I've called this meeting," Dominique said. "Given Paloma's situation, she won't be able to go on the meet-and-greet tour with Angel next week."

"Oh." Iris's stomach tightened at the mention of Angel's name. "Of course, that makes sense."

"I think it's best that you go in her place."

Iris balked. "*What?* Me?"

"Yes," Dominique said.

Iris shook her head. "I—but I'm not in PR." She turned to Paloma. "Wouldn't you rather have someone from your team go instead?"

"You helped plan the tour," Dominique said, not dissuaded. "It was your idea. You're the only person who knows the ins and outs as well as Paloma."

"There's no one else that I'd trust to do this," Paloma said. "We want a more senior person there to make sure everything goes smoothly. And since you already have a connection to Angel through your sister, we thought it made the most sense."

The issue wasn't that Iris didn't understand their reasoning. The meet-and-greet tour was a big deal for the company's future, whose reputation currently hung in the balance, and after everyone's hard work it made sense that someone at Iris's level would take the baton from Paloma to ensure that the tour was a success. And personally, Iris wanted to protect her own reputation. No one at the office had blamed her for what happened in Turks and Caicos, and it wasn't like she could have done anything about the resort choosing to switch kitchen management, but she was still frustrated that something so chaotic had happened on her watch. The skincare line's success was imperative.

But agreeing to the tour would mean spending a week with Angel. Who'd written a song about her. Possibly. Or possibly not. Angel with his golden voice and soft eyes. The thought of him made Iris feel flustered, and she *hated* feeling flustered.

"I know that making accommodations this late might be difficult, and if there's anything that you need for Calla, we're happy to assist you," Dominique said. She leaned back in her chair and folded her hands, analyzing Iris. She looked at Paloma. "Paloma, hun, can you give Iris and me a minute?"

Paloma nodded and rose from her seat. She gave Iris an encouraging smile before she left the room, closing the door behind her.

"You know that I take my role as your mentor very seriously, don't you?" Dominique asked.

"Yes," Iris said. "Of course."

"I'm aware that this is all very last-minute and Calla's graduation is coming up soon. I know that you're a long-term planner. But not just anyone can accompany Angel and see things through. You're the one that I count on time and time again." She smiled. "You know I've felt that way about you from the beginning."

Iris nodded. She had always known how much Dominique valued her and her work ethic. Over a decade ago, months before she'd graduated from Princeton, Dominique spoke at a seminar on campus, sponsored by the alumni association. Dominique had talked with fellow Princeton graduates on a panel about business practices, and Iris had been captivated by the Black beauty industry mogul who'd broken barriers by creating an inclusive makeup brand that celebrated everyone's inherent beauty, with the motto *it's your skin, but better*. Iris wasn't necessarily passionate about makeup herself at the time. At most, she wore lip gloss and mascara and added eyeliner on special occasions. But she was intrigued by Dominique's ambition and power. She wanted to be just like her one day.

After the panel ended, Iris had shouldered her way through the room until she was right in front of Dominique. She'd boldly asked for an informational interview, and surprisingly Dominique had agreed, saying that she rarely turned down the opportunity to speak with young Black women who were interested in forwarding their careers. Iris took the train into the city and met Dominique at the Crosby Street Hotel, where she told Dominique that she wanted to learn from her and would do anything for the opportunity. Dominique had been so impressed with Iris's straightforward ambition, she'd offered her a marketing assistant position once she graduated.

Under Dominique's mentorship, Iris had thrived at SFB. Her original plan had been to stay at SFB for a few years and then take what she'd learned and break into other industries, like tech or market research, while keeping her mentor-mentee relationship with Dominique intact. But then she'd gotten pregnant and later Terry had passed, and trying to switch into a new industry not only seemed impossible, it felt too risky. She knew SFB and she leaned into that secureness. Dominique and the rest of the team were there for Iris during one of the worst periods of her life, and because Dominique understood that Iris wanted to channel her energy into work, she continued to give Iris new projects and promote her. Iris owed so much to Dominique and SFB, and she didn't want to see the company fail.

She needed to get over herself and quick. Refusing to go on the tour was simply not an option. Too much was at stake.

After a lengthy pause, Iris said, "Okay. I'll do it."

Dominique smiled, satisfied. "There's my girl. Thank you. I knew I could count on you. Can you tell Paloma to come back inside, please?"

Iris gulped and nodded quickly. She was a professional. She could spend an extended amount of time with Angel as the company representative for his tour. Everything would be fine. Now that she thought about it more, it was silly to think that he'd written the song about her. Realistically, the song was probably about a model named Jasmine or Daisy whom he'd met at a famous-people party and she'd happened to also wear a champagne-colored gown. It was summer. Everyone wore champagne gowns to parties. Iris was simply overreacting.

This logical reasoning soothed her fluttering stomach. Taking a deep breath, Iris opened the door for Paloma and shared the news that she'd agreed to go on the tour. Paloma threw her arms around Iris, which was an impressive feat given that her belly was lodged between them.

"Thank you so, so much!"

"You're welcome," Iris whispered, eyes once again drawn to the Angel cutout. She forced herself to look away.

"Paloma, I trust you'll catch Iris up on the specifics for our meeting this morning," Dominique said.

"What meeting?" Iris asked.

"It's the last preliminary meeting with Angel's team," Paloma explained. "We weren't going to bother you with it because your schedule is already packed, and you don't usually deal with talent care. It was supposed to take place next week, but we moved it up because Angel had a schedule conflict."

Against her will, Iris's heartbeat quickened. "Angel will be at this meeting?"

"Yep!" Paloma beamed. "Isn't that so cool?"

"*Today?*"

Paloma nodded. "I know, shocking. He couldn't make any of the meetings before, but he'll be here. People in the office don't know, for security reasons. It's very hush-hush." She mimed zipping her lips.

"They'll be here in about an hour," Dominique said, checking the time. "Paloma, why don't you get started on updating Iris?"

Paloma jumped in, and after a delayed moment, Iris pulled out her legal pad to scribble notes. The fact that she somehow managed to absorb anything that Paloma said was a miracle because two thoughts ran on a constant loop in her brain.

Angel will be here.

You thought he wrote a song about you.

All too soon, a call came in from the front desk. Angel and his team were arriving. They were going take the freight elevator up for security.

Paloma needed to run to the bathroom before the meeting, so Iris was alone as she walked to the freight elevator bank to greet Angel and his team. Sweat gathered in the palms of her hands.

Be cool. She just needed to be cool. She could do this. It was no big deal, really.

The elevator doors opened, revealing a handful of people. A building security guard, a short, dark-haired woman, holding a phone to her ear. A blonde woman, texting feverishly. A tall, bulky man with light brown skin and neck tattoos. And in the middle of them stood Angel. He wore a dark brown short-sleeved leather button-up and matching leather pants. Sunglasses dangled from his shirt's collar. His gaze landed on Iris and his eyes widened. Iris's heartbeat decided to perform a drum solo.

"Iris?" Angel said, smiling as he stepped toward her. It was a relieved smile, like he'd been hoping to see her but wasn't sure if he would.

The tempo of her heart's drum solo quickened.

"Hi." She stared up into his face, feeling a little breathless. "Welcome to Save Face Beauty."

"I didn't know you'd be at this meeting," he said, looking at her with such focused attention, she felt glued to the spot under his gaze. "I'm really glad to see you."

Oh no, why did he have to go and say *that*? Her heart's drum solo added tambourines and a team of majorette dancers. They kicked and jumped around inside of her chest cavity. *Angel* was glad to see *her*. Her initial response was pure joy. Because being face-to-face again, she realized that she was glad to see him too.

But then she glanced at the team of people standing behind him, who were also looking at her, and she snapped out of her daze. She forced her heart's halftime show performance to pack it up and go home. This was her *job*. She needed to stop gazing at Angel like an awestruck fan.

"I'm glad to see you too," she said in the most professional tone possible. She cleared her throat. "And actually, I'll be joining you on your meet-and-greet tour."

"Really?" The smile that he gave her was so bright and full of life, it jolted her entire system.

"Really," she said, swallowing thickly. "Please follow me to our conference room."

5

MAYBE IT WAS FATE.

Or maybe it was simply a coincidence.

Iris did work for the company, after all. But either way, Angel wasn't going to question it. What he knew was that Iris was here, in this conference room, sitting only a few chairs away from him at the other end of the table. He hadn't planned to come to this meeting originally. Usually his team presented him with an endorsement opportunity and gave him a rundown of the brand and their mission. They talked numbers, he signed off on paperwork and showed up to set for photo shoots, commercial tapings and promotional events, and then he moved on to the next thing. But he'd joined today's meeting at the suggestion of his manager, Valerie, who knew he was climbing up a wall. After the success of "Summertime Fine," people were all abuzz. His fans wanted to hear more music, and if they had their way, they'd have his next album immediately. The issue was that his label was back to rejecting his songs. "Summertime Fine" had worked for them only because it had the pop R & B sound that they wanted. He'd been stressed, and it was messing with his creative flow, so he'd joined the meeting today as a way to give his mind a break.

Now his attention was focused on Iris. They were about to spend a week together on the campaign tour. He couldn't believe it.

"I'm so sorry that I won't be able to travel with you like originally planned," Iris's colleague Paloma said. "But you're in the best hands with Iris."

Iris sat with her back ramrod straight, her hands folded in front of her. She looked at Angel and his team and nodded in confirmation. Angel bet that she'd been the ideal pupil in school, earning straight As and a perfect attendance record. The thought made him smile. When he and Iris caught eyes, she blinked, and her cheeks flushed. She glanced at her hands before bringing her gaze back up to his, offering a soft smile of her own. The small act melted him. He wished they were the only two people here and that they weren't separated by a large conference room desk. He wanted to ask how she'd been. Had she thought about him over the last couple weeks? He'd certainly thought about her. He wanted to know if she'd heard his song. If so, did she know that it was about her? Did she like it? Or wait, what if it had made her feel uncomfortable? Crap, he hoped not.

"Just as another refresher, these are the products we'll be promoting," Paloma said, grabbing Angel's attention by placing three small brown containers onto the table. "Cleanser, moisturizer and SPF."

Valerie Marks, Angel's manager, unscrewed the cap of the moisturizer. Her pale blonde hair was held back by her black-framed glasses that she never seemed to actually wear.

She sniffed. "Smells delicious. Like brown sugar." She passed it to Angel. "Here, smell this."

He took a whiff as well. He'd smelled the products before at the campaign shoot weeks ago, but he'd since forgotten the scent. The brown sugar aroma wafted up his nostrils. "Yeah, it smells amazing. Like something you can eat."

"Thank you," said Dominique Johnson. She'd been introduced to Angel as Save Face Beauty's CEO.

Valerie passed the product to Angel's publicist, Claudia Chin, who sat to his right. Claudia dipped her finger into the moisturizer cream and rubbed it between her fingers. "Ooh," she said. "I love this consistency." She then passed the container to Ray so that he wouldn't feel left out.

Valerie and Claudia were the women who helped Angel keep his life in check. Valerie had been Angel's manager for the past three years, ever since he'd ditched his previous manager, Eddy. Valerie was a business veteran and a straight shooter. She'd done a world of wonder for Angel's career in a short time period. And Claudia was the reason that Angel was here at the Save Face Beauty's offices to begin with. She'd handled every detail of his ambassadorship while he'd been performing and recording and traveling over the past several months.

Valerie and Claudia were protective of Angel, because he had this little problem where he tended to say yes to everything, even when he was exhausted. Even when an event occurred on his birthday. Like the Atlanta stop of this meet-and-greet tour. He didn't usually make a big deal of celebrating his birthday anyway, so he didn't mind. He'd rather make more money than rest.

Paloma moved on to explaining the tour's logistics to

refresh everyone's memory. They'd start in Los Angeles, and then continue to Seattle, then onto DC and Atlanta, finishing in New York City with a final event attended by beauty influencers and sweepstakes winners, where Angel would perform a set for the crowd.

"This goes without saying, but can we make sure the stores are playing his music at each location?" Claudia asked.

"Absolutely," Paloma said, nodding. "Or if Angel would like to curate a specific playlist, we can share that with the stores too."

"Curating a playlist would be cool," he said.

Claudia raised an eyebrow, looking at him. "Are you sure you have time for that?"

"For sure."

Paloma clapped. "Awesome! If you can share the playlist with us within the next couple of days, that'd be great."

Claudia and Angel nodded. He let his eyes drift briefly toward Iris again, who was already looking at him. Her gaze moved across his face, and he stilled, letting her study him, wanting to be studied by her. He remembered how it had felt to hold her while they danced together. Had she thought about that moment as much as he had?

"Will there be a limit to the number of fan photographs?" Valerie asked, pulling Angel's attention away from Iris.

"A limit?" he repeated.

"We don't want to exhaust you," Valerie said gently. "Having him take pictures with the first one hundred fans at each store seems like a lot."

He appreciated Valerie's intention, but he'd hate for anyone to travel to see him and not get a chance to speak to him. "I think I'll be okay."

Iris spoke up, still looking directly at Angel. "If you decide that one hundred people is too much, please let me know. Your comfort is our priority. If there's anything you need during the autograph signing or photo ops, please don't hesitate to ask. If you need to take a break at any time, just say the word."

"Thank you," he said, and Iris nodded. Their gazes held for a beat before Iris looked at Valerie, who confirmed her satisfaction with Iris's answer.

To Angel's disappointment, the meeting ended soon after.

"Since we've finished a little early, we'd love to record some quick content for our social media with Angel," Paloma said, as everyone stood. "If that's okay."

"Yeah, of course," Angel said, before Valerie or Claudia could answer for him.

"Great! I'm going to quickly run to the restroom and then I'll escort you down to our studio," Paloma said.

"Actually, I'd be happy to escort them," Iris cut in. She went to the door and waited for Angel and his team, smiling patiently. Angel smiled back as he approached her. He felt a crackle between them, some kind of force that drew him to her. They fell into step together with Valerie, Claudia and Ray walking behind them.

Now it was Angel's turn to study Iris. Her short hair was tied back today in a low bun. She wasn't wearing as much makeup as she'd worn at the wedding. She was beautiful.

"So how's Maxine?" she asked.

Angel's brows rose. She'd remembered his dog's name. It

was such a small thing that made him so happy. "She's great. Missing me right now, like I'm missing her." He smiled. "How is everything with you?"

"Good," she said. "I've, um, been doing good."

She glanced back toward Valerie and Claudia, who were deep in discussion, looking at something on Claudia's iPad. Iris looked at Angel again.

"I wanted to apologize to you," she said quietly, leaning closer.

He took the chance to lean closer as well, taking in her floral-scented perfume. "Apologize? Why?"

"The way I reacted at my sister's wedding. How I ran away from you after we danced. It was unnecessary."

Now that he had some context about her not being in a place to date, he'd never hold her reaction against her. "It's okay. You don't need to apologize about that."

She gave him a doubtful smile. "You probably think I'm the most awkward person on the planet."

He shook his head. "Not at all."

"You were just trying to be kind to me when it was clear that I was having a bad day, and I appreciate that." She laughed softly. "This morning, I even convinced myself that your new song was about me."

"It was," he said honestly.

Iris's steps faltered and she stared at him. He stared back. "But . . . why?" she whispered.

"I felt like you could use a song."

Her lips parted. She blinked once, twice.

"Did you like it?" he asked. He held his breath, nervous and all too eager to hear her answer.

"I—" She glanced at his team again. They were nearing

the elevator now. Some of her colleagues were rising from behind their cubicles, looking at Angel, discreetly holding up their phones. But Angel didn't care about that. He was focused on Iris. She cleared her throat. "Yes, I did. I do."

Warmth spread throughout his chest. Iris liked the song. Even if *Pitchfork* or *The Fader* reviewed it and tore it apart, he wouldn't care. Because the song was about Iris and she liked it and that was all that mattered to him.

"Good," he said, grinning at her. "If you hated it, I'd have to quit music altogether and when people asked why, I'd be too embarrassed to tell them the truth, so I'd have to lie and say I'd decided to pursue other passions, like making home-made soap."

Iris burst into surprised laughter and quickly covered her mouth with her hand. "Why *homemade soap*, of all things?"

"Everybody likes being clean, don't they? I'll never go out of business."

"It's not a terrible idea," she said. "But if you decide to mass-produce it—because you have to assume that all of your fans will want some of your soap—could you keep the integrity of your brand? Natural ingredients can be costly. Once you get big, you'll probably end up adding synthetic ingredients." She tapped the side of her head, mouth curving into a smile as she looked at him. "Just something to consider."

"Wow, nah, those are good points." His grin widened, delighted that she was entertaining this fake idea of his. "You sound like you know what you're talking about. We should discuss it more over coffee."

Once he said that last sentence, he immediately regretted it. He'd meant it as a joke, because he knew from Violet that Iris wasn't dating right now. But it was clear that Iris thought that he was being serious. He watched in dismay as her smile fell a fraction and she bit her lip.

"Angel, I think you're great," she whispered with furrowed brows. "I mean, obviously you're great. But this is my job, and even if it wasn't, I don't . . . we . . . I mean, I . . ." She trailed off, obviously struggling for a way to let him down easy. Her cheeks flushed again.

Although it stung to hear this, he remembered what Violet had said about not taking Iris's rejection personally.

"I get it," he said, eager to put her at ease. "I hear you loud and clear. I'll be a perfect gentleman on this tour. I want you to know that." He smiled and added, "I won't ask you for any more dances at twilight."

Iris laughed, and the light sound relieved him. Her shoulders relaxed as she sent him a grateful look. "Thank you for saying that."

"Of course."

They faced each other as they waited for the elevator to reach their floor. Iris was still smiling. Her eyes began to roam his face, pausing at his hoop nose ring and then lingering on his mouth. She bit her lip again and rubbed the back of her neck.

Angel might have grown up as a sheltered kid, and he might not have had his first kiss until he was eighteen. But he knew enough now to recognize when a woman was interested in him.

He had a feeling that Iris was interested, or at the very least, intrigued. But she was determined not to act on it.

He had no choice but to respect that.

"Thank you for waiting!"

Angel blinked and Iris turned abruptly. Paloma was rushing down the hall toward them as fast as she could move. Dominique was right behind her, glancing between Iris and Angel with a quirked eyebrow.

The elevator finally reached their floor and opened its doors. Iris looked at Angel again, and he was suddenly filled with reluctance to leave her.

"Iris, can I speak to you for a moment before my eleven o' clock?" Dominique asked.

"Oh, of course," Iris said. She spared one more look at Angel. She smiled, and it zapped him straight in the heart. "Thank you for coming in today. I'll see you next week."

She held her hand out toward him. Angel took her hand in his, and he felt a rush as their palms pressed together. Her skin was soft and warm.

"See you then," he said.

Iris stared up at him. Their handshake was lasting longer than necessary but neither pulled away.

"Iris?" Dominique prompted.

Iris blinked and dropped his hand, taking a swift and sudden step backward. Immediately, he missed her touch. She cleared her throat and waved goodbye to him and his team. Angel held his hand at his side, palm tingling as he watched her walk away with her boss.

Funny that he was surrounded by people all day long, and in the few minutes he'd talked to Iris, he'd felt less lonely.

He hoped that by the end of the tour, they might at least become friends.

6

IRIS HAD CONFIRMATION NOW. ANGEL HAD WRITTEN THE song about her.

He said that he'd written it because he felt like she could use a song, and she could tell that he hadn't been lying. He'd *wanted* to write the song about her. She'd been on his mind heavy enough that she'd inspired an entire song. She pictured him in the studio piecing the lyrics together. Her body buzzed until her limbs started to feel like jelly. Angel creating that song was one of the loveliest things that anyone had ever done for her. It was wild! It was unbelievable! It was—

"Iris?" Dominique said, looking at Iris expectantly.

Iris blinked, once again on the other side of Dominique's desk because she'd wanted to quickly chat before her eleven o'clock meeting, and Iris was too busy thinking about Angel to pay attention to whatever her boss was saying.

"I'm sorry," Iris said. "Can you please repeat that?"

"I said that I wanted to discuss something with you about next week's tour."

Now Dominique had Iris's full attention. She sat up straighter.

"From what I observed in the hallway just now, you and

Angel seem to get along pretty well already, which is great. I know that you're familiar with each other because of the work that he does with your sister." Dominique paused and drummed her fingers against her desk. Iris's stomach clenched, anxious to hear what her boss would say next. She'd probably witnessed Iris staring at Angel with googly eyes. "Angel is obviously very charming and we all know that he has a bit of a reputation for dating beautiful women. Spending time with an attractive, famous man who is known for his romantic pursuits can have its . . . let's say, *temptations*. Now, I know that I'd never have to worry about this with you, but regardless, I must remind you that things need to stay professional during this tour. We can't have any inappropriate behavior reflecting poorly on the company. We've already been through enough this year."

Iris gulped and nodded quickly. "Yes, of course. I wouldn't think otherwise."

On cue, the tune of Angel's song began to play in her head. She shoved it deep into the back of her mind. Yes, the song did make her happy, and seeing Angel just now had made her happy too, but she couldn't entertain anything beyond that. They had to work together and there was too much at stake.

Dominique smiled, appeased with Iris's answer. "I'm glad we're on the same page."

Iris knew she'd have to keep the truth about the song to herself.

WELL, SHE DID reveal the truth to someone. Her therapist, Marie. Iris had started seeing Marie six months after Terry's accident. Iris had searched far and wide for a Black woman therapist who specialized in grief therapy *and* took her work's insurance. She and Marie had developed a comfortable rapport over the years, a rapport that Iris cherished because Marie had helped see Iris through some of her darkest days.

Later that afternoon, as Iris sat in Marie's office, she recounted the story of hearing the song for the first time this morning and her subsequent conversation with Angel.

"Do you like the song?" Marie asked. She had dark brown skin and a low-cut Afro. Her long nails had a new, elaborate design every month. Most recently, they were painted a shiny, cobalt blue with silver stars.

"I do," Iris answered honestly, sitting on the couch in Marie's cozy office. "It's very catchy. And, I mean, obviously I like that it's about me."

She laughed, a little embarrassed at admitting this, and Marie smiled.

"And how do you feel when you listen to it?" she asked.

Iris picked at a piece of lint on her skirt, thinking. "I feel admired and paid attention to. It was really sweet that he took notice of me and that I was on his mind. The song is beautiful." She took a breath and paused.

Marie tilted her head. "I feel a 'but' coming on."

"*But* I'm trying to be realistic about this situation. The song *is* beautiful, and I love it, but Angel is a celebrity. It wouldn't make any sense for me to pursue him because he's our brand ambassador, and professionally that's a line I won't cross, and two, he's not the kind of partner that I have in mind to join my and Calla's lives."

Marie nodded, aware of the qualities that Iris was looking for in a future partner. Stability and a similar lifestyle being the main factors.

"But Angel taking notice of you is a good sign, wouldn't you say?" Marie said. "It could be an indicator that others might notice you as well and appreciate your qualities if they spend time with you."

"I suppose," Iris said. Beyond creating a profile on Meet Me, a popular dating app, she hadn't made much progress on the Attempting to Date Again front. The thought of starting all over kind of exhausted her. But it wasn't like she could wake up one day in a healthy, long-term relationship. If she wanted companionship again, which she did, she'd have to put in the effort to find it.

"I'm working on it," she said, although she was hardly doing the bare minimum.

OVER THE NEXT few days, it was as though Iris heard Angel's song everywhere. Not just on the radio but playing in Duane Reade as she waited in the checkout line, and a group of teens had blasted the song on a loop while she rode the subway. She still hadn't told anyone outside of Marie about the song. She especially hadn't told her sisters because they'd make a big deal out of it and she didn't want to deal with the fuss or questions.

Sunday evening, the night before the tour started, Iris brought Calla with her to her parents' house for Sunday dinner, which was really an excuse for her mother, Dahlia, to force Iris and her sisters to listen to her plans for the annual July 15th barbecue that she and their father threw every year to celebrate their joint birthdays.

"Since your father and I are turning sixty-five this year, I think we should do something big," Dahlia said. "Like hire one of those Prince impersonators to perform."

Iris paused in the act of slicing tomatoes for a salad. There were so many ways that an impersonator could go wrong. Especially with Prince. Not everyone could hit those high notes. She glanced across the kitchen table at Violet and Lily, who looked back at her with varying degrees of amusement on their faces.

"I love it," Violet said, grinning mischievously. She was sun-kissed and glowing, having recently returned from her honeymoon with Xavier in St. Barts. They'd come back just in time for Calla's graduation a few days ago. "Why stop at Prince? You should add Rick James and Sheila E. too."

"You think so?" Dahlia asked, not picking up on Violet's sarcasm.

Lily turned away, hiding her grin as she laughed quietly.

"Vi is *joking*," Iris said, rolling her eyes, but trying not to laugh too.

Dahlia swatted at Violet, who continued laughing and dodged out of the way.

"It could be fun," Lily said, trying to appease their mother and find common ground.

"What if we hire a really good DJ who can play some Prince instead?" Iris suggested. It was usually her job to see reason.

Dahlia pointed at Iris. "That's what we'll do."

As their mom went to the oven and pulled out the roast chicken, Violet and Lily grinned at Iris knowingly. They had a running joke that Iris was Dahlia's favorite. Iris didn't think that was the case. She just made things easy and always had. When her Ivy League–educated parents pushed her to get straights As in school and join every extracurricular that would look good on college applications, Iris had thrown herself into pleasing them without complaint. Her parents had struggled with Violet, who'd always marched to the beat of her own drum, and Lily, who'd rather disappear for hours with her books. Iris had been a steady, reliable fixture, and they'd depended on her to help steer her younger sisters in the right direction. They still depended on her for that now.

Dahlia slid open the patio door and called, "Dinner's ready!"

First, Xavier and Nick walked inside. They'd been playing a pickup basketball game in the driveway. Years ago, Iris hadn't known why her father had bothered setting up the hoop since neither she nor her sisters played basketball. But his patience won out in the end, because Xavier and Nick were finally making use of it.

"Smells good in here," Xavier said, going to the sink and washing his hands. Xavier taught English and coached varsity basketball at Willow Ridge High School. He used to live in town too, but now he and Violet lived in Jersey City, since it was the middle point between Willow Ridge and Violet's work studio in New York City.

"Is there anything that I can do to help?" Nick asked. He stood beside Dahlia and offered a small smile.

"No, you sit yourself down, Mr. Bestseller," Dahlia said. "I don't need any help but thank you."

"Okay." Nick rubbed the back of his neck as he sat beside Lily. The second book in his popular fantasy series had landed at the top of the *New York Times* bestseller list recently, but you wouldn't know that by talking to Nick. Iris didn't think she'd ever met anyone who hated attention more than her youngest sister's boyfriend.

Lily patted Nick's hand and smiled at him lovingly. Xavier kissed Violet on the forehead as he took the empty seat next to her. Iris felt that familiar tug of loneliness in her stomach as she watched them. She loved Xavier and Nick, and even more, she loved that they made her sisters happy. But sometimes, being around all four of them at once only reminded Iris of her singleness.

Their father, Benjamin, came inside, rubbing his lower back. Calla followed behind him. She'd been helping him outside in his garden. He was testing new soil that they were considering selling at the shop.

"Grandpa said his back hurts," Calla announced to the room.

"I'm fine." Benjamin waved away everyone's looks of concern.

"You sure?" Iris asked, eyeing Benjamin as he washed his hands before taking his seat at the head of the table.

Benjamin nodded. "Yeah, just getting old. Nothing special."

Iris smirked and shook her head. Her dad was turning sixty-five in a month, and he still insisted on being hands-on with everything. Her parents ran the shop themselves, even though Iris and her sisters had been trying to convince them to hire a full-time manager.

"You and Mom need a vacation," Iris said, adding her chopped tomatoes to the salad in the middle of the table.

Dahlia laughed. "If we could trust someone to run the place when we're not here, we'd take one."

"I can help you find someone," Iris offered. She wanted to be able to help in some way, since it was unrealistic that she or her sisters would be able to watch over the shop while their parents were gone.

"Don't you worry about that," Dahlia said. "You've got too much on your plate as it is." When Iris began to protest, Dahlia refused to hear any more on the subject and told everyone to make their plates.

AFTER DINNER, IRIS offered to wash dishes. She wanted her parents to rest, especially since they'd agreed to watch Calla for the week while she traveled for work. Lily dried dishes. Xavier and Nick had joined Benjamin in the living room to watch the Yankees game, and Dahlia was upstairs with Calla, helping her unpack.

Violet sat at the kitchen table, using Iris's phone to play music. They were listening to a playlist that the app automatically generated based on what Iris had been listening to lately. So she shouldn't have been surprised when she heard the familiar opening tune of "Summertime Fine." She pictured Angel's handsome face, smiling at her in front of the elevator at the office earlier that week. Her pulse pounded.

"Ooh, turn that up," Lily said. "I love this song."

Violet complied and swiveled her hips in her chair. "It's so good, right?"

At the sink, Iris swallowed thickly. Maybe she should just tell them about the song and get rid of the elephant in the room that only she could see. She took a deep breath and turned around.

"Iris . . ." Violet said, staring at Iris's phone. "What is this?"

"What is what?" Iris dried off her hands and walked closer. Ridiculously, she worried that somehow the truth of the song's origins had materialized on her phone screen for Violet to read.

Violet flipped Iris's phone around. "Is this the Meet Me app?"

"Oh," Iris said, releasing a sigh of relief. Then, "Yes."

Lily's eyes widened as she held a plate and dishrag to her chest. "You're on a dating app? Since when?"

"Since a few weeks ago," Iris said. "I'm trying to put myself back out there slowly. It's something I talked about with my therapist . . . I wasn't going to say anything to either of you until I'd officially set up a first date."

When the three of them were together, they tended to weave a web of constant chatter. But now her sisters stared at her in silence. They exchanged a glance.

"Wait, this is huge," Violet said softly. "The fact that you feel ready enough to take this step. I'm really proud of you."

Lily nodded eagerly. "Me too."

"Thank you." Iris chewed the inside of her cheek. "I at least want to try. But that's a process too."

"Can I look at your account?" Violet asked.

Iris nodded and stood behind Violet. Lily stood on Violet's other side as they hovered over Iris's phone. For her profile image, Iris had chosen a picture she'd taken at last year's SFB holiday party. She was wearing a white sweater and wine red lipstick, laughing at something Paloma had said.

"That's a pretty picture of you," Lily said, and Violet voiced her agreement.

"Thanks," Iris said, watching as Violet continued scrolling to the "about me" section.

"Why is this part blank?" Violet asked.

"I'm not sure what to put yet." Iris sighed and bit her lip. "I know that on paper, I look accomplished with my work stuff, but I'm not sure if I'll sound very interesting."

"What do you mean? Of course you're interesting!" Lily protested.

At the same time, Violet said, "You, my dear sister, are a badass MILF. Put that in your 'about me' section. 'I'm Iris and I'm a MILF.' The men are gonna come running."

Iris snorted and shook her head.

"It's true!" Violet said.

"She has a point," Lily said, laughing.

"I don't know if this app stuff is really for me," Iris said. "I want to meet someone the old-fashioned way. In person."

"You'd have to go out for that to happen," Lily said. "If you ever want me to go out with you, just let me know. There are some really cool bars near me in Brooklyn."

"You'd need *me* to come with you too because I'm the friendly one," Violet said. She angled in her seat, looking at Iris. "What kind of guy are you interested in?"

"I guess someone who wants commitment," Iris said. "He needs to have a job, obviously. It would be nice if he had a career that he felt fulfilled him. Someone who wants a family and simplicity, and Calla would have to approve of him, of course. He'd have to be someone that I can talk to." An image of Angel in the vineyard, talking with her easily, materialized in her mind. Goose bumps spread across her skin and she rubbed her arms, shaking off the thought. "A normal guy."

Violet tilted her head and squinted at Iris. She opened her mouth, then closed it. "I—never mind."

"What?" Iris said.

"Nothing. All I'll say is that the person who might be the one for you might not come in the package that you're expecting."

"Hmm," Iris said noncommittally. It was a nice thought, and not one that she necessarily disagreed with on principle, but she had a pretty good idea of the kind of partnership that she wanted.

"Wow, Vi," Lily said. "That was pretty profound coming from you."

Violet gasped. "What is that supposed to mean? I can be deep when I want to be. I read that poetry book you gave me."

Lily blinked. "You did?"

Violet looked away. "Well, no. But I plan to."

While her sisters latched on to a new topic, Iris took her phone and slipped it in her back pocket. That was enough dating-app talk and talk about her in general for the night.

She had to get going soon anyway.

She needed to pack for what was sure to be an interesting workweek with Angel.

7

IRIS WAS POSITIVE THAT SHE'D NEVER SEEN SO MANY PEO-ple in one place. And she'd certainly never heard so much *screaming*.

The Refine store on Rodeo Drive was filled to the brim with Angel's fans who packed the space and spilled outside onto the sidewalk. The crowd consisted mainly of people in their late teens and early twenties, mostly women, but some seemed to be around Iris's age or a little older. The playlist that Angel had curated played overhead. People took turns posing beside his life-size cutouts. Influencers were easy to spot as they held up their phones, recording everything. Iris hoped the night would go off without a hitch and that the influencers wouldn't have anything negative to post. But right now, they seemed happy. The giddiness in the room was palpable.

Iris stood at the register in the center of the store, hold-ing a mic in her hand, waiting for a break in the pandemo-nium so that she could quickly give her opening spiel before introducing Angel. He obviously needed no introduction, but there had to be some sort of order to these things. An-gel, the reason for the screaming, stood to Iris's left. He wore a slim-fitting white T-shirt underneath an oversize dark blue denim jacket with matching jeans. A pair of sunglasses were pushed up onto his head. He grinned at the crowd, almost boyishly. A foot or two behind Angel stood his hulking bodyguard, Ray. His gaze was laser trained on the crowd. He wore a black suit and kept his arms crossed in front of him. He looked fierce and imposing now, but earlier when Iris had spoken to him in the hotel lobby, he'd been downright jovial, joking that by the end of the tour, he'd probably become a makeup influencer.

Despite Ray's current steely outward appearance, Iris could tell by the energy in the store that one of Angel's fans would be willing to face off with Ray in order to get to Angel.

As the shouting continued, Iris looked around for assistance. Bree, who was joining her this week, was recording videos of the crowd for Save Face Beauty's social media accounts. The Refine employees scurried through the thicket of fans, obviously overwhelmed by foot traffic. The store manager, Danica, was too busy gazing at Angel to take control of the crowd.

Finally, Iris put her fingers in her mouth and whistled like a sports coach, right into the mic. Suddenly, the room fell silent. Hundreds of curious eyes swiveled in her direction.

"Hi," she said, clearing her throat. "Thank you so much for coming to hear about Save Face Beauty's new skincare line. I'm so excited to introduce our brand ambassador, Angel—"

Her voice was drowned out by another round of intense cheers. *Sheesh.* She'd barely said more than three sentences before they'd started up again. Was this what Angel dealt with all the time? He lifted his hands, calling for quiet, and miraculously, his fans listened.

"Thank you," she whispered, and he nodded, motioning for her to continue.

"Today, the first one hundred people who purchase a special edition Save Face Beauty skincare bundle will get a picture with Angel and a signed autograph." More screaming. Iris silently counted to five before plowing on. "In this skincare bundle, you'll receive face wash, moisturizer and SPF." She picked up each container as she spoke, turning them in her hands to show the audience. "Now I'm going to get out of the way and let Angel say hello to you."

She held the mic toward Angel. He stepped forward and Iris quickly moved off to the side, taking the spot beside Bree, grateful to resume her usual place behind the scenes.

"What's up, y'all?" Angel said.

More screaming. Lots more. The odds of Iris having a migraine in the morning were increasing by the second.

"So, I'm not gonna lie, I didn't really think much about skincare until very recently," he said, and his fans laughed. "But I've learned that skincare is something we should all incorporate into our daily routine. These Save Face Beauty products are clean, vegan, and cruelty-free, which is something I can get down with. And just so y'all don't think I'm lying, I *have* been using the products, and I can say that my skin definitely feels smoother." He grinned as he caressed the sides of his face. Iris watched as several fans visibly swooned. She felt the corners of her mouth turn up. He knew how to work a room.

"Show us how you apply the products!" a fan shouted.

Angel chuckled. "Oh, so y'all want to make sure that I know what I'm talking about?" The audience cheered, and Angel nodded. "Okay, okay."

He reached for the face wash, and a seed of apprehension sprouted in Iris's stomach. Demonstrating the products was not part of the agenda.

"What's he doing?" she whispered to Bree. "He's not supposed to actually use the products here. And why is he starting with the face wash? We don't have anything for him to wet or dry his face with!"

Bree shrugged and laughed nervously. "I don't know. Do you want me to stop him?"

"One thing to know about Angel is that he has a hard time saying no," Ray explained, appearing out of nowhere, keeping his eyes on Angel as he spoke. "Especially when it comes to his fans."

Behind the register, Angel lifted his cleanser-dipped fingers to his face, and Iris hurried to intervene.

"Here, let me help you," she said, grabbing a wad of cotton pads from behind the register. She wiped off Angel's fingers, and he smiled at her quizzically but didn't resist her hold. "We're actually going to start with the moisturizer today."

"Oh, sorry." Angel glanced toward the crowd. "Looks like I needed some help."

His fans laughed as Iris placed the moisturizer onto the counter in front of him. She began to step away again, but then she held back a shriek as he used three fingers to scoop out an unnecessarily generous portion.

"Too much, *way* too much," she mumbled, grabbing more cotton pads to wipe his fingers again. She pivoted her face toward his so that the audience couldn't read her lips. To him, she whispered, "Is this how you've been applying the moisturizer?"

He nodded, smiling. "Yeah, why?"

"Oh goodness," she said.

Angel laughed, his whole face lighting up. "Uh-oh."

"You only need a decent amount on your fingertips," Iris said, unable to hide her own smile. She used the pad of her middle finger to gather some moisturizer, and then lightly dotted Angel's forehead, the center of both cheeks and his chin. "And you want to rub it in slowly, like this."

Her voice picked up over the mic, and Angel remained perfectly still as Iris gently rubbed in the moisturizer. Angel's skin was mostly smooth, and his complexion was even. His skin looked good in pictures but so many images of celebrities were altered, so Iris had no way of knowing what was real. There was a small pimple on his right cheek and another on the bottom of his chin. Angel was beautiful. That much was obvious. But it relieved her to know that in this small way, he had flaws too, like everyone else.

She leaned back, double-checking that she'd applied the product effectively, and when she brought her eyes to his and noticed how closely he was watching her, she felt her cheeks warm.

"What's next?" he asked quietly.

"The SPF." She pivoted sideways to face the crowd. "You want to make sure that you apply SPF to your face and neck every day. The great thing about our SPF is that it leaves no white cast."

She handed the SPF bottle to Angel, but he shook his head and gestured toward her.

"You're the expert," he said, mouth curving into a grin.

"Not an expert, just a company representative." But she picked up the bottle and applied the SPF to Angel's face as well. Then she rubbed it onto his neck. She brushed her fingers over his Adam's apple and it bobbed as he swallowed. Her fingertips were buzzing.

He tilted the mic away from his mouth and lowered his voice. "Am I doing a good job?"

She glanced up. "Yes, of course."

She lowered her gaze as she refocused on his skin. But she heard the smile in his voice. "Thanks. I'm glad I have your stamp of approval."

That made her laugh. "Well, my approval doesn't really matter."

Satisfied that she'd thoroughly applied the SPF, she stepped away and screwed the cap back onto the bottle.

"Sure, it does," he said.

He was still smiling at her when she looked at him again. To be the recipient of such a smile was enough to make a person dizzy. It had the power to hypnotize. Distantly, somewhere far off in the back of her mind, Iris remembered that she and Angel were standing in front of at least a hundred people, with even more waiting outside, eager to get a chance to see him.

She blinked and forced herself to pull her gaze away. She waved to the store manager, Danica, who jogged over immediately. "We're all good to start the signing now," Iris said.

The Refine employees tried their best to make a single-file line throughout the store. The loud chatter of Angel's fans created a constant buzzing in the room. Iris and Bree worked to make sure that the line moved at a steady pace, while Angel was positioned in front of the register with Ray right by his side. Fans openly sobbed as they greeted Angel. Some hugged and jumped on him. It seemed like such an invasion of space, but Angel's smile didn't drop from his face even once.

After two hours passed, Iris stepped forward to ask how he was doing. There was still a significant number of people waiting in line.

"Do you want to stop signing at a certain point?" she asked.

He shook his head. "I'll stay until I see everyone."

Iris admired how he remained calm and amiable, but once he started rolling his shoulders she could see that he eventually grew fatigued. Bree brought him a new water bottle and he smiled at her gratefully. He whispered something to her and nodded toward Iris.

"Is everything okay?" Iris asked as Bree walked back over to her.

"Yeah, Angel invited us to the club tonight," she said. "He said his producer is in town and has a table at Oasis. I hear celebrities always go there."

Iris hid her inner grimace. She'd accepted years ago that she wasn't a club person. She preferred small get-togethers where you could actually enjoy someone's company and didn't have to shout to be heard over the music. But Angel was inviting them out, and declining would probably be bad talent care. Her distaste for clubs could not outweigh her work ethic.

"Sure," she said, hoping that she didn't sound as reluctant as she felt. "Let's do it."

AFTER INTERACTING WITH HIS FANS, ANGEL ALWAYS FELT the same fulfilling yet bone-weary exhaustion. He'd refused to leave the Refine store until every fan got their picture. His face hurt from smiling. He probably should be back at his hotel room, sleeping before their early-morning flight to Seattle. He wanted to FaceTime Leah and Maxine. But at the moment, he was standing in VIP at Oasis because his producer, Malik, happened to be in LA tonight too, and he'd hit Angel up, inviting him out. Angel was drained, but he couldn't say no to Malik. "Summertime Fine" was still sitting high on the charts, thanks in large part to Malik's producing.

Malik and his friends were pouring up and taking shots of D'Ussé. Angel spotted Ray in the corner of their section, talking with Iris and Bree, who were sitting on the couch. Ray leaned down as he spoke, and whatever he'd said made Bree burst into laughter. Iris smiled and sat up straighter, casting a glance at the crowded dance floor. People had their cameras angled toward their section—toward Angel, specifically. He was used to the attention by now, but he could see how it might make Iris uncomfortable.

He'd been uncomfortable when he'd first moved to LA. He'd felt like an outsider who didn't have the right lingo or the right look. Shortly after he'd been signed to Capitol, a label executive had taken him out to the club, along with some of his new label mates. Angel had never seen so much expensive liquor in one place. That night, he'd gotten way too drunk, and the label exec had sent him home in a cab. His life had changed a few months after that night.

He'd gone from being a nobody to a Somebody. Suddenly, he was recognized while waiting at the red light in traffic. Fans would scream from the street that they loved him, that they would do anything for him. The new burst of attention had taken Angel off guard. It soon became clear that he couldn't do normal things anymore, like grocery shop or go to a public gym. At least not in LA. New York City was a little easier. Thinking of New York made him miss his bed and his place.

His gaze returned to Iris. Earlier, he'd been mesmerized by her featherlight touches across his skin. She'd smelled like flowers again. Intoxicating. But he reminded himself that she wasn't available, and he'd made a promise to her that he'd be a gentleman. He'd invited her and Bree out tonight as a kind gesture, a thank-you for accompanying him this week and taking care of everything.

"You good?" Ray asked, suddenly appearing in front of him. He did that a lot. He was like a big, silent ninja.

Angel nodded. "Yeah, I'm cool, bro. Why?"

"You were staring."

"What?"

Ray smirked. "At Iris."

Angel took a sip of his drink and said nothing as his cheeks warmed.

"The Save Face Beauty executive," Ray continued.

Angel laughed and shook his head. "I'm aware of what her job is."

"Okay. Just thought I'd remind you."

As if Angel needed reminding of the current boundaries in place. "I know."

"Anyway, what do you think of Bree?"

"You mean the Save Face Beauty executive assistant?" Angel asked, brows raised.

"Not the same thing," Ray said. "It's different for us."

"How so?"

"We're the help. We're in the trenches together so we want to spend time with someone else who understands our struggle." At Angel's amused expression, Ray added, "Well, not *my* struggle. You know I love my status as your best friend on payroll."

Angel snorted. "Yeah, *sure.*"

"I'm gonna ask Bree to dance," Ray said. "You don't mind, do you? Just one song and I'll come right back."

"You're good, bro," Angel said. The club already had enough security on deck. "Go have fun."

Ray saluted Angel and grabbed one of the many bottles on their table, pouring a shot and pounding it back. "Wish me luck."

"Good luck," Angel called after him as he made his way back over to Bree and Iris. He said something to Bree and pointed toward the dance floor. Bree hopped up immediately, leaving Iris to sit by herself.

There was no harm in going to sit with her, was there? In fact, wouldn't it be rude if he saw that she was alone and didn't at least offer to keep her company?

"Hey," he said as he approached Iris.

She looked up at him with a smile. He pointed to the open seat beside her.

"Yes, please, go ahead." She scooted over and made room for him.

"Are you having a good time?" he asked.

Her eyes shifted, and she noticeably hesitated before answering, "Yes."

"You don't sound very confident about that," he said, laughing.

"Okay, I'm not having a good time." She laughed too and smiled sheepishly. "Sorry. Clubs aren't my preferred setting."

"No need to apologize," he said. "But what is?"

"I'm sorry?" she asked, slightly raising her voice. She scooched closer, and he smelled her floral perfume again. She was wearing the same black dress from earlier. It was long sleeved with a scoop neck, and the hem fell to her knees. Plain and professional. He'd seen women wear way more tantalizing outfits, but he couldn't take his eyes off Iris and her Corporate America dress. He swallowed thickly and cleared his throat.

"I can barely hear you."

He moved closer as well, making sure to leave a few appropriate inches between them. "I said, What's your preferred setting?"

"My back patio. Especially at night during this time of year. I invite my sisters over for dinner outside. Sometimes it's just me and my daughter. She likes to wait for the fireflies."

He remembered the little girl who'd been in Violet's wedding.

"How old is your daughter?" he asked.

"Six." Iris smiled softly. "She just finished kindergarten."

"Wow. On to the big leagues."

Iris nodded. "Yeah, it feels like just yesterday I was holding a newborn, wondering why the hospital was letting us take her home to care for her on our own. Life comes at you fast."

He caught her uses of *us* and *our*. He wondered what the situation was with Calla's dad.

"My little sister is a junior at NYU," he said. "One day she was sucking her thumb and asking me to read to her, and the next she was lecturing me about composting and how I'm an uncool millennial. She likes to boss me around."

"See, my situation is the opposite," Iris said, smirking. "My little sisters always say that *I* boss *them* around."

Angel shook his head. "Why are little sisters always so opinionated?"

"I have no idea." Iris's smirk widened to a grin.

Someone shouted Angel's name and he waved at two fans who had their phones facing him. When he turned back to Iris, her smile had given way to an uneasy expression. His intention had been for her and Bree to have fun tonight, but he was realizing that his plan might have backfired where Iris was concerned.

"You didn't have to come out tonight if you didn't want

to," he said gently. "They set us up in a nice hotel. You could be there, relaxing."

Iris bit her lip, and damned if he didn't catch the motion. He blinked and forced his gaze back up to her eyes.

"I didn't want to be rude," she said. "Or to offend you."

"I wouldn't have been offended. I'd rather you be happy."

Iris opened her mouth to reply, but she was interrupted by the DJ, who took that moment to shout out Angel before he switched the song to "Summertime Fine." The crowd went wild, and Malik and his friends rushed over to Angel and pulled him to his feet. Angel waved at the crowd before sitting down again. He could go to the club and be on the scene anytime, but right now, he was in the middle of a conversation with Iris and he didn't want it to end prematurely.

"I really do like this song," she said. She glanced down at her hands in her lap, then looked up at him through her lashes. "Thank you again."

"Thank *you*. I have to follow the inspiration when it strikes."

He watched as a deep flush crept up her neck.

"You're welcome. I, um, that's—it's really flattering." She cleared her throat, and he felt his mouth curve into a smile. Watching well-spoken Iris become tongue-tied was endearing.

"Do you write all of your songs?" she asked.

"Most of them."

"Was this song hard to write?"

"Nah, I came up with the lyrics while playing the piano first."

She leaned back slightly in surprise. "Wait, I had no idea you played. For how long?"

"Since I was about eleven. I can play a little guitar too." He shrugged. "Nothing crazy, though."

"'Nothing crazy,' he says." She shook her head with a light laugh. "Wow."

He tried not to show that her reaction was a direct boost to his ego.

"So . . . 'Summertime Fine' was written as a slow song first?" she asked.

He nodded. "It was."

"Sorry," she said, smiling sheepishly again. "Whenever I become interested in a topic, I ask a ton of questions. Lily and Violet call me the inspector."

His lips formed into a grin. "Inspector Iris."

She grinned too. "But . . . I'd like to hear that version of the song, actually. The piano version."

"Really? I—"

He was about to say that he'd let her listen to it whenever she wanted, but he was interrupted as one of Malik's drunk friends tripped and fell onto the floor right in front of them. His drink splashed and hit Iris's legs. She jumped up and Angel stood immediately, hastening to find something to help wipe her off. Malik pulled his friend to his feet and apologized to Iris on his behalf.

"I think it's best if I call it a night," Iris said, wincing as she looked at her soaked legs.

Angel grabbed a fistful of napkins from the table and crouched down to wipe her legs.

"I'm really sorry," he said.

"You don't have to do that." She reached out and touched his hands. "It wasn't your fault."

But he kept wiping until her legs were dry. When he stood again, he averted his gaze, unable to look at her, afraid of what he'd see in her expression. He'd invited her out to a place where she didn't really want to be and now look at what happened.

"I'll get you a car back to the hotel, okay?"

"Oh," she said. "Um, yes. That would be great. Thank you."

He spotted Ray on the dance floor and waved him back over. They arranged for a car to take Iris to the hotel.

"Ray is gonna walk you toward the exit and take you to the car waiting outside," Angel told her.

"Okay. Thank you." She looked at him, trying to catch his eye. "Is everything—are you okay?"

"Yeah, yeah." He forced his easy smile and gestured for her to follow Ray, who stood behind him.

"Iris, do you want me to come with you?" Bree asked, gathering her purse.

"No, it's okay," Iris said. "Stay, have fun."

She looked at Angel again, gaze searching. "Have a good night."

He forced another easy smile. "You too. Sorry again."

She glanced back at him once before Ray unhooked the rope from their section. She still looked slightly confused at the sudden change in his demeanor. Angel's chest deflated as he watched her go.

He was embarrassed. He'd invited Iris to the club, and someone had spilled a drink on her. What was *he* even doing at the club right now? He heard his mom's voice in the back of his head, reminding him that he was living his life wrong. That he couldn't deserve a woman like Iris.

He rubbed a hand over his face. He didn't want to think about his mom or her judgments.

He grabbed the bottle of D'Ussé and took a huge swig, already knowing he'd regret it in the morning.

9

IRIS AND RAY SEEMED TO BE THE ONLY TWO PEOPLE IN their group who were awake and alert on the flight to Seattle the following morning. They were concealed away in first class, which was new for Iris, who'd experienced only business class and economy. Dominique had pulled out all the stops to ensure Angel's comfort. Last night, the LA Refine store had not only sold out of the Save Face Beauty's skincare bundles they'd had in stock, they'd sold out of all their Save Face Beauty inventory, period. If this kept up during the rest of the week, and the hype from the tour continued to influence online sales, they'd hopefully be able to get the company back on track.

Iris startled as Bree let out a loud snore beside her. Bree leaned her head against the window and snuggled deeper beneath her airline-gifted blanket. In the aisle across from Iris, Angel was fast asleep as well, with Ray seated in the row behind him, sitting upright and looking out the window. Iris's gaze lingered on Angel. His hood was pulled over his head, and his eyes were concealed behind sunglasses. His chest rose and fell in a measured rhythm. Earlier in the hotel lobby before their flight, he'd said good morning to

Iris and smiled briefly before putting on noise-canceling headphones and climbing into the back of the SUV that took them to the airport.

Iris couldn't help feeling like she'd somehow offended him last night at the club. She'd been enjoying their conversation up until the moment when that guy had fallen and spilled his drink on her. She'd been annoyed at first, but she'd quickly gotten over it. What had troubled her was the way that *Angel's* demeanor had changed. His mouth had been set in a concentrated frown as he'd wiped off her legs, and it was almost like he'd purposely avoided making eye contact with her. Growing up with two younger sisters meant that Iris had gotten very good at taking the temperature of a room, determining who needed what and when, if someone was in a certain mood and why. But she couldn't get a good read on Angel right now. If she didn't know any better, she'd think that he'd felt embarrassed last night, which didn't make sense because it wasn't like *he'd* spilled a drink on her. Maybe she was overthinking this.

Maybe he was just really hungover.

What she *should* be doing right now was focusing on her work.

She pulled out her laptop and began drafting an email to Dominique and Paloma, sharing the success of last night's event. She checked the weather in Seattle. The forecast called for rain, which was unsurprising. Iris's loud, quick typing must have disturbed Bree's sleep, because she stirred and rubbed her eyes. Her locs were pulled away from her face in a low ponytail. She adjusted her clear-framed glasses and sent a shy glance toward Iris.

"I don't usually go out much, just FYI," she said quietly.

At twenty-four, Bree was eight years younger than Iris, and Iris wouldn't fault her for taking advantage of a night with free food and drinks, especially since Bree was a good assistant. Iris had chosen Bree from a pool of almost twenty candidates when she'd hired her two years ago. Iris dug through her purse, pulled out a Liquid I.V. packet, and handed it to Bree.

"Here, take this," she said.

"Thank you." Bree smiled gratefully and shook the contents of the packet into her water bottle.

"Did everything go okay last night after I left?" Iris asked.

"Yeah. I left not too long after you. Angel and Ray made sure I got home safe. I'm not sure when they got back, though." She lowered her voice to a whisper. "Angel got pretty drunk last night. The DJ asked him to get on the mic and sing."

"Did he?" Iris asked.

Bree nodded. "He sounded good too, even though he was slurring the words a little."

Iris glanced over toward Angel again. He stretched his arms high and blinked slowly as he roused. He stretched his neck from side to side, and his gaze locked with Iris's across the aisle. He gave her a small smile before reclining in his seat and closing his eyes again. She started to wonder about what had gone through his head last night before she'd left the club.

Spending time with an attractive, famous man who is known for his romantic pursuits can have its . . . let's say, temptations.

Dominique's warning. It reminded Iris of the other reasons why she and Angel wouldn't make any sense together, so there was no use in pondering.

Iris refocused on her email and didn't lift her eyes from her screen until she hit send.

IRIS KNEW TO brace for rain, but it was *pouring* in Seattle. Rain fell from the sky in heavy sheets and rushed down the streets into gutters. People who dared to venture outside walked briskly in their raincoats or struggled with umbrellas against the wind. Iris had traveled to Seattle a handful of times for work conferences, and she'd experienced Pacific Northwest rain, but nothing like this. They were on their way to the Refine store, not too far from the University of Washington. The car ride was quiet as everyone stared at the rain. Iris winced down at her white Stan Smiths, wishing that she'd thought to pack rain boots.

"It's really coming down out there," Angel said softly. He was seated beside Iris in the back of the SUV.

This was the first thing he'd said to her all day since their brief exchange at the hotel in Los Angeles earlier that morning. Then again, he'd made a general statement just now, so it was possible that he wasn't even talking to her. She turned slightly. He was looking at her instead of at the rain.

"Yeah, it is," she agreed.

His forehead pinched as he frowned. "I wonder if people will still come."

"Of course they will."

Iris and her team had specifically picked the Refine store closest to the university because they'd expected a ton of college students to show. Her theory was proven right when they arrived, and his fans stretched for several blocks, don-

ning raincoats and ponchos. They shouted and waved as
the SUV came to a stop. Ray opened the passenger door and
exited, letting out Bree, who'd sat behind him. Wind and
rain whipped into the car as Ray held the door open for Angel, who tugged his oversize leather jacket closed and waved
to his fans. Ray procured an umbrella from seemingly nowhere and held it over Angel's head. Iris scooched toward
the door and braced herself for the downpour, but Angel
held his hand out to her and didn't move until she was safely
out of the car. He thanked Ray for the umbrella and held it
over Iris as they rushed into the store.

"Thank you," she shouted over the rain.

"No problem," Angel shouted back.

The umbrella hardly helped. They all got soaked. Water
seeped into Iris's sneakers, dampening her socks. Angel
wiped his face, and Iris realized wryly that today would
have been the perfect day for him to demonstrate how to
use the face wash.

The rain was loud and threatening as it pounded against
the roof. A rumble of thunder shook the entire store.

"Uh . . ." Bree said. "Is this the rapture?"

"Everything's fine," Iris reassured their group, just as another roll of thunder was followed by a strike of lightning.

Iris bit her lip and looked around the crowded store, trying to locate the store manager, Gia, whom she'd been
emailing with. She spotted Gia's short form hurrying toward them, blonde curls bouncing as she walked, followed
by . . . a police officer?

"Iris, hi," Gia said. She shot a quick, enamored glance at
Angel. "Hi, Angel, thank you so much for coming to our
store!" Her expression sobered as she turned to Iris again.

"I'm so sorry, but Seattle PD showed up minutes before you arrived. We have to shut down the event."

"*What?*" Iris gasped, and Bree sucked in a breath.

"We have a flash flood warning for this area," the police officer explained. He wore one of those bright green heavy-duty rain jackets. "It's a hazard to have this many people in the store and outside at once. There's a storm coming. We need people to be safe and inside."

"It doesn't usually rain *this* much here," Gia explained. "They're saying on the news that we're experiencing record-breaking weather. It's definitely not something that we anticipated."

Iris blinked, speechless. Her first concern was the inventory. The skincare bundles stacked behind the register. If the event was canceled, how would they sell the product? People would buy it over time, sure, but that could take months. What was she going to tell Dominique?

"What about the fans waiting outside?" Angel asked, breaking her train of thought. "They've been out there for hours, some since this morning. Is there something we can do for them?"

Gia sent a hesitant look to Iris, obviously not wanting to displease Angel.

Think, Iris, think.

"Can we give them the option to buy the products without coming into the store?" she asked. "Do you have one of those portable card readers?"

Gia bit her lip and shook her head.

"I'll buy them," Angel said. "I'll buy all of the bundles, and we can hand them out to the fans before we leave."

Iris turned to him, stunned. "What?"

"I'll buy whatever skincare bundles they have here and give them to the fans as a thank-you for waiting." His gaze was imploring. "That's something I can do, right? It won't be an issue with your boss?"

"No, not at all," Iris said quickly. His generosity would save their revenue.

She turned to the police officer. "Can we get at least another twenty minutes to hand out products to the fans?"

The officer sighed and glanced outside at the rain. "Twenty minutes and that's all I can give you."

They quickly jumped into action. Gia went to the register to handle the bundles, and Iris and Bree, along with a couple Refine employees, began piling the small boxes onto trolley carts. Gia gave Iris and Bree black ponchos with the Refine logo printed in the center.

"I'm coming with you," Angel said, following Iris outside.

"You don't have anything to cover yourself with," she protested as he shrugged off his leather jacket and lifted it over his head. "Your jacket will be ruined."

"I'll donate it to a fundraiser."

Their voices were quickly drowned out by the rain and the shouting crowd. The police officer announced to the fans that the event was being canceled, and disappointed murmurs rose around them, but when the fans learned that they'd each receive a free skincare bundle while supplies lasted, the cheers were thunderous—in addition to the actual thunder as it tore across the sky.

"We'd better hurry," Iris said.

Gia, Bree, and the Refine employees handed out the bundle packages, and Iris went down the line behind Angel, dutifully snapping pictures of him and his fans. Ray attempted to hold an umbrella over Angel, but it was impossible to keep Angel dry as he kept moving to hug his fans and lean down and pose with them. Plus, he insisted that Ray hold the umbrella over Iris, instead. Eventually Ray permanently positioned himself beside Iris. Angel was getting completely drenched. Raindrops slid down his face, but his smile didn't falter, even as his fans grabbed at him and screamed happily in his face.

The rainfall worsened. Bree confirmed that they'd given out every bundle package in stock. Angel wouldn't be able to get to each of his fans, and his dispirited expression moved Iris. But he was also shivering at this point. He didn't resist Iris when she grabbed his hand and pulled him back toward the waiting SUV. She instructed him to climb inside, and she asked the driver to blast the heat. Angel took off his wet jacket. Iris shrugged out of the poncho and used her cardigan sleeve to wipe Angel's face. Ray stood outside of the door, guarding them. Iris angled the vents so that the heat blew directly onto Angel. Underneath his jacket, he'd worn only a thin white T-shirt.

"My sister needs to start dressing you in warmer clothes," she said. Violet usually accompanied Angel for his album press tours and at fashion shows, but for the Refine campaign, they'd chosen each of his outfits ahead of time since Violet was taking her extended honeymoon sabbatical.

Angel laughed through his shivering. "You and me m-make a g-good team," he said.

Iris glanced up at him, and he was beaming at her. She was surprised at the deep sense of relief that she felt to see him smiling at her again. She returned his smile with a soft one of her own.

"We do," she said. "That's why we need to keep you healthy. I can't bench my star player."

He laughed again, then fell silent as Iris rubbed her hands up and down his arms, attempting to generate warmth. Her palms tingled as she rubbed his smooth skin. She could feel him staring at her.

"I'm sorry if I was being weird today," he said.

Iris stilled. She wasn't sure what to say. Should she acknowledge that she'd felt the difference in his demeanor? Angel must have taken her silence for confusion because he spoke again.

"Last night before you left the club, I got in my head about some stuff," he explained. "I'm not even sure if you noticed, but I got weird with you, so I wanted to say that I'm sorry. I feel like I'm finally getting out of that funk."

"I did notice," she admitted. "And it's okay. I know what it's like to be stuck in your head. It's why I pay for therapy."

She'd said that last part sardonically, and then she realized that her dry humor might not land properly without the context for why she needed therapy in the first place.

"I've been thinking about going to therapy for a while now," he said.

"Really?"

He nodded. "My parents basically disowned me for a few years."

She stared at him, blinking slowly. "I'm really sorry to hear that."

"Yeah," he said quietly. "We're okay now, I guess. But you don't forget something like that."

She admired him for sharing that information so effortlessly, because displaying vulnerability hadn't always come easily to her. Through therapy, she'd discovered that this stemmed from childhood. She'd had to set an example for her sisters, who'd watched her every move. She hadn't cried when she'd fallen off her bike or bruised her knee on the jungle gym because she'd had to show her sisters that they could fall and get right back up too.

For years, she'd thought that showing her soft underbelly was a sign of weakness—at times, she'd doubted if her underbelly even existed. But Terry's death had pushed Iris to examine herself in new ways. Her underbelly was there; she'd just gone through great lengths to protect it. She still struggled with discussing her feelings, but Angel had shared something vulnerable with her. She wanted to do the same with him.

"I'm in therapy because my husband died in a car accident five years ago," she said. "We were married for less than two."

People tended to treat her like fragile china once they learned about Terry. But Angel didn't look at her with pity or tilt his head and frown in that way she'd become accustomed to. Instead, his gaze was soft as he gently took Iris's hand in his, not breaking eye contact.

"I'm so sorry, Iris," he said.

She breathed deeply. "Thank you."

"What was his name?"

"Terry."

Angel nodded silently. They sat there, hands clasped together, honoring the silence, until Bree pulled the door open and interrupted them. Heart pounding, Iris quickly pulled her hands away and rested them in her lap.

"They're already talking about this online!" Bree said,

climbing through to the back row with Ray following behind. Bree's poncho dripped onto the seats. She showed
them a video of Angel shielding fans from the rain as he
took a picture with them.

"They're calling you Saint Angel!" she said.

Angel shook his head, smiling somewhat bashfully.

"It's great publicity for us too," Bree said, looking at Iris.

Iris nodded in agreement, clasping her hands together.
As their driver started the SUV and pulled into the street,
leaving the Refine store behind, the car jostled over a pot-
hole and Angel's arm brushed against Iris's. He touched her
hand once more, lightly, for only a second, before pulling
away.

When she shivered this time, she couldn't blame the
rain.

10

BACK AT THE HOTEL, IRIS TOOK A HOT SHOWER AND wrapped herself in a fluffy hotel robe. While responding to emails, she scarfed down the burger and fries she'd ordered through room service. Afterward, she FaceTimed her mom to speak to Calla, and she was surprised when Violet answered, holding a thirty-two-ounce mason jar filled with water.

"Do you know how many quarts are in a gallon?" Violet asked, in lieu of a hello.

"Four, I think. Why? And why are you answering Mom's phone?"

"I'm trying to drink a gallon of water a day, but it's hard, so I thought maybe if I separated it into quarts, I'd have better luck." Violet brushed her silk-pressed hair over her shoulder and smiled. "I'm answering Mom's phone because she and Calla are preoccupied with baking."

Violet angled the phone so that Iris could see the scene behind her. Dahlia and Calla were at the kitchen counter, rolling out cookie dough onto a flour-covered cutting board. Dahlia was still wearing her Greenehouse T-shirt.

"Cookies before dinner?" Iris asked, raising an eyebrow.

"Don't kill the messenger," Violet said. "Calla, your mom is on FaceTime."

Calla looked up and ran over to the phone, beaming at Iris, which always warmed Iris's heart in an indescribable way.

"Hi, Mom," she said. "We're baking sugar cookies and snickerdoodles."

"We're eating them *after* dinner," Dahlia called.

Iris smiled, satisfied with this. "That sounds good. Can you save me some, baby?"

Calla nodded solemnly. "I'll hide some for you in a good spot so Pop Pop won't find them."

Iris and Violet laughed, well aware of their dad's sweet tooth.

"I heard you had some bad weather over there in Seattle," Dahlia said, coming closer into view.

"Yeah, we had to shut down the event, actually," Iris said. "But Angel was really great about it. He bought every skincare bundle and gave them to the fans for free."

"Wow," Dahlia said, inclining her head.

"That sounds like something he would do," Violet added.

Calla was eager to continue baking, so Iris promised that she'd call again tomorrow. Calla and Dahlia returned to the kitchen counter, while Violet took the phone with her into the living room and settled onto the couch.

"Why are you at Mom's on a weekday evening?" Iris asked. Since Violet had taken an extended vacation from work post-honeymoon, Iris figured that Violet and Xavier would still be wrapped up and secluded away in newlywed bliss.

"I tagged along with Xavier to his summer league game,"

Violet said. "We stopped by Mom and Dad's on the way back."

Xavier appeared suddenly and leaned down into the camera. He kissed Violet on the forehead and smiled at Iris. "What's up, Iris?"

"Hey, Xavier."

"I told your dad that I'd keep him company outside, so that's where I'm headed," he said. "Just wanted to say hi."

Violet smiled adoringly at her husband as he walked out of view. In the background, Iris heard the sound of the front door opening and closing.

"Lily just got here," Violet said, craning her neck to see better. "Oh, and she brought Nick."

"I guess everyone is there without me, huh?" Iris said jokingly, but she felt loneliness creep across her skin.

Seconds later, Lily plopped onto the couch beside Violet. Nick followed after her, hugging Violet and waving at Iris.

"Nick made his deadline for his next book," Lily said, smiling proudly. "So we're celebrating."

"By coming to Mom and Dad's?" Violet scrunched her nose. "That's boring."

"By eating a home-cooked meal with family," Lily corrected.

"That's awesome, Nick," Iris said. "Congrats on making the deadline."

"Yeah, thanks," Nick said, smiling shyly.

"Xavier is out back with our dad if you want to spend time with the menfolk," Violet said to Nick.

Nick laughed, shaking his head. "I should say hi to everyone." He squeezed Lily's hand and waved goodbye to Iris.

"What's Dad doing outside anyway?" Iris asked.

"Gardening, last time I checked," Violet said.

"Isn't he tired from being at the store all day?" Iris thought of Benjamin's persistent backaches. "One of you should check on him. I think he's been working himself too hard."

"I'll check on him after we hang up," Lily said. "How's everything going with the tour?"

"It's going well, thankfully. We're only on day two, but I'm hoping that the strong sales continue. Angel's got some diehard fans, that's for sure."

"How is Angel?" Violet asked. There was a certain twinkle in her eyes that went beyond normal curiosity.

"Today he stood outside in the pouring rain and took a million pictures with all the fans. It's a miracle that he hasn't caught the flu. I think he's doing a great job."

Violet and Lily exchanged a look, quick and imperceptible to the naked eye. But Iris knew her sisters.

"What was that?" she asked.

"What was what?" Violet blinked innocently. Lily remained mum.

"Why did you look at each other like that just now?"

"I have no idea what you're talking about," Violet said.

At the same time, Lily blurted, "I'm pretty sure he's into you."

Violet nudged Lily in the side and Lily winced.

"Why do you say that?" Iris asked. Her voice sounded like a squeak.

She knew that Angel had expressed interest in her before, which was already mind-boggling enough, but she didn't know that her sisters were also aware. Had they somehow seen the two of them dancing together outside at

Violet's wedding? Had they seen the way that Iris had gazed at him, completely awestruck? Had they seen the way he'd stared deep into her eyes, mesmerizing her? If so, she had no clue how to explain herself. Her stomach muscles tightened as she looked at her sisters.

Violet and Lily exchanged another glance.

"It's not that big of a deal," Violet said, attempting a diplomatic tone. "He asked me about you and I told him that you weren't really in a place to date, but that was before I knew you wanted to start dating again."

Against her will, Iris's heart dusted off its drumsticks for another solo routine. "W-when did he ask about me?"

"It's happened more than once over the years. First, after he met you at my anti-wedding party. Then sometime after his first album dropped. Most recently at my actual wedding a few weeks ago . . ."

Iris blinked, piecing this information together slowly. Her brain was doing mental gymnastics. All this time Angel had been asking about her? Even earlier than their conversation in the vineyard? She couldn't believe it. But it had to be true, because Violet wouldn't lie to her about something like that.

"When you told him that I wasn't in a place to date," she said, trying to fight through her shock, "did you say why?"

Violet shook her head. "I didn't tell him about Terry, if that's what you mean."

"Oh," Iris said.

Violet and Lily watched her silently, their eyes round and alert.

"Angel is a good guy," Violet said. "If you're curious to know what I think."

Iris thought of Angel's reaction earlier when she'd revealed that Terry had died. She remembered his patient expression and softened voice.

"I know that he's a good guy," Iris said. "Of course he is. But that's not . . . I'm just not looking for something like that."

"'Like that' meaning . . ." Violet rolled her hand in a circling motion, urging Iris to elaborate.

"A relationship with a . . . celebrity," Iris said. "It wouldn't make sense for me or for Calla. And anyway, he's my company's brand ambassador. It would be inappropriate."

Violet frowned. "I guess that makes sense."

"You look really cozy in that robe," Lily said, changing the subject. "I hope you're getting some rest."

"Yeah, you know, I think I'll relax and watch a movie or something," Iris said.

Lily smiled softly. "That sounds nice. We'll text you later?"

Iris nodded. "Okay."

"Have a good night, love you," Violet said. She glanced at Lily and mumbled something to her as they ended the call.

Iris sighed and lay back against the plush pillows. She didn't want her sisters to feel like they had to walk on eggshells around her when it came to Terry or her love life.

She wouldn't pretend that it wasn't wild and ridiculously flattering that Angel had had his eye on her from afar for the last *three* years. She was still trying to let that realization set in. She thought back to their first conversation at Violet's anti-wedding party, and how Angel had saved her from a fall. He'd been so sweet to her that day. The more time that she spent around him now, the more she realized that not only was he still that same sweet, handsome guy, he was charismatic and kind and gracious. But there was no point in thinking about what logically couldn't and wouldn't be. It was better to be realistic.

She took a deep breath and forced herself to open the Meet Me app, curious to see what type of men Seattle had to offer. She'd read plenty of success stories about couples who'd met on this app, but she felt no excitement as she swiped past dozens of faces until her vision blurred. Maybe it was best to try again once she was back home.

Tossing her phone to the side, she reached for the television remote and flipped through the channels. Maybe she should order a glass of wine from room service. Having a nice glass of wine in a comfy hotel bed with a huge television before her would usually sound divine. But as rain pounded against the windows, Iris turned off the television and shifted onto her side, staring at the storm.

She couldn't stop picturing the look in Angel's eyes as he'd taken her hand earlier in the car. She felt restless. Antsy. She needed to get out of this hotel room.

Grabbing her phone again, she almost texted Bree and asked if she wanted to get a drink at the hotel restaurant, but it had been a long day, and Bree probably wanted time to herself. As Bree's superior, Iris didn't want Bree to feel obligated to hang out with her. She'd sit at the restaurant bar by herself instead.

She got dressed and went downstairs. The upscale downtown Seattle hotel was only a ten-minute walk from the waterfront, but the restaurant was nearly empty, thanks to the storm. Iris took a seat at the bar, which was nearly empty as well, save for a Black man with a thick, long beard, who was seated several chairs down from her. He wore a baseball cap pulled low and a track suit jacket zipped up to his neck. He was writing something down on a notepad. When he lifted his head to scratch his chin, Iris saw that he was wearing aviator sunglasses. Inside, when the sun wasn't even out. Okay. She had to admit that was a little sketchy. Maybe he was meeting someone here in secret. Or maybe he was a writer who had very specific rituals that he had to adhere to in order for his creative juices to flow. Nick had told Iris all kinds of stories about the interesting authors he tended to meet at festivals and conferences.

Iris looked away from the man as the bartender approached and asked what she'd like to drink. She looked over the cocktail menu and realized that what she actually craved was a simple Shirley Temple. The bartender slid the red, fizzy drink in front of her and she smiled as she took a sip. Shirley Temples reminded her of her family, and tonight her family was together without her. She tried not to feel so bummed about being alone.

A prickle suddenly spread across her skin, and she had the sensation that she was being watched. She glanced to her right, and the bearded guy with the sunglasses was looking at her. He nodded his head, and Iris smiled back, polite but tight.

I do not feel like having small talk with a stranger right now, sir. Please don't come over here.

The man stood, picking up his notepad and his drink. Iris groaned inwardly as he moved closer to occupy the seat next to her. He sat down, bringing the scent of cinnamon with him.

"This weather is a trip, ay?" he asked in a smooth, deep timbre.

She froze and turned to him fully, taking in the beard, the hat and glasses. The nose ring. His familiar build and voice. Iris squinted.

"*Angel?*" she whispered.

Angel lowered his glasses, revealing his brown eyes. He smiled and lifted his index finger to his lips.

"What in the world are you wearing?" she asked, right before she burst out laughing.

"*Shhh,*" Angel said, grinning from ear to ear. "This is my disguise."

"Your disguise?"

"I wear it to the movies. The pet store. Central Park. Target. Nobody ever recognizes me. *You* didn't."

They were whispering, even though there was no need to speak in hushed tones. They were the only patrons in the restaurant, and the bartender was at the other end of the bar, preoccupied with his phone.

"You shop at Target?" Iris asked.

"Who doesn't shop at Target?"

"Good point." She reached out and lightly touched the thick, fake beard. "Where did you get this? It looks real."

He smirked. "I ordered it online. What are you drinking?"

"A Shirley Temple."

He lifted his brows, amused. "I haven't had one of those in a minute."

"It's a comfort drink," she said. "My parents used to take my sisters and me to Friendly's after we got our report cards every marking period. I always got a Shirley Temple with the chicken tenders and fries basket. I take Calla there sometimes. She loves it."

"What's Friendly's?"

Iris blinked at him. "You've never heard of Friendly's?"

He shook his head. "Should I have?"

"It's only one of the finest North American food establishments to ever exist." She grabbed her phone and searched Friendly's website, checking their locations list. "Oh, wait. Looks like they've never been in Georgia. That's unfortunate. You truly haven't lived until you've had a Friendly's mint cookie crunch sundae."

"Nah, mint ice cream shouldn't exist."

Iris paused. She pivoted in her seat and sipped at her drink. "Oh, I see."

She could feel Angel smiling at her. "You see what?" he asked.

"You're one of those people who thinks mint and chocolate don't go together. I bet you hate Peppermint Patties too."

"The only person I know who actually likes Peppermint Patties is Mrs. Thurman, who played the organ at church, and she's gotta be almost ninety years old now."

"Correction: *me* and Mrs. Thurman are the only people you know who like Peppermint Patties."

Angel laughed. "Will you take me to Friendly's, the home of the mint cookie crunch sundae?"

"I don't know," Iris said primly, fighting her smile. "You're judging one of their most popular desserts and you haven't even tried it yet. I'm not sure if you deserve the chance."

"I think I do." The way he looked at her, so intent and delighted, made her stomach flutter.

"What about you?" she asked, clearing her throat and pointing to his glass. "What are you drinking?"

"Club soda. I'm done drinking alcohol for the week. I overdid it last night."

"I heard that you sang for everyone."

He grimaced and rubbed a hand over his face. "I saw a video of it this morning. My only saving grace is that my voice sounded okay." He glanced at her, sidelong. "I don't get drunk like that a lot. If you were wondering."

"It's not my place to judge you even if you did." She nodded at his notepad, noticing his neat penmanship. "What are you writing? If you don't mind me asking."

"Song lyrics. Not having much luck, though."

Is it another song about me?

The thought popped into her head, quick and unwarranted. She had enough sense not to give voice to the question. It was too presumptuous. He might have asked about her on and off over the past three years, but since she'd turned him down to his face at the office last week, she doubted that she'd be the inspiration for any more of his songs. And if he was writing another song about her, that would only complicate things more. She shouldn't want that.

"Oh, look," the bartender said. He pointed to the windows. "The rain stopped."

Iris and Angel turned in their seats. The sky was darker now as evening turned to night. But it was no longer raining. Finally.

Iris spun back around to face the bar. Her Shirley Temple was almost finished. There was hardly anything left of Angel's club soda. She didn't want to go back to her room yet. And . . . she liked talking to him. There was no harm in that, right?

"Do you want to go for a walk?" she heard herself ask.

It wasn't until the words left her lips that she realized

the irony of her question. She'd turned down Angel's invitation to go for another walk another day, at Violet's wedding, and he'd promised her that he wouldn't ask her to go for any walks at twilight. Now that she was the one asking, would he turn her down? She wouldn't blame him if he did. Her stomach seized, and the seconds felt infinite as she waited for his answer.

"As long as I get to keep on my disguise," he said, smirking as he stood. He placed a few bills on the counter, paying for their drinks. When Iris started to protest, he waved her away. He slipped his notepad in the back pocket of his jeans and held his hand out to her. She felt herself smile as she accepted his hand and scooted off the barstool.

"What should I call you once we're out in public?" she asked.

"Hmmm." He tapped his chin as they walked toward the exit. "Tom Wyatt."

Her surprised laugh echoed throughout the hotel lobby.

11

ANGEL STUFFED HIS HANDS INTO THE FRONT POCKETS OF his jacket as they walked along the waterfront. A handful of people were enjoying the break in the rain and walking their dogs. Beside him, Iris was gazing at the Pacific Ocean and the lit-up Ferris wheel in the distance. He was glad that she'd asked him to walk with her.

After learning about her husband's death, he looked at her in a new light. He couldn't imagine what it must have been like to experience a major loss like that so young, especially when you had a child to raise. He now understood why Violet had said Iris wasn't looking to date. He felt grateful beyond words that Iris had shared that bit of herself with him.

"What song are you humming?" she asked.

He hadn't realized he'd been humming aloud. "'Adore' by Prince. They were playing it in the hotel lobby. It's been stuck in my head."

"I love that song," she said. She tilted her head, looking at him more closely. The corner of her mouth lifted in a smile. "You have a soothing hum."

"I used to get in trouble for it in school. Lots of detentions," he said, liking that she'd paid enough attention to notice this small detail about him. "You ever get detention for a weird habit?"

"Never."

She said it so quickly, Angel laughed.

"Well, I came close to getting detention once," she amended. "While taking one of those standardized tests in seventh grade, I realized that this boy Sean Davis was cheating off me. I got so angry, I stood up and shouted at him to stop. Then I shoved his pencil and test to the ground."

She winced, like this was the worst possible act that she could have committed. Angel laughed harder.

"You laugh, but I'm serious! It was bad!" she said, giggling herself. "I was really scared that I'd get in trouble."

"What happened after that?" he asked.

"Sean and I were pulled out of the classroom. He got detention. I was reprimanded for yelling, but that was basically it."

"So what I'm hearing is that you liked school," he said.

"I *loved* it."

Angel smiled. "Were you a teacher's pet?"

"Yes," she said, answering honestly. "But only because I worked really hard. I didn't go out of my way to receive favoritism or anything."

"I believe you."

They passed by a group of teens gathered on a bench, laughing loudly. Angel tensed and automatically steeled himself for an interaction. But he remembered that he was wearing his disguise and he relaxed. The teens didn't spare him a glance. He and Iris walked on without interruption.

"It really works," Iris whispered, gesturing to his outfit.

"Every time."

He told her about how he'd created the disguise on his first R & B tour. He rarely got to enjoy the scenery of each city because his presence in public caused too much of a stir. One night while in Philadelphia, he'd wanted to see the Liberty Bell, but he wanted to go there unnoticed. He'd joked to Ray that he'd be better off wearing a costume. Then he'd realized maybe that wasn't such a bad idea. He'd borrowed a fitted hat from one of his backup dancers, and his tour manager had somehow found a fake beard. Angel had shrugged on a hoodie, and he and Ray walked to see the Liberty Bell. Then they walked to the Museum of Illusions. He'd gone unrecognized the entire time.

He'd since improved the disguise, getting a better-quality fake beard and adding a pair of sunglasses. He wouldn't trade his life, but sometimes he missed the ability to easily blend in.

"Speaking of your clothes," Iris said. "I talked to Violet earlier."

"How is she?" Angel hadn't seen Violet since her wedding. They didn't have another fitting scheduled until after he returned to New York.

"She's good." Iris slowed her walk and shifted to face him. "She said that you've asked about me a couple times over the years."

"I have," he said.

Iris laughed softly and shook her head like she was confused. "But why?"

"Why? Have you looked in the mirror lately? You have to know that you're beautiful."

A reddish undertone flushed her brown cheeks. "Thank you. But still, I'm me and you're you."

"What does that mean?"

"It means you're famous and attractive in a way that normal people aren't." She sputtered to a stop and squeezed her eyes closed. "I can't believe I just said that out loud. What is wrong with me?"

A grin spread across the bottom half of Angel's face. "I didn't mind hearing it."

Iris bit her lip and opened her mouth to respond, but she paused as two women jogged in their direction. The soles of their sneakers thwacked against the pavement. Angel and Iris moved aside, and Iris waited until the women passed before she spoke again.

"Let me rephrase," she said, holding up her hand. "You are famous. I am not. While I am secure in my physical appearance and am aware that people generally find me attractive, I recognize that you are not good-looking in a normal-people way. You are celebrity attractive."

"Celebrity attractive," Angel repeated, still grinning.

"Yes. The kind of person who gets scouted at the mall or on the street. Plucked from obscurity to become a big star." She squinted at him. "Surely you know this about yourself. I mean, come on! Look at you!"

Angel was laughing now. "My mom used to warn me that I was too handsome for my own good. Just kidding, she never said anything like that to me."

Iris snorted. "Well, I don't know about that saying either way in your case. Your handsomeness seems to do a lot of good for loads of people."

He laughed again, watching her as she watched him.

"I guess what I'm trying to say is that I was surprised that you took notice of me," she said. "You've dated beautiful actresses and models." She paused, frowning. "Now it sounds like I think that you're shallow, and I don't think that about you. I'm sorry. I don't really know what I'm saying."

She continued to frown, muttering to herself. Angel secretly enjoyed that he was the reason that she couldn't seem to get her thoughts straight, but ultimately, he wanted to put her at ease.

"It's okay," he said. "Being told that I'm celebrity attractive is one of the best compliments I've ever received. Thank you."

"You're welcome." She rolled her eyes at his sarcasm and laughed.

Every time that he made Iris laugh, Angel felt like the sun had peeked out from behind the clouds and beamed down on him. He had a feeling that Iris's laughter wasn't easily won. The fact that he'd caused her to laugh more than once over the last couple days seemed like a victory.

"When I first saw you, there was something about the way you carried yourself," he said. "You seemed so confident and grounded. I really lacked those qualities at the time, and I wanted to know more about you, and I enjoyed talking to you, even for those few minutes. It didn't matter to me that you weren't a celebrity, and stuff like that doesn't matter to me now."

Iris nodded slowly, eyes trained on the ground. His words lingered in the air between them. He'd spoken with bald honesty but skirting around the truth wasn't his usual method of communication.

"So, it is true that I've asked Violet about you," he continued. "But she told me that you were unavailable, and especially after what you shared with me about your husband's passing, I don't want you to worry about me trying you or anything. And we have a working relationship. I respect that."

"I'm not worried." She finally lifted her face to him. "What I remember about our first meeting is that I thought you were handsome and sweet, and I hoped the best for you and your career. Then one day, I turned on the radio and there you were, singing."

His mouth curved into a smile. "I'll take handsome and sweet."

Iris laughed, and he once again appreciated that he had the ability to get that reaction out of her.

Soon, they came upon the big Ferris wheel. It was lit with blue and purple lights.

"It's called the Great Wheel," she said, pointing. "This is my fourth time in Seattle, and I've yet to ride it."

Angel tilted his head back, appraising the Ferris wheel. "You want to ride it now?"

Iris thought about it for a moment. "Yeah, let's do it."

They walked down the pier and waited in line to buy tickets. It wasn't a typical Ferris wheel. This one had small, enclosed cabins with benches inside. It reminded Angel of a smaller version of the London Eye, which he'd ridden before on his first visit to the UK. He and Iris got a cabin of their own, and they sat with their faces pressed against the window as the wheel lifted them higher into the Seattle night sky.

"Calla would love this," Iris said, taking in the view of the city. She snapped a few pictures on her phone.

"What's your daughter like?" Angel asked, turning to her.

Iris smiled, but it was a different smile. One of deep fondness and love.

"Calla's inquisitive and gentle," she said. "She loves the color pink, her favorite picture book is about a girl who attends a princess academy, and she loves ballet, but she decided that she just wanted to focus on karate this year. She'll sit up for hours watching *The Twilight Zone* with my dad whenever she stays the night with my parents. She likes challenging herself and always wants to try things on her own before asking for help. I guess she gets that from me. And her dad."

Iris shifted closer to Angel, brushing her arm against his, as she scrolled through her camera roll and showed him a picture of Calla wearing a white karate gi. Calla was cheesing at the camera, one hand on her hip, the other holding a trophy.

"This was after her first karate tournament last year," Iris said. "At this age, the kids aren't involved in matches yet. They show their technique to the judges. She got second place. She used to be really shy but being involved in different activities has helped her come out of her shell."

Angel leaned over to get a closer look at the photo. Calla had some of Iris's features, the shape of her face and the color of her eyes, and there was a certain determination to Calla's smile that Angel recognized in Iris. But other parts of Calla, like her nose and her long limbs must have belonged to Iris's husband.

"How did you and your husband meet?" he asked.

Iris stilled, and Angel immediately wished that he could backtrack. His curiosity had influenced him to bring up a topic that she might not want to discuss. He was about to tell her that she didn't have to answer his question if she didn't want to.

"We went to business school together," she said. She was gazing out at the city again. "One night he walked me to the subway when it was raining."

"That was kind of him."

"He *was* kind. And patient. He was driven too. Fundamentally, we had a lot in common." She smiled a little. "Neither of us was looking for a relationship when we met. But life happens. First came love, then baby, then marriage. Then . . . well."

Angel murmured softly that he understood what she'd left unsaid. Silence settled between them. But it wasn't an awkward silence; it was considerate and accepting. If Iris wanted to talk more, he would listen. If she didn't, that was okay too.

"It took me a long time to stop talking about him in the present tense," she continued. She inhaled and exhaled, slow and deep. "After he died, it was hard to get a grip on reality. It was bizarre to me that the world kept turning and life continued on while he was no longer here, and I was angry that was he was taken away from us so suddenly. But Calla needed me, and focusing on her well-being kept me afloat. What makes me sad now is that she doesn't really remember him, and he was a wonderful dad. He loved her so much."

"I think she'll carry that with her, though," Angel said quietly. "The way he loved her? She'll always have that."

"I like that idea." Iris pivoted, facing him instead of the city view. "It's nice to talk about Terry with someone who didn't know him. Now you have a piece of him in your memory too."

Angel didn't think he was capable of truly expressing

just how grateful he was that she'd shared this with him. But he would try.

"Thank you for telling me about him," he said. "Really."

She nodded. "Thank you for listening."

They eventually made their way back to the bottom of the wheel and exited their cabin. They walked down the pier in the direction they'd come, but this time, Angel spotted something he hadn't seen before. He pointed at the SEATTLE BAY CREAMERY sign.

"Well, well, well. What do we have here?" he said. "An ice cream shop. You think they have mint chocolate chip?"

Iris pursed her lips, but her eyes were smiling. "What difference is it to you? You made it clear that you don't like mint and chocolate."

"You've convinced me to give it another try."

She smirked. "Okay, then."

Despite the night chill, they both ordered scoops of homemade mint chocolate chip in waffle cones.

"This is delicious," Iris said. Her eyes lit up as she enjoyed her cone.

Angel was convinced that he was actually eating sweet toothpaste. He grimaced before tossing his cone in the trash. Iris burst into laughter, and Angel's heartbeat quickened. He wanted to make her laugh like that all the time. But that wasn't his role to occupy. He'd settle for being able to make her laugh right now.

"It's just nasty," he said. "I'm sorry. But who thought of that flavor? What's wrong with them?"

"You hate mint chocolate chip almost as much as Lily used to hate those SpongeBob SquarePants Popsicles. Remember those?"

Angel frowned, shrugging.

"What?" she said, peering at him.

"Nothing. It's stupid." He sighed. "*SpongeBob SquarePants* references bother me."

Her brows furrowed. "Why?"

"I didn't watch a lot of TV when I was younger, and everyone at school loved SpongeBob. To this day, people regularly quote lines from the show and I see clips online all the time, and I feel out of the loop."

"So you don't know about Handsome Squidward?"

"Who?"

"Never mind, not important." She waved her hand. "Why don't you watch the show now? It's probably streaming somewhere."

"There's almost thirteen seasons! It's too much. I'd never have enough free time to watch it in chunks like I'd want to."

Iris ate the last bit of her cone and dusted off her hands. "*SpongeBob* was okay, but if you want to make up for lost time on kids shows, I'd start with *Hey Arnold!* Or maybe *Doug.*"

"I've heard of them." He pulled out his phone and made a note of the shows she'd mentioned. He also made a note about Friendly's.

"Were you not allowed to watch TV?" Iris asked as they walked back toward the hotel. "I remember you mentioned before that your mom was really religious."

"It's not that I wasn't allowed. We only had one television in our house, and we didn't have cable because my parents only needed to watch the news. I don't think they would have had a problem with SpongeBob because it seems innocent enough, but you never really know with my mom. Anything that she considered indecent wasn't allowed, and her definition of indecent varied. I used to secretly listen to R & B music at night while my parents were sleeping. *That* wasn't allowed. Sometimes I think I grew up in an alternate universe."

"Was it hard growing up like that?" Iris asked.

"It was. I felt stifled, but it was all I knew. I see now that they thought they were protecting us." He paused, looking up as the moon peeked from behind the clouds. "But I think there's a way to love God without having to give up so much else too. My mom doesn't really agree. She judges me."

"Because of what your life is like now?"

"Yeah," he said. "She doesn't approve of me singing secular music and wishes I still sung gospel. That definitely caused a rift between us and it's why we didn't talk the first few years I was living in LA. After my first music video came out, she almost had a heart attack. She thought it was too racy, I guess. She said I embarrassed her and she could barely look her church friends in the eye. Sometimes she acts like I was corrupted or something."

Iris gently touched his elbow. "I'm sorry she treats you like that. You don't deserve it."

"Thanks," he said. "I try to put myself in her shoes sometimes in order to see where she's coming from. She's always tried to use her life as a cautionary tale to me and my sister. She ran away from home when she was seventeen and bounced around from state to state. She partied a lot and I guess she had a nihilistic approach to life because she didn't care about what happened to her. Then she ended up in Maren and met my dad. When she got pregnant with me, she decided to change her life. I get why she acts the way that she does. She doesn't want me making the same mistakes that she made, but that's not what I'm doing. I wish that we could agree to disagree."

They were nearing the hotel now. Angel slowed his walk, aware that he didn't want to part from Iris yet and return to their separate rooms. To his relief, she matched his unhurried pace.

"How often do you see her?" Iris asked.

"Only on Christmas. It's all I can handle, to be honest," he said. "I'll see her next month, though. My hometown is honoring me because I donated money for church renovations and to the youth music programs. What I do for charity is the main reason that my mom started talking to me again."

Iris nodded, taking this in. "For the record, I liked your first music video. 'Better For You,' right?"

He smiled. "Yeah—and thank you. I worked *really* hard to learn that choreography," he said. "You wouldn't believe what they put me through to get that six-pack. I felt like I was training to be a gladiator."

Iris snort-laughed, covering her mouth. Angel couldn't help the smile that overtook his face. Seeing her laugh so openly did something to him. It made him want things that weren't meant to be his.

They walked into the hotel lobby and Angel finally removed his hat and fake beard.

"It's nice to see your real face again," Iris said.

Angel smirked. "Now that you know my secret, you have to promise not to tell anyone."

"Not only do I promise, I swear." She held up her fist,

lifting her pinky finger. "I'll even pinky swear like I do with Calla."

Angel laughed and looped his pinky around hers, feeling the warmth and softness of her skin. Iris smiled at him and their gazes held. Then, all too soon, she let go of his hand, and Angel tried his best to pretend that he wasn't affected by something as simple as linking pinkies.

Tonight, he'd learned a few things about Iris. She was a great listener, and with time, she gave you the opportunity to be a good listener as well. She liked Shirley Temples and mint chocolate chip ice cream. She wasn't afraid of heights. Talking to her made him feel stable and grounded.

She also loved her husband, and she might not have more room in her heart for anyone else.

And that sucked for Angel. Because after tonight, he only liked her more.

12

THE FOLLOWING MORNING, IRIS JOLTED AWAKE AS HER
alarm blared. Her limbs were tangled in the sheets and her
sleeveless nightgown was pulled askew. She'd been in the
middle of a dream. One where she and Angel were riding
the Great Wheel again, but this time he wasn't in a disguise
and they weren't separated by polite distances or covert
glances. In her dream, they were huddled side by side in the
small Ferris wheel cabin, so close they were breathing each
other's air. Angel was staring at her, staring at her mouth,
specifically. Iris gazed back, heart pounding in her ears as
he inched closer. His hand skated up her thigh, slow and
gentle before giving her flesh a firm squeeze. She gasped
and brought her hand up to his face, rubbing along his
square jaw, and she leaned forward and kissed him. His
mouth was wet and hot against hers. She lifted her hand
under his shirt, rubbing that six-pack he'd worked so hard
for. Then he was kissing her neck, sucking her skin. She
climbed into his lap—and then her alarm shook her awake.

Iris pressed her fingers to the base of her throat and felt
her rapid pulse. Breathing deeply, she checked the time and
hurried to shower. She closed her eyes as the water ran over

her skin, cooling her down. That dream was *hot*, and she hadn't had one like it in forever. She hadn't had sex in a long time, not since Terry. Five years.

Thank goodness for vibrators.

She'd learned in college that casual hookups didn't do it for her. In order to feel aroused enough to actually enjoy sex, she needed to have some kind of emotional connection with the other person. It seemed her dream was trying to tell her that she had an emotional connection with Angel, which made sense after how much they'd shared with each other last night. But she couldn't hook up with Angel in *real life*. The idea was absurd and illogical. She had to put it out of her mind immediately.

But things only worsened from there. On the flight to DC, Iris assumed that she'd sit with Bree again . . . but Bree sat with Ray. They grinned and whispered to each other, full of energy in the early-morning hours. Angel eased into the seat beside Iris, smiling at her with his gorgeous face, having no clue about her hornball dream. Iris smiled back, swallowing hard, and retrieved her laptop to email Paloma and Dominique. Angel slid on his noise-canceling head-phones and pulled out the same notepad from last night. Focusing on work wasn't usually a struggle for Iris, but she could hardly type a sentence of her email. She was more in-terested in glancing at Angel and observing the slope of his jawline and how he moved his shoulders when he shifted in his seat. How he nodded his head while listening to his mu-sic. The flick of his wrist as he scratched out a lyric that he didn't like. The way his large hand flexed when he got a cramp from writing too quickly. She couldn't stop thinking about how her skin had buzzed to life when they'd locked pinkies last night.

Then she zeroed in on his mouth. He bit his full bottom lip as he read over his lyrics, and heat prickled her skin. This was *terrible*. She was objectifying him! The current Save Face Beauty brand ambassador! She deserved to be fired.

Angel glanced up, reaching for his water bottle, and looked at Iris. She was caught red-handed, staring at him with her greedy, greedy eyes. She turned her head quickly and fidgeted with the screen on the back of the seat in front of her, searching for a movie. Something serious and very unsexy, like a bird documentary. She picked *March of the Penguins*. She'd seen it at least a dozen times, back when Calla went through a penguin phase after seeing them at the zoo.

Angel leaned his arm on the armrest between them. Iris held her breath. When he tapped her shoulder, she nearly jumped out of her skin.

"Whoa, sorry," he said, laughing. "What are you watching?"

She glanced at the screen. The emperor penguins were waddling across an expanse of snow in Antarctica. She glanced back at Angel and flashes from her dream accosted her brain. His hand on her thighs. His mouth on her mouth . . . What was the name of this documentary again?

"Um, it's called *March of the Penguins*?" she said, like she was unsure of the title.

"Is it good?"

She nodded.

"Cool." Angel smiled easily and slipped his headphones back on.

Get a grip, Iris.

———

HOURS LATER, THEY arrived at the Refine store in Georgetown, DC. Angel's fans began screaming as soon as he
walked through the doors. After three days, Iris had grown
a little more used to the commotion. She gave her opening
spiel and introduced Angel, who entertained the crowd
during his demonstration. During the meet-and-greet portion, Iris stood off to the side, observing, ready to jump in if
needed.

A fan reached the front of the signing line, and she froze
in front of Angel, like she couldn't believe that he was a real.
She had braces and long red Senegalese twists. She didn't
look older than sixteen.

Angel smiled warmly. "What's up?"

"Oh my God!" she shouted, bringing her hands to either
side of her face like Kevin McCallister. "I love you!"

She turned to her friends and screamed again. While
her friends encouraged her to get herself together, Angel
looked over his shoulder and met Iris's gaze. He nodded his
head in a quick motion, discreetly beckoning her toward
him.

"Yes?" she said, coming to his side.

"Guess what?" he whispered, leaning down so that only
she could hear him.

He smelled divine. She inhaled, exhaled. Blinked at
him. "What?"

"I did some research. There's a Friendly's an hour away
in Maryland."

She cocked her head to the side. That was the last thing
she'd expected him to say. "Really?"

"And guess what else?"

"What else?"

"It's right next to a skating rink."

Her forehead wrinkled. "I'm not following."

"When's the last time you went skating?"

She couldn't remember. Maybe at a birthday party for one of Calla's classmates, but she hadn't skated herself. "It's been a while."

He wiggled his brows. "Wanna go?"

Iris laughed, surprised at the question. Taking a trip to Friendly's and going skating with Angel had nothing to do with their reason for being in DC. But then again . . . wasn't accompanying Angel part of talent care? If Angel had asked Paloma to go skating, wouldn't she have prioritized his request? Keeping the brand ambassador happy was important.

At least that was what Iris told herself as she answered, "Yes."

Angel grinned, but their conversation was cut short as his fan, now properly ready for her moment, launched herself into Angel's arms. Ray tensed, watching the exchange. Angel hugged the girl back and winked at Iris over the girl's head. This drew the attention of the girl's friends. They gawked at Iris, a woman in her plain, professional black ensemble, who'd somehow elicited a wink from their beloved Angel.

Iris didn't want any smoke. She stepped aside again and noticed Ray glance at her with his mouth curved in a small smile. Before Iris could ask what that was about, Bree tapped her shoulder.

"Iris, do you know that woman?" Bree asked, pointing. "She asked me to get your attention."

Iris followed the direction in which Bree pointed. When her gaze landed on a familiar face, her heart leaped. Staring directly at her, dressed in a pale yellow Chanel suit, was her mother-in-law, Elaine. Iris would have been less surprised to see Michelle Obama staring back at her. Elaine was the kind of person who caught the train to New York City to buy makeup over the counter at Bergdorf Goodman, recommended by a top-end aesthetician. In one hand, Elaine held a shopping bag from J.McLaughlin. In the other, a classic black Chanel flap bag. Pearls adorned her ears and perfectly coifed dark curls framed her face. She wore peach lipstick that complemented her light brown complexion. She lifted her hand and waved excitedly. Iris waved back.

"That's my mother-in-law," she said to Bree. "I'm going to speak to her. Can you keep an eye on things?"

Bree nodded eagerly. "Yes, of course."

Elaine and Terry's father, Terrance senior, were supposed to come up to New Jersey for Calla's graduation last week, but Senior had experienced an arthritis flare-up the evening before and hadn't been fit to travel. Elaine had chosen to stay by his side. Throughout their decades-long marriage, they rarely spent a night apart, but Calla was their only grandchild, so they'd been devastated to miss her graduation. Iris and Calla saw Elaine and Senior a handful of times throughout the year, on holidays and for long weekends.

"Elaine!" Iris said, smiling as she reached her mother-in-law. "Hi! I'm surprised to see you."

"I'm surprised to see *you*," Elaine said, wrapping her arms around Iris. "You're in town and didn't say anything, miss."

"I know, I'm sorry," Iris said sheepishly. "I'm only here one day for work, and I knew I wouldn't have time to see you."

"Calla is with Dahlia and Benjamin?" she asked, and Iris nodded. "We're still so sorry that we missed her graduation."

"We know, it's okay, really. How's Senior?"

"Curmudgeonly, per usual. But he's not in much pain today. I told him I'd stop by Georgetown Cupcakes before I went home."

Iris smiled. The first time she'd visited DC with Terry, he'd taken her to Georgetown Cupcakes. His favorite flavor had been red velvet.

"I'm glad to hear he's feeling better," she said.

"I'll tell him that you asked about him." Elaine winked. "He'll be so jealous that I got to see you and he didn't."

Iris chuckled. Terry's parents had always treated her with such kindness, and although they were pretty traditional, they hadn't objected when Iris chose to keep her last name after she and Terry married. Elaine and Senior were old-money DC and came from families where everyone went to Howard or Hampton and the children were members of Jack and Jill. They lived in a beautiful home in DC's Crestwood neighborhood. Terry had been their only son, and after he and Iris had earned their business degrees, he'd worked remotely in New Jersey for his father's firm. Iris and Terry had assumed they'd eventually end up living in DC once it was time for Terry to take over the business completely, and Iris would take her talents to a new city. Now, Senior was close to retiring and he was grooming one of his trusted mentees to take his place in a few years.

A new burst of screams from Angel's fans made Iris and Elaine jump.

"It's quite the event happening here, huh?" Elaine said. "You remember that I volunteer with Girls of the Future?"

Iris nodded vaguely. Elaine volunteered for several organizations. "Can you remind me which one that is?"

"It's a nonprofit that helps young women prepare themselves for college," Elaine said. "They went on a field trip to the Alexandria Black History Museum today, and so many of them were crushed to miss the opportunity to see Angel in person. They just *love* him." She smiled and lowered her voice. "I have to admit that I didn't know who he was until they told me. I promised to come by and get a picture, but this line is so long. I guess I spent too much time doing my own shopping."

Elaine laughed easily, and Iris assessed the meet-and-greet line. Angel was taking a picture with a group of college students wearing Georgetown sweatshirts. There were at least thirty people left waiting.

"Follow me," she said, ushering Elaine through the store.

"Oh no, Iris, it's okay. I don't want to cut the line," Elaine whispered, but she was smiling, and she didn't resist as Iris steered her toward Angel.

"Hey, my mother-in-law would like to get a picture with Angel for a local nonprofit," Iris said to Bree once they reached her. "I'm going to quickly slip her in front. She'll be in and out."

Thankfully, Bree didn't bat an eye and nodded. She walked over to the fan who was next in line, a tall skinny boy with his hair dyed burgundy just like Angel's and asked him to wait just a moment. Iris quickly brought Elaine to Angel.

"Angel, this is my mother-in-law, Elaine," Iris said, making a fast introduction, aware that they had to be swift with this interruption to not upset his fans or the overall flow that they'd established. "She volunteers with Girls of the Future, an organization that helps prepare young women for college."

Elaine stuck out her hand toward Angel and smiled, warm and welcoming. "The girls that I mentor love you so much. They had to miss today's event due to a previously planned trip, but I told them I'd come by and get a picture of you."

She pulled a white T-shirt out of her shopping bag. It said **GIRLS OF THE FUTURE** in thick, black script.

"Would you mind holding this up?" she asked.

"For sure." Angel took the shirt and smiled at Elaine. He held up the T-shirt as she snapped a picture of him.

"Thank you," she said. She handed him a marker. "Would you mind signing the shirt as well?"

"No problem." Angel signed the shirt in a quick flourish. "Do you want a picture too? With me, I mean?"

"Oh no, that won't be necessary." Elaine laughed. "I'm just here on behalf of the youth. It was lovely meeting you."

"Same." Angel returned Elaine's smile and looked at Iris.

Iris mouthed *Thank you* and directed Elaine off to the side and signaled to Bree to let the next fan forward.

"I'll walk you out," Iris said to Elaine.

The midday DC sun beamed down on them as they stepped onto the sidewalk. Iris pulled at the collar of her black sleeveless turtleneck dress. Elaine folded her newly signed T-shirt and placed it back in her bag.

"It's actually a bit serendipitous that I saw you today," Elaine said. "Because I was planning to call you this week." She cleared her throat. "Senior and I are selling the house. We'd hoped to tell you in person after Calla's graduation."

Shock rendered Iris momentarily speechless. Her stomach sank. "What? But you love that house."

Their home was Elaine's pride and joy. It was an interior designer's dream.

"We do, and we always will," Elaine said. "But it's too big for us and it's getting harder for Senior to walk up and down the stairs." She smiled softly. "I want you and Calla to come and go through Terry's things soon. Take whatever you wish."

Elaine and Senior had left Terry's bedroom untouched. His posters of the Wizards and Nationals were still tacked to the wall. His handful of Hampton sweatshirts hung in the closet. There were the odd items that every adult left behind, knowing they'd be forever secure at their parents' home.

A person was not their things. But it had comforted Iris to know that a part of Terry's memory was preserved at Elaine and Senior's home. Soon, that would be gone too.

"Of course we'll come," she said quietly.

Elaine took Iris's hands in hers and gave them a firm, loving squeeze. It reminded Iris that the decision to move probably hadn't been easy for Elaine. The new house wouldn't have any traces of Terry.

"Good. Just let me know the day," Elaine said. "Now I really must get going or else Senior will be calling me soon and asking about those cupcakes."

They hugged tightly, and Elaine slipped on her sunglasses. "Give Calla a kiss for me," she said.

She crossed the street, heading for a black Audi that waited for her, with a driver who would take her to get cupcakes and then back home to Terrance senior. Iris waved goodbye as the car pulled off.

She wondered what Terry would think about his parents selling the home that he'd grown up in. She thought about how Calla would no longer be able to make similar memories there of her own.

It was silly to feel sad. It was just a *house*. But Iris felt sad nonetheless.

Sucking in a deep breath, she breezed back inside the store, forced a smile, and resumed her place beside Bree. The meet and greet was almost over, with only a few fans left in line. Iris tried her best to focus on the success of another event. She tried not to think of the first Christmas she'd spent with Terry's family, and how holding Terry's hand in front of the sparkling fir tree had felt magical, how Elaine and Senior's house had felt like a home away from home to her and Calla over the past five years. Iris tried not to think of these things, but it was easier said than done.

"You okay?" Angel appeared in front of Iris. His voice was soft, attentive.

The last fan was leaving the store, armed with a Save Face Beauty skincare bundle and a deeply satisfied smile.

Iris blinked at Angel. Where had the last five minutes gone?

"I'm okay, thanks," she said.

"Okay." But he didn't look like he believed her.

She *was* fine. She was just having a minor moment. She'd deal with her feelings once she was in her hotel room.

Back at the hotel, Iris made a beeline for the elevator, politely begging off when Bree and Ray asked if she wanted to get a drink. She expected Angel to stay behind with them, especially after he was approached by a fan in the lobby, but as Iris stepped onto the elevator and pushed the button for her floor, Angel eased through the doors right before they closed. Concern was written all over his face.

"Angel, I'm okay," she said, although now her voice was shaky.

"You don't look like you're okay." Angel paused. Quietly, he said, "Is this because of your mother-in-law? You seemed different after you talked to her."

Iris bit her lip. "She told me that they're selling their house and it made me think of Terry's things and how someone else will be living in his childhood home." She took a shuddering breath and tried to smile. "It's silly, I know. Sometimes these little moments jump up and startle me. But I'll be fine."

She wiped at her eyes, growing frustrated when she realized she'd started tearing up at some point.

Angel didn't say anything as he stepped forward, cautious and quiet as a cat. Slowly, he wrapped his arms around Iris and pulled her into his embrace. Her first instinct was to squirm away, because his attentiveness only caused her tears to flow more freely. But soon, she melted against him. The truth was that it felt good to be held, to be comforted. And as much as she disliked crying in front of people, she felt safe to cry in front of Angel.

The elevator opened to her floor. Iris sniffled and stepped away from him.

"Thank you," she said. She offered a weak smile.

"You're welcome." Angel kept his gaze on her.

He walked with her down the hall to her room, saying that he wanted to make sure she got in okay. When she fumbled with her key card, he gently took it from her and opened the door, letting them both inside.

Iris had a standard king-size room. Clean, efficient. It was probably nothing compared to the suite they'd booked for Angel. She slipped off her heels, sat on the bed and massaged her temples. Crying always gave her a tension headache.

Angel moved around the room silently. He grabbed a glass off the table and opened the mini fridge. Then he sat next to her, holding a glass of water.

"Thank you," she said, taking it from him gratefully.

She felt like she owed him an apology. The behavior he'd witnessed just now had been a bit unprofessional.

"I'm really sorry—"

"Who takes care of you?" he asked.

Iris paused. "What?"

"When you're upset, who takes care of you?"

"I—" She didn't know how to answer that question. Because she didn't have an answer.

"I get the sense that you're used to taking care of everything for everyone else," he continued. "Your daughter, of course, and Violet told me that you're like a second mom to her and Lily, and I see how you handle things at work. I know you said you're in therapy. But outside of that, who takes care of you when you need it?"

Iris sniffled again, wiping her eyes. She shrugged. "I take care of myself."

"Yeah, but we all need help sometimes."

She knew that he was right. She'd been taking care of herself for so long, she struggled with asking for help and couldn't recognize when she needed it. This was something she'd discussed with Marie. Ever a work in progress.

"You know what I think you need?" he said, easing back on his elbows. He grinned softly as he looked at her.

"A nap?" she said.

He laughed. "Maybe. I was going to say a nice, clean skate."

She blinked. Then she remembered. "You mean the skating rink in Maryland?"

"Yeah. We'll bring Bree and Ray." He smirked. "You ever seen a six-foot-four, two-hundred-fifty-pound ex-bodybuilder on skates?"

Iris shook her head as she began to smile. Angel seemed to move through the world with such light and ease. She wished to be more like him, if even for a moment.

"Me neither," Angel said. "We should go for that image alone."

She recognized that he was trying to cheer her up and she appreciated it. And his suggestion was probably better than staying in her hotel room, replaying her conversation with Elaine over and over.

"Okay," she said. "Let's go."

13

THE SKATING RINK WAS LOCATED IN A SUBURBAN MARY-land shopping center, squished right between a Dollar Tree and a Michael's. Angel wanted to be as inconspicuous as possible, so they'd rented a car. Ray drove, and Angel sat in the passenger seat, while Iris and Bree sat in the back. As they pulled into the parking lot, Angel was hit with a wave of nostalgia. Skating rinks reminded him of his childhood—particularly trips to the indoor skating rink during the summer. His church used to throw seasonal birthday parties for the Sunday school kids. One Saturday every June, the church van pulled up in front of Angel's house, and he joined the other summer birthday kids as one of their Sunday school teachers drove them to the skating rink. They skated for free and shared a big sheet cake. His parents didn't do parties and cakes for his and Leah's birthdays. They thought it was frivolous. The skating rink trips had been the highlight of Angel's summers.

He was turning twenty-nine tomorrow.

Ray knew this, of course. But Angel hadn't mentioned anything to Iris or Bree. Maybe it was a holdover, but making a big or small deal out of his birthday didn't come naturally to him. He'd looked up Friendly's out of curiosity, intrigued by Iris's stories of chicken tender baskets and ice cream sundaes, and when he'd found a location not too far from DC, he'd been eager at the idea of spending more time with her at a restaurant that held sentimental value for her. Its proximity to a skating rink had been an added plus.

But going skating felt more imperative now. It wasn't just a way for Angel to secretly celebrate his impending birthday. He thought Iris needed a night of pure fun. Seeing her cry earlier had done something to him. He'd wanted to protect and comfort her. He wanted to be the person she came to for protection and comfort, even though he knew there was little to no chance of that happening.

As they walked toward the skating rink entrance, Angel slipped on his baseball cap and long, fake beard.

"Tom Wyatt again?" Iris asked. She seemed in slightly lighter spirits, although there were dark circles around her eyes.

"Figured it would make things easier for everyone," he said.

He'd promised that if he was recognized and things got out of hand, they'd leave immediately.

The lights were dimmed when they stepped inside, and "You're All I Need to Get By" by Marvin Gaye and Tammi Terrell played overhead. A disco ball spun from the ceiling above the rink.

"Oooh, it must be oldies night," Bree said, shimmying her hips.

There was something else that Angel noticed as he

looked around. The crowd was older. His mouth slowly curved into a grin.

"I'll be right back," he said, removing his hat and fake beard.

"Wait, where are you going?" Ray asked, taking Angel's disguise pieces.

"I promise I'll be quick."

Ray raised an eyebrow but nodded, positioning his arms akimbo and standing with his feet planted. No one turned in Angel's direction as he crossed the floor. No one pulled out their phone to take his picture. He spotted two women standing at the vending machines, and he decided that they would be the subjects of his experiment. They wore matching gold sweatshirts and black jeans. They looked to be in their early sixties maybe, but with Black women you never knew. They could be closer to their late seventies yet looked ten years younger.

"Good evening, ladies," Angel said.

The women glanced at him. They smiled but there was no flash of recognition in their eyes.

"By any chance, do you know who I am?" he asked.

The women exchanged a look. "Should we?" said the shorter of the two.

Her friend squinted at Angel. "Wait . . . I think I've seen you before. You play basketball, right?"

Angel shook his head, grinning.

"Maybe he has one of those faces," the other woman mused.

"Wait!" The taller one snapped her fingers. "You're a rapper."

That answer was close, but not close enough. "Nah," he said. "Not me."

He wouldn't have to hide here. The people of this generation didn't know him without context. The last place they expected to see a famous person was at their local skating rink on oldies night.

This was amazing.

"Thank you for answering my questions," he said with a smile. "Have a good night."

"Now, hold on a minute," the shorter woman said, and her friend chuckled. "Why'd you come over here if you're not gonna tell us who you are? If you wanted to get your skate on with some grown women, that's all you had to say."

Angel laughed. "On another night, I'd join you, but I came here with friends. And I'm nobody important, trust me."

He said goodbye to the women and beamed as he rejoined his group. But he frowned when he noticed that Iris was missing.

"Where's Iris?" he asked.

"She's at the bar," Bree said. "She said that she'd skate later."

Angel turned around and found Iris sitting at the bar, nursing a big slushie. A sign above her said DRINK AND SKATE AT YOUR OWN RISK.

"What did you say to those women?" Ray asked.

Angel pulled his attention away from Iris. "I asked if they knew who I was, and they didn't. The people here don't care about me. It's all good."

"Okay, let's get our skates, then," Bree said. "I haven't skated in forever. I was never that good at it."

Ray smirked coyly. "Don't worry. I'll make sure you don't fall."

Bree laughed and batted her long eyelashes at Ray. Angel suddenly felt like a third wheel.

"I'm gonna check on Iris really quick," he said.

Iris noticed him walking toward her and she waved. Almost half of her slushie was already gone. He sat on the stool beside her.

"Hey, you okay?"

She nodded and rolled her shoulders. "I wanted a Dr Pepper, but Howard said that this spiked slushie is their special." She nodded toward the bartender, an older white man with tattoo sleeves and a thick, gray handlebar mustache.

"Is it good?"

"Mhmm." She pushed the bright red drink toward him. "Here, taste it."

He lifted her drink and paused before putting his mouth on her straw. But she motioned with her hands for him to go ahead. He placed the straw in his mouth, leaving his lips right over her lipstick print, where her own lips had been just moments before. Iris watched his mouth while he sipped. The air felt intimate and heated. He was playing with fire.

"It's sweet," he said, sliding the drink back to her. "And strong."

"You think so? I can barely taste anything."

Angel laughed. "That's probably a problem, then."

She smiled at him, and she was so beautiful, for a second, all Angel did was stare.

"Wanna come skate?" he asked.

"I will in a bit. It's been a long day, so I just want to sit for a minute. You go ahead. I'll join you later."

He slid off his stool. "I'm gonna hold you to that."

She gave him a thumbs-up as he walked away. He stood in line to rent skates from an attendant who barely glanced up at him, too busy reading a thick book. Something about elves living in a place called Ceradon.

Out on the rink, he caught up with Bree and Ray. Ray held Bree's hand as they skated slowly. Bree was shaky on her skates. Angel swerved around until he was in front of them and skated backward.

"Wow, you're really good," Bree said.

Ray scoffed. "He's a show-off. He used to do speed skating contests when he was younger."

"I'm sorry, I think what you're actually trying to say is that you're a hater," Angel said, zipping out of the way as Ray moved to grab him.

They looped around the rink as a Stevie Wonder song played. Iris waved at them from the bar. Howard slid another slushie in front of her and she grinned.

"Is Iris okay?" Bree asked, waving back at Iris as they skated farther away. "She seemed a little upset earlier."

Angel didn't want to betray Iris's confidence, so he didn't say anything.

"She definitely deserves a break tonight," Bree said. "She's such a saint. Everybody at the office loves her. She works so hard and she always finds the time to help other people too. You know she fought to make sure that I wasn't let go in the most recent round of layoffs? Dominique runs the place, but Iris is her right hand. She'll probably be Dominique's successor if she doesn't start her own company first. I'd leave SFB to work for Iris."

Angel looked over toward Iris again. She was in the middle of an animated conversation with Howard, nodding eagerly as he told her a story that required him to use his hands while he spoke. She looked so serious, her forehead wrinkling as she listened.

"What does she do for fun?" Angel asked, looking at Bree again.

Bree frowned. "Well, she and Paloma go to Pilates sometimes on their lunch breaks, but otherwise, I have no idea, actually. Iris is pretty private."

From what he could tell, Iris needed more fun in her life. He skated a couple more laps around the rink with Bree and Ray, then he slowed his pace as he spotted Iris at the rink's entrance, holding on to the rail as she tested out her skates.

He stopped once he reached her. "Ready to come out?"

"So those slushies *were* strong." She frowned at her skates.

Angel stepped onto the carpeted floor and rolled over to her. "You don't have to skate if you don't want to."

"I *do* want to." She looked up at him, sporting a newly determined expression. "I drank some water and Howard gave me a soft pretzel, on the house. I've been fed and hydrated and now I have to prove to myself that I still remember how to skate."

Angel raised his eyebrows as Iris removed her grasp from the rail and held on to him instead.

"Come on," she urged. "Please."

If she wanted to skate after the day she'd had, Angel wouldn't tell her no. He'd just do everything he could to make sure that she didn't fall. They carefully stepped onto the rink and Iris's left foot slid from under her immediately. Her butt would have smacked the floor if Angel hadn't been there to catch her.

"Whoops!" Iris threw her head back and her laughter was so uncharacteristically loud and carefree. She clasped Angel's hand tighter and his pulse spiked. She regained her composure and quickly tried for a focused expression.

"I can't laugh," she said. "This is serious."

"Why?" he asked, smiling at her as he began steering them slowly around the rink. She kept her arm looped through his and held on tightly.

"I can't leave here tonight without managing to skate well. I've made it a personal challenge."

"A personal challenge?"

"But I'm a lightweight, and my equilibrium is off." She sighed dramatically. "So that's a problem."

His smile widened, observing her downturned expression.

"I usually stick to wine," she continued. "Sometimes I'll have a hard seltzer, but did you know that alcohol is terrible for your skin? It can make your skin dry and wrinkled or bloated and puffy. I learned that at work." Her ramble came to an end with a surprise burp. She quickly covered her mouth, eyes widening in embarrassment. "That was gross. I'm so sorry."

Angel was too busy laughing. Tipsy Iris was funny. "You're good," he said. "What else?"

"What?"

"What other skincare facts do you have for me?"

"Oh, I love this question," she said, brightening. "Applying moisturizer and SPF daily is one of the best things that we can do for our skin, specifically for our faces and necks. A lack of sleep can affect our skin too. Hmm . . . oh, this is my favorite one: dancing makes your skin glow."

"*Glow?* Really?"

She nodded. "Well, exercise in general. It boosts blood flow, and sweating removes toxins and dead skins cells." She peered up at him. "Which probably explains why you have great skin. You're a good dancer."

He grinned at her compliment. "Thank you."

"You're wel—"

A four-man skating crew whizzed by, startling Iris. She threaded her fingers through Angel's, keeping herself upright. His large palm was covered with calluses from lifting weights, while her skin was soft and smooth. He swallowed thickly as his heartbeat accelerated. Over the past couple years, he'd had his fair share of thrilling encounters with beautiful women. But here he was, feeling giddy because Iris was simply holding his hand.

A song by the Temptations began to play, and the floor filled with more skating crews. Angel and Iris continued to loop around the rink at their steady pace. He spotted Ray and Bree getting snacks from the vending machine.

"I should have known that you'd be a graceful skater," Iris said. Her attention was fixed on Angel's feet. "Have you done this a lot?"

"I used to when I was younger. I won a couple competitions."

"Really?" Her eyes lit up. "Did you get a trophy?"

"No, but I won some medals."

"Pshh. Winners deserve trophies."

She stumbled again, and Angel's hands promptly went to her waist, keeping her in place. Her waist was slim, her hips generous. She smelled like the sweetest, most alluring flower. He exhaled deeply.

"You should probably sit down," he said.

"No, one more time around." She clutched his wrists, keeping his hands at her waist. "I promise I won't fall."

He shook his head with a laugh. "You're really taking this personal challenge to heart."

"I take all of my personal challenges to heart," she said, dead serious.

He liked that she continued holding on to him. "Okay. Don't worry. I've got you."

They skated even more slowly now, at a tortoise's pace. "If This World Were Mine" by Luther Vandross and Cheryl Lynn played overhead. Some couples stopped to slow dance in the middle of the rink, but Angel figured that would be too advanced for Iris. Plus, he'd promised no dances at twilight. Instead, he began to hum, catching Luther's harmony.

"You have a beautiful voice," Iris said quietly.

"Thank you."

This wasn't the first time that someone had admired his voice, but the compliment felt more special coming from Iris. She didn't seem like she often said things that she didn't mean.

"It's like you have a superpower." She looked up at him. "Do you use your powers for good?"

He laughed softly. "I think so."

"You mean you've never serenaded a girl to make her fall for you?"

He shook his head. "Honestly, no. I wasn't always smooth."

Iris craned her neck a little, trying to get a better look at him while keeping her balance. "I don't know if I believe you."

"I'm so serious. I didn't know the first thing about girls for a long time."

"Hmm." She squinted at him.

"We can test it out, though," he said. "See if my singing works on you."

He was joking . . . but at the same time, he wasn't.

Iris raised an eyebrow, recognizing the challenge. "You can try."

Angel smiled and lowered his lips to her ear. He sang along with Luther and Cheryl, leveling his voice in a deep baritone. Iris's grasp on his hand tightened, and he felt her breathing slow as he sang to her about how he'd give her anything if this world were his. Iris leaned into him and he watched goose bumps spread up the slope of her neck.

When he stopped singing, he pulled back slightly and looked at her. She angled her face toward his. She blinked, lost in a daze. Their mouths were mere millimeters apart.

"Did it work?" he whispered.

"I . . ."

Iris tripped over her skate and they both went crashing to the floor. Angel scrambled onto his knees and reached for Iris.

"Are you okay?" he asked, moving to help her up.

Iris covered her face with her hands as her shoulders shook. Angel's stomach seized. Was she crying again? But then she lowered her hands, and he realized that she was laughing.

"I'm a *terrible* skater," she said, wiping her eyes. "Are *you* okay?"

"Yeah," he said, and he started to laugh too. They were a laughing, tangled mess.

Ray rushed over to help them up. Iris winced as she held her elbow.

"Just a little bruised," she said, noticing their looks of concern.

Angel frowned, sticking close to Iris as they made their way off the rink. He waved toward Bree. "I think we should call it a night."

Back at the hotel, Angel helped Iris get ice for her elbow. In her room, she took some ibuprofen, kicked off her shoes and lay down flat on the bed, closing her eyes. Those slushies really took her out. Angel had a feeling that haphazardly discarding her shoes that way wasn't part of her normal routine. He grabbed her plain black heels and lined them up by her suitcase.

He sat on the edge of the bed and leaned down toward her. "I'm gonna leave now."

She opened her eyes and curled onto her side, staring at him. Softly, she said, "Thank you for taking me skating."

He smiled. "You're welcome."

Her eyes drooped closed again. "Your superpower is probably real, by the way," she mumbled.

"What?" He blinked at her.

But she was already fast asleep. Her chest rose and fell as she breathed. A string of lyrics came together in his mind as he watched her. He grabbed the hotel notepad from the bedside table and quickly jotted down a few lines. He ripped the page from the pad and left it on Iris's pillow.

He planted a brief, gentle kiss on her forehead before quietly slipping out of her room, wishing more and more for things that didn't belong to him.

14

IRIS WASN'T ONE OF THOSE PEOPLE WHO WAS UNABLE TO remember anything after a night of drinking. Her brain was too organized for that.

The minute that she opened her eyes the next morning, she recalled every detail from the night before. Crying in front of Angel in her hotel room after her talk with Elaine. Drinking those spiked slushies. Skating arm in arm with Angel. Angel singing to her before they fell.

She sat up slowly. Sunlight peeked through the blinds. Her elbow was a little sore, but otherwise, she felt fine. No hangover headache, thankfully. She wiped her eyes. Mascara residue appeared on her fingers and she sighed. She, of all people, knew how important it was to remove makeup before bed. She glanced over and noticed a piece of paper on her pillow. She peered at it and recognized Angel's handwriting.

If I had a superpower, I would use it for you
Anything you wanted, anything you needed, I'd
   get it for you
If I had a superpower, there's nothing I wouldn't do

Without context, it might seem like a poem. But Iris knew that they were song lyrics.

Her chest tightened fiercely as she ran her fingers over the page, tracing his words. She imagined him singing them to her, softly in her ear, like he'd done last night. She'd gone into some kind of trance while listening to him. His voice had literally caused her to lose her balance. Her skin flushed hot now just *thinking* of him.

Angel was so different from what she'd expected from a celebrity of his magnitude. Most of the time when it was just the two of them, she forgot that he was famous. He was kind and thoughtful and caring. He listened—*really* listened—to her when she talked . . .

Frowning, she hopped out of bed and unzipped the back of her dress. They had to be at the airport soon for their flight to Atlanta. She needed a shower. She needed to get ahold of herself.

Her thoughts were beyond unprofessional. Dominique had trusted Iris to successfully carry out this tour and re-store SFB's reputation, not form a crush on the brand am-bassador.

Ignore him, she told herself as she got dressed. *You will just have to ignore him.*

But she couldn't do that. Ignoring Angel would be just as unprofessional as harboring a crush.

She shrugged on her airport clothes and carefully folded Angel's note, placing it in her wallet. She'd read the note only a couple times, but she already had the lyrics commit-ted to memory. Another side effect of her organized mind.

Before leaving her room, she called her mom to check in with Calla, and after Calla shared how excited she was to visit the Liberty Science Center that afternoon at day camp, and she and Iris exchanged *I miss you*s and *I love you*s, Iris finished packing and left for the hotel lobby. Bree was already there, waiting, and Iris smiled as she walked over to her. When Angel and Ray stepped off the elevator, Iris took a deep breath and reminded herself to be polite to Angel, but not to treat him any differently. Then his mouth tipped up in a grin, aimed at her, and her limbs loosened slowly, like she was melting.

"Good morning," he said to the group, eyes lingering on Iris.

He stood beside her, smelling once again of cinnamon. Someone with a weaker willpower would have trouble fighting the urge to sniff him like a bloodhound.

Iris began to question her own willpower.

Gulping, she straightened her posture and smiled. "Good morning."

She kept her gaze forward, even as his presence surrounded her and invaded her thoughts.

"HAPPY BIRTHDAY TO *you. Happy birthday to you. Happy birthday, big brotherrrr. Happy birthday to you!*" Leah sang to Angel. They were on FaceTime, and Maxine bumped her way into the camera's view and sniffed the phone.

Angel was in his Atlanta hotel room, sprawled across his bed. He grinned at his sister and their dog. "Thank you. That was beautiful."

"Yeah, right. We know you're the singer of the family," Leah said. She was at his apartment once again, as opposed to her dorm. "And you're getting old. Pretty soon you're gonna have dentures."

Angel snorted. "Wow, that hurt my feelings."

"Sike, sike. Your birthday gift will be waiting for you once you get back."

"You know you didn't have to get me anything."

"I know you don't like gifts," Leah said, sighing impatiently. "But I got you something anyway. It's a pack of those notebooks from Kinokuniya that you like. More space for you to write down your angsty lyrics."

Angel laughed, shaking his head. "Thank you."

"How's the makeup stuff going?" she asked.

"Skincare," Angel corrected. "It's cool, I—" He stopped abruptly as another call came in, interrupting their conversation. His muscles tensed. "Uh, hey, Mom's calling me. I'll call you back."

Leah mouthed *Yikes* and said that she'd text him later.

Angel sat up. He breathed deeply and counted to ten before answering. It wasn't that he was surprised that his mother was calling him. It was his birthday after all. Usually Angel was able to prepare before their interactions. He liked having a ready script on hand; that way he was able stay on track without being ruffled by the inevitable little comments that she made. But being so relaxed while talking to Leah had thrown him off. He'd have to quickly adjust.

"Hey, Mom," he said.

"Happy birthday, son."

Angel automatically straightened his posture even more at the sound of Cora's stern voice. He cleared his throat. "Thank you."

He heard the banging of pots and pans in her background. Gospel music played faintly from the small radio that she kept on the kitchen counter.

"Do you mind if we pray?" she asked.

Angel walked across his suite to the balcony. The sun was shining. Birds were chirping. It was a beautiful Georgia day. He tapped his knuckles against the sliding glass door. He took another deep breath.

"Okay," he said.

Cora began her prayer with thanks that Angel had made it to twenty-nine years, and then she quickly slipped into asking God to remind Angel that it was never too late to change his ways and repent. Angel zoned out as she continued talking. He stared at a blue jay that was perched on a tree branch below, ready to take flight. Whenever he spoke to his mom, he felt like a bird with clipped wings.

"Amen," she said, finishing her prayer.

Angel didn't say *Amen* back. "Okay, Mom, I've gotta—"

"I'm cooking for Mr. Price," she said. He heard more pots banging. "His wife passed a few days ago."

Mr. Price had been one of Angel's Sunday school teachers in high school. He and his wife had always been so kind to him and the other kids.

"I'm really sorry to hear that," he said. "I'll send him some flowers."

"A call would do better," Cora said. Pointedly, she added, "He hasn't heard from you in so long."

Another deep breath. "Yeah, that's true."

"You'll be able to give your condolences in person anyway. Mr. Price is planning to be at the ceremony next month."

"Oh," Angel said. "Right. So I'll see him then. Mom, I really can't talk right now—"

"Mhmm. Now, where are you gallivanting to today?"

Angel closed his eyes and leaned his forehead against the cool glass of the sliding door. If he were someone else, he would lie. But he couldn't. Another steadying breath. "I'm in Atlanta, actually."

Cora's pause was considerable. "You *are*? Doing what?"

Angel swallowed and cleared his throat. "I'm working."

She breezed right over that answer. "You're less than two hours away. Did you have any plans at all to see your own mother?"

Angel rubbed a hand over his face. Years ago, she'd refused to see him. It wasn't until he started making regular donations to their church that she'd decided to be part of his life again. He wouldn't mention this, though. Technically, he *could* see her. The event at Refine was later in the evening. He hadn't planned to do anything today prior to that, other than get brunch with Ray.

"I—um, yeah. I can see you."

"Good. But come soon. I'll be leaving in a bit to drop this food off at Mr. Price's and I have several volunteer activities with the church group, as you know."

He promised his mom that he'd leave soon. After they hung up, he sat on the bed and held his face in his hands. What had he just agreed to?

A knock at his door startled him. He stood and opened the door for Ray.

"I'm hungry as fuck," Ray said, walking into the room with his loud, heavy footsteps. "Ready for brunch, birthday boy?"

"Uh." Anxiety spread in the pit of Angel's stomach. "I just did something really stupid."

"What?" Ray wasn't looking at him as he grabbed a water bottle from the mini fridge. "Accidentally post a nude online?"

Angel smirked, but the humor didn't reach his eyes. "No. Worse. I agreed to visit my mom."

Ray whipped around. "*Today?*"

"Yeah," Angel said, sighing deeply.

"But she drives you nuts. Why would you ruin your birthday like that?"

Angel laughed, but reality was beginning to set in. His anxiety worsened.

"You go to brunch," Angel said, looking for his sneakers. "Don't lose the reservation. Take Bree."

Ray stared at him, raising an eyebrow. "You sure?"

"Positive." Not everyone's day needed to be ruined. "You think you can help me get a rental car? I'd rather drive myself."

"For sure. The event starts at seven, so you'll need to be back before then."

Angel checked the time. He had a good six hours. "Okay."

"If Iris and Bree ask where you are, I'll come up with something."

"You can tell them the truth," Angel said. He thought of Iris and the open, calm expression she wore whenever he spoke to her. "Actually . . . I'll tell Iris myself."

He wanted to reassure her that he'd be on time for the event and that being on time was important to him. He didn't want her to worry about his absence.

Ray nodded and moved toward the door. "I'll get on renting a car for you." He paused and doubled back, embracing Angel in a tight bro hug. "Happy birthday. Don't let your mom and her shit get to you."

"Thanks, bro," Angel said. Ray was the only person who could hug him and make him feel short.

Ray patted Angel's back as he pulled away, saying he'd let Angel know details about the rental car soon.

After he left, Angel slid on his sneakers and threw on a hoodie, pulling the hood over his head so that he wouldn't be recognized in the hall. He was going down to Iris's room to tell her where he planned to be this afternoon. But he also wanted to apologize about leaving that note on her bed. In hindsight, he knew he'd overstepped. She hadn't mentioned anything about it this morning on the way to the airport, but he wanted to apologize for being so forward. They were developing a friendship now and he needed to be okay with just that.

He went to her floor and knocked lightly at her door. He heard the sound of her feet padding against the carpet. After a brief pause, Iris opened the door. She wore the same plain white T-shirt and jeans that she'd worn on the plane. Her short curls were pulled behind her ears by a thin black headband. Her brown skin was smooth and blemish free.

"Hey." She glanced up and down the hall before looking at him. "Everything okay?"

"Uh, yeah. I wanted to let you know that I'm driving to Maren. It's about two hours from here." He added, "Maren is my hometown."

"I know. The internet, remember." She tapped her temple and smiled. She tilted her head. "Are you going to see your family?"

"Yeah, my parents."

Iris let this information settle. "Is Ray going with you?"

"Nah, just me. I'll be back before the meet and greet tonight. I just wanted to let you know."

He recalled the other reason that he'd shown up at her door. He wanted to apologize about the note. "About last night—"

"Do you want some company?" she asked.

His heart stuttered as he blinked. "You want to come with me?"

"If you don't want to go by yourself," she said. She bit her lip. "But I understand if you'd rather go alone, of course. It sounds very personal."

His knee-jerk reaction was to tell her no. His mom was a hard pill to swallow and he was nervous about introducing her to Iris.

But then he thought about taking the two-hour drive with Iris. Uninterrupted time, just the two of them. He thought about showing her around his hometown, a place that still held a small, special place in his heart, even though he didn't make a habit of returning.

There were only two days left in the campaign tour. Selfishly, he wanted to soak up as much time with Iris as possible.

"I want you to," he hastened to say. "I'd like that."

"Okay." She flashed a quick, relieved smile. "Let me grab my bag."

He nodded and waited for her in the hall. She returned,

slinging her purse over her shoulder. She closed her door and glanced up at him as they fell into step together.

He'd meant to apologize about the note, but now as he looked at her, new lyrics formed in his head.

> *Do you want some company?*
> *That was what she asked me . . .*

It was almost like she was becoming his muse.

15

RAY RENTED ANGEL A BLACK BENZ WITH TINTED WIN-
dows. During the drive, Angel didn't have much time to focus on his frazzled nerves, because Iris kept him busy with
questions. She wanted to know the main differences between a town like Maren and a major city like Atlanta. His
answer: Almost everything. What was Maren's population?
He'd guess a little less than four thousand. How about the
demographics? Mostly African American. Did he like growing up there? Yes and no. Would he ever consider moving
back? Probably not.

The questions continued, but Angel didn't mind. He
liked that he was the object of her undivided attention. As
they came upon the exit for Maren, his stomach muscles
tensed again. He reminded himself that he was only visit-
ing, and he wouldn't be here for long. He had no reason to
be nervous.

An old fading sign that said WELCOME TO MAREN greeted
them as they came off the highway. They drove down a long
road, woods on either side of them for miles. He rolled down
the windows. It was still, quiet. The air smelled fresher

here. The woods continued until a FedEx warehouse appeared on their right.

Angel pointed to it. "A lot of kids from high school got
part-time jobs there once they turned eighteen."

Iris looked at the large facility and the white FedEx
trucks parked outside. She turned to back to Angel. "Did
you work there?"

"Nah, I worked at Cook Out, remember?"

She smiled. "Oh yeah."

"Speaking of." He pointed to the Cook Out on their left
as they came to a traffic light at the end of the street. A line
of cars wrapped around the pale brick building. The scent
of French fries and burgers wafted through the air. The
smell immediately brought back memories of wearing red
polos, black pants and no-slip shoes.

"I worked *there*," he said.

Iris closed her eyes and grinned. "Hold on. I'm trying to
picture it."

"Welcome to Cook Out. What can I get for you today?"

She opened her eyes and laughed. "There's the accent."

Angel's eyes twinkled as he watched her, pleased once
again to have made her laugh.

They continued on. Angel pointed out his high school.
They drove by the Kroger's, which still looked the same, although some of the businesses in the shopping complex had
closed down. He looped around and down a back road,
showing Iris where he used to cut through the woods on his
walk home from school. He drove by the K–8 school and the
field where he sang the national anthem before annual
Fourth of July celebrations. Iris listened intently to Angel.

He liked that she was interested in the things that he shared, no matter how insignificant or mundane.

Whenever he came home, he felt like he was hovering above the town and observing it from a bird's-eye view. He was a product of Maren, but he was no longer part of its ecosystem. In reality, he felt farther from Maren than ever. He didn't think that was necessarily a bad thing, and that made him feel guilty.

"Where's your church?" Iris asked.

Angel paused. Mount Olive wasn't that far away—nothing was too far from one point to the next in Maren. He hadn't been sure if he wanted to drive by the church, especially since he'd be back in a few weeks. But Iris was here with him now, and she wanted to see it, so he'd show her.

Mount Olive was in the same neighborhood as his parents' house. He made a right onto Mount Olive's street and he slowed to a crawl as they came upon the church. He'd visited last Christmas before the renovations. It used to be a simple building, but thanks to Angel's donations, they'd built a second story with space for a nursery and a new Sunday school room. It was newly painted a fresh, bright white. They'd replaced the generator, renovated the first floor and basement and repaved the parking lot to remove the potholes. The parking lot was empty. A sign outside read, GOD LOVES. GOD FORGIVES.

"This is my church," he said to Iris. "Mount Olive."

She leaned past him to get a better look. He watched as she took in the space, gaze roaming. "It's beautiful," she said.

He turned to look at the building again. "Yeah," he replied quietly. "It is."

He thought of the many days and nights he'd spent here, attending weekly Bible study and vacation Bible school in the summers. Doing his homework in the pews and watching over Leah after school while they waited for their parents to finish work. His mom worked as the church secretary and his dad had been a custodian. Growing up, he'd spent more time at church than he had anywhere else. That was why he'd stepped in to help with the much-needed renovations. Despite how his memories of church all felt tainted with Cora and her judgmental ways, Mount Olive would always be an important chapter in his life.

"You want to get out?" he asked Iris. She nodded.

They walked to the front door and found that it was locked, which made sense. It was a random Thursday afternoon and there wasn't a reason for the church to be open to the public. Gravel crunched under their feet as they walked around the side of the church. Angel pressed his face up against the glass-pane window and peered inside at the pulpit and organ and the raised pews for the choir.

Iris moved next to him and peeked through the window too.

"So, this is where you started," she said.

"Yeah." He'd never felt nervous to sing in front of a crowd. Not even when he was a kid. Singing always felt bigger than him. It made him feel like he had a purpose in life to bring people joy.

Iris smiled. "Well, then, I guess the world should thank your church for encouraging your gift."

He looked at her. He didn't know if it was a trick of the light or what, but it almost seemed as though she was glowing. He had the strongest sense that this was where he was meant to be at this exact moment, with her. The feeling of rightness overwhelmed him. It made his hands tingle and his heart pounded harder.

Unaware of the emotions that he was experiencing, Iris pulled out her phone and checked the time. Her brows pinched together a little as she looked at him again. "You should probably stop by and see your parents now," she said. "That way you'll have enough time with them before we have to head back."

He deflated, remembering the real reason that they were here to begin with. "Yeah, you're right."

Softly, she said, "I don't have to come inside or anything. I can wait for you in the car."

He thought again about how he'd rather not have Cora meet Iris, or anyone from his new life, frankly. But he didn't regret bringing Iris home with him. He'd liked showing her the places that were once important to him and had contributed to the fiber of his life.

And he didn't want Iris waiting around in a car in a neighborhood that was unfamiliar to her while he talked to his parents. Plus, he'd already called ahead of time to tell his mom that he was bringing a friend. They didn't have to stay long, and he definitely didn't plan to.

"You can come inside with me," he said. "It's okay. They know you'll be with me."

The smaller ranch-style houses on his parents' street looked the same. He pulled up in front of his childhood home. He'd offered to buy his parents a new house, but they'd declined. They wanted to stay on their street. Instead, he'd paid for renovations to their house. They'd knocked down the back wall to add more kitchen space and a full dining room. For all her opinions about Angel's career, Cora didn't turn down his offers to update the interior and exterior of their home.

The front door opened and his father, Percy, lifted his hands above his brows, shielding his view from the sun as he looked at Angel's idling car. The windows were tinted enough that he couldn't easily see inside. Percy was in his late sixties and still had a full head of thick hair, although it was graying. He had the same brown complexion as Angel and tall, like Angel, too.

"Is that your dad?" Iris asked.

"Yeah." His nerves rocked around inside of him like a ball in a pinball machine. He mentally counted to ten, then turned to Iris. "Ready?"

She nodded, gaze searching. "If you are."

"Okay." He opened his driver's side door. "Oh, by the way," he said quickly, "today's my birthday. They'll probably say something about it."

Iris gaped at him. "*What?*" she whispered.

But Angel was already climbing out of the car. Percy walked down the driveway to greet them. His eyes widened as he took in Angel's nose ring and burgundy-dyed hair. Usually, when Angel visited, he toned down his appearance. But coming here today had been so last-minute, he didn't have time to make changes. He fought the urge to quickly pull out his nose ring or throw on his hood. He reminded himself that he had nothing to be ashamed of.

"Angel," Percy said. "Good to see you, son. Happy birthday."

"Thanks, Dad. Good to see you too."

Percy wasn't a physically affectionate person, whereas Angel always had been, and there was an awkward beat as

Angel tried to determine if he should initiate a hug. In the end, they hugged, brief and light.

"How've you been doing?" Angel asked. "The new medication okay? You like your new doctor?"

Angel had arranged for Percy to start seeing a specialist in Atlanta to treat his type 2 diabetes.

"I'm fine," Percy said. "I like the doc good enough."

Angel glanced at Iris, who hung back, watching them. He beckoned her over. "Dad, this is my friend Iris," he said. "She made the drive with me from Atlanta. Iris, this is my dad, Percy."

Iris stuck her hand out for a shake, offering a smile. "It's nice to meet you."

"Likewise," Percy said, nodding as he shook Iris's hand. He looked at Angel. "Well, come on inside. Your mom is waiting."

Angel and Iris followed Percy to the front door. Iris brushed her hand against Angel's. She smiled at him softly, reassuringly. He smiled back, calmed some, but he nervously flexed his hands as his dad opened the door.

The front room smelled of sweet potatoes and ham. New furniture, sleek and modern, was arranged in the space. Framed pictures of Angel and Leah were tacked to the walls. He spotted the familiar photographs of him at church, as well as his picture-day portraits from middle school and high school. There were no pictures of him within the last five years, though.

Gospel music played in the kitchen. He heard his mom humming along. They followed Percy and found Cora at the sink with her back to them, shucking corn. The white granite countertops sparkled. There were brand-new appliances and a new stovetop, oven and fridge. Percy tapped her, and she glanced up, turning around. Cora favored Leah with her full, round face and light brown eyes. But where Leah was wiry, Cora was full-figured. Her coily hair, graying at the temples, was pinned back in a low bun.

"Well, here he is," Cora said, untying her apron and washing her hands. She opened her arms toward Angel and hugged him. He was enveloped by the smell of her jasmine perfume and olive oil hair spray. She leaned back and blinked at him, analyzing his face, his hair.

Angel physically tensed, bracing himself, waiting for whatever inevitable comment she'd make.

"You've still got that nose ring, I see," she said, tutting. "And this hair. It doesn't even look natural!"

Ah, there it is.

"It's good to see you, Mom," he said, forcing himself to brush off her opinion about his appearance. "How are you?"

"I'm getting along. Thankful to see another day. But your sister! Goodness gracious, she went and shaved half her head! She sent me a picture!" Her expression grew pinched. "Did you have anything to do with that?"

"No." He shook off the implied accusation and released a deep breath. "This is Iris, the friend I told you about. Iris, this is my mom, Cora."

Iris stepped forward, her smile polite and steady. "It's really nice to meet you. You have a beautiful home."

"Thank you." Cora did a quick sweep of Iris from head to toe. At least by appearance, she must have passed Cora's test, because Cora allowed herself to smile in return. "Nice to meet you too. Please, let's sit down. I'll get some drinks. Lemonade all right with you?"

Angel and Iris confirmed that lemonade was fine. In the living room, they sat side by side on the long couch, while Angel's parents sat on the love seat across from them.

"So, what work brings you to Atlanta?" Cora asked. She sat forward in her seat, looking at Angel closely again, eyes lingering on his hair, or rather, the shade of his hair.

Angel held his cup in his hands. He took a sip and hid his wince. Cora always made her lemonade too sweet. "I'm promoting skincare products with Iris's company."

"Skincare?" Cora frowned. "What do you mean?"

"Moisturizer, sunscreen, face wash," Angel recited.

Iris smiled at him proudly. "I work at Save Face Beauty," she explained. "I'm not sure if you've heard of it? Angel is our new brand ambassador and we've been doing meet and greets at a few stores across the country. Today's stop is in Atlanta later this evening. You're both more than welcome to come. I can even see about getting some complimentary products for you, if you'd like."

Cora shook her head. "I don't mess around with putting anything on my face but some Vaseline when it's cold outside. No, thank you."

If Iris caught Cora's disapproving tone, she pretended not to, but hearing her dismiss Iris's work that way bristled Angel.

"The products are good stuff," he said.

Iris smiled at him. "And you're doing an amazing job at promoting them." She turned to Cora. "You should see how much Angel's fans love him."

"His fans," Cora repeated, barely hiding her grumble. "Let me show you something."

She went to the entertainment center and pulled down a CD case. Angel sighed, already knowing what she was holding. She brought his gospel CD to Iris. The album was self-titled. What was better than a gospel singer named Angel? On the cover, he was smiling off in the distance as the sun shone behind him. He looked so young.

The truth was that he loved his gospel album. He loved making the music. He just hated that Cora had been his manager.

Iris ran her fingers gently over the album case, looking down at it.

"You keep that for yourself. I have a lot," Cora said. "This is Angel's best work. Before he started wasting his talent."

Iris's head snapped up. Her mouth fell open slightly as she glanced between Angel and Cora.

Angel wished that he could feel as surprised as Iris, but he didn't. This was a normal comment coming from Cora. He blew out another deep breath and tiredly rubbed a hand over his face.

"Mom," he said. "Not today."

"What?" Cora said. "I'm only speaking the truth."

How could she declare it as truth so easily? What gave her the right? He hated how she always thought that she knew best and that her way was the only one worth doing.

"It's your *opinion*," he said.

Cora put her hands on her hips. "You're going to talk to me like that in my own house?"

Her house where he paid the bills with the money he earned by using his *wasted talent*? He almost said it. The words were fighting to break through his lips. But he didn't want to start a full-blown argument. Not here, not in front of Iris.

"I'm not talking to you any kind of way," Angel said, working to keep his voice even.

Percy reached for his wife. "Cora, come on. Calm down."

Angel looked at Iris, embarrassed that he'd ever thought bringing her here with him might somehow turn out okay. Iris was frowning, her attention focused on Angel's face. Suddenly, she hopped up.

"Actually, we have to leave," she said to his parents. "I just remembered that we need to meet with my assistant to go over some last-minute details back at the hotel." She looked at Angel again. "It totally slipped my mind. I'm sorry."

It was unlikely that anything slipped Iris's mind ever. Angel recognized the out that she was giving him.

"Yeah, we'd better get going now," he said, standing as well. He looked at his parents. "I'll see you in a few weeks at the ceremony."

They exchanged stiff hugs goodbye. Cora was clearly still upset and turned away, bustling back toward the kitchen. When he and Iris stepped outside, Angel felt like bricks were being lifted from his shoulders. Silently, they returned to the car. Angel took one last look at his parents' house before he started the engine and pulled away. He was so relieved that he didn't have to live there, that his life existed elsewhere now.

He looked over at Iris, who was chewing her bottom lip, frowning fiercely at a spot on the dashboard in front of her. Not only had he thrown off his day, he'd thrown off hers as well. He wanted to apologize.

"Your mom," Iris said finally, shifting to look at him. "I'm sorry that she treated you that way."

Angel released a heavy sigh. "Me too."

"Is she always like that?"

"Every time I see her."

Iris shook her head. Then, "Why didn't you say anything about it being your birthday?"

He lifted his shoulders, tired, half-hearted. "I don't like to make a big deal out of it."

They fell quiet again.

Iris reached across the center console and rested her hand on top of Angel's. He turned his palm up and threaded his fingers through hers. She kept her hand there for the entire drive back to Atlanta.

16

A DIFFERENT KIND OF ENERGY BUZZED THROUGHOUT THE Refine store in Atlanta. Georgia was Angel's home state and his fans carried that pride. Their love for him was unmistakable as they lined the street and crowded the aisles inside the store. Angel lit up as he spoke to each of his fans, giving them a warm smile and his full attention, but Iris recognized his almost imperceptible air of melancholy. There was a strain in his eyes and his posture was more rigid than usual. After his visit with his parents, she couldn't blame him if he didn't feel 100 percent. She hated to see his joy dimmed.

Goodness, his *mother*. What a piece of work. And the thing she'd said about him wasting his talent? What a hurtful, untrue comment to make. Iris couldn't imagine ever dismissing Calla that way. Couldn't Angel's mom see that he was an amazing person, regardless of what genre of music he sang or if he decided not to wear a shirt in his music videos?

And today was his *birthday*. The only reason that Iris hadn't been aware of that important detail was because the wrong birthday was listed on his Wikipedia page. Based on how Angel deliberately hadn't mentioned a thing to anyone today, she doubted that he cared to fix the online mistake. She felt terrible that his birthday had taken such a stressful turn. And here he was working instead of vacationing on some island or in the South of France.

He'd cheered her up last night when she'd needed it. She wanted to do the same for him. She caught eyes with Bree and beckoned her over.

"What's up?" Bree asked.

"Today is Angel's birthday," Iris whispered. "I think we should do something to celebrate."

Bree's eyes popped. "It's his *birthday*? What should we do? Reserve a table at a fancy restaurant? Go to the club again?"

Iris observed Angel's tired form. "I think we should do something chill. He said he doesn't like to make a big deal out of his birthday. We should surprise him." The idea seemed better the more that she thought about it. "A small birthday get-together, with just us and Ray."

Bree nodded. "What do you need me to do?"

They huddled together to develop their course of action and looped in Ray. Bree would make a reservation at one of Angel's favorite soul food spots in Atlanta, and Ray would take him to dinner. Meanwhile, Iris and Bree would stay behind and decorate his hotel suite.

When the event finally wrapped up, Ray informed Angel of their last-minute dinner plans. Angel asked Iris and Bree if they wanted to join, but they lied and said that they needed to discuss work. Their group split. Angel and Ray went to the restaurant, while Iris and Bree went to the nearest party-supply store.

The aisles were filled with Fourth of July decorations, which was still weeks away. Iris and Bree hustled through the store, picking up cups and plates and birthday hats and a birthday banner, and Iris realized that they were gathering a colorful hodgepodge of random birthday decorations and their party didn't have a theme. The lack of uniformity made her skin itch. The parties that she planned for Calla were organized to a T. Calla's Gracie's Corner birthday party earlier this year had been the stuff of legend. Iris had hand-drawn Gracie's face and her cute little hair puffs onto each cupcake. But there wasn't enough time for something so detailed tonight.

Angel loved music, that much was a guarantee. Iris turned down the entertainment aisle and added a mini karaoke machine to their cart.

Ray gave Iris and Bree the spare key card to Angel's suite, so they let themselves inside, lugging balloons, bags of decorations, a nondescript vanilla cake and two bottles of champagne from Whole Foods.

"Whoa, this is huge," Bree whispered. She turned in a slow circle and gazed around at Angel's suite. "Dominique really pulled out the big guns."

They were staying at the St. Regis, one of the most expensive hotels that Atlanta had to offer. Angel's suite *was* enormous. The living room area had a large, plush, cream-colored couch and a matching armchair that looked big enough to seat two people. Angel's laptop and his notepad were placed on top of the dark oak desk. A short walkway led to the bedroom area. At a quick glance, Iris saw his king-size bed, covered in a plush, cream duvet.

"You have to see this bathroom," Bree called.

Iris followed the sound of Bree's voice. She found her standing in the center of the bathroom, eyes widened in awe. The bathroom had white marble walls and floors. A sparkling white claw-foot tub was positioned in the middle of the room, separating his-and-her vanity sinks.

Iris's room looked nothing like this. It was nice, of course, but standard. Comfortable and clean. Though she was valued by the company, she didn't imagine that they'd spend *this* kind of money on her. And while she made a decent salary, she couldn't afford a room of this magnitude on her own without breaking the bank. Angel probably stayed in rooms like this every time that he traveled. That was another difference between them.

Not that it mattered.

"Let's start decorating," she said.

She and Bree hung decorations in the living room area, along with a HAPPY BIRTHDAY banner on the wall. They blew up balloons with handheld balloon pumps. Soon, Iris's phone vibrated with a text from Ray.

Walking to the elevator.

"They're here," Iris said.

She and Bree slipped on their party hats. As the door opened, they shouted, "Surprise!"

Angel stumbled backward into Ray. He blinked, taking in Iris and Bree and the balloons behind them. He stared at the HAPPY BIRTHDAY banner. A slow smile crept across his face. He opened his arms and hugged Iris and Bree.

"Thank you!" he said, laughing. "Y'all scared the crap out of me!" He spun around to Ray. "Did you know?!"

Ray nodded, laughing as he glanced into the hallway, doing a quick check before closing the door.

"I hope you didn't eat too much at dinner because we have cake," Bree said. "And a karaoke machine!" She pointed at the mini speaker and microphone. "If you didn't already know every song on TLC's greatest hits album, you're about to know them now."

Bree hooked up the karaoke machine, and Ray followed her to help.

Angel stood by Iris and wrapped his arm around her shoulders. She felt his body heat radiate through his clothes.

"Thank you," he whispered in her ear. His cool breath fanned against her neck and she shivered.

"You're welcome," she said, attempting to keep her composure. "Happy birthday."

She placed a party hat on top of his head, and he held her gaze, his face inches from hers until Bree snapped them to attention to sing karaoke.

As promised, Bree performed "Diggin' On You," "Creep," and "Baby-Baby-Baby." Iris was surprised to learn that Bree could carry a decent tune. Ray sang a couple of Angel's songs, trying his best to mimic Angel's choreography, making everyone laugh. Angel blew them all out of the water when he sang "All My Life" by K-Ci & JoJo, reminding Iris that legit singers shouldn't be allowed to sing karaoke.

But Angel didn't stick to only ballads. He and Ray performed a duet of Pretty Ricky's "On the Hotline." Angel sang all of Pleasure P's parts, and Ray rapped. Iris was grateful that they'd chosen the edited version, because as Angel danced around in front of them, tossing his denim jacket to the side and slightly raising his shirt, heat prickled across

Iris's skin and crept up her neck. At any minute, she might burst into flames.

As Angel, Ray and Bree switched the mic among them, Iris was content to watch. She hadn't actually planned to sing when she'd purchased the karaoke machine. She didn't have the best singing voice and she wasn't going to let everyone else know that too. But Angel noticed that too much time had passed without her participation. He grasped her hands and pulled her to her feet.

"You're singing too," he said.

She shook her head and tried to sit down again. He held the mic out to her and smiled, innocent and sweet like a puppy dog.

"Please," he said. "It's my one birthday wish."

"Sing with her, Angel!" Bree said. "Be her Ja Rule!"

Bree played the instrumental beat to Ashanti and Ja Rule's "Mesmerize." Iris hadn't heard this song in over a decade. Angel burst into laughter and put his hand on Iris's waist. He spun her around to face the television as the lyrics rolled down the screen. He sang, mocking Ja Rule's deep, exaggerated voice. When it was her turn to sing Ashanti's part, Iris's cheeks flamed.

"Sing, Iris!" Bree called, clapping.

Iris cringed before she began to sing in a low, flat monotone. Angel watched her with pure delight. He danced around her, rapping Ja Rule's lyrics, not needing to look at the screen. Iris turned in a slow circle, following his movements. He did a little dance with his hips and Iris couldn't help but laugh.

When Ashanti's part returned, Iris closed her eyes and tried to stop worrying about how she sounded. They were all just trying to have fun. She didn't need to be perfect. No one cared that she sang off-key. She almost forgot that, technically, she was working.

She and Angel turned to each other, singing the last of the hook together as the song ended. She was breathless as he reached for her and dipped her in a sudden flourish. She and Angel held hands and bowed, while Bree and Ray cheered. As Angel smiled at her, she was so relieved to see that his melancholy from earlier had vanished.

At two a.m., they sang "Happy Birthday" and ate cake. Ray and Bree killed most of the champagne, so they were laughing uncontrollably as they sucked helium from the balloons and spoke to each other in high-pitched voices.

Iris didn't want their behavior to lead to a noise complaint for Angel's room, so she suggested, "Why don't you two head out? I'll clean up."

Bree straightened up immediately. "Are you sure?"

Iris nodded, and Ray and Bree took their chance to leave and presumably hang out some more.

Then it was just Iris and Angel.

Iris gathered the paper plates. Angel took them from her, and their fingers brushed. He didn't immediately step away.

"Ray told me that tonight was your idea," he said. "This was really thoughtful of you. Thank you. For real."

Her heart was stretching and twisting, doubling in size. He was looking at her so intently.

"Of course," she said, struggling not to feel so affected by his attention. "After what happened earlier, it was the least I could do to turn your birthday around."

"This is the first birthday party I've ever had."

Iris blinked, stunned. "What? How?"

"I didn't have any as a kid. When I was old enough to do them myself, I didn't bother with it. So tonight means a lot to me."

Moved by his words, Iris stared after him as he tossed the used plates in the trash bin. She realized that she was still wearing her party hat, and she slipped it off and placed it on the desk. She gathered the balloons and popped them as quietly as possible. Angel took down the banner and carefully folded it together. The cleanup process was fairly easy. It took less than ten minutes.

Angel kicked off his Lanvin sneakers and sat on the couch, leaving enough space for her to sit beside him if she wished. She knew that she should return to her own room now. Her presence here was no longer needed. But she leaned against the desk and watched him, stalling.

"Why do you have that look on your face?" he asked.

"What look?"

"Like . . . you're in a bakery and you're staring at a treat that you *really* want but you promised yourself that you wouldn't eat it."

Heat crept up Iris's neck as her eyes widened. Angel laughed. "I'm joking," he said.

But they both knew that he wasn't. Iris was fully aware that the truth of her attraction to him was written all over her face. She should *definitely* leave now. She pushed up off the desk and cleared her throat.

"What do you like to do for fun?" he asked suddenly.

Iris paused, thrown by the question. "For fun?" she repeated. He nodded. She pictured the plants and flower bushes in her backyard. "I like to garden."

He leaned back, relaxing more. "What do you like about gardening?"

She moved closer and sat on the other end of the couch. There were at least two feet of space between them. "It's calming. And it's rewarding too. There's something special about watching a plant grow from a seed or seeing flowers bloom again in spring." She smiled wryly. "I know that must sound very boring."

"I don't think it sounds boring at all." He shifted, facing her. He leaned his elbow against the back of the couch and rested his chin in the palm of his hand.

"What do *you* like to do for fun?" she asked.

"Chill with my sister and my dog. What's your favorite color?"

She smirked. "Are we playing twenty questions?"

"Maybe." He watched her. "Is it black? All your clothes are black."

"Technically, black is the absence of color, but yes, black is my favorite," she said. "If we're going to play, you should know that I don't play games like a normal person. I'm too competitive. My family banned me from playing anything with them."

Angel smiled. "How can you be too competitive at twenty questions?"

"By skipping over softballs," she said. "What's your biggest fear?"

"Wow." He laughed. Then he paused and squinted. "I guess my biggest fear is that I'll never realize my full potential or release the kind of music that I really want to make."

"What do you mean?" she said, frowning. "What about the music you're making now?"

"I want to explore a soul R & B sound, but my label wants me to stay in the same lane. I can't blame them because what I'm doing now is working, but I don't know. Sometimes I don't know if my frustration is real or if I should just shut up and be grateful."

"I think that your frustration is *very* real. I'd feel the same way."

"Thank you for the validation." Then he shook his finger at her, smirking. "That was two questions in a row. Is that the real reason your family doesn't want you to play with them? Because you cheat?"

Iris sucked in a breath. "I do *not* cheat. *Ever.*"

"Hmm." Angel rubbed his chin. "What was that kid's name who you said cheated off you in middle school? Maybe it was really the other way around."

"Accusations!" Iris said, laughing as she reached out and softly pushed Angel's shoulder. He laughed too, gently catching her hand in his. Then his expression turned serious.

"Thank you for coming back home with me earlier," he said.

He was still holding her hand. She felt like her palm was on fire and the heat was spreading up her arm. She didn't let go.

"Of course. It was nothing."

"It wasn't nothing," he said, shaking his head. "I hate that you had to witness my mom talking to me like that, but I'm glad that you came with me. It was pretty remarkable of you to offer, Iris. *You're* remarkable."

She blinked, taken off guard by the directness of his compliment. Her heartbeat picked up its pace.

"I think you're remarkable too," she said quietly.

Angel sat forward, watching her with new intensity. His gaze stretched across the space between them, and Iris felt the sizzling spark of their connection, electric and alive. She breathed deeply and tried to calm her rapid pulse. Their hands remained pressed together. This was *dangerous*. Still, she didn't move.

When Angel spoke, his tone was low and urgent. "I'm feeling you, Iris. I really am," he said. "I hope that my honesty doesn't come across as disrespectful. I just couldn't go another second without telling you."

A swarm of butterflies took flight in Iris's stomach. They spread from her abdomen to each of her limbs. Angel's admission tugged forcefully at her heartstrings. After Terry, she couldn't have predicted that she'd feel such an acute attraction to another man. Particularly, a man like Angel. Famous, beautiful, younger. But Angel had woken something in her that she'd worried had disappeared for good.

"Angel, you—I—" she stammered, at a loss for how to respond. She stood and began to pace. Angel watched her, brows inching up his forehead.

"I know maybe you're not in a place where you want to get involved with anyone right now," he said. "But—did I upset you? I didn't mean to upset you."

"I'm not upset." She paused in front of him, wringing her hands anxiously. "You must know it would not look very good for the company if I, a senior-level executive, became involved with our brand ambassador. Earlier this year we went through a big controversy after influencers got sick on a brand trip. We're just now finding our footing again with you and the new skincare line. But aside from that, there are other reasons why something between us wouldn't be a good idea."

Angel's watchful expression didn't change as he waited for her to explain further.

"Our lives are incredibly different and probably wouldn't mesh well," she said. "I have a six-year-old, and our—"

"I know. I love kids."

"—privacy is important," she continued, even as her heart melted, realizing he genuinely meant what he said.

"I would never intentionally put you or your daughter in a position where your privacy would be threatened." He started to reach for her but paused. "Can you sit down?"

Iris nodded, biting her lip as she sat beside him. "The truth is that I am trying to work myself up to dating again, and I think you're so wonderful, Angel." She glanced at her lap as a warm flush spread across her cheeks. "In another life, maybe. But in this one, we're kind of impossible."

Angel was quiet. She was afraid to look up at him, afraid that she'd renege on everything she'd just said.

"I don't think we're *impossible*," he said, after a moment. "But I also think it would be hard to convince you otherwise."

Iris finally brought her gaze upward and nodded.

They stared at each other in weighted silence. Admitting that they couldn't go anywhere should have dulled her attraction to him, but it seemed to do only the opposite. The plain truth was that she liked being around him too much. She felt drawn to him, and despite the reasons that they'd never be together, she didn't want to leave his presence just yet. After their last tour stop tomorrow, she'd probably never see him again. The realization weighed heavily on her. They wouldn't get another moment like this alone, just the two of them.

Angel was still looking at her, worrying his bottom lip between his teeth, like he wanted to say something but was unsure if he should. Her eyes focused on the fullness of his bottom lip.

She wanted to kiss him.

The impractical thought pulsated in her mind. She was usually so clearheaded and firm in her convictions, but Angel jumbled her thoughts and knocked her off-balance. He made her want things that made no sense.

She hadn't been kissed in years. *Years.*

Her heartbeat thundered in her ears, pumping blood fiercely through her veins. She felt like her skin was vibrating with the desire to touch him.

Leave now, the logical part of her brain said. *Leave before you do something stupid.*

She stood abruptly. "I should head back to my room."

Angel nodded quietly, keeping his eyes on her. "Okay."

"Good night." She quickly walked to the door, then spun around when she realized that she'd forgotten her phone. She crashed right into Angel.

"My bad," he said, placing his hands on her shoulders and steadying her. "I was going to walk you to your room."

"Oh." She was pressed flush against him. They breathed hard as they stared at each other. He smelled *so* good. He was so beautiful. He mesmerized her simply by existing.

Silently, he brought his hand up and gently cupped her cheek. His gaze was locked on her face. Her body lit with anticipation. She felt as though all the air had been sucked out of the room. He pressed even closer to her, lowering one hand to her waist. She wanted to stay right here like this. She wanted *him.* She swallowed thickly as her willpower slowly dissolved.

Just once, she promised herself as she stood on tiptoe. *Just this once.*

Softly, she pressed her lips against his, and Angel sucked in a surprised breath before he began to kiss her back. The kiss was slow, almost questioning, as their mouths grew accustomed to each other. Angel's lips were warm and smooth. Iris loved the feel of them. Goose bumps spread across her skin, and her heart pounded. He slid both hands down to her waist, gripping gently at her sides. He angled his head, deepening the kiss. He parted her lips with his tongue, and when her tongue met his, she moaned. She felt more than heard Angel's sharp intake of breath. His mouth tasted sweetly of birthday cake.

Desire ran through her as she looped her arms around Angel's neck. "The couch," she said, briefly breaking their kiss.

Angel's eyes were wild, his lips flushed pink. "You're sure?"

"Yes." She kissed him again as he walked them back to the couch.

He sat down and pulled her toward him. She drew to him like a magnet, shifting and climbing into his lap, until she was resting her thighs on either side of him. His hands gripped the fabric of her dress at her waist. He kissed her like it was an art, tonguing her down as he lowered his hands, squeezing the bare skin of her thighs.

Warmth pooled between her legs. Angel eased backward, pulling her flush against him, not breaking the kiss. He touched her so reverently, activating all of her senses.

She zeroed in on the feel of his lips and hands and could think of nothing else. She began trailing kisses down his neck, first featherlight, then deeper, licking and sucking his skin. He groaned and gripped her ass, pulling her even closer against him. She felt the bulge of his erection through his jeans. Emboldened, she grinded her hips against him as she continued to kiss his neck. Angel placed his hands on either side of her face and lifted her mouth to his again, kissing her with more urgency.

Their movements bordered on frantic as they reached for each other. She wanted to feel more of him, to be skin to skin. She lifted the hem of his shirt and brushed her fingers over his tight lower abdomen. He pulled at the hem of her dress and she raised up, hiking her dress farther up her thighs until it bunched at her waist. He squeezed the soft flesh of her thighs, and she moaned in his mouth, still grinding against him. She was behaving so unlike herself and she could not be bothered to care.

He slid his hands up her stomach and cupped her breasts. The fabric of her dress created an unwanted barrier. Hastily, she unzipped the back of her dress and eased out of her sleeves, shoving the material down to her waist and leaving her breasts covered by only her strapless black bra.

Angel gazed at her and licked his lips, palming her breasts in each hand.

"You are so fucking beautiful," he whispered.

She'd never heard him curse before until now. He brushed his fingers over her nipples and she sucked in a breath as he pulled down her bra, exposing her breasts fully. He brought her closer and kissed each of her breasts before putting one nipple fully in his mouth and sucking languidly.

"*Angel*," she murmured, breathless.

He moved to suck her other breast as he slipped his hand between her thighs, brushing his fingers against her opening through her underwear. She felt a new wave of heat pool at her center.

Angel continued to kiss her breasts, and when he slid her panties to the side and sank a finger inside of her, she could only think *More, more, more.* She ground against his hand, moaning, unable to control herself. She was the only person who had touched herself there in years. He added another finger, moving at a slow, torturous rhythm. She felt wanton as his lips returned to hers, tongues knocking wildly against each other.

"You're so soft and wet here," he whispered in his deep, beautiful voice. "I love touching you."

She couldn't think straight, couldn't respond. She felt like she was going to explode.

"Does that feel good?" he asked.

"*Yes.*"

He increased the pressure of his fingers. Pleasure washed over her, thrumming from the top of her head to the depths of her toes, and she cried out as she came in a swift strong wave. She struggled to catch her breath as Angel eased his hand from beneath her, resting his wet fingers against her thigh. She lay against him and their hearts pounded quickly in tandem. He turned his face toward hers, pressing his lips against her cheek.

In that moment, she existed in pure bliss. Nothing beyond their connection registered.

It wasn't until her pulse slowed and her thoughts cleared that reality finally settled over her.

Angel was the first man she'd kissed or touched intimately in so long. She'd opened herself up to him and had officially stepped into new territory, which was overwhelming in and of itself. But it was *Angel*. She'd spent so much time reminding herself of the boundary between them, and within seconds, she'd let that boundary crumble right between her fingers so that she could freely reach out for him and pull him to her.

What had she done?

She eased off him, blushing fiercely as she adjusted her bra and zipped the back of her dress. She stood and brushed her short curls back behind her ears. Her face was burning. Dominique had warned her about this. She'd warned *herself* about this. How could she get so carried away? She felt no better than a groupie.

"I . . . well, I should really go this time," she managed.

Angel stared at her, still dazed. His erection was clear as day. He blinked and sat up straighter. "What?" He frowned as she hurried to slip on her black flats. "Wait, where are you going? You're leaving? *Right now?*"

"We have an early flight." Her mind was buzzing. It was taking all of her energy to keep her distance and not climb all over him again and rip off both of their clothes.

"Iris . . ." He stood too, approaching her slowly, like she was a bird in the wild that might take flight at any moment. "I don't think that what just happened between us is something we can move on from so easily. I know *I* can't."

Iris clasped her hands together and pressed them against her stomach, physically fighting the urge to touch him.

"Angel, please," she whispered, staring up into his gorgeous face. Her defenses were almost nonexistent. She was begging him to have mercy on her. "I'm sorry, I don't know what came over me. Please just . . . remember the things I told you. The reasons why we can't do this."

Angel's expression was stricken. His hands fell to his sides as he stared at her.

"We could make it work," he said quietly. "We could at least *try.*"

She held her breath, blinking. Her heart and her brain were dueling for control. This time, though, she let her brain win.

"We can't," she said, trying to sound as resolute as possible.

He opened his mouth then closed it, falling short of saying anything.

She backed away toward the door. "Please don't tell anyone about what happened between us."

Angel frowned. "I would never tell anyone."

"Thank you," she mumbled, nodding as her hand gripped the doorknob. She forced a weak smile. "I'll see you in the morning."

He looked like he wanted to stop her, but instead he said, "Let me walk you down to your room."

"No, no, I'll be fine," she said hastily. "Someone might see you."

But truthfully, she was afraid of what she'd do once they reached her room. She couldn't trust herself. Her resolve would disintegrate if they touched each other again.

"Okay," he said quietly, resigned. "Good night, then."

"Good night."

She slipped from his room and speed walked to the elevator. Usually, she relied on her own logic and wisdom to see her through any given situation, but logic had fled her mind tonight. How could she have let her desires overpower her like that? And now her desire for Angel wasn't something she'd be able to quickly get out of her system. If anything, he'd become only another focus of her single-minded brain. She'd want more of him, but she couldn't have him. Dominique and the rest of the team could *never* find out about this. Iris was so ashamed. Yet at the same time, she longed to return to Angel and fall into his arms.

When she got to her room, she took a cold shower. It did nothing to dull the memories of Angel's hands and lips caressing her body.

She crawled into bed and tossed and turned the entire night.

17

ANGEL WAS AN ABSOLUTE WRECK.

Last night had been so *confusing*. First, Iris had told him that they were impossible, and then she'd kissed him. Kissing her, *touching* her had felt so good. Better than anything he'd felt in his life. She'd melted in his hands and had given herself to him so openly. Then she'd run for the hills and begged him not to tell anyone about what they'd done. As if he'd ever betray her confidence that way.

He wanted to talk to her about what happened because they couldn't leave things like this. But she'd been avoiding him all day. They'd barely exchanged two words on the flight to JFK. She'd quickly taken a seat beside Bree and focused her attention on her laptop.

Now they were in Lower Manhattan at the Skylight at Essex Crossing venue. The large space was filled with media journalists, makeup influencers and the select fans who'd won the sweepstakes, as well as several Save Face Beauty employees. A huge SAVE FACE BEAUTY X REFINE neon sign hung on the wall. Fans took turns posing beside his life-size cutouts. There was a photo booth and a pop-up bakery shop that was making cookies in the shape of the skincare products as well as Angel's face. A DJ was there to liven up the crowd.

Angel stood toward the back of the venue by the small stage, where he'd perform in a matter of minutes. He was flanked by Valerie, Claudia and a handful of people from his label. Everyone was thrilled with the success of his single and how the meet-and-greet tour had helped with buzz. They chattered around him. "Summertime Fine" had spent another week topping the charts. Soon he'd return to the studio and continue working on his third album. He was back in the thick of it again. It had been nice to feel normal the last few days, spending time alone with Iris, simply talking. He would miss it. He would miss *her*.

Where was she? He scanned the crowd until he spotted Iris standing with Dominique, talking with a group of makeup influencers. Iris was smiling and nodding along as one of the girls spoke. She was dressed in her usual professional yet plain attire, a short-sleeved black button-up blouse and another black pencil skirt. He remembered how it had felt to hike up her dress and run his fingers over her soft thighs, to hold her close.

Please look at me.

He willed her to turn in his direction. But at that moment, Dominique glanced over and happened to catch Angel staring. Soon, she was pulling Iris toward him. Iris sported a strange deer-in-headlights expression as they approached, but she fixed her mouth into a pleasant, composed smile as she and Dominique greeted their group. Iris and Angel locked gazes briefly. Color rose to her cheeks as she quickly glanced away. Why was she trying so hard to hide her feelings from him? Was it really just about her job and their different lifestyles or was there something else?

"How is everyone doing tonight?" Dominique asked. She looked at Angel specifically. "Ready to serenade us?"

Angel smiled. "Absolutely." He looked at Iris, who pointedly kept her attention on Dominique.

"Thanks for taking care of our guy," Valerie said to Iris.

"Of course," Iris said. Her gaze briefly flitted over to Angel. "He made our jobs pretty easy."

Dominique proudly put her arm around Iris's shoulders. "We armed Angel with the best of the best."

Iris smiled. Angel didn't want to stand in the way of her career, but he still wanted a chance to talk to her alone, at least one more time.

"We have to continue making our rounds and speak to some of the influencers," Dominique said, steering Iris away. "Can't wait for your performance, Angel!"

She waggled her fingers as she and Iris melded back into the crowd. Angel kept his eyes on the back of Iris's figure. If he let tonight go by without finding a chance to talk to her, who knew when he'd get the opportunity again? Soon, he'd be placed back on the racetrack that was his life. He had to act now.

He excused himself from his group. As he started for the crowd, Ray was right behind him.

"I'm cool, bro," Angel reassured him. "I just need to talk to Iris alone for a second."

"Nah, it's too many people in this room," Ray said. "You know I always give you your space but right now, it's my job to protect you."

Ray had a point. Angel nodded. As they made their way through the crowd, Angel's fans called out to him, some moved in front of him, posing for selfies. Angel obliged, flashing quick smiles. All the while, he was in turmoil. His gaze was fixed on Iris as she stood on the opposite side of the venue, engaged in a conversation with Dominique.

He hadn't made much progress toward Iris before another person stepped in his path and threw their arms around him. Ray launched forward but froze abruptly once he realized who the woman was. Angel blinked, surprised to find himself face-to-face with his stylist and Iris's sister.

"Hi!" Violet said, taking a step back and observing Angel's outfit. Tonight, he wore a black Louis Vuitton jacket and kilt with black loafers and shin-length white socks. "I'm glad we went with the kilt. It was definitely the right choice."

"Me too." He hugged Violet distractedly, glancing up to make sure that Iris still hadn't moved.

"How was it?" she asked.

He looked at Violet again. "Huh?"

"The meet and greets," Violet said. "Everything go okay? My sister said you were amazing."

"She said that?"

Violet nodded. "A few days ago. I'm hype that she got me an invite tonight. I'm gonna get *so much* free stuff. Hey, are you listening to anything that I'm saying?"

Violet waved her hand in Angel's face, but he was looking at Iris. She was moving farther away. He'd lose his chance if he didn't chase her. He planted a brief kiss on Violet's cheek.

"Sorry, I can't talk now but I promise I'll find you later."

Violet pouted. "Okay, fine."

Angel squeezed Violet's shoulder, and he followed Iris's retreating form through the crowd. It seemed to take him forever to reach her. Finally, he placed his hand on her elbow and she turned around. Her eyes widened.

"We need to talk about last night," he whispered. He affected an easy smile for the onlookers, but he focused directly on Iris. "Please stop avoiding me. Just give me five minutes."

Iris blinked. He watched her pulse thud at the base of her throat. He wondered if she would refuse him.

"Okay," she said. "Yes."

He sighed in relief, but before he could decide where they'd slip away to, Claudia appeared, and Angel was swiftly pulled away to perform.

18

IRIS STOOD STIFFLY IN PLACE AS SHE WATCHED ANGEL GET pulled toward the stage. His fans shouted his name and reached out to touch him, but their attempts at contact were thwarted by Ray.

Iris knew that Angel deserved an explanation after the way she'd reacted last night. She hadn't spent the last few years in therapy without learning about the power of communication. But how could she face Angel? Her job had been to make sure that things went smoothly this past week, to make sure that he had everything he needed. That did not include climbing into his lap, shoving up her dress and letting him finger her into another blissful dimension.

She should feel ashamed of herself and her behavior. She *had* felt shame last night, but as the hours passed and she continued to think of Angel nonstop, her feelings of shame were slowly replaced by a fantasy. A fantasy life where she and Angel gave this thing between them a chance and they were happy somehow.

That was what scared her. The fantasies and delusion. Because how could that ever be real life?

Her gaze was still fixed on Angel when Dominique re-appeared with the sweepstakes winners in tow, three young women who looked to be in their early twenties. They were armed with Save Face Beauty goody bags.

"These ladies are from all over the country," Dominique explained. "Krystal here is from Arkansas. Delia is from San Antonio and Myra is from Montana."

"I can't believe I'm here!" Krystal said, bouncing on her toes. "I've never been to New York City before. I feel like I'm in a movie."

Delia was less enthused as she sifted through her goody bag. "Yeah, real cool to be here. A few months ago, people were saying that Save Face Beauty was over, but this event is fire, and the skincare products are actually dope. I'm not gonna lie, I'm shocked."

"I love Angel so much!" Myra added.

Dominique looked like she was going to burst into a pile of confetti. She proudly patted Iris on the shoulder. The event *was* fire. Their skincare products *were* dope. And people loved Angel. The meet-and-greet tour had been a success. Iris's hard work had paid off. So then why did she feel zero sense of relief?

Dominique ushered the sweepstakes winners away toward the pop-up bakery. Realizing that she had a few moments to herself, Iris walked to the bar area and ordered a club soda to help calm her nerves. As she sipped her drink, someone tapped her shoulder. She turned to see Violet.

"Oh, hey," Iris said.

"'Oh, hey'? That's all I get?" Violet frowned. "It's a party. Why do you look like you're in the waiting room at the dentist?"

Iris tried her best to smooth her expression into one of ease. "I'm fine. Where's Lily?"

"Couldn't make it," Violet said. "Something about too many people being here, didn't have extrovert energy. Et cetera, et cetera. You know how she is."

Iris nodded, but she was hardly paying attention. Her eyes were glued to the stage. "Right."

"Okay, what is up with you?" Violet folded her arms across her chest and gave Iris a pointed look.

"What do you mean?"

"You're being weird and distracted." Violet frowned again. "Angel was acting the same way . . ." She trailed off, then squinted. "Wait a minute. Something happened between the two of you, didn't it?"

Iris gulped as her stomach seized. She was a bad liar, and Violet knew this, so Iris neither confirmed nor denied Violet's accusation. Instead, she averted her eyes and continued to sip her soda.

"I fucking *knew* it." Violet flashed a victorious smile. "This is amazing! Two of my favorite people finally came together . . . literally?"

Iris swatted Violet's arm. "Stop talking like that. I'm working," she whispered. "I don't want to talk about it, and I don't want you talking about it either."

"Why not? This is a good thing." Violet's voice softened. "Isn't it?"

Iris didn't speak. She gripped her plastic cup tightly in her hands. Her emotions warred inside of her. Violet moved closer to Iris and gently placed her hand on her shoulder.

"Do you care about Angel?" she asked.

"Yes," Iris said quietly.

Violet peered at her. "Then you should be happy, right?"

Iris bit her lip, unsure of how to respond. Buried beneath her worry and doubts, she *did* feel happy. Happy that she'd managed to connect with Angel so strongly. But what was she supposed to do with that connection if it couldn't go anywhere?

"He wrote 'Summertime Fine' about me," she said eventually.

Violet's eyes widened. Then she laughed quietly. "Oh, he is *so* sneaky. And romantic! This is wonderful."

"Is it?" Iris asked, voice strained. "How can it be wonderful if our relationship would create a conflict for my job, and there's a very low chance that Angel and I would last because our lives are so different? What about Calla?"

"You don't have to marry him," Violet said gently. "You've been wanting to date again. Maybe this can be your way of getting back out there. Maybe you and Angel can just spend time together when you can and have fun. It doesn't have to be serious." She wrinkled her nose. "And you're better than me because I would not give a flying fuck about my boss's thoughts on my personal life."

A loud, thundering cheer rang throughout the room as Angel walked onto the stage. He took his place behind the mic and smiled and waved. The beat for "Summertime Fine" began to play, and Angel serenaded the crowd, making eye contact with the fans in front, singing to them directly. He breezed across the small stage, wrapping everyone in his charismatic web, sounding beautiful as he sang the song that he'd written about Iris.

Her heart pounded painfully as she watched him. Over the last week, he'd not only made her feel happy, he'd made her feel understood. And Violet had a point. Iris wanted to put herself back out there. Why not try with someone who she genuinely liked? Angel might not be able to live a simple, low-key life alongside her, and he wasn't the long-term partner whom she'd envisioned, but to Violet's other point, it wasn't like Iris needed to marry him. She didn't have to introduce him to Calla or anything so serious.

And in terms of her job . . . she realized it was unprofessional to pursue Angel, reckless even. So unlike her. But regardless of how unprofessional or reckless it may have been, she wasn't ready to let go of him yet. She'd put her job above her personal life for years, and she'd been so lonely. What if they found a way to spend time together that didn't affect her job or draw the attention of his fans?

After everything she'd been through, couldn't she keep this thing that made her happy, even if for a little while?

"You're right," Iris said to Violet.

Violet was bobbing her head and singing along with Angel. "Of course I'm right. Aren't I always?"

Iris laughed.

When the song ended, the crowd erupted into a new round of cheers. Iris wondered if Angel could see her. He paused in her general direction for a moment before he spoke again.

"Thank y'all so much for coming out and for showing love to me and Save Face Beauty," he said. "I promise you my next album is on the way—" He was cut off by more cheers. He laughed and spoke louder. "Thank you. Have a good night."

The audience's cheers shook the room. Iris watched as

Angel basked in his fans' love. His smile lit up his entire face.

Iris hugged Violet goodbye. "I'll text you later. Get home safe."

"Go get your man, girl," Violet said, eagerly clapping her hands.

Iris moved through the crowd toward the stage, and she waited patiently as Angel spoke with his team. When he glanced over and noticed her there, he made a beeline for her. She kept her smile polite, knowing that people were watching.

"You did a really great job," she said.

His gaze was focused, questioning. "Thank you."

She backed away a little, easing behind Ray, and Angel followed, picking up on her desire for a bit of privacy.

"I'm sorry about how I left you last night," she whispered.

He leaned down closer to her. "What happened?"

"I freaked out." She bit her lip as she stared up at him. "I just wanted to apologize to you now. But maybe we can talk later if you have more time."

Angel peered at her silently. Then, "What about tonight?"

"Tonight?"

"Can you come over tonight?" he asked. "So that we can talk more?"

Her parents were watching Calla until tomorrow. She was free tonight.

Last chance to get off this train.

She could walk away and let him go and spend the rest of her life wondering what might have been. Or, for once, she could take a chance and live in the moment. She figured she'd earned that much.

"Yes," she said. "I can come over."

He lightly touched her elbow before dropping his hand. "Okay."

ANGEL LEFT BEFORE the event ended. Long after the influencers and fans departed with their free gifts and aesthetically pleasing pictures, Iris dutifully stayed behind with Dominique and the rest of the SFB team. Dominique gave a special toast to Iris and Bree, praising them on the well-executed and profitable meet-and-greet tour. Iris accepted everyone's congratulations and she was trying her best not to appear jittery with impatience.

Finally, she was able to slip outside into the town car that waited to bring her to Angel's condo in Chelsea. Once she reached his building, suitcase in tow, she went to the front desk attendant, who'd already received instructions from Angel. He directed Iris to the elevator and she rode it up to the penthouse floor.

Am I really doing this? Her stomach tied and untied itself in knots, a mixture of both nervousness and excitement. By the time she reached his floor, her entire body buzzed in anticipation.

Angel was waiting at his door, leaning against the doorjamb. He'd changed out of his stylish outfit and into a black T-shirt and sweatpants.

"Hey," he said. He smiled at her softly.

For some reason, she suddenly felt bashful as she walked toward him. "Hey."

He pulled her into a hug and they stood there, embraced for a few silent moments. They were alone again. They didn't have to worry about who was watching or listening. He pressed a soft kiss to her temple and pulled away, taking her suitcase from her.

"I'm really sorry in advance," he said, lowering his voice. "But my sister is here, and she refuses to leave until she meets you."

Iris blinked. "Oh."

"She's nosy but mostly harmless. I'm going to kick her out ASAP."

Iris laughed as she followed Angel inside. His penthouse was spacious and pristine. He had massive floor-to-ceiling windows with an immaculate view of the city. The interior was well decorated with nude-toned furniture. A massive television hung against the wall above a modern fireplace. A piano was by the window.

"It's beautiful in here," Iris said, looking around.

"Thanks." He smiled and lifted his shoulder in a shrug. "I can't take any credit, though. I hired someone to do all of this. I also feel like I'm not here enough to enjoy it."

Iris startled as a dog came barreling toward her. The boxer jumped up on its hind legs and smacked its paws against Iris's thighs, barking and wagging its tail. Iris recognized the dog from the pictures Angel had shown her—Maxine.

"*Max*," Angel scolded. He crouched down and pulled the dog away, holding her to his chest. "You have to pretend like you have some manners, okay?"

In answer, Maxine whimpered. She thumped her tail against the floor and gazed at Iris with thinly veiled enthusiasm. Iris crouched too and brought herself eye level with Maxine.

"Hi, Maxine." Iris rubbed her hand over Maxine's head. The dog whimpered louder, inching closer to receive more pets. She lurched forward and licked Iris's face. Iris laughed, and Maxine took that as her cue to jump on Iris again.

"Okay, okay," Angel said, pulling Maxine away. "Sit . . . *sit*."

"You know she doesn't listen to you." A girl with a half-shaved head and several hoop earrings in both ears walked toward them. She wore a sleeveless leather minidress and black Dr. Martens. She smiled brightly at Iris. She and Angel had the same smile, warm and inviting like they'd been waiting for the moment to talk to you. "I'm Leah. Angel's favorite sister."

"Only sister," Angel said, smirking.

Iris stood and held out her hand. "It's really nice to meet you."

Leah shook Iris's hand in quick, hearty pumps. "I've never seen Angel clean his place so quickly in my life," she said. "He must really like you."

Angel shot his sister a look, and Iris laughed.

"In fact," Leah continued, "I *know* he really likes you because he said—"

Angel grabbed Leah's backpack and slung it over her shoulder as he directed her to the door. Maxine trotted after them, wagging her tail. "Don't you have an exam to study for or something?"

"Nope." Leah twisted around, looking at Iris again. "You're really pretty, by the way."

Iris smiled. "Thank you. So are you. I really love your hair."

"Thanks!" Leah grinned and then she turned to her

brother, who held the door open. "Okay, I'm going! *Jeez.* No need to escort me out. Bye!"

Leah closed the door behind her, and Maxine whined. Angel ran a hand over his face, exhausted, but he smiled at Iris.

"See," he said. "Mostly harmless. Can I get you something to drink?"

"Water is fine." She followed him into the kitchen area, which was sparkling white. "I wanted to hear the rest of what your sister was going to say."

Angel poured her a glass of water and handed it to her. "She was probably going to say that I told her I was nervous."

"Really?" Iris asked. Angel nodded, and she swallowed thickly. "I am too."

Angel stepped closer to her, but Maxine nudged her way between them. Angel picked up a toy and threw it. Maxine flew across the room and gripped the toy between her teeth. She dragged it to her dog bed by the living room windows and chewed. The toy squeaked with each bite. Iris squinted, trying to get a good look at the toy.

"Is that a lizard?" she asked.

"It *was* a fish." Angel motioned for Iris to come with him into the living room. "But she bit its head off."

They sat on the soft, plush couch. Iris wondered how to bring up their conversation from earlier. Thankfully, Angel wasted no time.

"So, what else did you want to tell me?" he asked.

Iris took a deep, steadying breath. "First, I want to clarify something that I didn't say last night," she said. "I do like you."

"Okay." The corners of his mouth lifted slightly, but it

was almost like he wouldn't allow himself to smile fully until she'd said all that she had to say.

"I would like to keep spending time with you," she continued. "I wonder how you feel about us finding time to see each other when we can and see where things go. But we'd have to keep it between us."

His brows raised. "So you want us to be a secret?"

Putting it that way made it sound like she was ashamed of him, which she certainly wasn't. What she didn't want was for anyone to be in their business.

"My job can't know about us," she said. "And I don't want your fans to know about me. I have to protect my and my daughter's privacy."

"I understand that," he said. He stared at her fixedly, and she waited with bated breath as his heavy pause stretched between them. "I want to keep spending time with you too. We can keep this between us."

Instant relief washed over her. Iris bit her lip as she looked at him. "I'm sure you've guessed this, but I haven't dated in a very long time. I don't really know how to go about this."

"We can take things slow then," he said, moving closer to her. "You want to watch a movie?"

She stared at him, thinking of how he'd touched her last night. "Not really."

He chuckled softly. "Yeah, me neither."

He lifted her feet into his lap and began to massage her arches. She relaxed against the couch, watching him. His lashes lowered as he stared back at her. He eased his hands farther up her legs, over her knees and settling against her thighs. The air thickened. Her breath hitched as his fingers brushed against the hem of her skirt.

Maxine gripped her toy and shook it between her teeth. She plopped it by the couch and stared at Angel and Iris expectantly. Iris laughed.

"I think maybe we need a bit more privacy," Angel said, smirking.

He picked up Maxine's toy and led her back over to her dog bed. He placed more toys around her, and he spoke to her in a lower whisper, using that baby voice. Maxine beat her tail against the floor as she basked in his attention. When he stood, and Maxine remained where she was, chewing mindlessly on two toys, Angel smiled at Iris and walked back over to her, holding out his hand.

She placed her hand in his, and he led her down the hall. They walked by a glass case displaying his album covers and awards. He led her into his room. A king-size bed was covered in a similar nude comforter, and his dressers were a dark brown. A walk-in closet to their left, which was almost half the size of her old Lower East Side studio, housed racks and racks of clothing.

They sat on his bed, and Iris felt that unmistakable spark between them again.

"I should tell you that it's been a while since I've had sex," she said, exhaling a breath. "A few years. Not since Terry."

Angel was quiet, watching her. "Okay." He moved closer and brushed his fingers against her collarbone, placing a soft kiss against her neck. "Like I said, we can go slow."

He continued to kiss her neck as he unbuttoned her shirt, and as she eased out of the sleeves and slipped off her

bra, he lowered his mouth, pressing kisses in the space between her breasts. Iris closed her eyes and breathed him
in. She loved the way that he touched her. She unzipped
her skirt and stood, easing it down. She hadn't been naked
like this in front of a man since Terry. She had stretch marks
on her stomach and thighs. She didn't usually feel self-
conscious about them—they were part of life and motherhood. Angel pulled her to him and kissed her stomach and
the tops of her thighs as she slid off her panties. Bringing her
back down next to him on the bed, he kissed her lips and
neck, moved to her shoulders, then trailed down between her
breasts. He pressed his palm flat against her stomach, easing
her backward until she lay on her back. He moved over her,
continuing to kiss his way down her body. When he kissed
her between her legs, she gasped as his tongue brushed
against her heat, and he used his fingers to touch her.

"I've thought about this all day," he whispered, looking
up at her.

She breathed deeply, too aroused to respond.

He lifted her legs to rest on his shoulders as he continued to lick and kiss her there so intimately. When she felt
like she might fall apart, Angel finally released her and
stood, shrugging out of his clothes too. They gazed at each
other, completely naked and exposed. Her breath hitched as
she observed him, his strong arms and powerful legs. Angel
lowered himself back onto her, closing the space between
them with a deep, hungry kiss.

His body rocked against hers in a soft, slow rhythm. She
couldn't help herself as she reached down and wrapped her
fingers around his length. Angel sucked in a breath, and she
moved her hand up and down on him. He groaned and

kissed her neck again, biting at her soft, supple skin. When her touches became too much, he reached up to his nightstand and pulled out a condom. Iris watched eagerly as he slid the condom on and reached for her again.

"I want you to tell me if it hurts, okay?" he whispered, placing a tender kiss against her mouth. She nodded and placed her arms around his neck.

He sank inside of her slowly. Beads of sweat dotted his brow and he closed his eyes. Her flesh was tight, and she winced at first. Angel froze.

"Are you okay?" he asked, voice strained.

"I'm okay," she said, breathless. "Keep going."

Slowly, he began thrusting at a deep, thorough rhythm. Her muscles gradually eased to accept him. Slight pain turned into intense pleasure. He kissed her mouth, her jaw, her cheeks, her forehead and neck. She arched into him and he moaned as his hips surged faster. She hitched her legs to his waist, taking him deeper. He groaned in her mouth and held her face between his hands, sealing his lips over hers. She felt so cared for, so adored.

Soon, she felt the intensity of his thrusts build to a peak inside of her. They locked eyes as she came in hard, wrenching spasms. The intimacy of it was too much for him to last longer.

"Fuck," he hissed. He groaned her name and his thrusts turned shallow and erratic as he came.

She wrapped her arms around him and they breathed together unsteadily. After a moment, he eased out of her and she already missed being connected to him there. She buried her face in his neck, breathing him in. Angel squeezed her closer, and she felt the pounding of his quick heartbeat.

She felt brand-new, like someone who'd woken out of a deep slumber to find that everything around her had changed. She held on to him tighter. Angel sweetly kissed the top of her head.

A loud bump sounded against his bedroom door, followed by the squeeze of Maxine's toy and her bark.

Angel lifted his head and they both glanced at the door, laughing.

"I hate to say this, but I should probably take her for a walk," he said. Reluctantly, he sat up and gazed down at Iris. He gently brushed his fingers across her hip. "Can you stay over?"

She'd probably be sore in the morning. She'd need to take a hot bath. But for now, she wasn't thinking about that. She just wanted to be closer to him.

"Yes," she said.

His smile was the perfect reward.

19

AT THE OFFICE, IRIS WAS A HERO.

The meet-and-greet tour and the ambassador partnership with Angel had raised the company's profits, and it seemed that the Turks and Caicos food poisoning fiasco was all but forgotten. As Iris walked through the halls, her colleagues smiled at her and went out of their way to say hello. Dominique started every conversation with, "Here's my star!" Paloma, who was officially working from home, sent Iris a beautiful bouquet and made plans to take her out to lunch.

And everyone—seriously *everyone*—wanted to know about Angel. What was he like behind closed doors? Was he nice or was he an asshole? What did they do in their downtime on the tour? Did they hang out? Did he try to hit on her or Bree?

Iris gave the same boring, succinct response every time: "Angel was sweet and very easy to work with."

No one would have guessed that she knew him much better than she let on. And why would they? She was Iris. Dependable, straightforward Iris. It was like she had a secret, all to herself.

It had been a week since she'd stayed over at his place. While her life had more or less returned to normal—dropping Calla off at day camp, commuting to work—Angel had been constantly on the go. He'd traveled to Los Angeles for business meetings, to London for a movie premiere because he'd been featured on the soundtrack, and from there, he'd flown to Paris with Violet to visit a fashion designer's showroom.

Iris kept in touch with him through text. Throughout the days, her phone vibrated with alerts. To avoid drawing suspicion, she had him saved in her phone under the name Tom Wyatt.

MONDAY, 3:21AM
Just left the studio in LA. Omw to In N Out. You ever try it?

WEDNESDAY, 3:00PM
This is what the sky looks like in London right now. Nonstop rain!

THURSDAY, 4:41AM
Ayo, Leah just sent me this pic. Maxine ripped one of my Jays in HALF!! Idk what to do with her sometimes. You wanna dog sit? I feel like you could turn her into a proper lady ☺

His texts made Iris smile wide and goofy. Other than her sisters, Angel was the only person she'd texted with consistently in years. It was nice to have someone to message about the random musings of her day, like how she almost always burned her tongue on her tea in the morning, or that she needed specific scented candles for her office because certain scents gave her a headache.

He liked hearing about everything, from what she ate for breakfast to what she did to unwind after dinner. He wanted to see pictures of her office and he teased her about how it looked even more organized than he'd imagined. He wanted to know every mundane detail—things that Iris thought most people would find boring. But through Angel's eyes, she wasn't plain, serious, rule-abiding Iris. She was someone who was interesting.

He'd returned to New York late last night. Currently, he was uptown at the recording studio. She wished that she could stop by and see him, but she had other responsibilities. She needed to hop on the express train after work to get Calla from her parents' house because they were picking her up from day camp. Iris wasn't entirely sure when she'd see Angel again. It made her skin prickle with longing.

She was rereading their text thread when a knock at her office door caused her to look up.

"Hey, ready for the meeting?" Bree asked. She tilted her head. "You must have gotten some good news. Your smile is on a thousand!"

Iris felt her face grow warm. "Just texting my sisters."

She grabbed her notepad and followed Bree into the hall. Today's meeting was a strategy planning session for the upcoming holiday season. Holiday sets were being revealed earlier and earlier these days. Some well before Halloween, and the SFB team needed to capitalize on their sudden renaissance and give the holidays their best shot.

"Here's our star," Dominique sang, gesturing toward Iris

as she walked into the conference room, like she was a prize on *The Price Is Right*.

Pat Jones, SFB's CFO, and Ed Brown, the COO, sat on either side of Dominique. They looked very similar, tall white guys with graying blond hair. In her early days with the company, Iris had struggled to tell them apart.

"Sales are still way up," Pat said. "Not just on the skin-care products but makeup products across the board."

"Google hits on Save Face Beauty are through the roof." Ed grinned.

Iris could see the dollar signs flashing in their eyes. Before, she would have eaten up this kind of praise. But as she sat down across from them, she didn't feel that spark or excitement from an achievement. She'd thought after the meet-and-greet tour that some of her inspiration might come back. But so far, nothing.

Maybe she was just tired. She probably should have taken a vacation this week.

The marketing team kicked off the meeting, and Iris jotted down notes as they spoke. Her phone vibrated in her lap with a new text from Angel.

Any chance you have time this afternoon to stop by
the studio? I'm about to take a break.

Iris bit her lip. If only that were a possibility. After this meeting, she'd eat a quick lunch before her weekly check-in with Bree.

Probably not, she texted back. I'm sorry.

It's cool, came his reply. I just miss you.

She stared at her phone. He missed her. It meant that

she'd been on his mind, that the lack of her presence was felt. She felt the same sense of longing for him. The sound of her colleagues' voices were drowned out completely as she reread his text.

I miss you too, she responded.

She opened her calendar. This current meeting would end exactly at noon. Her meeting with Bree was at one fifteen p.m. Usually, she worked through lunch and ate at her desk because it gave her a chance to catch up on emails. But she wanted to see Angel. Would it really be so difficult to use her lunch hour to stop by the studio and say hi?

Actually, I'll come by during my lunch break, she texted. But I can't stay long.

For real?? Great! Can't wait to see you.

The rest of the meeting dragged. Iris tried to suppress the urge to bounce her feet. By the time the meeting ended, she practically flew from her seat. Dominique called her name, and Iris sputtered to a stop at the door.

"Want to get lunch?" Dominique asked. "How about Selene? My treat."

Iris felt like a wide-eyed deer stuck in oncoming traffic. She wanted to see Angel but at the same time, how could she refuse lunch with her boss?

Iris fumbled for a reply. "I—um . . ."

"You know what, I forgot I have that call with a new investor," Dominique said, waving her hand. "Tomorrow, yeah?"

Iris released an imperceptible sigh of relief. "Absolutely."

Angel offered to have a car pick Iris up, but she was

worried that would be too conspicuous. Instead, she took the N train uptown. When she reached the studio, Ray was standing outside, smoking. He tossed his cigarette and crushed it beneath his boot. He flashed Iris a wry grin.

"Well, hello, hello," he said.

Iris cleared her throat, suddenly self-conscious. It hadn't occurred to her that someone else who knew her might see her here. "Hi, Ray. How are you?"

"I'm doing just dandy. How are *you*?"

Oh, the way he smiled at her. He knew why she was really here. She still felt the need to save face, though.

"I'm well. I'm here to see Angel. He left something at the event last week, and—"

"No need for all that," Ray said, opening the door for her. He tapped his temple. "I know what's going on. I hope you'll forgive me for poking my nose into your and Angel's business. It's my job to know."

She nodded silently, cheeks heating, as she stepped inside.

"Had to run a background check on you," he said.

She whipped around to face him, eyes wide. "You *did*?"

"Yep. Don't worry. You passed with flying colors." He winked and pointed to the elevator. "Angel's on the third floor. First door to the right."

"O-oh," she stuttered. "Okay, thanks."

She followed Ray's directions and exited the elevator on the third floor. She stopped at the first door on the right and knocked lightly before turning the knob. Angel was standing in the recording booth and his producer friend, whom she'd met at the club in LA, was seated in front of the mixing board.

Angel glanced up at her, and the smile that he gave her was worth a million bucks.

ANGEL'S WEEK HAD been filled with work on top of work and with missing Iris. Wanting her, wishing he could be next to her, and now she was here. He felt an intense rush of euphoria as he looked at her.

He eased off his headphones and stepped out of the recording booth. Iris stepped farther into the room and Angel walked over to her.

"Hey," he said, once he reached her. He was trying his best to contain the eagerness of his smile. He was physically buzzing with the desire to be closer to her.

"Hi." She sounded a little breathless as she looked up at him through her lashes.

He hugged her and was careful to keep his touch light, knowing that Malik was watching. Only he and Iris knew the truth about their relationship. And Ray, of course. He had to tell him. And Leah. And he figured *her* sisters probably knew by now too . . .

Iris felt so soft as she hugged him back, and she smelled amazing.

"You remember, Malik, right?" he said, reluctantly pulling away. "Malik, this is Iris."

Malik stood and shook Iris's hand. "Sorry again about my boy splashing you that night."

Iris smiled. "It's okay. Already forgotten."

Malik told Angel that he was going to grab food and would be back later. Once they were alone, Angel and Iris turned to each other. Her gaze roamed his face. He wondered if she knew how starved she looked for him.

He opened his arms and she stepped into his embrace. He held her closely, tightly like he'd been wanting to. He used his index finger to tip her chin up, lifting her face toward his. He bent down and kissed her deeply.

"How's your day been?" she asked when he pulled away, brushing her fingers across his collarbone.

"Hectic." All week he'd been running around like a wild man—a well-dressed, supremely groomed wild man—but that was his life, where the world felt like it was spinning at three times its normal speed. "How about you?"

"It's been okay." She walked over to the mixing board and ran her hands over the keyboard. She leaned down and peered at the computer desktops, which showed his layered vocals. "What have you been working on?"

He walked closer. "You wanna hear?"

She nodded, shoulders hitching up in excitement. She was so adorable, he couldn't help himself as he kissed her again.

They sat down, and Angel played back the song they'd been working on for the past few hours. He'd temporarily titled it "Us, Me, You." It was a song about seeing a girl every day by chance and loving her from afar. He'd written it while on the flight from Paris. It had a slow, funky beat, sort of Marvin Gaye but with a modern R & B feel. He watched Iris's face as she listened quietly and nodded to the beat. He bit his lip, anxious to know if she liked the song. He wanted to impress her, this woman who was not so easily impressed.

When the song ended, she beamed at him. "I love it."

"Really?" At first, he tried not to show how he hung on

her praise, but then again, he was never one to play it cool. He pulled her close and kissed her. She laughed, cradling his face in her hands, kissing him back.

"I'm glad you like it." He leaned his forehead against hers before he pulled away. He sighed. "The label won't."

"Right," she said quietly, placing her hand over his. "You said they want you to stay in the same lane."

He sighed again, rubbing his jaw. "Yeah, and as a creative, there's no excitement in that. But I don't want my sales to drop. That's what they're worried about."

"I think that you know yourself better than anybody at your label," she said. "And I witnessed firsthand how much your fans adore you. I think they'll love whatever you put out, so why not make the music you want, especially if it's this good?"

She had such a clear-cut way of seeing things. He wished he could be the same. He slid her chair closer to him. He toyed with the hem of her skirt. "You make good points."

"I usually do," she said, smiling. "Everybody at work keeps asking me about you."

"Hmm." He smirked. "What do you tell them?"

"That you were a pleasure to work with."

He raised an eyebrow. "A *pleasure*. Wow."

She laughed. "Honestly, I kind of like when they ask about you, because it adds some excitement to my day. Otherwise, at work, I feel so . . . blah."

He cocked his head to the side. "Blah?"

"Yeah. You'd think that with the success of the skincare-line rollout, I'd jump at coming up with some new ideas, but I don't have any and I don't really want to spend time working on a new project, which is so wild to me, because I used to live for that. I'm *bored*." She looked at him and laughed wryly. "I know, it's a corporate office job, so boredom is to be expected. But I used to come to work energized every day."

"It'll come back," he said. "Or you'll find something else."

"Something else," she repeated. "It's weird but for a long time, I haven't imagined anything other than being at SFB."

"Well, if you decide to leave, I know any other company would kill to have you."

He spread his hand over her thigh, and he watched as goose bumps appeared on her skin at his touch. Over the past week, he'd thought of them naked in his bed more times than he could count.

"Can I go in the booth?" she whispered, pulling his mind from his fantasies.

He smiled. "Yeah, come on."

He led her into the booth and placed the headphones on her ears. "I'm gonna play a beat," he said. "You can sing, rap, whatever you want."

"Sing?" she said, turning to him with a laugh. "You know I can't sing."

"Your voice isn't *terrible*," he said. "Could you use some lessons? Probably, but I'll give them to you for free."

She playfully smacked his arm, and he returned to the mixing board and turned up the volume on her headphones. He played one of Malik's beats, and Iris held the headphones to her ears. She couldn't hear him while in the booth, so he held up his fingers as he counted her in. She nodded along to the beat and started to rap.

"My name is Iris, and I . . . like Angel. He looks so good . . . I want a bagel."

Angel burst out laughing. Iris covered her mouth with

her hands, laughing too. Her smile softened as she looked at him. His laughter quieted as he gazed back at her.

Come here, he mouthed, curling his index finger and beckoning her to him.

She took off her headphones and left the booth, returning to him. He pulled her into his lap and brought her lips to his. Their tongues brushed against each other and Iris adjusted herself, moving closer, and he grew hard instantly. He pulled back and used the pad of his thumb to remove the smeared lipstick from her chin.

"You've got some lipstick on your face too," she said, gently brushing her fingers over his mouth.

He kissed her fingers, and his heart pounded at a steady rhythm as his hands roamed down her waist to her thighs. She leaned forward and kissed him again, pressing her breasts against his chest. She began to rock in his lap, a sensual back-and-forth motion that drove him mad. He adjusted her so that she straddled him. She gazed at him, biting her lip.

"Do we have time?" Iris asked, breath hitching.

"Yes," he said, against her mouth.

They kissed again, groping at each other, knocking hands as she hiked up her skirt and Angel reached for his zipper. He kept one hand on her as he leaned down to retrieve a condom from his leather duffel bag on the floor. He turned, eager to kiss her again.

"Wait, wait. I meant to ask, are you seeing anyone else?" Iris said. Her chest fell and rose quickly on deep breaths. "I should have brought this up before. But it just occurred to me to ask, and if you don't mind, I would prefer to be exclusive—"

"I'm not seeing anyone else," he said, pulling her close again as he slipped on the condom. "Only you."

Her relief was obvious, and it touched him. "Only you," he repeated.

She reached down and brushed her fingers against his hardness. He slid her panties to the side, and she lifted up and sank down onto him slowly. He loved being inside of her. The exquisite feel of her made him see stars. She moaned quietly and let her head fall back as she rode him, and he couldn't take his eyes off her. He was no match for her when he watched her like this. He touched her at the space where they were joined, feeling her wetness. As her quiet moans grew more ragged, she whispered his name, and he came hard, unexpectedly. She kept riding him until she found her release as well.

Then she lay against him and they breathed deeply, hands clasped.

An alarm sounded on her phone, startling both of them.

"I have to get back to work," she whispered.

Angel hooked his hands behind her back, kissing her, wishing that she could stay. But he knew he'd have to let her go. He sighed, and Iris slowly eased off him. They stood and righted their clothes. He tossed the condom in the trash bin, reminding himself to dispose of it before Malik came back. Although what he and Iris had just done felt amazing, he wanted more than just a quickie with her in the middle of the day before they both went back to work.

He wanted more from her in general. She wanted to see where things went. The question mark hovered above his head, and he craved a more definitive direction for them. But he knew that if he were to ask her for more, it might not end well. If she wasn't ready, she might shut them down alto-gether. He rolled his shoulders and shook off those thoughts, focusing on how she was here with him now.

She smiled sadly. "I'm sorry I can't stay longer."

"It's cool," he said, hugging her close. "I'll call you to-night. It might be late."

"I'll answer."

They shared one last hug and kiss before Iris slipped out of the room.

20

"I FEEL . . . WELL, I GUESS THE PLAINEST WAY TO PUT IT IS that I really, really like being with Angel," Iris said.

She was sitting on Marie's comfy leather couch. There were many things that Iris appreciated about having Marie as her therapist, but high on the list was that Marie kept Saturday hours during summer. That way Iris could meet with her on Saturday mornings while Calla was at karate.

"You look very at ease," Marie said, observing Iris with a smile. Today her nails were painted hot pink. "You're glowing, actually. I don't think I've ever seen you like this."

Iris glanced at her lap, feeling herself blush. "I do feel at ease . . . but I would be lying if I said that I wasn't also feeling cautious."

"Cautious, okay," Marie said. "Can you explain further?"

"My job doesn't know about us, and I don't like that I'm lying by omission to my boss." Iris bit her lip. "People are so invested in Angel's personal life, so I'm not sure how long someone like him can keep a relationship secret. He's been pretty low-key while working on his album, so he's not out and about that much right now, and we've been really careful, but I'm not sure how long this phase will last. At the same time, I'm just trying my best to focus on the present and enjoy my time with him while I have it."

Marie nodded. "I think it's important to acknowledge the progress that you've made here, Iris," she said. "You've put yourself back out there and you're trying. That's something you didn't always know if you were capable of."

"Thank you," Iris said quietly. She glanced at the framed photograph on Marie's desk of her young son and their border collie puppy. "Sometimes I wonder what Terry would think of this whole thing. What he'd think of Angel."

Marie tilted her head. "What do you think he'd say?"

"I think he'd be really surprised." Iris laughed softly to herself. "*I'm* surprised. Terry was . . . well, he was my type, I guess. And I didn't think that Angel was my type, but it turns out that he is too. They're so different." She stopped herself. "I don't want to compare them."

"It's natural to compare them," Marie said easily. "Terry was your first love and Angel is the first person that you've shown real interest in after Terry."

Iris nodded, conceding Marie's point. The truth was that she wasn't exactly sure what Terry would think about her and Angel. But she hoped that he'd be relieved to know that she was spending time with someone who really cared about her and who made her happy.

AFTER THERAPY, IRIS drove to pick Calla up from karate. She waited in the dojo parking lot along with the other parents and stayed in her car to avoid running into Janet and Viv. Through the windows, she could look inside the dojo and see Calla punching and kicking, sporting her focused expression.

Look, Terry, Iris thought to herself, smiling. *Look at our baby. Isn't she so amazing?*

Calla's instructor ended class and Calla and the other pupils bowed. Calla glanced out the window and spotted Iris's car. She waved and rushed outside, bouncing on the balls of her feet as Iris unlocked the door. Calla climbed inside the backseat, tossing her duffel next to her.

"Burger Hero?" she said eagerly.

"Burger Hero," Iris replied, grinning.

It was their post-karate Saturday tradition. Turkey burgers and fries from Burger Hero, the fast-food chain restaurant that existed only in North Jersey.

Iris took a picture of her Burger Hero curly fries and sent it to Angel.

In addition to Friendly's, you're missing out on Burger Hero.

He'd told her that he'd be in the studio all day, so she wasn't expecting to hear from him for a while. They'd seen each other once more since she'd visited him at the studio. She'd briefly stopped by his condo after work one day last week. She'd helped him give Maxine a bath, which Maxine hated. She'd jumped on Iris, wetting her button-up and skirt. Of course, then Iris had to take off all of her clothes and put them in the dryer, and while she waited for her clothes to dry, she and Angel conveniently found their way to his bed.

Her phone vibrated a few minutes later with his response: Promise you'll take me there.

She smiled and texted back, Promise.

After eating, she and Calla stopped at the grocery store to buy snacks. They were having a girls' night tonight, just the two of them. The deal was that they each got to pick a movie. Calla had already made her choice: an animated movie, *The Good Dinosaur*. Iris was still deciding between *13 Going on 30* and *10 Things I Hate About You*. Both seemed like appropriate choices to watch with her six-year-old.

The last stop before heading home was to swing by Greenehouse so that Iris could pick up fertilizer. When they arrived, Iris breathed in the familiarity. The smell of soil and plants, the natural light and warm breeze thanks to the high ceilings and open windows. She knew this place better than she knew her own home.

Saturday was usually the busiest day of the week, but this was something else. Customers filled the aisles, holding various plants and flower bouquets. Iris held on to Calla's hand as she maneuvered through the store. Amina and Harry, employees and local college students, buzzed around, assisting customers. Iris spotted her dad at the register, rubbing his lower back as he rang up a customer.

"Hey, Dad," Iris said as she and Calla approached.

"Hi, Grandpa," Calla said, standing right beside him. She was fascinated with the workings of the computer register. She stared at the numbers on the screen, barely noticing when Benjamin bent downward to hug her.

He kissed Iris on the cheek before helping the next customer in line.

"You okay?" Iris asked, eyeing him. "I see you rubbing your back."

"I'm fine, Iris," Benjamin said. He gave her a look. "Don't fret over me. You sound like your mother."

Iris decided to drop the issue with his back, for now. "It's really busy in here."

"The Flower Studio in Bridgewood closed down."

Iris blinked. For years, the Flower Studio had been Greenehouse's main competitor in their area.

"What happened?" Iris asked as Benjamin swiped the customer's credit card. Calla followed the action with her eyes and looked at the computer screen. She grabbed the receipt and handed it to the customer, who smiled at her. "Was business bad?"

Benjamin shook his head. "The family moved to Texas. I think they might be planning to open something down there."

"Wow."

So now Greenehouse would get double the business. This was even more reason for her parents to hire a manager to help them. But Iris didn't want to start a heated discussion, especially not right now when Benjamin needed to focus on the store.

"Can I help?" she asked.

"No, you go on about your day," Benjamin said.

"Is that my grandbaby I hear?" Dahlia poked her head out of the back office. She hurried forward and Calla skipped, meeting her halfway. Dahlia scooped Calla up in her arms and squeezed her.

"I want to take Calla with me to the floral show up in Averton tonight," Dahlia said. "I just got the invite."

Calla looked to Iris, her expression filled with hope. "Can I go, Mom?"

"What about our movie night?" Iris asked.

"Maybe we can do movie night next Saturday," Calla suggested gently.

Iris smiled at her sweet, thoughtful daughter who didn't want to hurt her feelings. Iris *had* been looking forward to movie night, but of course she would let Calla attend the floral show.

She brushed her hand over Calla's hair. "Okay, that's fine."

"Thank you!" Calla beamed. "Can I stay over at Grandma's too? That way I can have her Sunday pancakes for breakfast."

Iris looked at Dahlia and raised her eyebrow in question.

"You know you don't have to ask," Dahlia said.

They discussed what time Dahlia would get Calla for the show. And suddenly, Iris had a Saturday evening to herself.

HOME ALONE, IRIS was flipping through channels. She'd just ordered a pizza and wanted to find something to watch before she went to pick it up. Suddenly, Angel popped up on her screen, starring in an energy drink commercial. He was dancing in the studio, sweating and looking focused. Then he paused and grabbed the energy drink and flashed his gorgeous, blinding smile as he took a huge swig.

She'd seen the commercial dozens of times in the past, but that was before Angel had become hers.

I'm dating him right now.

This beautiful man who had a golden voice and made regular appearances on her TV screen was the same person whom she texted on and off throughout the day and whom she spoke to every night on the phone until she was so sleepy, her eyelids drooped closed. It was still so surreal.

Iris's body ached with how much she missed him, how much she wished he were here with her now. So naturally, she went on YouTube and looked up his music videos. She started with the videos from his debut album. Then she went deeper and found footage from his old gospel performances. He looked so young, barely older than a teenager. He was skinnier, less well dressed, but he sang with such passion. That passion for singing was present in all of his songs, Iris realized.

Wryly, she was starting to wonder if she was no better than an obsessed fan.

Her phone vibrated, interrupting her video. Angel was FaceTiming her.

"I was just watching videos of you," she said as she answered.

He smiled as he lounged on his couch. "Which ones?"

"All of them. Even your gospel ones." She peered at his background. "You're home?"

"Yeah, just got back from the studio." He was still smiling. "What did you think of the videos?"

"I think that I could watch clips of you singing all day."

His grin widened. "I hope I'm not interrupting movie night."

"Nope. Calla's with my mom and they're having a sleepover. I'm here alone and I guess I don't know what to do with myself."

He wiggled his eyebrows. "You've got a free house? You should throw a party."

Iris laughed, shaking her head.

"Or . . . I could come over," he said.

Iris paused. She stared at Angel and quietly, he stared back. Her heartbeat picked up pace. Was she ready to have him in her space this way? She was here alone, and she wouldn't have to worry about introducing him to Calla. The plan was to pick her up from her parents' shop tomorrow afternoon.

And she *missed* him.

"I like that idea," she said.

Angel sat up. "Really?"

She nodded, and he hurried to say that he'd be there soon. After they hung up, Iris sent him her address and rushed to her private bathroom. She brushed her teeth and combed her curls into a presentable bun. She was wearing an old Greenehouse T-shirt and sweats.

She threw off her clothes and changed into the only sexy lingerie that she owned. She'd bought them on sale at Macy's last year. Then she slipped into a silk robe and realized that it might look like she was trying too hard. She shrugged on her Greenehouse T-shirt again but instead of sweatpants, she changed into biker shorts that made her butt look great.

By the time that Angel rang her doorbell, Iris's harried feelings melted away. She opened the door and Angel hugged her, and she eased into his embrace. A fancy-looking black car was parked in her driveway.

"I drove myself," he explained. "I rarely get the chance to do it."

She nodded, impressed. "It's a nice car."

"Thank you," he said, grinning.

She stepped aside to let him into the foyer. Noticing the shoes by the door, he slipped out of his sneakers. His cinnamon cologne enveloped her. He followed her down the hall and paused at the photographs that lined the walls. There were pictures of Iris and her sisters and parents at various holidays throughout the years. Iris and Calla when they'd first brought her home from the hospital and later at her pre-K graduation last year. There was a photo of Iris when she was pregnant with Calla, sitting on the front steps of this very house, right next to the FOR SALE sign. And then there was a photo of her and Terry on their wedding day in Brooklyn, holding hands. Iris was leaning her head against Terry's shoulder. She wondered how these snapshots from her life looked to Angel as she stood beside him.

He pointed to the wedding photograph. "This is a great picture."

"Thank you."

He stepped closer, examining the pictures. A soft smile played out on his lips.

"Let me take your bag," she said, reaching for his duffel.

He backed away from the photographs and trailed after Iris into the living room. She left his bag by the couch and he joined her in the kitchen. She poured him a glass of wine as he sat at the island. He eased out of his jacket and folded it on the back of the chair.

"You have a nice house," he said. "It looks how I imagined it would."

Iris smirked, sitting across from him. "What does that mean?"

"It's neat and organized," he said. "And homey. It feels lived in. Like there are stories here."

Iris looked around at her kitchen, trying to see things through his eyes.

"I love this house," she said. "But it's a little big for just Calla and me."

"Have you thought about moving?"

She nodded. "Not right now, though. I don't have the time or energy to go through the moving and selling process. And . . . I want Calla to live in the same house where her dad lived for a bit longer."

She thought of how Elaine and Terrance senior were selling their DC home, and how she still hadn't settled on a date for her and Calla to visit and look through Terry's things.

"I get that," Angel said softly.

Neither of them bothered to drink their wine. Instead, they studied each other across the island.

"Do you want to have more kids?" Angel asked. "Then you might not need to sell the house."

"Sometimes I think it would be nice for Calla to have a sibling," she said slowly, intrigued that he'd asked this question. "Especially since my sisters and I are so close, and I know how important that bond is. But that's not in the cards for me at the moment." She tilted her head, looking at him. "What about you? Do you want kids?"

"I do." He smiled easily. "I want a big family. And I want my kids to feel loved and supported. Not judged."

She nodded. Given the current state of his relationship with his parents, Iris understood why he'd want his relationship with his own future children to be a lot different.

For a moment, she pictured it: Angel holding a chubby baby in his arms who looked like him, and who looked like her. Standing beside them, she saw herself, smiling with pride. And beside Iris, there was Calla. A happy, blended family. The image caused Iris's stomach to twist in wanting. *Foolish* wanting. She and Angel weren't working toward marriage and babies. They were having fun.

"I have to pick up the pizza I ordered," she said, changing the subject. "Are you okay to hang out here for a few minutes?"

Angel stood. "Nah, I want to come with you. I want to see Willow Ridge."

Iris paused and bit her lip, watching as Angel walked toward his duffel bag. "I don't know if that's a good idea. Somebody might see you—"

She stopped short as Angel produced a baseball cap, sunglasses and fake beard from his bag. The Tom Wyatt disguise. He turned to her as he began fastening the fake beard over his real one.

"If they see me, they won't know who I am," he said, lips curving in a grin.

Iris laughed, shaking her head as she looked at him. A feeling of lightness and warmth spread from her toes to the top of her head. *He* did that to her.

"Let me get my purse," she said.

She took the long way to Pat's Pizzeria, showing Angel around Willow Ridge the same way that he'd shown her Maren. She drove him by the high school where Xavier worked and the library where she'd spent so much of her youth. She drove him past Greenehouse and by Calla's karate dojo. Angel smiled, engaged and delighted, as he listened to Iris.

"What about the TGI Fridays where you worked?" he asked.

Iris laughed in surprise. She'd mentioned working at TGI Fridays once and he'd remembered. "That's near Princeton, where I went to college," she said. "I'll have to take you there another day."

He leaned back and nodded, smiling. "Can't wait."

And she knew that he actually meant it.

She pulled into the Pat's Pizzeria parking lot and left the car running as she went inside to get the pizza. Angel rolled his window down and looked around at the shopping complex. Thankfully, the pizza was ready, and Iris quickly paid after grabbing a two-liter bottle of ginger ale. She held the hot pizza box in one hand and the ginger ale in the other. She used her hip to open the door. Watching her, Angel got out of the car and jogged toward her, ready to help.

"Hi, Ms. Greene!"

Iris startled, fumbling with her pizza. She turned and saw Calla's friend Nena walking toward her . . . followed by her mom, Janet.

Oh God.

Panic overtook Iris as she glanced between Janet and her daughter, and Angel who came up to her, taking the pizza and soda from her hands. Her pulse slowed a bit when she remembered his disguise. But still, she was being seen with an unknown man in her town by the biggest gossiper in the karate mom group chat.

"H-hi, Nena," Iris said. She looked at Janet, who was staring at Angel, eyebrows lifted in intrigue. "Hey, Janet."

"*Hiiii,*" Janet sang. Her gaze was glued to Angel, flitting from his hat to his sunglasses to his beard. She looked at Iris and waited for an introduction.

"Oh, um, this is, uh—" Iris fumbled for a response. She hadn't expected Angel to get out of the car, and she certainly hadn't expected to run into Janet at Pat's Pizzeria of all places. She didn't even know that Janet ate pizza. At a dojo fundraiser last year, Janet had warned Iris that she shouldn't make a habit out of eating hoagies because bread contained too many carbs.

"I'm Tom," Angel said, easily smoothing over Iris's stalled sentence. He smiled as he shifted the ginger ale under his arm to shake Janet's hand. "Nice to meet you. Janet, is it?"

"Yes, nice to meet you too," Janet said, tilting her head slightly as she observed him. "Something about you is a bit familiar. Have we met before?"

Only Iris noticed the sly edge to Angel's smile. "No," he said. "I don't think we have."

"It was nice running into you," Iris said, placing her hand against Angel's back and steering him toward her car. "I'll tell Calla that you said hi, Nena."

Nena waved goodbye and Janet stared after Iris and Angel, sporting that same expression of shock and intrigue.

"How do you know her?" Angel asked as Iris pulled out of the parking lot.

"She's another mom from karate." Iris briefly glanced at her rearview mirror as she pulled out of the lot. "Is she still looking?"

Angel twisted to look out the back window. "Yep."

Iris groaned.

Angel gently placed his hand on her thigh. "She didn't know that it was me."

"I know," Iris said, resting her hand on top of his, grateful that he was trying to calm her. "She's just *very* nosy, and I try to tell her very little about my personal life because she can't keep anything to herself. The next time I see her, she'll probably ask about you until she's blue in the face."

On cue, her phone vibrated on her center console. At a quick glance, she saw that she'd received a text from Janet.

Girl!! He's cute!! Hard to tell with the big beard and glasses, but he definitely has a hottie vibe! What's the story there???

Iris groaned again, and Angel gave her thigh a squeeze. He sent her a soft smile. "Tell her that I'm a traveling salesman who stays at your house when I'm passing through town."

She snort-laughed, glancing at him, shaking her head. "Yeah, that would put an end to her questioning for sure."

Angel's smile widened into a full grin. He seemed satisfied that he'd managed to lessen her anxiety and make her laugh. And he was right. Janet hadn't recognized him, and it wasn't the end of the world if Iris was seen out with an unknown man. Janet and Viv would definitely gossip but they didn't have any facts. Their interest would die down in a couple weeks. And more important, Iris remembered that she wanted to be in the moment whenever she was with Angel. She didn't want to waste their evening together worrying.

She threaded her fingers through his. "I'm really glad that you're here," she said.

His expression softened. He lifted her hand to his mouth and kissed it. She shivered.

"Me too," he said.

Back at her house, they tried to find something to watch while they ate. They sat side by side on her couch.

"What are you in the mood to watch?" she asked.

Angel tapped his chin, thinking. "I don't know. What's good right now?"

"Oh!" Iris suddenly clapped her hands, and Angel jumped. "We can watch *SpongeBob*."

Angel laughed as he took a sip of his soda. His eyes lit up.

"Just one episode," Iris said. "A good one."

She found the show on a streaming app. She flicked through the episodes, trying to best determine which episode they should watch. She hadn't watched *SpongeBob* in years, but many scenes and lines of dialogue were imbedded in her brain, like every other millennial who'd grown up on Nickelodeon. Finally, she made her choice and pivoted to face Angel head-on.

"So," she said, "to give a quick overview. SpongeBob is a sea sponge who lives in a pineapple under the sea, and he works at a fast-food restaurant called the Krusty Krab, and the show is basically about him and his friends."

Angel nodded. "Okay. I knew that much."

"I'm sure there's plenty of debate about which *Sponge-Bob* episode is the *best*," she continued. "There's the classic episode when SpongeBob and his neighbor-slash-coworker Squidward deliver a pizza. There's the episode when he and his best friend, Patrick, go camping and Patrick accuses SpongeBob of eating his candy. So much Mermaid Man and Barnacle Boy. I don't think I can even get into that right now. Oh, then there's the episode when SpongeBob and Patrick basically become a couple and adopt a baby clam."

At this, Angel quirked an eyebrow. "Are they best friends or boyfriends?"

"You know, I'm not exactly sure now that I think about it," she said. "Anyway, I think the best thing for us to do is watch an episode that I remember as *my* favorite, and that's 'Karate Island.' SpongeBob and his friend Sandy Cheeks go on a journey because SpongeBob has been told that he's the king of karate, but Sandy is suspicious."

"Sandy Cheeks is the squirrel in the astronaut suit, right?"

"Yes." Iris cued up the episode. "Ready?"

Angel grinned and nodded. "Thanks for the presentation," he said. He slung his arm around her shoulders as she settled closer to him.

As they watched the episode, Iris realized that she'd forgotten that this show was hilarious yet unhinged. After being invited to Karate Island, SpongeBob was kidnapped, and Sandy had to fight several people in order to rescue him. As it turned out, SpongeBob was lured to the island for a real estate scam.

Angel was laughing so hard, there were basically tears coming out of his eyes by the time the episode ended.

"Wow," he said, sighing. "I can see why everyone at school was obsessed with this show."

Iris smiled at him, pleased that this small gesture had made him so happy. He set his plate on the coffee table and rolled his shoulders, wincing.

"Are you okay?" she asked.

"My muscles are sore from working out."

"Do you want me to run a bath for you?" Once the question

was out in the open, she realized that taking a bath with Angel was exactly what she wanted to do. She probably should have suggested that before *SpongeBob*, to be honest.

"Will you join me?" he asked, gazing at her.

A warm flush crept over her body. "Yes."

Upstairs in her bathroom, she ran the bathwater. Angel set his bag down by her bed and walked slowly around her room, looking at the items on her dresser, calling out to her that he wasn't surprised by how organized her bedroom was. When the water was hot, Angel joined her. He stripped, and Iris did as well. He marveled over her alluring black lingerie as he unhooked her bra and slid down her panties. He climbed into the tub and held her hand as she climbed in after him. They settled into the soapy water. She leaned her back against his chest. She could feel the steady pounding of his heartbeat, the hardness of his length poking her backside.

"I'm *really* glad I'm here," he said, voice husky at the curve of her ear, repeating back what she'd said to him in the car.

One hand lingered at the space between her thighs. He used the other to cup her breast.

"Me too," she whispered.

He kissed her neck and whispered to her too, telling her how beautiful and soft she was. He coaxed her to rise up on her knees and he played with her until she was pliant and moaning. He rose from the water and picked her up, wiping her off and carrying her into her bedroom.

"You have so many pillows," he said, smirking as he laid her down.

She twisted, looking at the various light blue and white

pillows that she kept stacked on her bed. "I know," she said, laughing quietly. "It's just that my bed is so big . . . and I guess the pillows make it feel less empty."

Angel paused in the act of pushing some of the pillows out of their way. He looked down at Iris, his gaze focused and warm. He cradled her cheek in his palm.

"Well, I'm here now," he said softly.

He *was* here, in her bed, in her space. It was a new level of intimacy. He was the first man who'd been here since Terry. She realized just how much she'd craved and longed for this closeness, to share this part of herself with Angel.

It felt like her heart was doubling in size as he bent down and kissed her, slower and deeper than before. He briefly broke away to grab a condom, and he returned to her. Together, they slid the condom onto him, and he covered her body with his own and entered her slowly, then pumping into her with deep, fast thrusts. She wrapped her legs around his waist, pulling him closer to her until they felt like one breathing being. She closed her eyes and bit his shoulder, languishing in the feel of their connection until it sent her over the edge.

Later, both exhausted, they climbed under the covers. Iris liked to have her many pillows situated behind her head, just so. When Angel reached for one of her favorite pillows, she bit her lip.

He paused, brows raised. His mouth displayed a hint of a smile. "Did I do something wrong?"

"I like this pillow," she said. She handed him a different pillow that looked identical to the one he'd reached for but inexplicably wasn't her favorite. "You can have this one. If that's okay."

"Thank you." He fluffed the pillow before lying back. He turned on his side, facing her. "Anything else I should know about your sleeping habits? Do you snore? Drool?"

She wrinkled her nose. "I don't *drool*. But . . . I do snore when I'm really tired."

Angel laughed. "Remind me to buy some earplugs for the future."

For the future. Those words ran on a loop through Iris's mind as Angel cocooned her from behind, one hand draped across her stomach, the other fitting behind her pillow. He fell asleep fast, breathing deeply behind her. Iris realized that this was something else that she had missed. Being held. With Angel, she felt taken care of.

For the future, he'd said. A future they most likely wouldn't have together.

She felt the deep twist of wanting in the pit of her stomach again. This time, it was much harder to ignore.

21

IN THE MORNING, ANGEL WOKE TO IRIS'S EMPTY SIDE OF the bed. He blinked and shaded his eyes from the sunlight, adjusting to the unfamiliarity of her bedroom. The walls had looked white last night, but in daylight, he could see that they were painted sky blue. There was no clutter in her room, just signature Iris orderliness. He smiled and turned over, letting out a deep, contented sigh.

Her house was quiet. Growing up, his Sunday mornings had been filled with his parents bustling around, blasting gospel music before church. And now, if he wasn't traveling for work, he usually woke to the sound of Leah and Maxine creating chaos. He sat up and rubbed the back of his neck, listening for the sound of Iris moving around somewhere in the house. When he still heard nothing, he swung his legs around the side of the bed and shrugged on his boxers and joggers.

He found Iris outside in her backyard. She wore the same long T-shirt from last night and pajama shorts as she crouched in front of a large bush with sprouting purple flowers, holding the water hose in one hand.

"Good morning," he said, stepping outside barefoot.

She turned, smiling at him as she stood. "Good morning. How'd you sleep?"

"Amazing." He gazed at her garden as he walked toward her. It was like a spring oasis, filled with green, purple, pink and yellow. He didn't know much about plants, but her garden looked well taken care of. "This is so dope."

She put her hands on her hips and glanced around. "Yeah, I try my best. Thank you."

He came behind her and wrapped his arms around her torso. He kissed the top of her head. "Which one is your favorite?"

She gasped, twisting to look up at him. "I can't pick a favorite. I love all of them." But her eyes went to the bush with the bundles of purple flowers. She lowered her voice and pointed. "Okay, maybe the hydrangeas. But only because they're so high-maintenance and I've managed to keep them alive."

"Why are we whispering?" Angel asked, the corner of his mouth pulling into a smirk.

"Because I think plants can hear us. I talk to mine all the time."

How was he not supposed to kiss her when she said endearing things like that? He tipped her chin up gently as he pressed his lips to hers. She dropped the hose and eased into him, turning and wrapping her arms around his neck. He loved that this felt like it was second nature to them already.

His stomach growled, and Iris laughed again between kisses.

"What do you want for breakfast?" she asked.

"Whatever cereal you have is fine with me."

"I've got lots of options in the cabinet," she said. "I'm

gonna hop in the shower. Feel free to help yourself to anything."

He followed her back inside and stopped in the kitchen while she continued on into the hallway.

"Wait, what time is your daughter coming back?" he asked, realizing that he wasn't wearing a shirt.

"In the afternoon," Iris called back. "She likes to be at the shop with my parents on Sundays. I'll pick her up in a couple hours."

"Cool."

He opened her cabinets, which were stocked with food. Lots of cereal options, like she'd said. He poured a bowl of Frosted Flakes and some almond milk. Out of curiosity, he took a peek inside her freezer. Yep, she had a tub of mint chocolate chip ice cream. Horrible. But he'd buy her a lifetime supply if it made her happy.

He sat at the island and ate his cereal. He liked the calm, the quiet. Most of all, he liked that Iris was somewhere here too, existing with him in the same vicinity. It felt domestic and normal. It was the kind of simplicity and stability he'd been craving for as long as he could remember. And they had all morning to lounge around. Maybe he'd convince her to get back in the tub with him . . .

The jingling of keys at the front door made Angel freeze, midchew. The door opened.

"Iris!" a woman called.

As her voice grew closer, Angel remembered that he was shirtless. He dived for his denim jacket that he'd left on the chair last night and hastily buttoned it up to his collar.

"Iris, where—" The woman stopped midsentence as she entered the kitchen.

It took Angel a moment to place her. Her features were familiar—the shape of her face and eyes. This was Iris's mother. He'd met her at Violet's anti-wedding party years ago and a couple months prior at Violet's wedding. Her name was Dahlia. She gaped at Angel.

Angel cleared his throat as blood rushed to his face. "Good morning."

Dahlia stared at him slack-jawed. "G-good morning."

Iris's daughter trailed into the kitchen behind Dahlia. Her head was adorned with braids and pink barrettes. She was holding what looked like a stuffed dinosaur toy, and her attention was focused on her grandmother, until she noticed Angel standing there. She blinked at him, her small eyebrows scrunching together.

"Who are you?" Calla asked.

"I'm Angel." He approached them with a smile. "I'm a friend of your mom's. It's nice to meet you." To Dahlia, he said, "Iris is in the shower. She should be down soon."

Dahlia's smile was slow and delighted, like that of the Cheshire cat. "*Oh*, I see."

He wasn't sure what to make of her smile. Here he was meeting Iris's mom and daughter while shirtless beneath his jacket and standing barefoot in her kitchen. What kind of first—or third, in Dahlia's case—impression was that? He cleared his throat again and let out a nervous laugh.

"Mom?" Iris called. Her feet pounded down the steps. She raced into the kitchen and sputtered to a stop. She'd thrown on a T-shirt and jeans. She looked fresh-faced and beautiful. She glanced from Angel to her daughter to her mother. Mild panic overtook her features. "I—I thought I was coming to get Calla this afternoon."

Dahlia's eyes lingered on Angel before she turned to Iris. "Your father pulled his back this morning."

"*What?*" Iris said. "Is he okay?"

"He's fine. We took him to urgent care and they gave him some pain meds. We had to close down the shop for the day and send the employees home. That's why I dropped Calla off. I didn't realize you were preoccupied . . ." She glanced at Angel again.

"Why did you close down the shop?" Iris asked, pointedly ignoring her mother's sly smile directed toward Angel.

"We don't have anyone to run it. I want to be home with your father."

Iris sighed, frustrated. "The store's going to be so busy today now that the Flower Studio is closed. This is exactly why I keep telling you and Dad that you need to hire a manager."

"And *I* keep telling you that *we're* the managers."

"Well, I'm going to run the shop today," Iris said. "I still remember how to do everything."

"No! You're busy!" Dahlia shot another glance at Angel. "I'll take Calla back home with me."

"I'm happy to help any way I can," Angel interrupted.

Iris turned to him sharply, eyes widening in surprise. "No, I can't ask that of you."

"It's really no big deal," he said. "I wasn't planning to head to the studio until later tonight anyway."

"If you want to keep the shop open today so badly, you could probably use him . . ." Dahlia said, raising her eyebrows.

Years ago, during one of their many fittings, Violet had mentioned offhandedly to Angel that her mom could be very meddlesome when it suited her. Now he could see what Violet meant. He had to admit that Dahlia's very obvious hints were kind of funny, though.

Iris frowned as she looked at Angel, then at Calla.

Dahlia's phone rang. "Oh, this is your father calling." She turned away and ushered Calla with her into the living room.

"I'm so sorry about this," Iris said quietly. "She has a key and sometimes she comes over unannounced, but it's always just me and Calla here. I wish that she would have called first."

In Iris's strained expression, Angel read what else she probably wasn't saying—that she hadn't been ready for him to meet Calla yet, which he understood. They'd agreed to take things slow, and meeting her daughter the morning after his first sleepover at her house was not very ideal.

Her dad injuring his back wasn't ideal either, and if Iris needed his help at the store, Angel wanted to give it.

"You don't need to apologize," he said. His heartbeat had finally regulated. If he'd been caught completely shirtless, it would have been a different story. "What are you gonna do?"

"Sunday is the busiest day of the week at the shop, and it's the middle of summer. If they close for the day, they'll lose a ton of business."

"So go to the shop and run it, like you said. I can come with you."

"I can't steal you away to work in my parents' shop." Iris shook her head. "You're even busier than me. Don't you want to rest until you have to be at the studio?"

"You're not stealing me if I'm offering," he said. "And I'd rather be here to help you out."

"I don't know. Are you sure?"

He saw how hard it was for her to accept help from him. He stepped closer, resting his hands on her shoulders firmly. "Yes, I'm sure. Let me help you."

She bit her lip. "Okay," she said finally. "I have to make sure that it's okay with Calla too."

"Of course." He kissed her cheek. "I'll still get dressed either way."

He jogged upstairs and threw on the jeans and T-shirt that he'd packed. He gathered his duffel bag too, just in case Calla wasn't comfortable with him joining her and Iris at the store. He hoped she'd be okay with it, but if she wasn't, he understood. He hoped he'd have a chance to meet her again under better circumstances.

As he came downstairs, he overhead Iris and Calla in the kitchen, midconversation, speaking in low tones.

"He's your friend?" he heard Calla ask in her light voice. "Like how Nena is my friend?"

"Sort of," Iris said softly. "We're getting to know each other more. I like spending time with him."

Angel felt himself smile at that. He leaned against the hallway wall, not wanting to interrupt them. In the living room, he could hear Dahlia talking on the phone to Iris's dad.

"He offered to help us at the store today," Iris continued. "But I only want him to come if you're okay with it too. And it's okay if you aren't."

Calla was quiet. Angel held his breath, anxious to hear Calla's response. Finally, she said, "If he's your friend and he's nice to you, I don't mind if he comes."

Angel breathed a sigh of relief, and his heart stuttered at the sound of Iris's laugh.

"He is very nice to me," she said.

"Okay. Good," Calla said simply.

Angel's mouth strained with the strength of his smile. He was grateful that he didn't have to be separated from Iris just yet, grateful to have Calla's approval for joining them this afternoon.

"Do you have any questions for me?" Iris asked.

"I don't think so," Calla said. Then, "Wait. Does he like dinosaurs?"

Angel held in a laugh and raised an eyebrow at that one.

"I'm not sure," Iris said. "But we can definitely ask him."

He took that as his cue to reenter the kitchen. At the same time, Dahlia ended her phone call and walked into the kitchen too. Three sets of eyes turned to look at him.

"Angel, I want to introduce you to Calla," Iris said. Smiling at Angel tentatively, she placed her hand on Calla's shoulder.

Angel recognized the significance of this moment, and he felt the weight of his hope for Calla to like him. He also knew that he probably wouldn't have been introduced to Calla this soon if it weren't for Dahlia coming over unexpectedly. But maybe meeting Calla right now was fate. He didn't know.

Calla was so small. Angel felt gargantuan as he stood in front of her. She craned her neck to look up at him. He wanted to look her in the eye, so he knelt down, meeting her gaze.

"Hey, I've heard a lot about you." He held out his hand. Calla gingerly placed her small hand in his and they shook.

"You look familiar," she said quietly, looking at him. She glanced up at her mom for further explanation.

Iris chewed the inside of her cheek and Angel wondered how she would handle this. Would she tell Calla that he was famous and that was the reason that he looked familiar? He didn't mind if Calla knew the full truth about who he was, but Iris knew best. He fell quiet, letting her take the lead.

"We've seen him on television before," Iris said. "He's a singer."

Calla turned to Angel again. "You can sing?"

He nodded.

"Can you sing something right now?"

"*Calla*," Iris said, laughing. But Calla continued to watch Angel, like he was a magician and she wanted to see a magic trick.

"Okay, sure." Angel began to sing a melody from "Summertime Fine," figuring it might be a song that Calla would recognize since it was more recent.

When he finished singing, Calla smiled. "*Wow.*" Then as if she remembered her manners, she said, "Thank you."

Angel felt himself grin. "You're welcome."

He didn't miss the way that Dahlia elbowed Iris and wiggled her eyebrows. Iris sighed and ignored her mom.

"Okay, let's go to the shop," Iris said, twirling keys in her hand.

Dahlia sidled up beside Angel as they walked outside. "Iris hasn't brought a man around in a long time," she said quietly.

Angel glanced at Iris's mom, unsure of what to say. It was obvious that Dahlia had no idea that he and Iris had been seeing each other. He'd promised Iris that he'd respect her privacy, and in a way, that meant even when speaking to her mom.

"How long have you been spending time with my daughter?" Dahlia asked.

"It's new," he said, offering a polite smile.

Dahlia eyed him. Her Cheshire cat grin returned. "I hope we'll get to see you around more often."

"Mom, please stop harassing Angel," Iris said, unlocking the car doors.

"*Harassing?*" Offended, Dahlia pressed a hand to her chest. To Angel, she said, "I wasn't harassing you, was I?"

Angel laughed and shook his head.

"I love your music, by the way," she said.

"Thank you."

"You're handsome in pictures, but they really don't do you justice. In person, you're just as gorgeous as can be!"

Iris looped her arm through Angel's and physically dragged him away from her mother.

"I'll drop the keys off later!" Iris shouted to Dahlia, as she, Angel and Calla climbed into her car.

On the way to the shop, Iris called her sisters on three-way and explained their dad's injury. Violet was hysterical and wanted to know if she should ask one of her celebrity friends for a back specialist referral. Lily fretted over what might have happened if the injury had been worse. Iris, who'd been upset about their father just moments ago, easily calmed her frantic younger sisters.

Angel reached for her hand, placed on her gear shift. At first, she glanced over at him, startled. But then she relaxed and smiled gratefully. *Who takes care of you?* He'd asked her that back in DC. She shouldered so many responsibilities. It was clear that she could take care of herself, and she probably prided herself on that. But he wanted to support her too, care for her when she needed it.

It wasn't until they arrived at the shop that Iris looked at Angel and gasped.

"We forgot about your disguise," she said.

They decided that he'd wear a bandanna over the lower half of his face and a Greenehouse baseball cap to cover his recognizable burgundy hair. He borrowed a pair of plain Wayfarer sunglasses that Iris kept in her glove compartment.

The shop quickly filled with churchgoers buying bouquets and people buying plants and flowers for their weekend gardening hobbies. Iris worked the register, while Angel helped pack carts and carry items to customers' cars. As expected, people asked *a lot* of questions about plants. Angel shrugged and apologized when he couldn't provide an answer, saying that today was his first day, which was technically true.

When a woman approached him, holding a large dark green plant with sprawling leaves and asked what kind of sunlight it needed, Calla appeared beside Angel and rescued him from having to say *I'm not sure* for the millionth time.

"That's a corn plant," Calla said, pointing. "Don't put it directly in the sun. It likes shade."

The woman smiled at Calla and thanked her.

"Thank you," Angel said to Calla. He grinned sheepishly. "I don't know nearly enough about plants to work here, obviously."

"My grandparents tell me a lot, and my mom," she said. She eyed Angel curiously. "Do you want to know something else that I know a lot about?"

"What?"

"Dinosaurs."

He blinked and then recalled her question from earlier about whether or not he liked dinosaurs. They must have been important to her. "What do you know about them?"

For the rest of the afternoon, Calla trailed after Angel and kept him entertained with her various dinosaur facts. Sometimes, he asked for more clarification on a fact—like if male and female *T. rex*es looked different from each other, and she'd scrunch up her face adorably and say that she didn't know but she'd look it up later and tell him.

At one point, he glanced over toward the register and found Iris was watching them, smiling softly.

"You raised a great kid," he said quietly, sliding up behind her once there was a brief break in customer traffic.

Iris looked at him over her shoulder with warmth in her eyes. "Thank you."

She reached back and squeezed his hand quickly, then let go as a new customer entered the shop.

By the end of the day, Angel's arms and knees were sorer from lifting and carrying heavy potted plants and bags of soil than they were after dance rehearsal or a workout.

"I can see why your dad hurt his back," he said as Iris counted cash from the register.

She sighed and looked up at him. "I know. They don't want to hire someone to run the shop for them. It's been frustrating, to say the least." She smiled tiredly. "Thank you so much for helping out today."

"Of course," he said. He glanced at Calla, who was busy sweeping behind the register. The broom was almost taller than her. Angel grinned. "It was fun, actually."

Her eyes widened. "Really?"

"Really. It was kinda peaceful. Simple."

Iris smiled and started to reply but glanced toward the door as one final customer walked in.

"Sorry, sorry, I know you're closing!" a woman shouted. She wore a blue sundress and a matching sun hat. She quickly picked up a pot of pink and blue morning glories and brought them to the register. "I drove almost twenty-five minutes to get here, and halfway I realized I needed to stop for gas. The Flower Studio was a five-minute drive from my house, but they're closed, so here I am." She cast a glance behind her, wiping the sweat from her brow. She turned back to Iris. "This is a lovely store."

"Thank you," Iris said as she swiped the woman's credit card. "If you don't mind my asking . . . Has a new florist or nursery bought the Flower Studio's retail space yet?"

The woman shook her head. "Not that I know of. The last time I drove by, a 'For Rent' sign was still in the window."

"Huh," Iris said. "Well, thanks so much for making the trip to Greenehouse."

The woman promised that she'd be back, and Angel carried her pot to her car. When he returned, Calla had progressed to sweeping the center of the store. Iris was leaning her elbows on the register, watching the woman drive away. Her brows furrowed.

"Would it be crazy if I suggested to my parents that we take over the Flower Studio's space and open up another Greenehouse location?" she asked.

Angel leaned his hip against the register, facing her. "No," he said. "But who would run it?"

"That's the problem. I can't because I already have a job."

She chewed her bottom lip, frowning, thinking. "It's just that . . . well, today I finally felt energized about work, and I haven't felt that way in so long. Anyway, it was just a thought. I'm sure someone else has their eye on the space." She smirked and nodded her head at her daughter, who was trying her best to maneuver the big broom throughout the shop. "I think Calla could probably use some help."

"On it," Angel said, saluting her, and she laughed.

Iris turned on some music and Angel hummed while he swept. Iris shimmied her hips and Calla skipped over and mimicked her mom. They laughed together, and the sound was so beautiful. Angel watched them, and his heart expanded.

For years, he'd been eager to carve out a piece of his life that grounded and sustained him—something to contrast with his usual hectic pace. This weekend with Iris had been just what he'd needed. He imagined a future where he came to the shop to help her and her family whenever he could. Returning from work trips and staying with her at her house. And eventually getting to know Calla better. He saw the ways that he and Iris could fit together.

As he watched her laugh with her daughter, he craved to know how he could make his place in her life more permanent. It was on his mind heavy, and it was the reason why he gave voice to a new question as they drove back to her house.

"The honor ceremony in Maren is next Saturday," he said. Iris looked over at him, then glanced back at Calla, who dozed in the backseat. "Would you like to come with me?"

Iris paused, and his stomach tightened as he waited for her response.

"We don't have to tell anyone the truth about us," he

said quickly. He suddenly worried that he was ruining the comfortable bubble that they'd existed in for the last twenty-four hours. But he wanted her to be at the ceremony with him, to have her by his side as he went back to Georgia and accepted an award that was important to his hometown.

"It's a small-town event," he continued. "Maybe the local newspaper will be there, but otherwise it's not a big deal. No paparazzi. Leah will be there and Ray too. We can say we're friends or even that you're a member of my team if someone asks. I'd just really like to have you there with me, and I know I'd regret not asking."

Iris was quiet as she focused on the road. When they reached a stoplight, she turned to him.

"I want to support you," she said, reaching over to squeeze his hand. A gentle smile played across her lips. "I can come, but I'll have to be on the first flight out Sunday morning."

"For sure." His relief felt palpable. "So . . . how would you feel if I bought you a lifetime supply of mint chocolate chip ice cream as a thank-you?"

Iris laughed so loud, she woke Calla, who wanted to know what was so funny.

22

THE CEREMONY WAS HELD AT THE HOLIDAY INN RECEP-
tion hall downtown. It was the same place where Angel had
attended his senior prom and received his first kiss from a
girl named Aliya Brown. Granted, Aliya had ditched Angel
after she'd been voted prom queen and she'd left early with
the prom king, but a first kiss was still a first kiss. After he'd
signed his gospel recording deal, Aliya, as well as several
other girls in his class who hadn't given him the time of day
previously, had suddenly started paying him a lot more attention. He hadn't known what to do with it.

But Angel took the attention in stride now as he spoke
to Aliya, who was also being honored tonight for her ac-
complishments with the elementary school's PTA. The ceremony hadn't officially started yet, and Angel was making
the rounds, trying to say hello to as many people as possible. Aliya's husband, a firefighter, was an honoree as well.
He was somewhere in the room too, but obviously far
enough away that he didn't see when Aliya lightly placed
her hand on Angel's arm.

"I'm *so* proud of you," she said, leaning in and giving his
biceps a covert squeeze. "I mean, you used to sing the na-

tional anthem at assemblies and now look at you." She slowly dragged her eyes up and down Angel's form. "We are all so, so proud."

Beside him, Ray snorted quietly. Angel elbowed him in the side as he smiled at Aliya.

"Thank you, for real," Angel said, easing his arm from her hold. "And congratulations to you too. It was nice talking to you, but I've got to . . ." He gestured around at the rest of the room, politely indicating that there were other people he needed to talk to.

"Of course," Aliya said, eyes twinkling as she waved goodbye.

"You're the belle of the damn ball," Ray said, snickering as they walked away.

Angel couldn't do anything but laugh because it was kind of true. Further proving Ray's point, a camera flashed in their faces, startling them. A photographer from the local paper circled them, snapping pictures. Angel posed and smiled. Already, he'd spoken to a couple local journalists. Claudia had worked with the ceremony organizers to make sure that the media list was selective. Angel hadn't wanted his hometown to be overrun with the media or paparazzi because of him.

"Great, thank you," the photographer said, giving them a thumbs-up. "Angel, can we get one with you and the mayor?"

Mayor Daniels suddenly appeared by Angel's side, and soon Angel was surrounded by his old teachers and classmates and other attendees. Everyone was trying to get their pictures with him before the ceremony began.

Across the room, he saw his parents talking with Trey Jones, Angel's old youth pastor at Mount Olive, who was now a senior pastor. He was presenting Angel with his award tonight. Leah stood by their parents, smiling yet somehow simultaneously looking bored out of her mind. At their mom's request, Leah had smoothed her hair down into a neat side bun on the half of her head that wasn't shaved. She'd refused to remove the row of hoop earrings in both ears, though. Of course, Cora had blamed Angel. *If she wasn't up there with you in New York, she wouldn't have all these piercings.*

Already, Cora had picked a fight with Angel about his outfit. He was wearing a double-breasted Versace suit, contrasting black and plaid and a black turtleneck. He thought that he looked good, low-key even. But Cora had asked why he couldn't have worn a "normal" suit. And couldn't he have died his hair a normal shade instead of that burgundy? She'd also wanted him to take out his nose ring. He wondered again why he'd bothered to come tonight and subject himself to her.

Other than saying hello to Reverend Jones and to his old Sunday school teacher Mr. Price, offering condolences on his wife's passing, Angel hadn't made small talk with many others from Mount Olive. Not because he didn't want to talk to them and hear about how they were doing, but because he was apprehensive that they'd treat him just like his mother did, and there was only so much of that he could handle.

The ceremony was starting soon, and the host asked everyone to take their seats. Angel glanced toward the door, looking for Iris. Her flight out of Newark had been delayed, so he knew she'd be late. She'd texted him a half hour ago saying that she'd just gotten to the hotel and was getting dressed. He was so grateful that she'd agreed to join him here tonight, even if they couldn't be honest with everyone about what they meant to each other.

Angel and Ray took their seats at the table, which was situated in the front of the reception hall. Soon, Leah and their parents sat down too.

"I wouldn't be here if I didn't love you," Leah whispered to Angel. She nodded her head at Cora, who leaned across her husband to continue her conversation with Reverend Jones. "She's driving me nuts."

Angel smirked at his sister, knowing exactly how she felt. "We'll be outta here soon."

Then, suddenly, Iris appeared at their table as dinner was being served. She looked slightly winded as she smiled and waved hello. Her hair was styled in a wavy bob. She wore a black turtleneck dress and heels. Instant relief swept over Angel. He immediately stood to hug her.

"Hey," he said, turning his face down to her hair, breathing her in.

She hugged him back. "Hi. Sorry I'm late."

"It's okay."

He realized he held on to her for a beat too long when she cleared her throat and lightly tapped his side. Reluctantly, he stepped back. "You remember my parents, Cora and Percy. And this is Reverend Jones. He's known me since I was a kid. This is my friend Iris Greene."

Reverend Jones stood, offering his hand to Iris.

It felt weak and empty to refer to Iris as his friend, but it was what Iris wanted.

"Nice to meet you," Iris said.

Reverend Jones smiled at her. "Likewise. Thank you for coming to help us honor Angel."

Iris nodded as she took the open seat on the other side of Leah. This had been part of the plan too. Iris wanted to look like a member of Angel's overall group and not make it obvious that she was his romantic partner. Angel hated that she wasn't sitting right next to him. But they'd be alone later.

The ceremony started with a welcome speech from the mayor, and awards were presented to each honoree. Angel tried not to keep glancing at Iris the entire time, wishing that he could be next to her and rest his hand on her thigh or loop his arm around the back of her chair. He craved her nearness and he wondered if it was obvious to everyone around him. But Iris was the only one who caught his gaze time and time again. Neither of them was paying attention like they should have been.

They'd saved Angel for last. Reverend Jones walked to the podium to present Angel with his award.

"I'm here to honor a young man by the name of Angel Hughes, but most of you know him simply as Angel now. I remember when Angel was this big." Reverend Jones lifted his hand to his waist, and a few people laughed. "He would stand up in church, clapping loud and singing his little heart out. Even then, he had a strong voice that carried. We all knew that he was special. His success should come as a surprise to no one. And he's paid his blessings forward by donating to Mount Olive and helping us in our time of need. He's also made it so that the young people in our community who are interested in music have the tools to learn and realize their dreams. I am so proud to present this Maren honoree award to the one and only Angel Hughes."

Angel stood to loud applause. Leah hopped up and hugged him, and he looked across at Iris, who smiled at him with such warmth in her eyes, he felt her happiness radiating out to him. At the podium, he hugged Reverend Jones and thanked him. He would keep his speech short and sweet.

"Thank you for this honor," he said. "Thank you, Reverend Jones, for your kind words, although I do remember being taller than that as a kid." He paused as people laughed. "I'd also like to thank my family and this community. In a way, everyone here in this room helped make me who I am today." He glanced up at Iris, who watched him. He wanted to thank her too, just for being here. But he knew that she wouldn't want him to do that and draw attention to her.

He held his plaque and thanked everyone again. As Angel stepped away, the mayor resumed his place at the podium and wished everyone a good evening. Then the ceremony was over. Angel had been so nervous about being back home because it meant having to be around Cora, but other than her usual nitpicking, tonight hadn't been that bad. Maybe his apprehension had been unfounded.

Iris smiled softly as she took Angel's plaque in her hands. She tested its weight. "This is really special," she said. "Are you going to put it in your award case?"

He nodded, looking at her. "I'm ready to go. Are you?"

"Yes." She handed the plaque back to him and he purposely brushed his fingers against hers, holding her gaze.

"You can go with Ray and Leah to the car," he said. "I'll just say bye really quick."

"Okay."

Angel was in a hurry as he went to say goodbye to Reverend Jones and his parents. He hugged his dad, then his mom.

"I'll see you soon," he said, kissing her on the cheek.

Cora stiffened and squinted at him. "Well, we both know that's a bold-faced lie."

Angel paused and let out a deep breath. Reverend Jones cleared his throat, and Percy sighed, looking at his wife.

"He'll fly all around the world before he visits his mother," Cora explained, turning to some of her friends from church. "It's the truth, and y'all know it is."

It had been a surprisingly good night. Angel wanted to spend the rest of it with Iris. He didn't want to let his mom bring down his mood.

"It was good to see you, Mom," he forced himself to say, easing away. To Reverend Jones, he said, "I'm sorry I can't stay around longer. I'll be back in New York tomorrow. I'm working on my next album—"

"Oh, a new album," Cora said. "Does that mean you're going to be naked all over television again?"

"Naked?" Angel turned to her sharply. "What are you talking about?"

"Close enough to naked. Singing about those things you do. All the women."

Angel closed his eyes and fought the urge to rub his temples in frustration. He wasn't surprised at Cora's words, but he was surprised that she was saying them in front of other people. Reverend Jones and his mom's church friends glanced away, making embarrassed and awkward eye contact with one another. Couldn't his mom see that she was making them uncomfortable?

It was like she couldn't take that he was being praised

for the positive things that he'd done. He didn't want to ar-
gue with her in public. He didn't want to have this conversation at all.

"Okay, Mom," he said, choosing to let it go, like always.

Cora placed her hands on her hips. It was like Angel's
refusal to engage her only rankled her further. Her voice
dripped in quiet disappointment as she said, "You know
that I raised you better than what you're doing. When's the
last time you've been to church? You don't go anymore. I
know that you don't."

It's because of you, he wanted to say. *I stopped going because of you.*

Her rules had gripped his throat like a vise. Growing up
here, he'd been stifled by her, and he'd tried to twist himself
into the version of the son that she wanted. But he didn't
want to change himself. He *liked* himself. He didn't think
that there was anything about him that would make God
love him any less. So why did she always give him such a
hard time?

"How could you be willing to miss out on the opportunity to get to know your son for who he is?" Iris said fiercely,
coming to Angel's side. He looked down at her in surprise.
He thought she'd gone outside already. A pink flush spread
across Iris's brown cheeks. "He's a good person. He's here,
and he's *alive*. You need to love him while you're still able."

Without another word, she grabbed Angel's hand and
together, they walked outside. Ray and Leah were already
waiting in the car. Leah had jumped at the first chance to
escape their mom.

Angel blinked at Iris as she walked briskly beside him.

"I can't believe her," she hissed, keeping her quick pace.

"I'm sorry to have spoken to your mother like that. I know it might have been disrespectful, and I'll probably apologize to her at some point in the future. But she treated you so horribly, I couldn't listen to another word!"

He didn't say anything. He was thinking, watching her. A realization crystalized in the forefront of his mind.

"I want you to look at me," she said, stopping abruptly. She lifted her hands and firmly rested them on either side of his face. "You are a wonderful person, and no one should ever speak to you like that, least of all your own mother."

Her chest rose and fell quickly on deep breaths. She was fuming, all because she was feeling protective over him. He stared at her, feeling too many things at once. He, who wrote love songs for a living, could only close his eyes and lean his forehead against hers and breathe her in.

"Okay?" she said, wanting an answer from him.

"Yeah," he said. "I hear you."

"Good."

He was beyond touched by her concern. She didn't resist as he took her hand and they walked together to the car.

Back at the hotel, Ray and Leah went to their rooms, and Iris went to hers before changing into flats and knocking on Angel's door. In the minutes that they'd been separated, he'd been able to think clearly about what he'd been feeling. He let her inside, and she lightly touched his cheek as she passed him. She sat at the edge of the bed and let out a deep exhale.

"I'm *exhausted*," she said, looking at him. "I'm sure you are too."

He came to stand in front of her. His heart pounded in a steady, strong rhythm.

"I want you," he said.

She laughed and raised her eyebrows. "Is this foreplay?"

"No, no, not like that," he said, shaking his head. She blinked, and he hastened to clarify. "I mean, yes, I want you in that way too. But what I'm trying to say is that I want you in my life, Iris. I don't just want to see where things go with us. I want to say, for real, that I'm yours and you're mine."

He watched her face change. Her smile slipped from her face as she gazed at him seriously.

"I know you probably don't want to be out in public with me because of everything that comes along with it, and I understand that," he said. "I won't ask you to go on red carpets with me or to places where there will be tons of paparazzi or people around hounding us. I can be so, so careful." He paused, looking at her. She was still listening with rapt attention. "Tonight, I wanted to sit next to you and hold your hand. I don't want to lie and say that you're just my friend. It feels like it's watering down what we have. I know you've been through so much, and I don't want to pressure you to do anything right now. I'm here and I'll wait until you're ready. I just needed to be real with you."

Iris was quiet for a long time, looking at him. As his adrenaline wore down, he realized how nervous he was to hear her response. He sat beside her and resisted the urge to touch her until she spoke.

"You and I came out of nowhere," she said quietly. "I never could have expected anything like this, and I'm honestly still trying to wrap my mind around it."

"I know," he said.

She placed her hand over his, and his pulse quickened again.

"It would be a *really* big transition for me to be known as your girlfriend," she said. "So if we're going to do this, we would need to take it very, very slowly."

"As slow as possible," he said eagerly. "Slower than a turtle. Slower than a *sloth*."

She laughed, and it was music to his ears.

"I'm serious," he said. "Whatever you need."

"The first step is talking to Calla about it," she said. "And then I have to find a way to bring this up to my boss. I have no idea what she's going to say. But I need time to think about how to tell her. We definitely should wait until your ambassador contract ends after the holidays. It will be less of a risk then."

That was months from now, but he would wait. Five months was nothing if it meant that he could really have her.

"Whatever you need," he repeated.

She leaned in and kissed him. He pressed his hand to her upper back and held her there against him.

"I appreciate you being so forthcoming with me," she said as their noses brushed. "It's one of my favorite things about you. I never have to guess how you feel or what you're thinking because you'll tell me."

"I will always be honest with you," he said.

Quietly, she whispered back, "I'll always be honest with you too."

He kissed her again, slow and sweet. Then exhaustion settled over him. He flopped down on his side, and Iris lay in front of him.

"You look as tired as I feel," she said, smiling.

He pulled her closer, inhaling her perfume. It made him dizzy with happiness. His eyes began to close as she wrapped her arm around his waist and crossed her legs with his. She rested her face in the space between his neck and shoulder. They built a comfortable cocoon.

She whispered something to him about needing to wake up at the crack of dawn for her flight. He nodded drowsily, too content to move with her there in his arms. He fell into the deepest, most soothing sleep of his life.

23

IN THE MORNING, IRIS WOKE TO FIND HERSELF WRAPPED
securely in Angel's embrace. Both too exhausted to get up
and change last night, they'd fallen asleep fully dressed. Angel
looked so peaceful while he slept. Gently, reverentially,
Iris touched his face, brushing her fingers across his brow
and his nose ring, down to his lips. This man wanted to be
hers and hers alone. He'd agreed to take things slow. Her
heart felt full, brimming over with joy and amazement.

When she looked at their situation from a bird's-eye
view, it almost seemed miraculous that they'd found each
other. But right now, as he dozed before her in the early-
morning hours before the sun had risen, she wasn't thinking about his fame or her ordinariness. She knew only that
she wanted them to have a fair chance at something real
and she wanted to be brave enough to try.

Angel stirred, blinking. He smiled sleepily at her and
nuzzled closer, placing a kiss against her collarbone.

"Good morning," he whispered.

"Good morning," she whispered back, reluctant to break
the spell. "I have to leave soon."

She was flying back to Newark. Angel had purchased her roundtrip flight, first class. His flight to JFK was later in the afternoon.

"Stay," he said, voice husky as he pulled her closer, until she was sidled up against him and there was no space between their bodies.

"I *really* wish I could."

But she had to get home. Violet had purchased a new car and had volunteered to pick Iris up from the airport and take her to their parents' house, where Iris would then pick up Calla and return home to go through her usual Sunday-evening ritual of preparing for work.

She slipped from Angel's embrace and her heart squeezed as he rose and drowsily kissed her. She promised that she'd call him once her flight landed. Angel planned to be in Manhattan all week at the recording studio, so they made plans to meet up again in a few days.

Iris slept during the first half of the flight, and she spent the second half thinking of what she'd say to Dominique about her and Angel. It racked Iris's nerves something serious to admit to her boss that she and Angel were in a relationship, but she was happy with him and she wanted to hold on to that, to preserve it. And since they'd agreed to wait until his ambassadorship ended in a few months, Iris had plenty of time to think about how she'd broach the topic with Dominique. She just hoped that her decision wouldn't impact Dominique's opinion of her.

The positive news was that Calla had met Angel and they'd gotten along. They'd looked so sweet together when they'd interacted at the store last weekend. It gave Iris hope.

With time, maybe she could have the partnership that she'd been looking for after all.

When the plane landed at Newark, Iris switched off airplane mode on her phone as her seatmates and others in first class stood immediately, even though the flight attendant hadn't opened the main door. Iris was rolling her eyes at their lack of patience when her phone vibrated again and again with alerts that she'd missed during her flight. There were over a hundred messages in the group chat that she shared with her sisters, as well as voice mail alerts from Lily and Violet. Angel had left her a voice mail too, and he'd sent a text. Call me ASAP.

Calla. Something happened to Calla.

It was Iris's first thought. But Calla was with her parents. And if something had happened to her, why hadn't Dahlia or Benjamin called?

With shaking hands, Iris started to call Dahlia, but her phone vibrated again. Lily was calling.

"Lily, what's going on?" Iris said, answering. "Is Calla okay?"

Her seatmate glanced down at her as he retrieved his suitcase from the overhead compartment.

"What? Calla's fine," Lily said, but there was a hint of nervousness in her voice. "Where are you? Are you still on the plane?"

"Yes, I just landed." Iris's shoulders sagged in relief, knowing that Calla was okay. "Why is everyone calling me? Is Dad okay? Did something happen to his back again?"

"Dad's fine too," Lily said. In the background, she could hear Violet saying something about their group chat. Lily asked, "Have you checked our messages?"

"No, I haven't had a chance to." Iris lowered her voice as people began to pass her as they exited the plane. "Why?"

There was a weighted pause on the other end of the line. Iris remembered Angel's text, asking her to call him ASAP. An eerie feeling overtook her.

"*Why, Lily?*" she prompted.

"Um, okay, so someone took pictures of you and Angel last night and it's all over the internet," Lily finally said. "We sent you links."

Iris jerked her phone away from her ear and opened the group chat. Violet had sent a link to a gossip blog, one that Iris didn't recognize because she didn't read gossip blogs for fun. But she did recognize herself and Angel in the photograph. It had been taken right after they'd left the ceremony. Angel was leaning his forehead against hers, closing his eyes, and her hands were placed on either side of his face. It had been an intimate, *private* moment, where she'd felt the need to protect him from whatever bullshit his mother had spewed. And now their moment was displayed for the world to see, along with a bold headline: **ANGEL SEEN NUZZLING NOSES WITH A MYSTERY WOMAN IN HIS HOMETOWN.**

Iris inhaled a shaky breath. Okay, it wasn't too, too bad. It was dark, and you couldn't *really* see her face. It could've been any woman.

She kept scrolling. Then she saw the second photograph of them walking hand in hand to the car, taken head-on. Here, her identity was unmistakable.

"*Oh shit,*" she whispered. Her breathing turned shallow. She dropped her phone in her lap.

She'd been so caught up in the moment last night, so

incensed and filled with fierce care for Angel, she hadn't even thought about how people might be around to see them, that someone would take a picture and share it.

"Iris? Iris! Can you hear me?" Lily was still on the phone.

"Ma'am?" A flight attendant appeared, leaning across the empty seat beside Iris. "We need you to exit the plane now. Do you need any assistance?"

Numbly, Iris looked around her. She was the only person left in her section.

"S-sorry," she stammered, standing on shaky legs. She got up and grabbed her suitcase, placing her phone between her shoulder and her ear. "Lily, I'm trying to get off the plane now."

"We're here waiting for you," Lily said.

Iris walked briskly through the airport in a fog of confusion. Pictures of her and Angel had made their way to the internet. She'd been called his *mystery woman*, but her face was plainly shown for everyone to see. For *her boss and colleagues* to see. She was supposed to have time to tell everyone in her own way—especially Calla. This was everything she'd wanted to avoid.

Fuck. Fuck. Fuck.

She spotted Violet's new sleek silver car as soon as she stepped outside.

Violet rushed to open her door and she ran to Iris and wrapped her in a hug. "Are you okay?" she asked, leaning back and looking at Iris in concern.

"No," Iris said.

Lily took Iris's suitcase and put it in the trunk. "Come on," she said. "Let's at least get out of the airport."

"This isn't the end of the world," Violet was saying as they got in the car.

"*It's not?*" Iris's heart was hammering so hard, like it was ready to burst. Like she'd run the world's longest marathon and her heart was seconds away from giving out. Her palms were drenched in sweat. She felt like she was seconds away from puking.

"Well, you look good as hell in those pictures," Violet pointed out. "The body is giving!"

"That's not helping!" Iris said, exasperated, terrified.

Lily turned around to face her. "The moment between the two of you looked so tender. I'm so sorry that someone took a picture and ruined it."

Iris's phone vibrated again, and her stomach seized. Angel was calling.

"Angel?" she said, motioning to Lily to turn down the radio.

"Where are you?" He spoke urgently, his voice dripping in concern.

"I'm on my way home from the airport. Have you seen that article?"

"I have," he said. "It's bullshit. I'm so sorry. We—"

"Are they allowed to do that?" Iris said, interrupting him. Her brain had shifted full throttle into problem-solving mode. "They can't post our picture like that without our consent, can they? Can we get them to take it down?"

Angel sighed in frustration. "I wish it was that easy. I really do. But it's not about our consent. All they need is consent from the person who took the picture, and we don't know who took it. It could have been anyone there last night." Softly, he added, "Either way, the image is already being shared online outside of that blog."

Iris blinked, staring blankly at the back of Violet's headrest. She leaned forward and rested her face between her knees. She felt dizzy.

"Oh my God," she mumbled.

"This is all my fault," Angel said angrily. "I shouldn't have asked you to come. I should have told you to wait to say anything until we got in the car. But I was being so selfish. I wanted you with me. I'm so sorry. But it's going to be okay. Iris, do you hear me?"

A dull buzzing had taken over her brain. She could barely respond. A block of ice lodged itself in her stomach.

"Iris, I have my publicist, Claudia, on the other line," he continued. "You remember her? I'm going to add her in, so that you can hear what she has to say, okay?"

Iris blinked and nodded, forgetting that Angel couldn't see her.

"Iris," a woman's voice said. Her tone was sharp, direct. "I'm Claudia Chin, Angel's publicist. I'm sorry that we're speaking again under such stressful circumstances, but I want you to know that we're containing this situation as much as we can. It's often best to wait until these things die down. Eventually, the media will move on to a new story. For the sake of your protection, we're going to put out a statement saying that Angel has no comment and to please respect his privacy. His fans don't have a history of harassing people, so that's good."

Iris's throat went dry. She'd been worried about Dominique, but she hadn't even thought about Angel's fans. She'd witnessed firsthand how much they loved him. Would they be upset that she was dating him? Were they looking for her online? Her barely used Instagram account was private, but would they still try to find out more about her anyway? What if they hacked into her account and found pictures of her and Calla? She tried to tell herself that something like that would be wild and unlikely, but it shook her nerves nonetheless.

"Iris?" Angel said, snapping her to attention. "Are you there?"

"Yes," she said, clearing her throat.

Claudia promised Iris that she'd check in again in a few hours. After she hung up, Iris swallowed, hard.

"This is so bad, Angel," she said quietly.

"It's going to be okay," he repeated. "I swear to you. I'm not going to let any of this affect you."

It seemed like such a silly thing to say. She wanted to believe him, but she couldn't.

"I'm on my way to the airport now," he said. "I'm going to come see you as soon as I land, okay? If you need anything— *anything*—please let me know, and I'll do it."

"Okay," she said. She hated how weak she sounded. She wasn't a weak person.

After she and Angel hung up, she bit the bullet and scrolled through social media. She searched Angel's hashtags and his fan accounts. She'd become well accustomed with this search during the planning stages of his brand ambassadorship. Back then she'd been looking through these accounts for business purposes. Now it was personal.

The pictures of them were everywhere. She knew better than to read the comments, but she did anyway.

Who is that girl???

She's pretty! Nice to see him with a normal person for once. Maybe I'm next!

She better get her hands off my man

I swear that's the girl who was at his Refine event in DC!! She was working the event! He was all up in her face!

The block of ice hardened in Iris's stomach. She imagined Dominique and everyone else at SFB reading these comments. She was *so* screwed.

"What did Angel say?" Lily asked.

"Why can't people just mind their business?!" Violet asked angrily. "Trust me, from experience I know how upsetting it is to feel like the whole world knows about your personal life, but people have short attention spans! They'll forget!"

"Are you okay?" Lily reached in the backseat and rested her hand on Iris's knee when Iris didn't respond to either of them.

Iris focused on breathing deeply, trying to calm her frantic thoughts. She felt like her head was going to explode.

"I—"

Her barely formed thought froze on her tongue as her phone vibrated again with a new alert. An email. From Dominique. She'd marked it as urgent. There was no message, just a subject line: I need to meet with you ASAP.

Not *first thing tomorrow morning*. Not *call me later*. She needed to meet in person with Iris *now*.

Iris's heart thudded rapidly. She steeled herself and looked up at her sisters.

"Violet," she said, trying to sound calm, although calmness was the last thing that she felt. "Can you turn the car around and drive me into the city?"

24

WITH SWEATY PALMS, IRIS WALKED THROUGH THE SAVE Face Beauty halls. Her footsteps echoed throughout the empty space. A ball of anxiety ping-ponged in her stomach. When she reached Dominique's office, she found Dominique leaning against her desk, wearing a purple tennis dress and a matching visor. Dominique played in a tennis league on Sundays. Iris had taken her boss away from her favorite pastime. Dominique looked up.

"Iris," she said, eyeing her. "Come in."

Heart hammering, Iris squared her shoulders and stepped inside. She glanced at the life-size cutout of Angel and her stomach squeezed. She quickly averted her eyes.

"Your personal life is none of my business, Iris, truly," Dominique said, folding her arms across her chest. "But these photographs of you and Angel . . . He's our *brand ambassador*. You are a representative of this company. How did this even happen?"

During the drive into the city, Iris thought about what she'd say to Dominique, how she'd explain herself. In the end, she decided that there was no point in lying. Dominique wasn't stupid. The truth was plain to see in the photographs. As complicated as it was, Iris was just going to tell the truth.

"While on the tour, Angel and I got closer and"—Iris briefly squeezed her eyes closed, hating that she'd have to admit this unprofessional truth—"things did turn romantic between us. It was completely unplanned. I was going to tell you once I figured out the right approach, but the pictures surfaced before I could say anything. We've been so careful, but last night was the one time that we weren't. I'm so sorry."

Dominique watched Iris silently. The silence was so loud and pointed, Iris wondered if Dominique could hear the sound of her frantic heartbeat. Then Dominique emitted a long, weary sigh.

"You're the *last* person who I'd expect to be caught up in something like this," she said. "You came up with this fabulous rollout plan that turned things around for the company. It was *amazing* work, Iris. But now all that anyone will be able to think about is that you had an affair with our brand ambassador. What if people assume that he only agreed to work with us because he's involved with you? It could jeopardize the legitimacy of our products and our reputation *again*." She shook her head, so sad, so dismayed. "When I saw you talking to him in the hall all those weeks ago, something told me that the two of you looked a little *too* friendly. But I thought, *No, Iris wouldn't cross the line.* I thought that you knew better."

"I *do*." Iris couldn't take seeing her boss and mentor so utterly disappointed in her. She ran an agitated hand through her hair. Suddenly, now face-to-face with Dominique, Iris realized the true idiocy of her actions. She'd been so starved for affection, she'd let herself get swept away by the idea of romance—with a *celebrity*, of all people—and along the way she'd lost sight of reality, thinking that somehow things would turn out okay in the end. She'd wrapped herself in a web of delusion. And now look what happened. It had all blown up in her face.

"I *do* know better," she said hoarsely, stomach sinking. "I don't know what I was thinking. I'm so sorry."

Dominique uncrossed her arms as she continued to look at Iris, pressing her hands flat on her desk. "I was planning to tell you this tomorrow, but I've been talking with Pat and Ed," she said. "We're creating a new VP of strategic initiatives position particularly for the online space. Unanimously, we decided that the role should be yours."

Iris blinked. It was mental whiplash. Her mouth opened and closed. She was so thrown, she didn't know what to say.

"Again, I was going to talk to you about this *tomorrow*," Dominique continued. "But given this current situation, I thought it would be best to let you know what's at stake. I can't tell you who you should or should not be involved with in your personal life, but what I will say is that the choices we make in our private lives can be held against us when they become public. My advice to you is to look at the bigger picture and determine what does and doesn't fit. Sometimes we have to make sacrifices that we regret in the moment, but we're thankful for them later. I've had to make many sacrifices to be in this position, believe me."

Iris wrung her hands together, harried and anxious as she looked at her boss. She remembered her ambitions from her early twenties, before Terry and Calla, before life had thrown her the sharpest curveball. She'd wanted corporate world domination. She imagined seeing her headshot on the company website with Vice President of Strategic Initiatives printed below her face. The mental image didn't bring on an effusive rush like it might have in the past, but . . . she had to be realistic. She was good at her job. Really good. She'd be good at this new position too and it definitely would come with a bigger paycheck. After what she'd done, it was a miracle that the job was even still on the table.

She'd spent the last few weeks living in a fairy tale, one where a seemingly untouchable prince had found a maiden and they'd fallen for each other despite the odds. But she wasn't Cinderella. She had a child and a mortgage. As much as it killed her, there were sacrifices that she'd need to make too. It was time to wake up and accept her reality.

She thought of Angel's face this morning, so peaceful and content as he'd slept with his arms wrapped around her. Her chest ached as she took a deep breath and nodded.

"I'm interested in the promotion," she finally said, swallowing hard.

Dominique's eyebrows raised as she tilted her head. "So, you understand what I'm saying."

It wasn't a question. Dominique leveled her eyes at Iris.

"I understand," Iris said. "My personal life won't be an issue moving forward." She cleared her throat and met Dominique's gaze head-on. "I'd love to talk more about the position tomorrow."

Dominique's lips curved into a satisfied smile. "First thing tomorrow, come see me and we'll go over details."

———

THE STREETLIGHTS WERE beginning to cut on as Iris looked out her living room window and watched Angel's car pull into her driveway. During her meeting with Dominique, Angel's team had put out a statement saying that Angel had no comment on the pictures and that he'd asked everyone to respect his privacy. The photos were still circulating online. Luckily, it seemed that people were more curious than anything. The discourse hadn't turned malicious. A few more people had recognized Iris from the Refine meet-and-greet tour, but so far, no one had come forward and identified her by name. That might have been the only saving grace.

Janet and Viv had seen the pictures, because of course they had. They'd blown up Iris's phone with text after text.

I knew that guy I saw you with last week looked familiar!!! Janet messaged. Why did he tell me that his name was Tom???

They were trying to keep things a secret, obviously! Viv texted. Iris, you have to tell us *everything* about him!! Dinner soon?!

Iris had groaned and immediately closed out of the group chat. Now she'd have to worry about the other parents in town gossiping about her. She prayed that their children wouldn't overhear them and say something about it to Calla at day camp.

At this point, Iris wasn't even angry with whoever took and sold the photos. Like Angel said, it could have been anyone. He was a public figure. It was expected that people would want documentation of having seen him in the flesh. The only person that Iris was angry with was herself.

Angel got out of his car and walked up the driveway. Iris's stomach twisted and turned.

She glanced at the staircase, confirming that Calla was still asleep upstairs in her room, and she met Angel at the door before he could ring the bell. He stood there, waiting, looking impossibly handsome as always. But he also looked haggard and exhausted. She let him inside and glanced up and down her street, making sure that they weren't being watched before swiftly closing the door behind him.

"Hey," Angel said softly.

He reached for Iris and she let him wrap his arms around her. He leaned his face against her shoulder and breathed deeply. She held on to him and cataloged his scent and the rhythm of his breathing, the tight, firm feeling of his embrace. She took a mental picture of it all, trying her best to commit everything about him to memory.

"Hey," she said, barely above a whisper.

She led Angel over to the couch and they sat down. He rested his hand on her knee, as if he couldn't keep himself from touching her.

"I'm sorry it took me so long to get here," he said. "How are you?"

Her voice shook slightly as she said, "I'm okay."

He tilted his head, looking at her more closely, like he didn't believe her, waiting for her to be honest.

"Well, I guess I'm not," she said, tugging her bottom lip between her teeth. "But how are *you*? Have the pictures negatively affected you in any way?"

He shook his head. "No, of course not."

He rested his palm against her thigh and shifted closer to her. His gaze was focused, direct. "I know that you were really worried about your privacy, and I feel so damn horrible that it was compromised. I'm really sorry, Iris."

"I know you are," she said softly. "But you don't have to apologize. It wasn't your fault."

He reached for her hands and held them firmly in his own. "I'm still sorry. Your privacy—your happiness—is so important to me."

The feeling of their hands pressed together, combined with his intense, tender stare was too much. It was making it harder for her to do what she knew she needed to do, what she wished that she didn't have to do. She took a sharp, deep inhale and forced herself to speak.

"I met with my boss today," she said. "She wants to promote me to a VP role."

Angel's face broke into a surprised smile. "For real?"

Iris nodded, beginning to feel miserable.

"That's so dope! Congratulations." He leaned in to hug her but paused as he observed her tight expression. "You were worried about how your boss would feel about our relationship, but if she's promoting you now, that's a good thing, right?"

"She wasn't thrilled about the pictures," Iris said quietly. "I didn't have the chance to tell her about us like I wanted to. She had to find out along with everyone else." Iris stared blankly at her lap. She couldn't look at him as she spoke again. "It was already risky enough with me being a director, but especially now at the VP level, I really have to be careful with the decisions that I make moving forward."

Angel fell quiet. Lowly, he murmured, "What are you saying?"

Iris swallowed thickly. The words felt too painful to speak. She briefly squeezed her eyes closed and reminded herself to be pragmatic, to be reasonable. She felt tears gathering at the back of her eyes.

"I think it would be best if we decided to just be friends," she said.

Angel stiffened. Iris gazed at his crestfallen face and hastened to fill the thick silence that had blanketed the room.

"I told you from the beginning that it wouldn't look good for me to be involved with you," she said. The words tumbled so quickly from her mouth, she could barely catch her breath. "I said it could only work if we kept this between us, and for a moment, I thought maybe if we had time to tell people, that wouldn't have to be the case, but now those pictures are out there, and everyone at my office has probably seen them. It's a miracle that my boss didn't decide to fire me, and instead, she remembered that I'm valuable to the company. But I'm not valuable if I'm involved in a relationship with someone we're paying to represent us. In a few months, you'll have to start promoting our holiday campaign, and—"

"So I'll stop being the brand ambassador," he said.

"*What?*" Iris cried, jumping to her feet. Angel stood as well. "No, *no*. You can't do that. There's a contract in place. You can't decide that you don't want to be the brand ambassador anymore right before our most important season. And you can't decide that you want to do that because of *me*."

"You're way more important to me than this ambassador deal," he said fiercely.

"Breaking your contract would only make things *worse*. Not just for me, but for the whole company. This ambassador deal was supposed to save us." She brought her hands to her temples. Voice cracking, she said, "We have to be sensible."

"I can't be *sensible* about you breaking up with me." Angel stepped closer to her. "I'm sorry for what I said about breaking my contract. I won't do that. But I finally have you, Iris. You can't really think that I'd be willing to let you go so easily. There has to be a way that we can make this work. If me being the ambassador is a problem, let's do what we said originally. We'll lay low until my contract is over. They won't care after that."

"Angel," she whispered. She closed her eyes again and wrapped her arms around her torso, physically pained. He'd made her so happy for a short time. She hated to give him up, but she *had* to. "It's not just about my job. Our lives are too different. It will be too hard. Please."

"Look at me," he said with a soft fierceness that made her open her eyes. He held her face in his hands. Goose bumps spread over her skin. Her brain was misfiring, fighting a torturous battle with her heart.

"I still mean everything I said last night," he said. "I'm yours and I want you to be mine. I want to come to your house and spend the weekend with you. I want to take baths with you at night and help you at your parents' shop in the morning. I want to get to know your family better, especially Calla. Yes, our lives are different right now, but *we* aren't different from each other. Not in the ways that matter. I see you and you see me." He lowered his voice, slowly bringing his mouth down to hers. "Think about it. Think about how happy we could be."

He kissed her with such passion, her knees buckled. She leaned into him and clutched at his arms as she kissed him back. Her natural response to him only increased her panic.

If she didn't push him away now, she never would. She'd end up compromising her place at Save Face Beauty and who knew what else. No matter how much she cared for Angel, she had to think rationally. She allowed herself these last few moments to kiss and hold him. She'd never felt such deep joy and sadness at the same time.

Finally, she forced herself to back away. "I'm so sorry," she said shakily. "I wish things could be different. Please listen to what I'm saying."

Angel stared at her fixedly. His hands opened and closed at his sides.

"I think you're making a mistake," he said finally with an air of defeat. "I really do. We've got something special. I've felt that since the first day we met, and I ran after you to give you the flower that fell out of your hair. I just wish you could see it too, but you won't let yourself. Why? What are you so afraid of?"

"I'm not afraid of anything," she said hoarsely, wanting so badly to believe that to be true.

He shook his head, gaze intent on her face. "I thought you said you'd always be honest with me."

She stood in silent agony as he bent down and kissed her on the forehead before he turned and walked out the door.

Iris held her breath until she heard his car start and pull out of her driveway. Then when she was sure that she was all alone, she placed her face in her hands and finally allowed herself to cry.

Tomorrow, she promised silently as tears ran down her cheeks. *I'll pull myself together and move forward with my life tomorrow.*

She didn't have any other choice.

25

HE WONDERED IF HE'D HURT LESS IF HE'D BEEN HIT BY A bus instead.

It had been a week since Angel had driven away from Iris's house, holding his bruised heart in his hands, and to put it mildly, he was struggling. This wasn't the first breakup that Angel had survived. He'd been dumped via text and voice mail, even over Instagram DM. But those breakups hadn't caught him by surprise. In his previous relationships, fun but fleeting, the realization that things had run their course had always been mutually understood.

But it had been different with Iris. It had felt *real*. He couldn't stop thinking about her. He felt like he was moving through quicksand every day, sinking lower and lower until missing her slowly consumed him. After the pictures had appeared online, he'd assumed that she'd want some space. He was sorry as hell that he'd put her in a situation where anyone could photograph them, that he'd thought a small event in his hometown would be safe. But he didn't think that Iris would end everything completely. She was concerned about her job and how things would look for her, and as much as it pained him, he understood where she was coming from. Fear that he'd push her away completely kept him from calling again and again, begging her to change her mind, for them to find a way to work things out. Because there had to be a way, right?

But Iris was steadfast. She knew what she wanted. What else could he do but respect her decision?

He'd done this to himself, really. From day one, she'd told him that she was unavailable. But he'd wanted her so badly, he'd hoped in vain to change her mind. He hadn't thought of the consequences.

If he'd known that he'd end up with his heart shattered, would he still have pursued her? Probably. He knew how stupid he sounded. But when things had been good, they'd been *good*.

"Angel, yoo-hoo." His manager, Valerie, reached across her desk and waved her hand in Angel's face. "You here with me?"

Angel blinked, taking in the surroundings of Valerie's office. They were talking about his next endorsement deal with a sneaker brand. He was scheduled to record a beauty secrets video for *Vogue*, using Save Face Beauty's products. And Valerie was pushing the label to pitch Angel for the Macy's Thanksgiving Day Parade or New Year's Rockin' Eve, preferably both. *Work. Right.* He should be paying attention to the business that paid him. He rubbed a hand over his face and sat up in his chair.

"Yeah, I'm listening," he said. "Sorry."

"No worries." Valerie eyed him. She hadn't said much about the pictures of him and Iris, because she usually didn't involve herself in Angel's dating life, but she wasn't oblivious to his unusually quiet mood. "You sure you're okay? You want some coffee or something?"

"Nah, I'm good. Honest."

Really, he just needed to channel his misery in the best way he knew how. He'd been writing sad love songs all week. He was anxious to record them.

"Just thinking about the studio," he said.

"About that," Valerie said, shuffling the papers on her desk. She gave Angel an uneasy look that rattled him. "You know that 'Summertime Fine' rose back to the top spot on the charts. The sales are still phenomenal. The label is over the moon."

Angel nodded. He was well aware of this. Wasn't it a good thing?

"I had a long call with the execs at Capitol this morning. They basically asked me to encourage you to drop the full-on soul angle," she said, wincing. "They've listened to the bundle of songs you sent recently, and while they agree that the songs are good, they see your soul songs not as singles but as tracks that flesh out the larger album. They aren't confident that an entirely soul album will pull in the same numbers, and they really want you and Malik to focus on the pop R & B angle again, because that's what's working. You know how they are about taking risks."

Angel rubbed his temples and let out a deep sigh of frustration. "But what about what I think?" he asked. "I don't want to be a one-trick pony who keeps doing the same thing over and over just because it's popular. I'm an artist. Don't I deserve the opportunity to evolve and expand?"

It seemed that at every stage of his life, someone was

always trying to control him or hold him back from reaching his full potential. He was tired of it.

"I'm working on it," Valerie said earnestly. "I promise I am."

Angel nodded but he wasn't sure where he could place his faith.

After he left Valerie's office, he rode downtown to Violet's studio for a fitting. He had an appearance on a late-night television show next week. Ray sat beside Angel in the backseat as Gabriel drove. Ray grinned and laughed quietly at something on his phone. Angel quirked an eyebrow, looking at his best friend.

"I wanna laugh too," Angel said. "What's funny?"

Ray glanced up and slid his phone into his pants pocket. "Nothing. Just texting Bree."

Angel blinked. "Is that a thing now?"

Ray nodded, shrugged. "We're chilling. It's casual, but I like her a lot. She's cool as hell."

Thinking of Bree made him think of Iris. Misery gripped him. But he wouldn't bring down Ray's vibe.

"That's good," he said. "Really."

Ray smirked but then glanced away. Almost like he felt guilty to be happy when Angel was not.

"Iris probably just needs some time, bro," Ray said. "I can tell that she really cares about you."

He knew that Iris cared about him. That was never the issue. Maybe they were just an example of right people but wrong time and wrong place.

*Wrong time, wrong place. I want to see her
    face . . .*

Song lyrics. He pulled his notepad from his back pocket and jotted down the lines. He was burning to get back to the studio, even if his label had basically said screw him and the music he'd been recording.

"Yeah, maybe." Angel shifted his gaze to the traffic on the street.

When they arrived at Violet's studio, they were greeted by her assistant, Alex. Music played in the wide space, and Violet was sorting through clothes on a rack. Angel hadn't seen her since the night of the Save Face Beauty party. He assumed she knew what had happened between him and Iris. When she turned and flashed him a sweet but anxious smile, his assumptions were confirmed.

"Hi," she said, walking over and hugging him. "It's good to see you."

"It's good to see you too." He hugged her back and they stood there for a silent moment.

Violet eased away but didn't release her hold on him. She looked at him closely. "How are you?"

"I feel like shit," he said, laughing softly.

Violet shook her head. "I'm so sorry about you and Iris."

"You don't have to be sorry about it." He forced a smile and nodded at the clothing rack. "What you got for me today?"

Violet eyed him for a beat before leading him over to the clothes. "I just received some new pieces from Prada today," she said. "I've also got these dope Phillip Lim jumpsuits . . ."

Angel listened attentively as Violet showed off the items that she'd curated for him. He tried on a handful of outfits and Alex and Ray weighed in with their opinions. Angel was grateful to be working, to be focusing on something other than Iris. But he couldn't stand in front of Iris's sister and pretend that he hadn't been thinking about her all day every day.

Violet was adjusting the collar on his tweed jacket. He lowered his voice and asked, "How is Iris?"

Violet's hands stilled as she looked up at him. She glanced around. Ray and Alex were standing by Violet's desk, too far away to overhear their conversation. She looked back at Angel.

"Iris is okay," she answered. "Sad. But okay."

On one hand, he felt relief, knowing that he wasn't alone in his grief over losing what they'd had, but hearing that Iris was also sad made him only feel worse.

"She misses you," Violet added quietly. "She hasn't said it, but I know she does."

Angel closed his eyes briefly, feeling another sharp pang in his chest. "I miss her too."

"For a long time, I thought of Iris as my strong, impenetrable big sister," Violet said. "But the older I get, the more I realize that Iris is just as vulnerable as the rest of us, maybe even more so. She's just better at hiding it."

He wished that Iris would let him be there for her. They could be so good together. But it wasn't what she wanted.

Right person. Wrong time. Wrong place.

"I feel guilty," Violet said, chewing the inside of her cheek. "I persuaded her to see where things could go with you, but it got more serious than I was expecting, and now you're both heartbroken." She frowned. "I'm really sorry."

"You don't have to apologize for anything." Angel hugged her sideways and smiled weakly. "If anything, I'm glad you convinced her to try."

Violet smiled back, although it didn't reach her eyes. He couldn't take her being sad too. He needed to lighten the mood.

He looked at his reflection in the mirror and flexed his arms.

"*Sheesh.*" He whistled. "I look good, don't I?"

Violet burst out laughing, which was exactly what he'd hoped would happen.

"You know that you do," she said, rolling her eyes. She fluttered around him, rolling up his jacket sleeves and inspecting the hem.

All the while, he counted the minutes until he could return to the studio and make something out of the sadness in his heart.

26

AT WORK, IRIS WAS THE ELEPHANT OF EVERY ROOM THAT she walked into. She could feel her coworkers' stares following her as she moved through the halls or took her seat at a meeting. No one outright asked her about Angel. Instead, when people spoke to her, they made a point to congratulate her on her new role. It was like there was an unspoken rule around the office. Iris probably had Dominique to thank for that. First thing Monday morning after the photo fiasco, Iris had officially accepted the promotion, and Dominique had sent an email to the entire company, sharing the news. She'd written, Iris has been an impeccable member of the Save Face Beauty family for nearly a decade. Her dedication and loyalty to this company are unmatched.

Her dedication and loyalty were the reasons she'd forced herself to let go of Angel, and in turn, she'd left a gaping wound in her chest. She missed him. Missing him had become a physical burden that she carried daily. She felt lethargic and unfocused. Miserable.

Shortly after Dominique's email went out, Iris's inbox filled with congratulatory replies. She didn't have the energy to respond to anyone yet. She walked to the bathroom on her floor and paused as she overheard two women discussing her in their respective stalls.

"How long do you think she's been messing around with him?" one woman asked. "You think they started hooking up during the meet-and-greet tour or after?"

"Who knows," the other woman responded. "But either way, I don't blame her. That man is *fine*, okay? I'd risk it all for him too."

They laughed, and Iris stood frozen in place near the sinks. By the time she snapped to attention as the toilets flushed, it was too late to move without being seen. The women stepped out of the stalls and startled at the sight of her. Faye and Meena. They were on the advertising team. Awkwardly, they glanced at each other, and Iris tried her best not to look mortified.

"Oh, h-hey, Iris . . ." Faye said, clearly fumbling. "Congrats on your promotion, lady!"

"Yes, girl, congrats! So amazing!" Meena said.

"Thank you." Iris forced a smile and hurried past Faye and Meena, escaping into an empty stall. She heard them whispering to each other as they left the bathroom.

That continued to be the way of things over the following days.

Online, it took only a little over a week for the buzz around their photos to die down. Mostly because another celebrity, a pop singer named Meela Baybee, had announced on a red carpet that she was pregnant by one of her backup dancers.

But in Willow Ridge, the interest didn't fade so quickly. Janet and Viv reached out multiple times, asking Iris if she wanted to get lunch or coffee, to which Iris responded that she was too busy with work. When she picked up Calla from karate, she noticed that some of the other parents who usually didn't say more than a passing hi or bye tried to go out of their way to make small talk with her. Even Dahlia's hairstylist drilled Dahlia with question after question during her most recent appointment. But Dahlia, being the loyal mother that she was, didn't give up any information, which annoyed the ladies at the hair salon to no end.

Angel hadn't called or texted. Not that Iris expected him to. She'd asked him to respect her decision, and that was exactly what he was doing. In a way, not hearing from him made things easier. If he came after her, she didn't know if she'd have it in her to turn him away. And their separation was probably for the best. Most likely sooner than later, he'd meet a woman who lived a similar lifestyle, one who didn't have a borderline panic attack when pictures of them appeared in the press. A woman who had a little less at stake. And when the moment arrived that Angel met someone new, Iris would steer clear of the internet so that she didn't have to see him being happy with someone else.

Marie had encouraged Iris to keep a journal to write down her thoughts and feelings about the breakup. She told Iris to write about the good parts of her relationship with Angel and the reasons why she felt they'd need to separate too. She said it was normal if Iris felt like her emotions were all over the place. Breakups were a different form of mourning, something that Iris was familiar with.

Iris figured that her feelings for Angel would ebb and flow until they receded into her periphery. Eventually, they'd shift out of focus so that they weren't constantly at the forefront of her mind.

This was what she told herself as she lay in bed at night, not sleeping. Staring silently at her ceiling, trying not to remember how it had felt to turn over and feel Angel's presence in the bed beside her.

IN HER NEW role, Iris's first order of business was to lay out new goals for the season's fourth quarter. The skincare bundles had sold out online during their Fourth of July sale, and after restocking, they'd almost sold out again. Now it was time to officially focus on the holiday campaign. They were adding a unisex mint-flavored lip balm to the skincare set.

Iris met with the marketing team, and they shared proofs from Angel's recent photo shoot. He was dressed in a shiny white bubble coat and white jeans, wearing fluffy white earmuffs. His lips looked smooth and moisturized as he displayed the new lip balm in his hand.

Iris stared at the photos for so long, her vision started to blur. She'd been trying to force herself to be strong and move on, but looking at his pictures, it hit her all at once just how much she *hadn't* moved on yet. She missed this face. She missed *him*.

She was aware that her coworkers were watching her, not only waiting to hear her opinions on the photos but secretly gauging her reaction. Iris knew that she should care about how she appeared in this moment, but her heartbreak eclipsed everything else.

"I think these look great," she said finally. She tapped a close-up photo of Angel. He was smiling with a mirth in his eyes that he used to direct toward her. "This one's a winner."

After the meeting ended, Iris slipped away into her office. She was supposed to meet Paloma for lunch because Paloma was officially on pregnancy leave and Iris probably wouldn't see her again until after the baby was born. But Iris knew that she'd be crappy company today. She almost wanted to cancel, but Paloma was meeting Iris near the office and she was coming from Long Island City. She was probably almost at the restaurant.

"Hey, Iris?"

Iris glanced up. Bree stood at her door, holding a stack of papers in her hands. She walked toward Iris's desk. "You left these in the conference room. Marketing said these proofs are yours to keep."

Bree slid the images toward Iris, and her heart squeezed as she once again glanced at Angel's smiling face. Iris looked up at Bree. "Thanks so much."

Bree lingered by the desk. "Can I get you anything before your lunch?"

"No, that's all right." Iris managed a smile. "Thank you."

Bree backed away slowly. When she reached the doorway, she turned around and quickly doubled back. "Iris, I just want to say thank you for keeping me on as your assistant instead of finding someone new when you got promoted. I really appreciate it, and I think you're a great boss."

Bree was so bright and chipper, bubbling over with energy. In contrast, Iris felt like a dying energy vampire. She needed some of those good vibes.

"Want to come to lunch with me and Paloma?" she asked. Bree was the perfect person to distract Paloma from Iris's sucky mood.

Bree blinked. "Seriously?"

"Yep. It's on me." Iris grabbed her purse and stood. She flashed her company Amex card. "Or it's on SFB, I should say."

"Of course!" Bree said.

"Great." Iris closed and locked her office door behind them.

They met Paloma at Harry's Italian. She was sitting in a corner booth, wearing a soft pink nap dress. She was positively glowing.

"Oh my God, you look even more gorgeous than the last time I saw you," Iris said as she hugged Paloma. She gingerly placed her hand on Paloma's slightly larger belly. "I'm so jealous. You know I looked like a hot mess when I was pregnant."

"You did not," Paloma said, snorting. "And anyway, I know you're just being nice. I feel like Mrs. Puff."

Iris ignored the prick in her chest at Paloma's *SpongeBob* reference. Had Angel continued watching the show without her?

"I invited Bree," Iris said, shaking thoughts of him away.

Paloma and Bree hugged hello, and then everyone sat down. The server came to their table and they ordered pizza and salad. After he returned with their glasses of water, Iris smiled at Paloma, grateful that seeing her friend had managed to lift her mood.

"How've you been feeling?" Iris asked.

"I'm fine. Switching to remote work was so much easier on my body. The baby's healthy, and my feet are swollen." Paloma took a long sip of her water and waggled her finger. "But I don't want to talk about me. I want to talk about you *and Angel*. I can't believe you held out on me like this!"

Iris's cheeks heated. Maybe if it were just her and Paloma

having lunch, she'd spill. They'd been friends for years. But Bree was here too. Iris glanced at her assistant, who looked back at her in wide-eyed silence. Clearly, Bree wanted to know about Iris and Angel too. Iris felt the need to set an example.

She returned her gaze to Paloma. "I don't know if it's appropriate to discuss that."

"I'm with Ray now," Bree blurted.

Iris balked, whipping her head to look at Bree. "You mean Ray, *Angel's bodyguard*?"

Bree nodded. To her credit, she looked a bit sheepish. "We hooked up during the tour . . . and now we're together."

Iris's mouth fell open. She'd noticed that Bree and Ray had been getting along fairly well . . . But how had she missed the beginning of their relationship when it had happened right under her nose?

Well, actually, she had the answer to that question. She'd been too busy paying attention to Angel.

Iris's knee-jerk reaction was to find fault with Bree, but what harm was there in dating a famous person's bodyguard? Ray wasn't the brand ambassador. Bree hadn't done anything wrong, really. And because Bree had come clean about her and Ray, Iris figured she didn't have much left to hide. Ray was Angel's best friend, so Bree probably already knew the truth anyway.

"Angel and I were seeing each other," she admitted. "It started on the tour and continued for a few weeks after."

"Iris!" Paloma clapped gleefully. "I have to be honest, I didn't know you had it in you, babe! But why are you speaking in the past tense?"

Iris cleared her throat. "We broke up."

Paloma gaped at her. "What? *Why?*"

"Because we didn't make a lot of sense together when it really came down to it. And it was unprofessional." She looked at Bree. "I know everyone is still talking about it. I bet people think I was promoted because of Angel's influence or something crazy like that."

"People *are* pretty curious about whatever happened between y'all. Those pictures were all over the Slack channels for days," Bree said. "But never, and I mean never, did anyone assume that his involvement had something to do with your promotion! You got promoted because you're amazing. You just happened to also be secretly hooking up with one of the sexiest celebrities alive. Both things can be true."

Of course, the server arrived with their pizzas at that exact moment. He looked at Iris curiously before serving each of them a slice and darting away. Iris's face was officially on fire.

"Okay, can I say something?" Paloma asked, dabbing her mouth with a napkin.

Iris nodded as she chewed.

"Do you even want to be VP of strategic initiatives?" Paloma asked. "You don't seem excited about it at all."

Iris shrugged half-heartedly. "It's a new opportunity and it's more money. Dominique handpicked me for it. She thinks this is the right next step, and she's never steered me wrong before." She glanced out the window, releasing a heavy sigh. "She was so disappointed when she found out about me and Angel. I wanted to crawl under a rock."

"Okay, you know I love Dominique," Paloma said. "Love her to pieces. But her being disappointed in you is kind of extra. I know we went through the whole Turks and Caicos drama earlier this year, and that shit sucked, but if *I* were the CEO and you, with your amazing self, as Bree said, were on my team, I would not care if you were dating the brand ambassador as long as you kept things professional in the office. You know why? Because he's only gonna be the brand ambassador for a limited period. Then we'll choose someone else. That's how these things work. You know this." Paloma paused, picking up another pizza slice. "It's obvious that Dominique has been grooming you for years to take her place one day. And I'm sure that your being involved with someone like Angel threw a huge monkey wrench in her plans of finding a successor who would have no desire for a personal life, just like her."

Iris blinked at Paloma's bluntness. But she remained silent, because she realized that Paloma wasn't wrong.

"And listen, I've been with SFB just as long as you have," Paloma continued. "Sometimes I think about leaving, but for now it works. I have all the respect in the world for Dominique. She's a wonderful leader and a great boss, and I know she loves having her life revolve around the company. That's cool. SFB is her baby. But my question for you is, Do you want to *adopt* her baby?"

Bree snorted at Paloma's analogy and Iris couldn't help laughing too.

"I'm serious, though!" Paloma said, smiling. "You're the kind of person who can do anything that she puts her mind to. If you decided that you wanted to run for president, I'd be like *Yeah, okay. That makes sense.* Why stay with SFB?"

Iris's laughter died down. Paloma's question was something that Iris had seriously thought about over the last couple weeks. Why stay if she wasn't happy or fulfilled? Her

initial reasons for staying had been her salary and the stability, which were still very true. But she could find stability
and good pay with another company too. So what was the
reason?

"After Terry died, my life turned upside down," she said.
"So much had changed. I was a new mom and I was a single
parent. But what stayed the same was being at SFB. It was a
relief to show up every day and throw myself into the next
task without having to think about everything that was
happening in my life. I've given so much to Dominique and
this company." She twirled her straw in her glass. "I know
SFB. It's all I've ever known. I thought accepting the promotion would make me feel excited again, but mostly I feel like
I'm wearing a pair of pants that used to be *really* comfortable, and now they don't fit me anymore." She looked up at
Paloma. "Sorry, I'm not as good at analogies as you."

Paloma smiled softly. She reached forward and patted
Iris's hand. "You'll figure it out. A new pair of pants is out
there waiting for you. You just have to want to go shopping."

Iris laughed. "You need to write a book of analogies or
something."

"Ooh, that's an idea." She drummed her fingers against
her belly. "Maybe a children's book. I should call your sister."

"Wait," Bree said, interrupting them. She turned to Iris.
"If you start your own beauty company, please take me
with you."

Iris and Paloma laughed, but Bree looked at Iris, straight-
faced. "I'm not kidding."

"I'm not sure if that's what I want to do," Iris said, answering honestly.

Just weeks ago, she'd told Dominique that she wanted to

ed under duress. She'd mostly been think-
ing about the pictures of her and Angel, and she'd wanted to
enact some kind of damage control over her life. So she'd
latched on to her job, just like after Terry's death.

She didn't know what would come next if she decided to
leave Save Face Beauty, but she didn't want to rush that decision.

If you leave, maybe you can be with Angel.

The thought suddenly took root in the back of her mind,
but she squashed it before it could fully take shape. Because
she also wasn't sure if she was truly ready for a life with
him, out in the open for everyone to see now that they no
longer had the option to take things slow.

And he'd looked so hurt after she'd broken things off.
He probably didn't want to hear from her anyway.

"I'm glad I came out to lunch with y'all instead of mop-
ing in my office," she said.

Bree smiled. "I'm glad you invited me."

"And *I'm* glad to get free lunch on the company." Paloma
raised her glass. "To Dominique."

"To Dominique," Iris and Bree repeated.

AFTER WORK, IRIS drove to pick up Calla from Greenehouse. These days she'd taken to driving with the radio off,
afraid to hear any of Angel's songs, which were played constantly.

Her parents were closing up when she arrived. The last
handful of customers trickled out the door, armed with
their new purchases.

"Hey, hey," Iris called as she walked through the aisles toward the register.

Calla beamed and hopped down from her stool to give Iris a hug. "Hi, Mom."

Today at day camp, they'd gone to the lake. Calla's skin was browner, and she smelled like sunblock and childhood. Iris hugged her close.

Her parents sported exhausted but satisfied smiles.

"Was it a good day?" Iris asked.

"A *great* day," Dahlia said. "We're making out like bandits since the Flower Studio closed."

Iris glanced around the store. She remembered how exhilarated she'd felt weeks ago when she'd ran things for her parents. There was potential here to do more.

"Have you thought about buying the Flower Studio's location?" she asked.

Dahlia and Benjamin paused, glancing at each other.

"We have thought about it," Benjamin said.

"But we just don't have the time," Dahlia said.

"Or energy," Benjamin added.

"Huh," Iris said, nodding.

I could do it, she almost told them. But would that be crazy? Would that be an instance of her overestimating her abilities, adding another responsibility to her already full plate?

Iris continued pondering this on their way home.

"Hey, mind if we make a stop on our way home?" she asked Calla.

In the backseat, Calla quirked an eyebrow. "No. Where are we going?"

"To look at a building."

Iris took the thirty-minute drive to Bridgewood and pulled into the Flower Studio's parking lot. A FOR RENT sign was in the window, and the outdoor greenhouse structure was still set up.

"Hey, wanna get out and look at this store with me?" she asked Calla.

Calla nodded, curious. "Okay."

They walked up to the large windows and Iris shaded her eyes as she peered into the store. It was a nice size, a little larger than Greenehouse. Iris could see where they'd add shelves and hang pots. She pictured rows and rows of colorful, beautiful flowers.

Somewhere along the way, she'd forgotten about her potential. She'd lost sight of the woman who'd moved to the city with big plans and big dreams and the grit and savvy to achieve them. Years ago, she'd eagerly started a marathon, then life had pushed her down. She'd gotten back up, but instead of continuing her race, she'd started running in place. Was she going to continue running in place forever?

"What are we looking for?" Calla asked, mimicking Iris and peering inside the empty storefront.

Iris turned to her daughter. "I'm wondering if Grandma and Grandpop should put another store here. What do you think?"

Calla scrunched up her little face, seriously considering Iris's question. "I think it could be fun."

It was such a pure, innocent response, Iris laughed and hugged her daughter.

27

AFTER ANOTHER DAY OF BEING SURROUNDED BY PEOPLE
for hours on end, Angel welcomed the silence around him
as he sat at his piano. Well, it wasn't completely silent. Maxine snuggled on the floor against his foot, squeakily chewing on her newest toy victim. She usually clung to him when
he was home, but lately, she'd made a point of cuddling with
him whenever she could. No doubt, even his dog could
sense his downcast mood.

He plucked absently at the piano keys, building a melody and jotting down lines as they came to him. Even if this
was another song that his label inevitably rejected, he didn't
have to record or release this song. Tonight, he was seated at
the piano for catharsis.

> *It was the wrong time, wrong place. I wish I could
> see your face.*

He sang quietly to himself, fingers brushing against the
keys.

> *I knew it wouldn't last, but I wish she could get*
> *past . . .*

He trailed off and leaned his forehead against the smooth hardwood of the piano.

"Okay, I've officially had enough of this," Leah said.

Angel jerked his head up and looked at his sister. She had her hands on her hips, frowning at him. Her black lipstick was fierce and severe.

"Huh?" he said.

"Come on." Leah tried to pull him to his feet, but he resisted. "You're coming with me and we're going for a walk to get you out of your funk."

"I'm not in a funk." Angel turned back to the piano. "I'm working."

"No, you're *sulking*. There's a difference," she said. When Angel sighed, she added, "You've been like this for weeks. I understand that you have a certain creative process as an artist, and I respect that, and you. But if you play that same sad melody one more time, I'm gonna call Iris myself and beg her to come over here and talk to you. And Max needs to go for a walk anyway."

At hearing her name and the word *walk* used in the same sentence, Maxine scrambled to her feet and raced to the door.

"Can't you walk her?" Angel asked.

"Yes, but I want you to come with me. If not to get some fresh air, at least for protection in case someone tries to mug me."

Angel gave her a look. Leah walked around the neighborhood by herself all the time.

"You won't leave me alone until I say yes, will you?"

She shook her head. "Nope."

Angel released a weary breath and slowly pushed away from the piano. The sooner they walked Maxine, the sooner he could come back and be left in peace. He grabbed Maxine's leash and slipped on a baseball cap, pulling it low over his face.

Outside, the mid-July evening air was thick and humid. They walked their normal route down West 20th Street toward the High Line. Maxine wagged her short tail and sniffed along the sidewalk. Multiple times, Angel and Leah had to stop her from ingesting an unidentifiable object.

"Okay. I have to be honest. I have an ulterior motive for asking you to go for a walk with me," she said, looking at Angel sidelong. "A few of my friends from church are getting together tonight for game night. You're welcome to come with me if you don't want to be alone."

"Nah, I'm cool." He shook his head. "But thanks for asking."

"You know, my church is really chill," she said. "It's just a bunch of us meeting up to sing and talk. Some of us met through school, and other people connected with the group through a friend of a friend. We're all from different denominations too, but we don't think about that. Everyone just comes together to hang out, and it's really nice. And they already know that you're my brother, so they won't be weird about asking for pictures or anything. We're meeting at my friend Imani's. She doesn't live too far from here."

Angel realized that he hadn't known any of these details about Leah's church because he'd never asked her. Honestly, he hadn't wanted to know. He'd envied that Leah found a new church that she liked and attended every week and that she could do so without hearing their mother's voice in her ear, picking her apart. Because that was how Angel felt every time he'd tried to go to church over the past few years, and it was what had stopped him.

He hadn't talked to his mom since the ceremony in Maren. She'd called and left voice mails, trying to guilt Angel into calling her back. He wasn't sure when he'd return her call, but he'd texted to say he'd reach out to her when he felt ready. What Iris said to him that night had been true. He didn't deserve the way that his mom treated him, and until she could treat him with more respect, he needed time and space from their relationship.

"I'm not sure if I'm in the mood for game night," he said. "But I'll walk you."

Leah's expression turned hopeful. "Okay."

Leah led them in the direction of her friend's apartment on Eleventh and West 23rd. They slowed their walk as they reached her friend's apartment building.

"You sure you don't want to come too?" Leah asked. "We can leave after an hour if you get bored. I just hate the idea of you sitting alone, being so sad!"

Angel smiled softly at his sister. He appreciated her concern, that she wanted him to be happy.

"How about this, I'll come up for a bit and leave after thirty minutes, and I'll take Maxine with me." He paused. "Wait, does your friend care if we bring Maxine?"

Leah shook her head. "Imani has three cats and they *love* Max."

They rang the buzzer and entered Imani's apartment

building. A short guy with dark brown skin and bright green hair answered the door. He had a septum piercing and thick silver hoops in both ears. For a moment, Angel wondered if he'd just willingly agreed to surround himself with Leah and her fellow Gen Z goths.

"Hey, Leah!" the guy said, throwing the door wider. He looked at Angel and his smiled widened. "Oh, and she brought her brother! And the dog!"

Maxine jerked herself free from Angel's hold and dashed into the apartment, barking excitedly. As he followed Leah inside, he was greeted by a handful of her church friends. Some looked to be around Leah's age, but others seemed older, in their late twenties or early thirties. They were a blend of smiling, welcoming faces as they urged Leah and Angel to grab some pizza and find a seat. Imani was one of the people around Angel's age. Chin-length braids framed her face, and as she hugged Angel hello, he remembered to take off his baseball cap.

"Do you know how to play Uno?" Imani asked him.

"He doesn't," Leah answered.

Angel elbowed her. "I don't." Another thing he'd missed out on growing up. "But I can learn quickly."

Imani smiled at him. "Perfect."

It was strange, really, how smoothly the night flowed from that point. They played multiple rounds of Uno (which Angel lost each time), and then they switched to Taboo, then Jenga. Like Leah had said, everyone was chill about Angel being there. Imani's cats made an appearance and surrounded Maxine, purring loudly like little engine motors, and Imani's girlfriend, Janay, plopped one of the cats

into Angel's lap, swearing that he didn't know true joy until
he cuddled with their tuxedo cat, Chester. Janay was right.
Chester was good at cuddling.

After a while, Imani turned on some gospel music,
and everyone started to sing together. From the way their
voices harmonized, Angel could tell that they did this a lot.
Jeremiah—the one with the green hair—in particular had a
strong tenor voice. Imani and another woman named Vee
were perfect altos.

At first, Angel sang along quietly to himself, keeping his
voice no higher than a slight mumble. He was content to
listen to everyone else. He loved the power and strength in
their voices. Hearing them and witnessing this was like a
gift. They were happy to be together with no sense of judgment. They were completely accepting of one another. And
they'd so easily accepted him.

Angel began to sing louder. Singing was *his* gift too, and
he'd been given an opportunity to share his gift with the
whole world. It didn't matter what kind of music he sang,
whether gospel or pop or soul. Despite what anyone said,
his music would still have meaning, whatever he chose
to do.

For too long he'd carried the burden of seeking acceptance. He'd fought for his mom to accept him as he was.
He'd been struggling to get his label to let him record the
kind of music that he wanted to make.

He'd even fought for Iris's acceptance. He'd wanted her
to love him despite their many differences. He couldn't help
that he lived the life that he did. He had little privacy and
sacrificed normalcy most days. But he couldn't change who
he was. He was doing what he loved.

He just had to hope that maybe Iris would come around to accepting him. But it was more important that he accept himself first.

And in that moment, he finally began to.

He ended up staying until game night was finished. Leah's friends hugged him goodbye and Imani forced him and Leah to take home extra slices of pizza wrapped in aluminum foil.

"Before you go," Jeremiah said, tapping Angel's shoulder, "I just wanna say that I'm a big fan of your music. The gospel and the R & B. I can't wait to hear what's next, bro! Keep doing what you're doing."

Maybe this was another one of those otherworldly, divine interventions. Angel didn't know. But it was exactly what he needed to hear.

"I will," he said.

28

BOXES LINED THE FOYER OF ELAINE AND TERRANCE SE-
nior's home. Most of their furniture was covered in shrink-
wrap. In less than a week, they'd be moving to a new town
house in the same neighborhood. It would be much smaller
and a better fit for just the two of them. And with shorter
flights of stairs, Senior would get around more easily.

Iris and Calla had finally come to visit and go through
Terry's things.

"My rosebush seemed to hate me this summer," Elaine
said as she walked with Iris around her garden in their perfectly manicured backyard. She plucked a rose loose, and
the dry petals floated to the ground. "It's like it knows we're
leaving."

Iris took the rose stem and twirled it in her fingers. "Will
you have a garden at your new place?"

"Yes, but much smaller." Elaine gave Iris a proud smile.
"I'll have to order my fertilizer special from Greenehouse
now."

Iris smiled back and winked. "You'll get the family dis-
count too."

After leaving the Flower Studio's vacant lot last week,

Iris had sat up all night, considering the possibilities. Eventually, she'd gotten out of bed and drafted a business plan. First, she just wanted to see if it would be a good idea. And once she realized that it wasn't only a good idea but that it could work *well*, fervor took over her. Bleary-eyed and invigorated, the following morning, she'd shown up at her parents' house before work to present her idea: not only could they rent the Flower Studio's retail place and open a new Greenehouse location, but *she* could be the one to run it. And maybe they'd be able to open more locations in the future.

At first, Dahlia and Benjamin had been shocked. For so long, Iris had a very specific life plan and joining Greenehouse long-term hadn't been part of it. They thought Iris was offering only because of the issues with Benjamin's back. But Iris convinced them that wasn't the case. She was ready for a new challenge—she'd been ready for a while. Then Dahlia and Benjamin had admitted that they were relieved that Iris wanted to join the family business. They wanted to retire in a few years, and when that day came, it meant that they could leave the company in Iris's capable hands.

Dahlia had been so excited, she'd plucked a bottle of champagne from the cabinet and popped it right there at the kitchen table, even though it was only seven thirty a.m. Iris laughed as she took a huge gulp, knowing that she'd need the liquid courage in a couple hours.

As soon as she entered the Save Face Beauty building, she requested a meeting with Dominique. And there in Dominique's office, she shared the news that she was resigning and switching gears to work with her parents.

Dominique had been shocked into silence. She'd literally stared at Iris, slack-jawed. Once she picked her jaw up off the floor, she'd overwhelmed Iris with questions. Wasn't she happy at SFB? Was it the new position? Did she want higher pay?

"No," Iris said as she sat on the other side of Dominique's desk. "I think it's time for me to move on and forge a new path. That's all."

Dominique leaned forward and looked at Iris closely. Finally, she asked, "Is this because of Angel?"

Iris swallowed and smoothed her hands over her skirt. "I'm not leaving *because* of him, but the fallout helped me realize more of what I genuinely want. The truth is that I haven't felt fulfilled here for a while."

"I'm really sorry to hear that, Iris." Dominique released a defeated sigh. "And I'm sorry that I didn't notice."

Iris smiled sadly and scooted forward. "Thank you for being the best boss and mentor. Everything that I've learned from you, I'll take with me."

"You're welcome." Dominique sighed again, but this time, she smirked. "And one day, when you turn Greenehouse into a nationwide chain store, I'll be able to say that I taught you everything you know."

Iris had agreed to stay on for another three months to help Dominique find and train her replacement.

"This heat is unbearable," Elaine said now, fanning herself. "How about we go in?"

Iris followed Elaine inside to the kitchen, where freshly squeezed lemonade waited for them. Their chef was preparing roasted chicken Caesar salads for lunch, and Senior and Calla were seated not too far away in the dining room. Calla was showing Senior how to play MASH. A counselor had taught the game to Calla and her friends at day camp a few days ago, and it was Calla's new obsession, next to dinosaurs.

Iris looked around Terry's childhood home, almost in disbelief that eventually someone else would live here. The first time she'd visited, she'd been awestruck by the sheer size of the house, and by the staff, which not only included a private chef, but maids and a chauffeur too.

"It's like a castle," she'd whispered to Terry as he'd shown her around.

Terry had smiled at her in his subtle way. "Then that would make you the new princess."

"I'm not a princess," she'd said, laughing.

A family of six would move in by August.

"You ready to take a look upstairs?" Elaine asked after she finished her lemonade.

Iris set her empty glass on the countertop. She'd talked with Marie about what today would entail. Marie had reminded Iris that if it made her emotional to look through Terry's things, that was okay. She reminded Iris that she'd already been through this once when she'd sorted through Terry's belongings at their home in New Jersey. Iris donated many of his clothes to shelters and charities that collected clothing for men who needed interviewing outfits.

Even though she might feel like she was here today to give more parts of Terry away, that wasn't true. He was so much more than his things. Iris squared her shoulders.

"Ready," she said.

They went upstairs and once they reached the top of the staircase, Iris heard the soft pitter-patter of Calla's feet as she hurried after them. Elaine opened the door to Terry's bedroom. It was one of the few rooms in the house that had been left untouched by the moving process.

Terry's room was like a post-college time capsule. His queen-size four-poster bed was covered in a red and navy blue comforter that matched the Washington Wizards poster on his wall and the space area rug situated between his bed and desk.

The last time that Iris had slept in his bed had been the Christmas before he'd passed. Now, when she and Calla visited, Iris slept in one of the guest rooms. Sometimes she'd hover in the doorway like she was doing now, or she'd take a slow walk around his room, remembering him. Remembering them.

Calla slipped between Iris and Elaine and went to Terry's desk. She touched the small basketball figurines that he'd hand-painted in high school. Iris always imagined a younger version of Terry working on the figurines, hunched over, holding a paintbrush with the utmost focus.

"I'll leave you to it," Elaine said softly. "I'll let you know when lunch is ready."

Iris smiled at her. "Thanks."

Iris walked over to Calla. Most of the items on Terry's desk were from high school and college. A stack of planners. An old TI-84 calculator. A pencil case, a mug filled with mechanical pencils. But these weren't things that Iris needed to look through for keeping.

While Calla played with the figurines, Iris walked to Terry's closet. It was filled with Hampton sweatshirts and T-shirts. A couple high school basketball and college jerseys. Iris grabbed a gray Hampton sweatshirt and lifted it to her nose. It didn't smell how she remembered Terry smelling. His sandalwood-scented cologne.

This version of Terry was unfamiliar to her. She hadn't known him then. She'd met him later, when Hampton had been in his past. Her time with Terry had been wonderful but so short. She hadn't been ready for marriage or motherhood. And she hadn't been ready to be a widow either.

Life with Terry, though brief, had changed her. She was a different person from the girl who'd stood with him in the rain outside of the library. For years, she'd thought that there was no one else who could take his place, and that was true. There would only ever be one Terry. She'd never have that same relationship again.

It was why she'd been apprehensive about using the dating apps. She hadn't known if it would be possible to find real love again. She'd wanted to meet someone new, but she hadn't really wanted to *try*. Instead, she'd focused on wanting someone with the qualities of her "ideal" partner. But, really, she had to admit that her list was based on wanting to find someone just like Terry, because that's what she'd been used to, and theirs was a love that she'd known to be real and true.

Yet somehow, against all odds . . . she'd fallen in love with someone new and completely different.

She'd fallen in love with Angel.

Angel might not live a simple life by Iris's original standards, but he had all of the qualities Iris had been looking for. Patience and intelligence. A kind heart and a desire for a family. He got along with Calla and wanted to spend more time getting to know her. Angel wanted simplicity at heart.

He respected her, and he hadn't wanted her to change.

He wasn't what she'd expected, but he'd been exactly what she'd needed. He'd made her feel alive again. With him, she felt truly seen. What she'd had with Angel *was* different from her relationship with Terry. But that wasn't a bad thing.

In retrospect, Iris had known that she loved Angel the moment that she'd stood up to his mom and talked to him outside of the ceremony. Because why else would she have involved herself in his family's business? And then those pictures had appeared online, and she'd freaked out. He'd accused her of being afraid, and she'd denied it, but he'd been right. In those pictures, she'd seen just how much she loved him, and she'd been afraid of loving him and then somehow losing him. It hadn't really been about her job or his different lifestyle. She'd used those reasons as a shield to hide the truth, which was that she'd been terrified, because after losing Terry, she hadn't wanted to face the possibility of loss again.

But now she knew what it was like to be without Angel, and weeks since their breakup, things hadn't gotten any easier. She was still heartbroken. By never taking another risk, she would resign herself to living the rest of her life on the sidelines. Maybe she would have been okay with that in the past, but that was before Angel had come into her life. She didn't want to go back to stubbornly being alone again, especially when he was still here to accept her love.

Knowing that she loved Angel struck her squarely in the chest. Her pulse thundered at the realization. She wanted to call him. But she'd made such a mess of things. What would she even say to him now? It was naive to think that telling Angel that she loved him would magically cure everything. He was probably so angry with her. *She* would be angry with *him* if he'd behaved the way that she had.

"Mom, are you okay?" Calla asked. Iris looked up. Calla was watching her, brows wrinkled in concern. "You got really quiet."

"I'm okay," Iris said.

Calla walked over and took Terry's sweatshirt out of Iris's hands. "This was Dad's too?"

Iris nodded. "Want to try it on?"

"Yeah." Calla shrugged the sweatshirt over her head. The hem fell to her shins and the sleeves flopped loosely. The garment swallowed her, but she smiled. "Can I keep it?"

"Absolutely," Iris said, laughing. She looked at her daughter, who had Terry's nose and his sweet empathy. She crouched down and hugged Calla. "I love you. And your dad loved you too. So much."

"I know," Calla said with such childlike simplicity, it made Iris laugh again. "I love you too. And Dad."

Iris glanced up when she heard a light knock at the door. Elaine was watching them. She smiled and sniffled, wiping her eyes.

"Lunch is ready," she said.

Calla spun around to face Elaine. "Grandma, look, this was Dad's. I'm going to keep it."

"And maybe you'll be a Hampton girl yourself someday." Elaine winked. "Just like Grandma."

"Or a Princeton girl," Iris added, standing. "Like her mom."

"'Or a Princeton girl,'" Elaine repeated, laughing lightly. But she looked at Calla and shook her head.

Unconcerned with college talk, Calla hurried downstairs, ready to have lunch. Iris joined Elaine in the doorway.

"We'll take a few of Terry's sweatshirts and probably his figurines," she said. "But the rest you can donate."

Elaine nodded. "Thank you for coming to look. I figured he'd rather have you go through his things instead of me." With a smile, she added, "He was always calling me nosy."

"I can only imagine what Calla will say about me once she gets older," Iris said, smirking.

Elaine looped her arm through Iris's as they stepped into the hallway. Arm in arm, they descended the stairs.

"Something I've been telling myself whenever I get sad about selling the house is that it's okay to adjust and embrace something new." She looked at Iris. "And that's what I'll tell you as well."

"Thank you." Iris smiled at Elaine gratefully.

It was exactly what Iris needed to hear.

29

"YOU SURE YOU'RE COOL WITH DOING THIS?" RAY ASKED.

Angel, Ray and Bree were huddled together at a table in the back of the room at Lover Underground, a bar in the East Village known for its open mic nights. Leah was the one who'd suggested that Angel come tonight, even though she couldn't make it herself. She was at Imani's again.

A handful of performers had already taken to the stage. Angel had gone virtually unnoticed thanks to the dim lighting and his baseball cap. He guessed that was the beauty of New York City. A celebrity could literally be sitting feet away from you, and you might not even know it.

He'd been writing furiously over the last few days, determined to keep making the R & B songs that his label didn't want to hear. He wanted to try the songs out in front of unbiased listeners to get an honest reaction. He was the most attached to a song he'd titled "Right Person, Wrong Time." He'd written it about Iris.

"I'm sure," he said, answering Ray. He lifted the brim of his hat and rubbed his forehead. His fingers came away damp. He was sweating. He laughed a little. "I'm kinda nervous. Not gonna lie."

"Good luck," Bree whispered. She held Ray's hand and smiled at Angel. They'd decided to officially start dating a few days ago.

A woman with a raspy voice was singing a neosoul song on her guitar. After she finished, the audience applauded, and the host, a short man with shoulder-length locs, returned to the mic and glanced at the sign-up sheet.

"Okay, next up we have . . . Angel." The host laughed. "That's it? No last name? I guess you must think you're like the singer, huh?"

Laughter peppered the audience, and Angel smiled, feeling flustered. Why was he so nervous all of a sudden? He'd performed in front of way bigger crowds than this one. Maybe it was because he was about to sing something new and vulnerable, and he *really* hoped that people liked it.

As he stood, his phone vibrated on the table. He stared wide-eyed at a text from Iris.

> Hey. I hope you're doing okay. I'd really love to talk
> to you if you have time. Can you please let me
> know?

In his haste to grab his phone, he accidentally knocked it to the floor. It landed with a loud, menacing smack.

"Damn, bro," Ray said, leaning over to pick up the phone. He whistled as he handed Angel's phone back to him. "Why don't you have a screen protector?"

There was a huge spiderweb crack in the center of his phone and his screen was completely black. Even when he hit the side buttons, nothing happened.

"*No, no, no.* Are you for real right now?" Angel hissed,

trying to get his phone to work. Iris had texted him. She wanted to *talk*. And now his phone was broken?!

"Angel? Is there an Angel here?" the open mic night host said, peering at the audience.

"We'll try to fix it," Bree said, taking Angel's phone from him.

"I guess, we'll move on, then . . ." the host said, looking at the sign-up sheet again.

"Sorry, sorry! I'm here!" Angel jogged to the stage and removed his hat.

A hush fell over the room.

"Oh shit," the host said as he handed the mic to Angel. "Y'all, please welcome *the* Angel to the stage!"

A loud cheer erupted. People whipped out their phones to snap pictures and record. Angel stood at the mic and cleared his throat.

"How y'all doing tonight?" he asked.

He was met with another round of cheers. Someone wolf whistled. Angel laughed and took a deep breath.

"I, uh, want to sing something new for y'all tonight," he said. "Is that all right?"

"Yes!" Bree shouted way in the back. Others cheered in agreement.

With shaking hands Angel sat at the piano, all too aware that everything he did tonight would be recorded and shared. But there was no turning back now.

He began playing the harmony of "Right Person, Wrong Time." The audience fell silent and his voice filled the room.

> *Wrong time, wrong place. I wish I could see your*
> *face . . .*

If only you knew how much it meant. I wanna
  relive the time we spent.

A few people in the audience caught the song's smooth rhythm and began to clap along. When Angel finished singing, everyone in the room jumped to their feet. *A standing ovation?* Angel laughed in disbelief as he pivoted toward the audience and humbly accepted their praise. He bowed, steepling his fingers under his chin.

"I wrote that song for someone who I love very much," he said quietly into the mic. "That song will always be for her, no matter what."

And as soon as he left this stage and got ahold of a phone, he was going to call her and say yes, he would love to talk. And he'd tell her that he loved her. But before that, he had one more song to play.

He sat at the piano again. "Do y'all mind if I play something that might sound a little familiar?"

The audience cheered once more. His fingers moved across the keys, and he began to sing the original, slower version of "Summertime Fine."

IRIS COULDN'T STOP checking her phone. Angel still hadn't texted her back. He was probably busy. He was probably *working.* She didn't need to stress or freak out or worry that maybe he was purposely ignoring her because he was done with her for good, right?

She was miles away in New Jersey in her parents' kitchen, removing a cake from its bakery box. It was her parents' annual July 15th birthday barbecue. The house and backyard were filled with family. But tonight, they were also celebrating that Iris was joining the family business.

Iris began to cut slices of cake, quietly contemplating if it would be completely unhinged if she showed up at Angel's building, when Violet and Lily entered the kitchen and crowded Iris's space.

"Um," Iris said, glancing left and right at her sisters. "I'm trying to cut the cake. Can you back up, please?"

"No, we cannot," Violet declared. "Because we're staging an intervention."

Iris frowned at her. "A what?"

"*Intervention*," Violet said. "Show her the clip, Lily."

Lily lifted her phone in front of Iris's face and pressed play on a video. Iris's heartbeat increased with longing when she immediately recognized Angel. He was sitting at a piano, singing a song about loving someone but the timing hadn't been right. She held her breath as he sang, and she gasped when he said, *I wrote that song for someone who I love very much. That song will always be for her, no matter what.*

Speechless, Iris gaped at Lily's phone screen. Her quickening pulse vibrated throughout her body. He loved her too.

"When was that video posted?" she asked hoarsely.

"About twenty minutes ago," Lily said. "He's at Lover Underground in the city."

"So this is where the intervention part comes in." Violet folded her hands in front of her diplomatically. "Angel loves you. You love him, and don't try to deny it because we know you do, okay? So why are you being so annoying about this?"

"*Violet*," Lily said. "Remember what we said about our delivery?"

"What? I'm being direct! If you love him, you need to tell him and stop wasting time." Violet glanced at the kitchen entrance and smiled. "Right, babe?"

Iris turned to see Xavier walking toward the fridge. Nick followed behind him.

"What are we talking about?" Xavier asked as he opened the fridge and grabbed a water bottle. He handed a second bottle to Nick.

"We're saying that Iris loves Angel, so she needs to get it together and tell him," Violet said.

"Oh, um . . ." Xavier glanced quickly between the three sisters. "Is this a trick question? Am I actually allowed to comment on this?"

"No," said Iris.

"Yes," said Violet.

"Maybe?" said Lily.

Nick stood by Lily and looked over her shoulder at her phone. "What's this video?"

"Angel was singing a beautiful song that he wrote for Iris," Lily explained.

"Ah." Nick nodded in a knowing way, which made it clear to Iris that Lily had shared Iris's business with her boyfriend. But Iris wasn't surprised. Nothing remained a secret for long in this family.

"Violet was a little blunt," Lily said softly. "But I agree with her. You spend so much time making sure that everyone else is happy, but you need to be happy too, Iris. And I think Angel made you really happy."

"And horny," Violet added. "Which is a good thing."

Xavier snorted and covered his wife's mouth with his hand.

"If you would have given me a second to answer, I would have told you that I *have* reached out to him," Iris said. "I do love him, and I want to meet up and tell him, but he hasn't responded to my text." She chewed on her lower lip as she looked at her family. "Should I just go to him now? Would that be crazy?"

"YES, GO," Violet and Lily shouted.

"Um." Iris placed the cake knife on the countertop. "Okay, yeah."

As she left the kitchen, Violet whooped behind her. Lily ran to get Iris's car keys and shoved them into her hands. Iris hurried to the living room. Calla was sitting on the floor in a circle with her cousins. They were playing MASH.

"No, that's not how you play," Calla said, taking the paper finger game from her older cousin, Jay. "You have to move your fingers four times, not three." She held up four fingers. "*Four.*"

"Goodness, sometimes she's like a mini-me isn't she?" Iris said to Violet and Lily.

"Yes," her sisters said. Lily said, "Go ahead. We'll watch her."

"Calla, honey, I have to drive into the city, but I'll be back soon," she said, hugging her daughter. "If you need anything, your aunties are here."

"The city?" Dahlia asked, walking into the living room. "Why? What's in the city?"

"Angel," Violet answered.

Iris didn't even have time to roll her eyes.

"*Oooh*, really," Dahlia said.

Benjamin, who appeared behind Dahlia, raised an eyebrow but said nothing.

"Your friend who helped at the shop?" Calla asked. "I liked him."

"Yes," Iris said, and Calla's answering smile took up her whole face.

Lily and Violet hovered by the door. Nick and Xavier watched the proceedings with expressions of mild amusement. That was what you signed up for when you fell in love with a Greene girl.

Iris paused in front of her sisters. "Wish me luck?"

Violet and Lily hugged Iris, wrapping her in a sister sandwich.

"You don't need luck," Lily whispered.

"Now go on, get out of here!" Violet said, affectionately pushing Iris outside.

Iris jogged to her car, started the engine and sped out into the street. She called Angel, but he didn't answer. She'd have to hope he'd still be at Lover Underground when she got there.

This was completely unlike anything she had ever done in her life. She was acting purely on instinct and adrenaline.

And love.

30

THIRTY-TWO MINUTES LATER, THANKS TO IRIS'S SPEEDING
and a surprising lack of traffic going through the Holland
Tunnel, Iris breathlessly ran into Lover Underground. A
spoken-word poet was performing onstage. Iris squinted as
she looked around the dimly lit room, failing to locate Angel. Was he still here?

"*Iris*," someone hissed.

Iris turned in the direction of the voice. Bree and Ray
were sitting at a small table toward the back of the room.
Iris hustled over to them, trying not to bring attention to
herself.

"Are you looking for Angel?" Bree asked. Beside her, Ray
smiled wryly.

Iris nodded. "Where is he?"

"He left about twenty minutes ago," Ray told her. "He
said something about getting his phone fixed so that he
could call you. I told him most phone repair shops were
probably closed by now."

"His phone is broken?" Iris asked.

Bree and Ray nodded. That would explain why he hadn't answered any of Iris's calls during her drive.

"Do you know where he went specifically?" she asked.

Ray shook his head, and Bree grinned. "He *flew* out of here after he finished singing."

"Check his place first," Ray said. "He might be there."

"Okay." Iris moved to leave, but she turned back to face them. They looked so blissful and content, sitting closely. "You're really cute together, by the way."

Ray and Bree shared a smile.

Iris raced back to her car. She hoped that Angel would be home. How many phone repair shops were there in the city? It might be impossible to catch him at one.

Finding parking on Angel's street at this time of night was a pain. She parked three blocks away and by the time she rounded the corner of his building, speed walking like her life depended on it, she was winded and sweaty. Her T-shirt and denim shorts clung to her skin.

The building's doorman was smoking a cigarette. He eyed Iris as she approached. Angel had no idea that Iris was coming over, so he hadn't given the building's staff a heads-up to expect her. Aware that she looked like a sweaty mess, Iris took a steadying breath and smoothed back her fraying curls.

"Hi," she said, "I'm here to see Angel. I'm a friend. Or, well, more than a friend, actually. An ex, kind of?"

The impassive doorman raised an eyebrow and crushed his cigarette beneath his shoe. "Is that right?" he said.

To him, she probably looked like a crazed fan. "I'm not lying, I swear."

He chuckled. "That's what they all say. I'm gonna have to ask you to move along, lady. I'm sure you can find something better to do besides stalking."

Iris frowned, instantly incensed. "Excuse me, I'll have you know—"

Her words evaporated on her tongue as Angel's black car emerged from the garage.

"Angel!" she shouted, running toward his car.

"Ma'am!" The doorman reached out to stop her.

Angel slammed on his brakes and lowered his window. "*Iris?*" He quickly got out of his car and waved his doorman away. "It's okay. I know her."

The doorman shrugged and resumed his post at the entrance.

Angel was wide-eyed as he walked toward Iris. She was so relieved to see him. Her gaze devoured him as he approached, taking in every detail that she'd missed during the last few weeks. His beautiful face and assured stride. He stopped in front of her.

"I was on my way to see you," he said breathlessly, clearly recovering from the shock of her presence. "My phone is broken."

"I know. Ray and Bree told me," she said. "I went to the open mic night to look for you. I watched the video of you singing the song that you wrote for me. It was so beautiful."

Angel stared at her. "Thank you."

She swallowed thickly as her pulse spiked.

"I have to tell you something," she said. "And I want to get it all out now so that there isn't any miscommunication between us, or confusion about how I feel."

Angel's expression turned apprehensive. "Okay."

"I've always been someone who is in control and in charge. I've been that way with my family and at work. I plan and plan and plan. That way I always know what to expect. But, Angel, you came out of nowhere, and I didn't know how to handle my feelings for you or how to control them. And that scared me. I was afraid of what I didn't know and what I couldn't predict." She inhaled deeply. "When I realized the true extent of my feelings for you, I was afraid that I'd lose you somehow and I didn't want to experience that loss after everything I went through after Terry died, so I pushed you away."

Angel's chest rose and fell on a deep breath. "Iris—"

"Hold on, please. I'm not done," she said gently.

He nodded again and dutifully returned his arms to his sides. She thought she saw a hint of amusement flash across his face, but he quickly schooled his features.

"I know now that never allowing myself the chance to love you would be worse than losing you," she continued. "I know that you might be upset with me, given how I handled everything. You have every right to be. I'm so sorry for how I acted. I was afraid to admit what I wanted then, but I'm not afraid now." She looked him directly in the eye, her gaze unwavering. "I love you. And if you'll still have me, I'm clearly and straightforwardly asking if you would like to be my boyfriend."

Angel was quiet for a moment. Iris anxiously clasped her hands together. Then the knot in her stomach loosened as a slow smile crept across his face.

"I—"

"Wait! Still not done, sorry," she said, and Angel bit his

lip, trying not to laugh. "If you say yes, I do think it's important for us to make sure that Calla's privacy is protected. That's a huge priority."

"Can I talk now?" he asked, quirking an eyebrow.

"Yes," she said.

But Angel didn't speak. Instead, he wordlessly wrapped Iris in his arms and kissed her. She startled in surprise but easily melted in his embrace, grasping his shoulders and returning his kiss. His mouth was soft and warm. It was the kind of kiss that stopped time and moved mountains. She didn't want to let go of him.

He pulled back and cradled her face in his hands. "I love you too."

She'd never thought of herself as the type to swoon, but she almost did right then.

"I will always do my best to protect your privacy and Calla's, like I told you before," he said. "I'm sorry about what happened at the ceremony. I know this life isn't for everyone. I won't make you do anything that you don't want to do. I just want us to be together."

"I know," she whispered.

"Then, yes, Iris Greene," he said. "I will be your boyfriend."

Joy seeped through her veins, traveling from the top of her head to the tips of her toes.

She looped her arms around Angel's neck and gazed at him with love.

"Kiss me again, please," she said.

Smiling, Angel brought his lips to hers and eagerly complied.

Iris was capable, reliable and a problem solver. Ambitious

and motivated. And she was brave. Brave enough to pursue a life where a dance with a famous singer at dusk one summer evening might eventually lead to a magical love affair.

This was her story.

EPILOGUE

One year later

IRIS KNEW BASICALLY EVERYONE AT THIS PARTY.

Big parties weren't really her preferred setting, but the party she was attending today was one that she couldn't miss.

It was a Saturday in July, the opening day of Greenehouse's new location in Bridgewood.

Mother Nature had gifted them with beautiful sunshine, and the store was packed. Iris took up residence at the register, and her new employees donned their bright green Greenehouse T-shirts. Among them were Lily and Violet, who'd volunteered to help out on opening day. Xavier and Nick had volunteered to help carry items to customers' cars. Dahlia and Benjamin greeted customers at the door. Now that Iris was a part owner of the company too, she'd finally convinced her parents to hire a manager at the Willow Ridge location.

Across the store, Iris's gaze fell on Angel and Calla. Calla stood by Angel's side, talking animatedly to Angel as he signed a few autographs for fans. Ray hovered nearby, making sure that both Angel and Calla were safe. All the while, Angel kept his ear bent toward Calla, listening intently as she talked to him about her most recent obsession, LEGO bricks. Last night, the three of them had sat around on the living room floor, helping Calla build a pirate ship.

Bree and Leah stood not too far away, talking and laughing, and Leah had brought Maxine too. She walked up to each customer, eager to be petted.

Iris had expected a high turnout for opening day. Over the past year, Greenehouse's business had been booming, and Bridgewood residents were happy to have a florist/nursery closer to home again. But Iris couldn't deny that another reason for their high opening day turnout was because Angel's local fans, who were in the know, wanted a chance at seeing him. As long as they didn't overwhelm the store and made sure to purchase something before they left, Iris didn't mind.

Angel glanced up and caught eyes with Iris. He winked at her, and she smiled back. A year later, she still got butterflies when she looked at him across a crowded room. No matter how many people were around, their relationship still felt like a private secret between the two of them.

Angel had been good at protecting Iris's privacy. They had an agreement that he didn't post pictures of her or Calla on social media. And even though she accompanied him to some events, she didn't walk the red carpet with him. Instead, she waited until he walked the carpet and she joined him afterward. She'd been his date to the Grammys earlier that year when he'd won Best Traditional R & B Performance for "Right Person, Wrong Time." He'd thanked her in his acceptance speech for inspiring the song, and as the camera panned to her, she'd felt like her cheeks were on fire. But that didn't outweigh how proud she was of him.

She was proud too of the way he'd handled his relationship with his parents. Although he still checked in with his dad, he'd set a clear boundary with Cora. Until she could speak to him respectfully, he didn't desire to have much contact with her. He was hopeful that one day his mom would come around to accepting him for who he was, but he wasn't going to let her lack of approval dictate his life. He was happy with himself and that was what mattered most.

After the viral success of the songs he'd performed at the open mic night, Angel's label had finally come around to backing him in the R & B soul direction. His third album was composed of the songs that they'd originally rejected. And like Iris knew they would, Angel's fans had supported him, and the new album brought sales success and critical acclaim. He'd be going on tour in September.

He would be really busy, and Iris was busy too, as always. But they did their best to make time for each other. And in those moments, when it was just the two of them cuddled in her bed with no cameras or fans watching, she got Angel all to herself. And she cherished every minute.

"Is this plant hard to kill?" Dominique asked, setting an orchid on the register with a frown. "Because I kill plants like it's nothing."

Paloma laughed and placed a prickly pear cactus on the counter beside the orchid. Her adorable son, Leo, was strapped to her chest in a baby carrier. "I told you to get a cactus like me."

"And accidentally prick myself trying to water it?" Dominique asked, aghast. "I think not."

Iris laughed. Every now and then, she missed being at Save Face Beauty. At first the transition had felt strange. Corporate America and the Save Face Beauty offices were all she'd known, and now she was a small-business owner. Her career path was different from what she'd envisioned in her early twenties, but she was a boss in her own right, and she was on a new journey that she was enjoying.

"Make sure to water the orchid once a week," she instructed Dominique. "And make sure it gets lots of sunshine."

Dominique frowned again, like she was unsure if she could handle those simple directives. "I'll try my best."

"The store is lovely, Iris," Paloma said, coming around the counter to hug her. Leo squinted up at Iris and grinned. Iris smiled back, lightly touching his soft, brown curls.

"Thank you both so much for coming," she said.

"Of course, you know we had to support you. Even if you abandoned us." Dominique sighed dramatically but smirked.

Iris laughed as she asked an employee to take over her register. She walked Dominique and Paloma to their cars and hugged them goodbye. When she came back inside, Violet and Lily were standing by the stacks of soil, chatting leisurely.

"Um, hello," Iris said, shaking her finger at them. "I don't think it's break time yet."

Violet rolled her eyes. "You can't fire me. I don't actually work here."

Lily smiled. "We just wanted to see how you're doing."

Iris looked at her younger sisters and smiled too. "I'm fine," she said. Then she amended herself. "I'm good."

A burst of laughter sounded from the other end of the shop. Calla was laughing at something Angel said to her. He was crouched in front of her. He placed a flower behind his ear and posed, holding his hands beneath his chin.

"She likes him a lot," Lily said. "That's a good thing."

"Yeah," Iris said softly.

She liked to think that Terry felt the same way. That he was grateful for Angel's presence in her and Calla's lives.

In the hallway of her home, they'd added another picture to the wall: a photograph of her, Calla and Angel standing in front of the *T. rex* skeleton display at the American Museum of Natural History. Angel's arm was looped around Iris's waist. They each had a hand placed on Calla's shoulders as the three of them grinned for the camera. Leah had taken it for them.

It was one of Iris's favorite pictures.

Violet and Lily ended their unofficial break, and Iris continued to ring up customers, grateful for the good business. When the afternoon rush ended, she felt a tap at her shoulder. She turned, and Angel was standing there, grinning at her, holding a pink rose.

"I think you might have dropped this," he said.

Iris laughed, remembering the black rose that he'd returned to her years ago. "Thank you," she said, taking the flower from him.

He wrapped his arms around her front and pulled her close, resting her back against his chest. He softly kissed her cheek.

"I'm really proud of you," he said.

She angled her head to face him. "And I'm proud of you."

She was well aware that people were watching them, but she was so in love, she couldn't bring herself to care.

He smiled as he leaned down and brought his lips to her ear.

Then he sang a little song that only she could hear.

Acknowledgments

It feels like just yesterday I was writing down bits and pieces of Lily and Nick's emails in my journal, working on what would become the beginning of *The Neighbor Favor*, and now here we are with Iris, the last Greene sister! I almost can't believe it. Writing this series has been such a wonderful experience. This book in particular was probably the toughest to write, and as always, I'm very grateful for everyone who helped me along the way.

Thank you to my editors Angela Kim and Cindy Hwang for your sharp insight and for pushing me to make this book the best that it could be with each draft. I'm so lucky to work with you, and the Greene sisters have the best home at Berkley.

Thank you to my agent, Sara Crowe, who is truly the best and always has my back!

Thank you to the larger team at Berkley: Dache' Rogers, Anika Bates, Christine Legon, Sammy Rice, Heather Haase, Brittney West, Emma Tamayo, Tawanna Sullivan, Gabi Jonikas, Lynsey Griswold, and Randie Lipkin. And thank you to Lila Selle for a third beautiful cover. And thank you as well to the UK team at Penguin Michael Joseph.

Thank you to my amazing friend and critique partner Alison Tergis, who has read early drafts of every single one of my books and handles my stories and characters with such care.

Thank you to my best friends, Shantel, Kenniqua and Corinne, who inspired bits and pieces of Iris and her journey in motherhood. I'm in awe of each of you!

Thank you to my family and Jason for your love and support.

Thank you so much to my readers. Whether you were already familiar with me from my YA books or you discovered me through *The Neighbor Favor*, thank you for taking the time to read my work. I feel extremely lucky to have this job.

Everything that I know about flowers and gardening, I learned from my mom and my grandma Peggy. Because of them, I've been surrounded by flowers and plants for much of my life. It's the reason the Greene sisters are named after flowers and why their parents own a nursery/florist. My grandmother passed away while I was working on this book, and in several ways, Iris's thoughts and feelings about grief mirrored my own. While I'm very sad that my grandmother won't be here to see this book on shelves, I'm really grateful for the support and inspiration that she has always given me throughout my career and my life in general.

KEEP READING FOR AN EXCERPT FROM

The Neighbor Favor

THE FIRST GREENE SISTERS NOVEL BY
KRISTINA FOREST,
AVAILABLE NOW FROM BERKLEY ROMANCE!

LILY WAS ALONE AS SHE WALKED INTO HER SISTER VIO-
let's fancy Union Square apartment building and got onto
the elevator, pressing number 14 for their floor. It was a
newer building with a housing lottery, so Violet had gotten
lucky and scored a deal on the rent, and Lily was happy to
temporarily live on Violet's pullout couch. She loved Union
Square. It was one of her favorite parts of the city.

Lily remembered the granola bar in her tote bag, and she
rummaged for it, gasping in delight once it was located. Hiding at Violet's engagement party meant she hadn't had much
time to eat. She took a large chomp, grateful and starving.
Then she jumped when someone suddenly shouted, "Hold
the elevator!"

A hand shot out, keeping the elevator doors from closing. And then Lily saw him.

Her neighbor who lived down the hall.

He was slightly out of breath as he stepped into the elevator, and he flashed a quick smile at Lily, so beautiful it was
nearly blinding. She tried not to openly stare at him. But
that was difficult. Because he was fine as hell.

Fine as Hell Neighbor was tall. At barely five three, Lily

had to tilt her head back a little to look at his face. And look she did at his smooth, medium brown complexion and his full goatee that actually connected. He was wearing a plain white T-shirt and blue jeans with black Vans.

"Thanks," he said, running a quick hand over his hair that was cut into a fade. "I appreciate you."

"Um," Lily uttered, her mouth full of granola. "You're welcome, um, yeah."

She did this every time she saw him, mumbled nonsensical replies. She was still looking at him now as he leaned back against the elevator wall, his posture indicating a slight aloofness about him. His limbs were long and muscular. Sometimes when she was lucky, she ran into him as he was leaving the gym on the ground floor of their building, and his skin would be damp and glistening with sweat. Her dignity was the only thing that kept her from drooling. She swallowed thickly at the thought now and glanced away. His presence always left her senses prickling with awareness. She felt like maybe they'd met before in passing but she couldn't remember when or where. He'd definitely popped up in her dreams a few times, dressed as an old-school, sexy elevator operator with a double-breasted jacket and matching hat.

Her confusing infatuation with him was low-key embarrassing because, in reality, they'd never exchanged more than polite greetings.

The elevator door closed, and they were alone. Lily's thoughts clambered over one another as she tried to think of something to say.

"Nutri-Grain," Fine as Hell Neighbor said, pointing at

the bar in Lily's hand that she'd forgotten existed. "I love those. I hate when the crumbs get everywhere, though."

She struggled to form a response and look at him at the same time. She glanced down, and that was when she noticed he was carrying a thick paperback. Fine as Hell Neighbor always had a book or a notebook when she saw him. Once, he'd been holding a copy of *The Fifth Season* by N. K. Jemisin, and Lily had been too tongue-tied to mention that it was one of her favorite books. She angled her head slightly, trying to get a better glimpse at the book he held now, when the elevator abruptly stopped on the seventh floor. An East Asian man, who looked to be in his fifties, stepped inside, carrying a tray of cupcakes. He sighed in visible relief at the sight of Fine as Hell Neighbor.

"You're just the person I wanted to see," the man said, hurrying to her neighbor's side. "I need your advice. It's a big night for me."

"What's up, Henry?" Fine as Hell Neighbor eyed the cupcakes. "Did you make these yourself? Can I have one?" He reached for the tray and Henry slapped his hand away. Lily laughed, and her neighbor's gaze shot to her. His lips spread into an embarrassed grin, and Lily's brain short-circuited.

"No, these aren't for you," Henry said. "They're for Yolanda. Today is her half birthday. I made these for her to celebrate. And because I am going to ask her out to dinner."

"For real? That's what's up, Henry!" Fine as Hell Neighbor patted the older man on the back. "It's about time. She's been giving you hints for a while."

Henry shook his head and pulled nervously at the collar of his shirt. "What if she says no? What if she hates the cupcakes? She said cupcakes were her favorite dessert, so I found this recipe on Google. I don't like sweets, so I didn't try the cupcakes myself. Remind me what to say. I forgot everything you told me. I'm not a ladies' man like you. You talk to women so easily."

Fine as Hell Neighbor glanced at Lily and coughed, scratching the back of his neck. "I'm not—you know I'm not a ladies' man, Henry." He smiled softly and placed a reassuring hand on Henry's shoulder. "Number one, you've gotta relax. You already know Yolanda likes you and she's been waiting for you to make the first move. Just tell her the truth. You like her, and you want to take her out for a nice dinner. Be yourself. You got this. You're the man. Come on, say it."

"Say what?" Henry asked.

"That you're the man."

"I'm the man," Henry said quietly.

"Nah, say it with *feeling*."

"I'm the man," Henry repeated, slightly louder this time.

"You're the man!"

"I'm the man!"

Lily laughed, watching the two of them.

Henry glanced at her and his cheeks flushed bright red. "Sorry," he mumbled. "I hope we aren't disturbing you."

Lily shook her head. "Not at all. Um, good luck with asking her out."

Henry smiled, although he still looked nervous. "Thank you."

The elevator finally stopped on the fourteenth floor. Lily's floor. And her neighbor's.

He turned to Henry one last time. "Remember, you're the man."

Henry nodded, waving at the two of them as they stepped into the hallway. The elevator doors closed.

Lily and Fine as Hell Neighbor weren't walking together, necessarily. He was a couple feet behind her, but she felt as though he were only inches away.

That was really nice of you to help him out, she wanted to say. *To be honest, I could use one of your pep talks.* But her tongue felt leaden, covered in molasses. Why couldn't she just be normal and talk to him?

She reached Violet's apartment and pulled out her keys. Taking a deep breath, she turned to her neighbor to say something, she had no idea what. But he was already walking past her toward his apartment, exactly four doors down and across the hall.

"Have a good night," he said, smiling politely.

"Me too," Lily said. "Wait, I mean, you too." She shook her head. *God.* She was the worst.

He nodded his head before slipping inside of his apartment. Annoyed with herself and her inability to say something dazzling or memorable, Lily groaned and entered Violet's apartment, slumping against the door. *One day soon.*

One day soon, she'd get up the nerve to actually talk to him.

Lily had run into Fine as Hell Neighbor in the hallway/elevator/lobby nearly every day since she'd moved in with Violet last month. And even more lately, since the other elevator had been out of service for weeks and there was only one way up, other than the stairs. And each interaction consisted of him being friendly and attempting conversation, while she became overwhelmed by his hotness and struggled to speak.

But with Fine as Hell Neighbor, Lily actually had something to talk about. Books. She could overcome her battle with casual conversation. And . . . wait.

Wouldn't that make him the perfect date for Violet's wedding?

They could talk about books all night. And even better, she didn't have to worry about trying to make anything work long-term because apparently, he was a "ladies' man," according to Henry. Lily had never seen Fine as Hell Neighbor with a woman herself, but Henry clearly knew him better than she did. If he was a serial dater, they could have a fun night at the wedding and then go about their lives. No yearlong email chains and no messy heartbreak.

And if it happened that before they parted ways, he told Lily she was the sexiest, most fascinating woman he'd ever met, and he passionately pushed her up against the wall, grabbed her face, covered her mouth with his and then completely ravished her, who would she be to complain?

"*Meow.*"

Lily startled and looked down at her sweet Tomcat, who was too hungry to wait for her to finish her daydream.

"Hey, bud," she said, as Tomcat affectionately bumped his head against her shin. "Let's get you fed."

Lily was the quiet sister. Or according to her family: shy. Or according to old classmates: mousy. She personally preferred the term *observant*.

She wasn't bold like Violet or strategic like Iris, but she'd have to be in order to ask out Fine as Hell Neighbor. And she'd start by learning his real name.

Steven Forest

Kristina Forest is the *USA Today* bestselling author of romance books for both teens and adults. She earned her MFA in creative writing at The New School, and she lives in New Jersey, where she can often be found rearranging her bookshelf.

VISIT KRISTINA FOREST ONLINE

KristinaForest.com
KristinaForest_
𝕏 KristinaForest
KristinaForest1

Ready to find
your next great read?

Let us help.

Visit prh.com/nextread

Penguin
Random
House